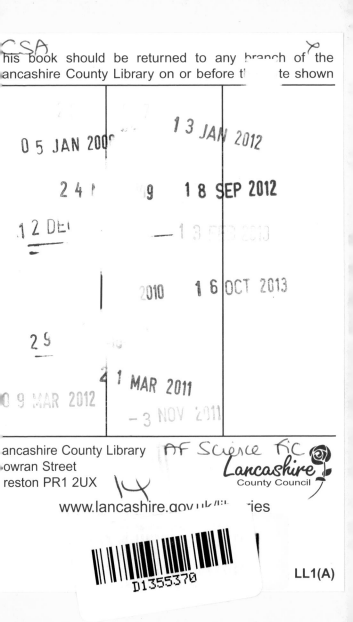

FIREMASK

THE LAST LEGION: BOOK 2

CHRIS BUNCH

www.orbitbooks.net

ORBIT

First published in the United States in 2000 by Roc,
Penguin Group (USA) Inc.
First published in Great Britain in 2007 by Orbit

A CIP catalogue record for this book
is available from the British Library.

ISBN 978-1-84149-627-6

Papers used by Orbit are natural, recyclable products made
from wood grown in sustainable forests and certified in accordance
with the rules of the Forest Stewardship Council.

Typest in Garamond by M Rules
Printed and bound in Great Britain by
Mackays of Chatham plc
Paper supplied by Hellefoss AS, Norway

Orbit
An imprint of
Lirrle, Brown Book Group
100 Victoria Embankment
London EC4Y 0DY

An Hachette Livre UK Company

www.orbitbooks.net

For
The Knicks
who've made life a lot easier:
Kelly, Ed
Erin and Ed Jr.

Before battle, meditate on the thirteen ways of fire:

1. Its power is far greater than any charger, yet it hides in a child's robes.
2. Bright, angry, it gladdens the heart of he who uses it.
3. Its sight weakens the foe, for he knows the mercilessness of what he faces.
4. Set properly, it will never surrender.
5. Once fire rages, the warrior may pursue his own course.
6. It needs little encouragement to shoulder its arms, little food other than a scattering of twigs, and fights on without rest until the end.
7. It fights its own battle, leaping here, there, and no sayer can predict its course.
8. It carries almost all before it, and they are its victims or allies; the wind becomes its steed, the earth its fortress, and only great waters are its final enemy.
9. Behind its mask the warrior can devise his own stratagems in leisure and concealment.
10. With fire guarding his flanks, the warrior may fight with all his heart, knowing he has given himself a perfect shield.
11. It attacks all that the enemy has, wagons, horses, victuals, as well as swordsmen and archers.
12. Even its wounding is terrible and few survive.
13. Its barren aftermath gives nothing to the host but desolation and despair.

Consider well the ways of fire, its masks and tactics, then make war with its soul in your belly.

> — *Maxims for a Lone Warrior,*
> *Fighting Against a Host*
> by Lai Shi-Min, later
> The Emperor T'ai Tsung
> (ca. 630 CE)

ONE

Langnes 37421/4Planet/Gathering

Starships snapped into real space, slashed toward the system's fourth planet. As they closed, bays slid open, and small C-shaped fighting ships, the lethal *aksai*, darted out and held close formation on their mother ships.

It could have been an attack, but was not.

The Musth clanmasters were assembling to decide what might be done with the humans occupying the far-distant Cumbre system.

Or, at least the clanmasters who felt the matter of interest or value; perhaps twenty percent of the Musth clans, no more. Others might choose to involve themselves later, might remain neutral.

To the Musth, 4Planet was held, in mythology, to be the homeworld, although most of their scientists believed the race had simultaneously evolved on a dozen, perhaps more, planets; proof the universe belonged to them, buttressed by the ease with which they had conquered their home cluster and expanded beyond.

4Planet was temperate, with large continents, low mountains, lakes, much of the land covered with veldt, grassy plains interspersed with small forests. The sun was

G-type, but the light was starker, more blue, than a Terran would feel comfortable under. Its climate was a bit chill for man, although it seldom snowed. Rainfall was seasonal, sparse but heavy when it came.

It had not always been like that. Over the millennia, it'd been plowed, mined, deforested, and built up, and then the Musth had gone out to the stars.

4Planet, almost abandoned, was encouraged to revert to its natural state. Cities were leveled, and the ravaged land contoured and planted, polluted rivers and lakes made to run clean, and the world was as it had been, at the dawn of Musth time.

With population pressure gone, the few million Musth who chose to remain on 4Planet built semi-underground villages, one clan holding each settlement.

Only one small continent still showed the Musth's technocracy. Here were military bases, great landing fields, roboticized factories and yards, and the slender bureaucracy the Musth needed to administer their thousand thousand worlds. This was Gathering.

In the center of it all was a two-kilometer-wide cylinder with a domed rotunda. This building, three hundred meters high, was where the Musth came to deal with problems beyond the immediate reach of a clanmaster, or to settle a feud when one or another of the warring groups requested intervention.

The building had no name, which the Musth found logical. As the only one in their empire used for these purposes, it needed none.

There was a wry Musth proverb: 'The only reason we Musth do not rule All-Cosmos is we need one eye for our race's future, one eye for our personal destiny, and one eye to guard our backs, and the First Cause only gave us two eyes each.'

In the cylinder's walls were suites, each with a small

landing platform wide enough for a pair of ships. A clanmaster could arrive, well guarded, and conduct whatever business was necessary without leaving his suite, using the elaborate electronics array. Each suite was completely independent, with its own power generator and available air supply for those who were worried about an enemy trying to gas them.

If the controversy was solved, then the masters, their subordinates, delegates or relatives, could choose to meet in the flesh.

There were almost five hundred clanmasters assembling. Some ruled several worlds, some controlled a trade or craft, others commanded fighting fleets.

While the *aksai* banked and circled overhead watchfully like Earth swallows, the clanmasters entered the building, each computer-routed so no enemies would find themselves sharing airspace and seizing the moment.

They came out of their small flits arrogantly, as befitted a master race; two meters tall, more when they reared back on their small tails, their coarse, yellow to reddish brown fur gleaming, small heads peering about on long, snakelike necks, quick in their motions as they moved into their quarters.

All wore weapons belts, none of their armament ceremonial in nature.

That night, before the assemblage began, coms flashed to and fro as strategies, tactics, and ideas were sent back and forth.

At sunrise, the meeting began.

Wallscreens opened, dividing as necessary as clanmasters appeared on them. Other masters activated their monitors but preferred to remain invisible.

Aesc, former 'ambassador' to the Cumbre system, presented the Musth's case. There'd always been tension between the humans and Musth, but within the last time sequence, it had exploded into violence as what he called the lesser beings, the 'Raum, slightly smaller and darker than other humanoids, had revolted against their masters. And they'd attacked the Musth.

'Why?' a clanmaster asked. 'I know little of humans, barely enough to loathe them. But I thought our differences were settled, at least in their eyes, when we made peace before.'

'The 'Raum,' Aesc explained, 'have a common belief, that they are destined to rule not merely their race, but all space, all time, all beings.'

There were noises of amusement, somewhere between purrs and growls. Someone said 'heresy,' and there was more mirth.

'Leader Wlencing had the opportunity to fight them on occasion,' Aesc went on. 'Once in league with the human army.'

'Your views, Wlencing,' a clanmaster, Keffa, requested.

'The 'Raum are what the humans call,' and Wlencing used a Terran word, '"wormsss," or slime beings. Cowards, who avoid face-battle, not much in the way of warriors when they're driven to combat. But they were able to hurt us quite badly when they sent a manned suicide bomb into our mining headquarters on the third world.'

'That,' Aesc said, 'sparked our withdrawal, as the documents provided show.'

'I have read them,' Keffa said. 'And you intervened when Wlencing had not finished my question. I care little of these fools who believe themselves superior, especially when you say they have been destroyed.'

'Not destroyed,' Wlencing said. 'Defeated, driven back into their warrens.'

'By the human army, which is my main interest and which my question was about,' Keffa said. 'What of them?'

Wlencing considered, head darting from side to side.

'As warriors, some fight very well, especially those who have been trained to seek personal battle. As an army, in prolonged war, I have less information. The fighting with the 'Raum was little better than a series of skirmishes.

'Against us? Since the Confederation that we once fought against seems to have withdrawn their support for this sector, their fighters are unsupported, frequently forced to improvise or do without. I will admit one advantage humans, or at least some humans, seem to have over our race is being able to find alternative solutions quite readily.'

'Perhaps,' an older clanmaster, Paumoto, said, 'because their tools are so frequently inadequate to the task.' There was a ripple of agreement.

Paumoto spoke for the most militant of the Musth those who wanted to devote all the race's energy to obliterating the stumbling block of humanity. Only Man had presented a threat to the Musth, and vice versa. Other intelligent races encountered were either unambitious, not imperialistic, far less advanced or, most commonly, not oxygen-based, and therefore welcome to the worlds Man and Musth found harsh, uninhabitable.

Thus far, Paumoto had gained only marginal support, most of his race either having no contact and hence no interest in humanity, or believing Mankind was a tottering, dying race that would vanish of its own stupidity.

One of Paumoto's strongest allies was Keffa, who unfortunately had far too much wealth and too little seasoning.

'That may be true,' Wlencing said once the amusement died down. 'But I do not take our enemies lightly. Still, I have full confidence that we can destroy them if we fight cleverly.'

'I admire you, War Leader,' Paumoto said, 'and your more perceptive fellows, for realizing what I've been warning for half a generation is the truth, that we must confront Mankind, on our terms, as soon as possible.

'This galaxy, and the ones around it, can support only one master, and we must put Man in his place before he can grow stronger! The perhaps-chaos of their Confederation offers us the perfect opportunity.'

'Thank you,' another clanmaster, Senza, said, 'but I must remind you what happened to make some of us worry about Man.'

Thirty-five E-years earlier, the Musth had sent a major colonization group into a mineral-rich cluster both races had discovered. They took over worlds already claimed by Man, began to exploit the system. The Confederation struck back hard, destroying most of the Musth force, and made a harsh treaty requiring them to cede half a dozen systems in the sector to the humans, as well as the systems that sparked the war.

The clanmasters shifted uncomfortably, some ears cocking in anger. No Musth liked to be reminded of the past, especially if it smelled of failure.

Senza was generally regarded as unbalanced, even a calamity bringer, and probably would have been brought down if he wasn't extraordinarily careful about his personal safety.

He was also grudgingly accorded respect because he was the unquestioned head of the ubiquitous and vital *Polperro*, or 'Reckoners.' The *Polperro* were a unique clan, able to recruit from any other of the Musth, since they were the race's diplomats and lawyers, the lubricant that kept the race from perpetual civil war.

Unlike most of the other Musth, Senza had voluntarily visited Man's worlds and returned impressed. He thought each race had much to learn from the other, and might consider an alliance rather than enmity. His views were popular only with the young Musth who could break from tradition, or the more radical elements of the clans, those who wanted change from the existing order.

'The past is dead,' growled Keffa.

Senza moved a paw diagonally, signaling doubt.

'It is,' Paumoto said with finality, 'as far as this debate. The question now is, what to do about the men in the Cumbre system? This moment, this chance. Suggestions?'

'We should return with warriors, not miners,' War Leader Wlencing insisted. 'Hit first, hit hard, and the system is ours. We already have listeners in place, so we shall face few surprises. If the Confederation still exists, they'll be faced with a done deed. If they do not' – he held out a paw, extended its claws – 'we will have returned to our former path of conquest. There does not seem to be another option, nor, if we take this way, the risk of us suffering any real damage.'

'What of the humans who don't conveniently die,' Senza asked. 'Should we set stinging-ones on them?' These near-insects were part of one of the Musth's less pleasant hand weapons. Held unconscious in grenades, they swarmed anything moving when the grenade burst.

'We are not monsters,' Wlencing said. 'I would hardly kill cubs or breeders without provocation. We could not allow them to escape after our victory, for fear they'd bring back the Confederation.

'But isn't there always a place for workers, doing tasks we would rather not? In the mines or even as serving class? Those who survive, and have no desire to oppose us again, might be more useful to us alive.'

'No!' Keffa snarled, eyes reddening in anger. 'When a Musth cannot do his own labor, whether it's clean or filthy, when we think ourselves too good for work, we are ready to pass on, to allow a stronger, more virile race to rule! Senza may have thought he was jesting, but I think he has the correct solution. Brutality now would prevent future complications.'

'Keffa certainly has confidence,' Senza said. 'As yet, we have mounted no campaigns, and already we are discussing the spoils and how we shall murder those we're too stupid to deal with in other ways.'

'Do you doubt our ability to conquer?' Paumoto demanded.

'Certainly not,' Senza said. 'If, and I emphasize *if*, we decide on war. Let me ask, before the words become more fiery, just how many of the clanmasters here want a fight with Man?'

'We've hardly begun to talk about—' Keffa said.

'That, certainly, is the direction of this meeting, so I think the amount of interest in such an extreme passage would be interesting. I call for such a consensus.'

That was Senza's right, and paws touched sensors in each suite.

Seconds later, a screen showed the tabulation:

About a third in favor, a third against, a third undecided.

'Our *great* race,' Senza said, putting slight emphasis on great, 'hardly seems to perceive Wlencing, Paumoto, and Keffa's destiny as obvious.'

'Are you saying we should accept our defeat?' Aesc said. 'Accept being driven from Cumbre?'

'According to the documents, you and War Leader Wlencing chose to withdraw, in order to consult with us. That is hardly being driven anywhere.'

'How do you think the humans will perceive it?' Aesc hissed.

Now there were rumblings throughout the building.

'I do not care how the humans perceive it,' Senza said. 'What they are is what they are. I happen to have far greater faith in the destiny of our race to worry overmuch about humans.

'I will also add I am not impressed by your perform-ance, Aesc, nor you, Wlencing. You involved yourselves in what was a most minor operation, seeing no doubt great advancement therein.

'I do not see many riches having been gained through your actions.

'Now, you want to increase our involvement in the system. I think this is foolish. I think we should pursue one of two courses, which I suggest to this gathering.

'First, we permit your involvement with the Cumbre system to continue, but with no greater commitment than before. I enter this for a vote at this time, but request my fellow clan leaders wait until my second sug-gestion is offered.

'That is that we retreat from the Cumbrian system entirely and restrict our presence there to a purchasing team or two, and trade for the minerals the system has.

'It is perhaps inevitable we shall encounter other races than the ones we have to date, races which are as ambi-tious as we are and who also share the same carbon-based cycle.

'If we can learn from Man, study their weaknesses, could not those same lessons be applied when we encounter other aliens, and decide whether they are our enemies or our allies?

'Think well on these two matters, clan leaders. We may, in what appears to be a very minor matter today be setting policies future Musth will praise or curse us for.

'Now I call for a vote.'

Senza was not surprised at all when both his measures failed handily.

'Now that that foolishness has passed,' Paumoto said, 'we can return to the real issue and forget cubbish sentiment.

I suggest we return to Cumbre, but with a larger force than before, one mostly composed of warriors. The detachment would be led by Aesc, since he is most familiar with the system, and his second-in-command would be Wlencing. Be aware I would like him to be the second in everything, not merely military.

'Rather than have our main elements stationed on Silitric, and our headquarters in a remote section of their home-world, we should establish posts in every city on the planet.'

'I don't understand their purpose,' Aesc said.

'On the surface,' Paumoto said, 'to attempt to lessen the tension between our two races. But in reality to monitor exactly what these men are planning, thinking, and to be ready for an instant, violent response if that is required.'

'Or, perhaps,' Senza added cynically, 'Paumoto is suggesting them as targets, so that if men wrong the Musth, they will have an opportunity close at hand, and we will then have enough reason to retaliate for such a massacre instantly.

'Is that an element of your thinking?'

'I would hardly allow myself to speak for a policy that might mean the deaths of some of our people, would I?'

'No,' Senza said. 'You would not *speak* about it.'

'There shall come a time, Senza,' Keffa put in, and, the clanmasters could see on their screens, his claws needled in, out, 'when your cleverness shall turn against you.'

'Is this a challenge?' Senza said. 'To my clan, or to myself? If you are challenging me personally, you should remember I said time past I would accept no offers to duel. Blood settles little, which you'll learn, Keffa, as you grow and age. If you age.'

'Enough,' Paumoto said. 'I would wish to put my suggestion to a vote, reminding those who are in favor of the measure they will be required to assist in the funding and equipage of this expedition.'

The tally was taken slowly, over several hours, as various factions argued back and forth or withheld their votes until one side or the other won the argument or presented recompense.

At the end of the time, 112 clanmasters involved themselves and their clans, with only a scattering of votes against the proposal. Senza, like most of the others, remained neutral.

'Is that enough?' Aesc asked Wlencing privately.

'More than,' the War Leader responded. 'For the ones who favor the measure are the ones rich in weapons, warriors, and power, and once the inevitable happens, the others will scratch to join us.

'This marks a new beginning.

'It shall not be long,' Wlencing said firmly, 'that all Musth will join us, and the day of man's removal from our path shall arrive.'

The next day, as Senza's mothership offplaneted, his aide, Kenryo, came to him.

'Your student Alikhan, Wlencing's cub, remained on 4Planet.'

Senza lifted a paw, indicating mild surprise.

'He's chosen to serve with his father, on Cumbre.'

'Which means we have lost another battle,' Senza said. 'Another one chooses the violence-way, the way that requires no thought, no reasoning.'

'You denigrate your teachings, sir.'

'In what way?'

'I do not think Alikhan is completely insensate, that his time with us was wasted, that your thoughts were ignored.'

'Thank you for the compliment,' Senza said. 'But if

you are right, then the cub may be troubled by the contrast between what we believe and what his father will practice.

'I fear,' he said somberly, 'his final decision, as many others he has made, has a strong probability of being made in blood.'

TWO

Cumbre/D-Cumbre

'And don't you love this peacetime army,' *Alt* Garvin Jaansma, Commanding Officer, Intelligence and Reconnaissance Company, Headquarters, RaoForce, panted. 'Duding in custom-tailored uniforms, ankling down a promenade, the rattle of good silver in your pants, every admiring eye on you, the goddamned palladium . . . whatever the hell that is . . . of all that's good, right, and just in society?'

'Shaddup and help me bang this friggin' form back where it's supposed to be before Monique buries us in quikset,' his executive officer, *Aspirant* Njangu Yoshitaro, grunted.

Both officers, barely twenty E-years old, wore torn, sweaty undershirts, work boots, and cement-stained pants.

Hosed down and in the midnight blue dress uniform of the Force, they would look a great deal better, particularly Jaansma.

He was tall, almost two meters, blond, with a natural weightlifter's body, and an open, firm face. If he lived long enough and didn't desert, he could end up in a high command position strictly on appearance. He was the descendent of a longtime circus family, and had enlisted hastily after setting Earth tigers loose on a mob.

Njangu Yoshitaro was a bit shorter than Jaansma, slender, dark-complected and -haired. He was less handsome than striking, and his eyes were constantly calculating. He never talked about his background, or about his criminal record that'd put him between enlistment or conditioning.

The two met as raw recruits, on the last troopship from the Confederation capital of Centrum, and had distinguished themselves enough as soldiers and covert operators during the recent 'Raum uprising to be offered commissions.

They were currently at the bottom of a five-by-five-by-six-meter hole that they, and a half-dozen other Intelligence and Reconnaissance soldiers had dug using explosives, antigrav hoppers, shovels, and obscenities.

A cool wind blew down the mouth of Dharma Bay, toward Chance Island and D-Cumbre's capital of Leggett. The sand was clean, the sky improbably blue, and the surf curling white against the ocean.

At the bottom of the hole, nobody could see anything entrancingly tropical, though. A battered, obsolete Cooke lowered toward them, its cargo bay filled with fresh concrete, First *Tweg* Monique Lir at the controls. Lir, if you discounted her muscles and steel-toothed attitude, looked less like the stereotypical hard-ass noncom than a model or actress.

'Ready to pour?' she called.

Njangu looked skeptically at the plas form around the pit.

'You realize if she screws it, and buries us alive, she'll take over the company, don't you?'

'Thank Allah and his all-girl band that she is happy

being the brains behind the scenes,' Garvin said, then shouted, 'Let 'er go.'

'So she claims,' Yoshitaro muttered, and whatever else he added was inaudible as concrete gushed down the nozzle held by a sweating striker.

'Why,' Yoshitaro tried, when the rumble died a bit, 'are we, two big-time, supposedly bright officers, standing underneath a goddamned Cooke, when we've done everything to get rid of the worthless bastards because they crash so much?'

'Pure intellect,' Garvin suggested. 'And it's my turn to ask questions: Who the hell came up with this idiot idea of leading by example?'

'You did, you dolt. I think you got it out of some manual.'

'What a dipsh,' Garvin said. 'We coulda been strolling around, supervising, with maybe a cold beer in each hand. Instead—'

'You mention beer and cold in the same sentence and I'm gonna throttle you, even if you do outrank me,' Yoshitaro managed, coughing as dust clouded them.

'Empty,' Lir called. 'Going for more.'

'Why are we so *special*?' Garvin said, then shouted 'Take it up!'

'Why's she driving, anyway? How'd that friggin' Dill manage to get out of the scut work flying cement around, anyway?'

'He's playing test pilot. This is his big day to Die Gloriously over on Mullion. So he's too busy and bigtime for us.'

'Asshole. Shows what happens when you commission an elephant.'

Lanbay Island, once utterly uninhabited and uninhabitable, was being turned into a tiny fortress, with half a dozen missile pits and a central command bunker being built on it.

On other islands, on the arms of Dharma Island circling the bay, on Mullion Island and many of the other islands and small continents sprayed across D-Cumbre's middle, more fortifications were being hastily built. Some would be manned immediately, but most would only be used if the Musth fulfilled their promise of months earlier, and returned with warriors.

Or if Alena Redruth, 'Protector' of Larix and Kura came back with warships and a stronger offer of 'protection.'

The Strike Force was very busy, and gloomily expected to be still busier in the future as it deployed out from the comfortable, easily targeted Camp Mahan on Dharma Island.

It'd once been called, rather grandiloquently, Swift Lance, the Confederation force holding the Cumbre system and keeping the colonists safe, as often as not from each other.

Two local years earlier, when Jaansma and Yoshitaro had arrived, Swift Lance had been the very model of a lazy, button-polishing peacetime garrison unit. But the 'Raum uprising brought reality in with a shock.

Now it was commanded by *Caud* Prakash Rao, and it was officially RaoForce, the Force, or commonly the Legion, when its soldiers needed a label that wasn't obscene.

It had taken massive casualties in the Rising, including its then CO and most of his staff, and surviving soldiers like Yoshitaro and Jaansma had been rapidly promoted. The formation was rebuilt with recruits from the local population. As Jon Hedley, once CO of I&R Company had predicted, a lot of them, frequently the best, came from the defeated 'Raum. If a recruit, man or woman, showed unusual familiarity with weapons or tactics, no one in the Force asked where she or he had learned, but instead marked them for early promotion.

RaoForce was nearly up to its authorized strength of ten thousand. But it was far weaker in equipment than before the shooting had started. There still was no communication, let alone supplies or equipment, from the Confederation, and the Force was learning to rebuild total wrecks, do without, or improvise from whatever could be found in Cumbre's civilian sector.

Everyone knew time was short, and wondered where the next enemy would come from, and whether it would be human or Musth.

Dec Running Bear stretched behind the controls of the sleek lim, now incongruously anodized in camouflage pattern.

'If you're stiffening up,' *Caud* Rao offered from the rear of the luxury lifter, 'I can fly this beast.'

'Nossir,' Running Bear said. 'Just reminding myself I'm not dreaming, and gonna wake up still flying a Cooke.'

Rao looked at him skeptically, went back to his quiet conference with *Mil* Angara, the Force executive officer, and his aide, *Alt* Erik Penwyth.

Rao, medium height, dark, stocky, early fifties, could have passed for a 'Raum. Angara's still-athletic body was beginning to lose the fight with gravity and desserts. Erik Penwyth had hair a bit long for an officer, a long aristocratic face and nose to match. Not your usual recruitment poster grouping.

Something had happened, Running Bear knew, something big. The evident casualness of the three officers was deceptive. But it wasn't his affair.

He thought about Rao's volunteering to take the controls of the lim. That was a change from the old days.

Caud Williams was nice enough, but he never would've thought to play driver.

Hell, pushing this lim around, a gift from the momentarily grateful Rentiers of D-Cumbre instead of a rickety Cooke dripping with autocannons, was a big change.

Running Bear touched his new rank tab and the Confederation Cross, the empire's highest award, on his breast. His wounds were bothering him a little, but he didn't really mind. The pain kept reminding him he should've been quite dead after doing a last stand like he was that white-eye Cutter or Cluster or whatever the guy's name was, and not be whining about whatever was bothering him.

Changes . . . he glanced out the driver's window to his left, at the beaches of Leggett, then the wasteland that'd been the 'Raum ghetto, the Eckmuhl, mostly destroyed in the 'Raum's final, desperate counterattack.

He still wasn't sure if he liked the idea of serving with people who'd been shooting at him not very long ago, but when he'd brought it up once to Rao, the officer had told him to never mind, and so he had. Especially after one of the 'Raum strikers in his section had taken him home on pass, and Running Bear had met the striker's sister.

Not that there was much to do even if you did somehow find a social life. Leggett was rebuilding. but not as quickly as anyone liked. The war had cost money, not just lives, and the ensuing peace hadn't brought much in the way of prosperity, since there still was no offplanet market for the minerals on C-Cumbre.

The AmerInd shrugged. Not his business, nor concern.

'Coming in, sir,' he said, and banked the lim down toward the new prefab that was Planetary Government, not half a kilometer from where the old building had vanished in a boil of flame, along with most PlanGov officials.

The lim grounded, and the three officers got out. Penwyth carried a small projector and screen.

'Find a shady spot and get something to eat from the canteen,' Rao said. 'This is liable to take all day.'

'Yessir,' Running Bear said, and lifted away.

'Here we go,' Rao said. 'Penwyth, kick me if I don't kiss the proper asses, since you know Rentier high society. We want to make sure they give us what we want.'

Penwyth grinned slightly, but said nothing. He was, indeed, part of D-Cumbre's upper crust. He'd enlisted in the military for no known reason, then been commissioned from I&R in lieu of being court-martialed for pretending to be an officer, since he got away with it.

'It'll be interesting to see what happens,' *Mil* Angara said. 'It's bad enough being isolated, without the nasty little secret we're about to hand them.'

'Especially since,' Penwyth said, 'a lot of people I know have friends, sometimes even relatives, on Larix or Kura. There'll be howling. But they'll have to recognize the truth.'

'With all this logic on our side,' Rao said, 'we've got to be doomed.' And on that note he led the way into PlanGov.

'They say,' *Alt* Ben Dill, Commander of the Mobile Scout Section recently folded into Intelligence and Reconnaissance, 'if it looks good, it'll fly good.'

'Can't flippin' argue with that,' said *Haut* Jon Hedley, head of the Force's II Section – Intelligence. Hedley was a gangling, profane, lazy man who somehow could hike any of his soldiers into the ground while yodeling and skipping backwards, then carry their packs into camp while they crawled home.

Both men were lying, both knowing half a hundred examples of air/space craft with lines that sang, and performance that killed.

Dill was not quite the size of a Terran elephant; late twenties, prematurely balding, and naturally big in every direction without ever having to work out. There were those who'd made the mistake of thinking anyone that big couldn't move that fast.

He'd commanded the Grierson – the standard Aerial Combat Vehicle – Garvin Jaansma had been assigned to when he joined the Force, showed talent as a covert insertion specialist during the 'Raum Rising, been commissioned and tasked to restructure I&R's new integral flight section. Despite his inherently casual attitude about everything, Dill could fly a Grierson, or anything else he'd gotten behind the controls of, through the eye of a needle without touching metal.

Dill ambled around the Musth *aksai* toward its command pod. It was one of half a dozen that'd been abandoned, in various shades of disrepair, when the Musth pulled out of the Cumbre system.

The Force had quietly taken the ships, as well as other scrounged or 'acquired' non-military aircraft and spaceships to a new, secret airbase hastily cut out of the jungle on Mullion Island. There, technicians began laboriously figuring out not only how the *aksai* flew, but how they kept on flying.

Hedley hoped they wouldn't need these ships, whose cost and maintenance were buried deep in the Force's classified intelligence budget, but preferred to prepare for the worst.

'Are you sure you're going to fit, Ben?' he asked. Unless around higher-ranking outsiders, no one in I&R ever called anyone other than his first name or just 'boss.'

'Be a bit tight,' Dill said. 'But I've laid off the beer for a week, so I should slide in, properly greased.'

Two techs stood nearby, next to a starter cart and a jury-rigged boarding ladder.

Dill walked once more around the *aksai*. 'Don't see anything dangling, so I might as well give it a shot.'

He checked his flight suit, made sure its various emergency devices were functioning.

'Tell Mother I died game,' he said, and went up the ladder to the cockpit. It creaked, but held.

The concave *aksai* varied from model to model as to the number of fighting positions, from one to four, all of them prone and in pods in various places along the body, about twenty-five meters from horn to horn. The pilot lay in his pod not quite in the center of the C-curve. Dill crawled backwards into the flight pod.

'I fit, I think. Nobody use the word "claustrophobia."'

He closed his eyes, let his fingers run over controls never meant for man. Dill had spent every minute the techs let him in the cockpit, memorizing the controls and the functions computer analysis, logic, and ground rehearsal suggested. Labels had been cut and stuck on the sensors to help him out. Dill preferred tactile memory.

'Start it up,' he ordered, touching the sensor that slid the clamshell canopy closed around his face. He keyed the human com that'd been welded into the cockpit, set on a seldom-used frequency.

'Chase One, this is Experimental-Alpha. How you hear this station?'

A civilian stuntcraft commandeered by the Force soared a thousand meters overhead.

'Ex-Alpha, Chase One. Strength Five.'

'This is Alpha. Engines being started. Let me know if any significant pieces fall off.'

A microphone click responded.

Dill felt the Musth ship vibrate, and watched the techs' hands swarm over the starter cart. Bar lights flashed on the canopy, were level with each other, went away. Dill appreciated the Musth instrument design. If it wasn't a problem, it wasn't there, and none of the bar lights were currently flashing violet, the Musth emergency color.

The vibration went away.

Dill touched sensors. Everything seemed to be as it should.

He keyed another Force-added box.

'Ex-Control, this is Ex-Alpha,' Dill said. 'Telemeters on. Beginning first flight test.'

On the ground, *Haut* Chaka, normally commander of Golan element, a heavy Zhukov section, touched his throat mike.

'This is Experimental Control. Telemetric recording 'kay. Standing by. Good luck.'

'All Ex stations,' Dill said. He frowned, annoyed that his voice had just a bit of hoarseness to it. He'd already done static and tethered ground-level tests on the *aksai*, so there wasn't any reason to be nervous. None at all. 'Lifting.'

His fingers brushed a control, and the *aksai* bobbed, then came clear of the ground. He touched it a little harder.

The fighting ship rose straight up, waggled a little.

'Landing gear up,' Dill said, and the skids slid into their slots. 'Switching to secondary power and beginning programmed test,' and the *aksai* accelerated, started to climb, wiggled frantically for a minute.

'Son of a bitch,' Dill muttered.

'This is Control,' Chaka's calm voice came. 'What happened?'

'Critter's about as easy to fly as balancing a plate on a stick. Shut up and let me concentrate.'

Haut Chaka ignored the insubordination, eyes fixed on the three screens showing the *aksai* overhead.

' 'Kay,' Dill muttered. 'Got it now.'

He pulled the *aksai* back into a climb, fed power.

'Ex-Alpha, this is Chase One,' the pilot of the stunt plane said. 'You went past me like payday. On full power, climbing after you . . . you're still pulling away from me.'

'Power setting, half-power, I think,' Dill said. 'The mother seems to work. Beginning aerobatic routine.'

He touched other sensors. and the *aksai* banked left, right, rolled, suddenly spun for an instant, corrected itself.

'Shit, this bassid's delicate,' Dill said. 'Try that one again.'

Once more he went through the memorized routine, at various altitudes, stages of power.

'She seems to want to motivate,' he said. 'First hairy routine.'

He nosed over, sent the *aksai* screaming toward the far-distant ocean below.

'Radar has you at Mach 7,' Chaka said. 'Passing through five thousand meters.'

'Feels like. Beginning pullout. Lemme know if the wings fall off, if that's what they call these wiggly guys on either side of me.'

Dill touched the base of a sensor, and the *aksai* lifted, bobbled, then smoothly swooped back up into the skies.

'Bird's got a nice gimmick,' he said. 'Antigrav cuts in when you pull more'n, guesstimate, five Gs. I could do this all day long and not puke more'n once or twice.

'Stand by Chase One, I'm gonna yump for space. Control, you've alerted Big Ears? I'd hate to get my ass shot off as an unknown intruder.'

'That's affirm,' Chaka said. 'Everybody's turning a blind eye.'

The warning stations at C-Cumbre's north and south poles and on the moons of Fowey and Bodwin had been alerted to see nothing and notify no one of the tests.

'Ears . . . eyes . . . what a confusion. Yow! Chase One, I just blew past you like you were parked . . . Chase Two, this is Experimental Alpha. Do you have me?'

A converted private yacht just out-atmosphere opened its mike.

'Have you roarin' and ready, Alpha.'

'Advancing to two-thirds drive,' Dill said. 'And let's see what Kailas looks like. Experimental One, clear.'

Two hours later, Dill touched his mike sensor.

'Experimental Control, Experimental Control, this is Experimental-Alpha, inbound from the far side of the moon.'

'I have you, Ex-Alpha.'

'This sucker scrambles,' Dill reported. 'Wish I had stardrive clearance. It'd be interesting to see what happens when I hit the big red button.'

'That's for another hero, later,' Chaka said. 'Bring it on home. It seems like we're a success.'

'Wait 'til I land,' Dill said. 'If I land. Then break out the champagne and promotions. But it does look like, assuming we can get those other sluts in the air, the Force has got some new toys.'

PlanGov at one time had been led by Confederation officials, most killed in a 'Raum suicide strike. Now PlanGov was a Council of some twenty men and women, all Cumbre natives. *Caud* Rao had to lay down the law quite firmly to keep the Rentiers, the self-appointed rulers of the system, from simply appointing twenty of their own, and had forced the aristos to put three 'Raum, one merchant, one fisherman, and two miners, both also 'Raum, on the board, as well as a nonvoting observer from the Force. The positions were initially named by caucuses of the various classes, but free elections had been promised within a year.

It didn't give the majority of the population majority rule, but it was a hopeful beginning.

The Rentiers had been hit as hard as anyone during the 'Raum riots, and so the Council members were mostly younger than traditional elitists.

Among the new executives were Loy Kouro, the dapperly handsome heir to *Matin*, Cumbre's biggest and most conservative news source and publishing trust, whose father had died in the blast that destroyed the PlanGov; and Jasith Mellusin, who'd become the heir to Mellusin Mining in the same explosion.

The two had another thing in common: Garvin Jaansma. Kouro had become his enemy after a minor brawl at a party; Jasith had been his lover, then suddenly broke off the relationship, without offering any explanation, when the fighting ended.

Caud Rao waited until the Council's normal business came to an end, then requested his matter be held in camera, which was promptly granted. It was still close enough to the insurrection that the Rentiers hadn't forgotten who'd kept their corrupt regime from being completely destroyed.

'There probably isn't any question more important to *us*,' *Caud* Rao began, 'than what has happened to the Confederation, or, rather, why Cumbre has been cut off from any contact with the mother worlds.

'We don't have a complete answer, but we have a partial one, with supporting evidence:

'The worlds of Larix and Kura, supposed longtime allies of ours, have been systematically cutting off any convoy or single ship passing through their sector.'

Rao paused, waited for the outrage and shock to settle. He nodded to Penwyth, who set up his equipment.

'Not only have convoys not been reaching us for more than two local years, but none of the starships offplaneting from Cumbre have returned, no matter what their destination within the Confederation.

'We determined to find out, if we could, what was happening. We acquired a small transport, roboticized its controls, and fitted it with the most elaborate sensors we have access to. A second, manned ship completed the task force.

'The first ship was programmed to follow the standard astrographic plots between Cumbre and Centrum, the Confederation capital. Most frequently, these plots pass close to Larix and Kura, with the third or fourth jump beyond Cumbre entering their system.

'The first ship was to make a jump, then, immediately on return to normal space, launch a missile with stardrive capabilities. All data received by the ship's sensors was to be 'cast on a tight beam to the missile. If the datalink was broken, the missile was to enter N-space, and send out a targeting signal for the second ship to home on.

'On the first jump, nothing happened, and the second ship's crew signaled the first to make another jump. Again there was nothing untoward.

'However, the third jump was very different. When still in hyperspace, the first ship was swept by detectors. When it exited N-space, it was immediately challenged. Since there was no crew aboard to respond, the ship was attacked.

'I have full records of events to this point for anyone interested. However, the most important data is from this point forward.'

He nodded to Penwyth, who touched sensors and the screen lit.

'This,' Rao explained, 'is a composite image from various sensors aboard the roboticized transport. Here, you can see a ship appear from hyperspace. This ship has been identified, plus or minus less than point-one percent, as being a Confederation *Remora*-class destroyer leader.

'The flagship of Alena Redruth's fleet is such a ship, the *Corfe*.

'This isn't necessarily conclusive, however. Over two hundred of that class DL have been commissioned in the last twenty years, and some might have fallen into the hands of pirates, if such exist.

'At this point, our transport has been electronically challenged, ordered to take up a certain orbit and prepare for inspection. The challenge is preemptory, and no part of the signal says who the challenging party is.

'Of course, our ship failed to respond.

'Now, you *see* three other ships, here, here, and here on-screen? These are very unusual, brand new *Nirvana*-class patrol boats.

'Now, these ships are very new, very classified, and all are supposedly reserved for Confederation Homeworld troops.

'How my predecessor, the late *Caud* Williams, learned of their existence, how he was able to request some of them, is beyond my ken. But he did, and those ships were also on the *Malvern*, the mysteriously highjacked ship, together with other supplies and more than seven hundred fifty fresh recruits.

'Only three of those recruits, incidentally, were able to evade the "pirates," and make their way in a lifeboat to Cumbre. Two of them still survive, serving in the Force. The third man, an experienced Confederation soldier, absolutely identified one of the "pirates" as being another Confederation veteran who'd left the service to join Alena Redruth's forces. Unfortunately, this third man didn't survive the recent ... unpleasantness. However, his friends did, and one of them positively identified this soldier as being among the "pirates," and later saw him some months ago, as part of Alena Redruth's staff when they visited C-Cumbre.

'The reason that none of you have heard of these three is because the late Planetary Governor Haemer and *Caud* Williams ordered them to keep silent.

'Those *Nirvana*-class ships, by the way, accompanied Protector Redruth on the *Corfe* when he visited the Cumbre system last. I don't know if *Caud* Williams failed to recognize those patrol craft, or chose to keep quiet, or possibly informed Planetary Governor Haemer of them. Both men are dead now, so it doesn't matter.

'But the evidence now is quite clear. Our supposed friend, Alena Redruth, is the pirate, the one who's successfully blockading Confederation ships, if any, from reaching us and vice versa.'

The Council grew into a hubbub of shock, disbelief. Rao waited patiently.

Kouro was the first to speak or rather wail, somewhat coherently.

'But what does this *mean*?'

'It means, just for openers,' Rao said, 'we've got more than one enemy to worry about. The next time Protector Redruth offers his support, I imagine it will be made in even stronger terms than before. A man who's willing to chance angering the Confederation certainly will have no hesitation seizing Cumbre's resources, given half a chance.'

'And what will we do?'

'I've taken a vow to the Confederation,' Rao said. 'As have all my officers. If anyone attempts to overthrow the legal government of Cumbre, we'll fight.'

'But they've got starships, heavy equipment, a far

larger army, don't they?' This came from another Council member.

'So the fiches tell us,' Rao said.

'Can we beat them?' This was from Jasith Mellusin.

'I don't know,' Rao said honestly. 'That's why I came here. We need to put Cumbre on a war footing immediately, or face the likelihood of attack, possibly invasion.'

'Another question,' Jasith said. 'This is important to me, and to my father's mining companies, which I've inherited. Before the war, when Protector Redruth visited us, he said that he wanted to increase the amount of ore shipped to his system, that he was going to build a lot more ships than he had.

'But this hasn't happened. My advisors told me the matter was never brought up again to my father, and we can't find any memos or contracts in our files. Do you have any idea what might've happened?'

'I don't know,' *Caud* Rao said. 'If I were cynical, I'd say that Redruth is waiting for a more favorable opportunity.'

'Like just taking them?' Jasith asked.

'I'd guess that thought must've occurred,' Rao said.

Jasith made a face, but said no more.

'One question that's a little aside from the main matter,' a woman asked quietly. She was new to the Council, a 'Raum appointee, and Rao puzzled for her name. Jo Poynton.

'Yes?'

'I'm not familiar with interstellar travel,' she said. 'Is the only route, if that's the correct word, through Larix and Kura?'

'No,' Rao said. 'But it's the most economical and commonly used by far.'

'If the Confederation was still intact, or still concerned about frontier systems like Cumbre, and if they had repeatedly tried one route without success, wouldn't they most likely try a second, or a third?'

'I certainly would, if I were a Confederation official.'

'Yet nothing has come from them since the *Malvern*,' Poynton said thoughtfully.

'So even if we believe your investigation, which certainly sounds credible, the question remains: Something must have happened to the Confederation, to the thousand thousand worlds of our empire, something beyond the petty machinations of this Redruth.

'We know from reports by newly assigned troops and emigrants there were civil risings throughout the empire, including major riots on Capella. Many worlds were put under martial law. There were unconfirmed reports that entire sectors of the empire dropped out of contact or, worse, declared some sort of unilateral independence.

'But what catastrophe could have produced this sudden silence, this complete breakdown of all communications?

'I wish,' *Caud* Rao said slowly, 'I could even hazard a guess. But I cannot.'

THREE

Njangu Yoshitaro leaned against the orderly room railing, listening to the clerk call the mail list: 'Irthing . . . Bassas . . . Fleam . . .'

He pared his nails with his combat knife, wondering what it'd be like to get a letter from someone, tried to pretend it didn't matter that he never had.

'. . . Bayle . . . *Alt* Jaansma . . .'

Njangu looked up with a bit of surprise. Garvin got no more mail than he did, and Yoshitaro wondered who it could be from. Probably a dun from a tailor – Jaansma insisted on dressing like the illegitimate son of a Star Marshal that he occasionally claimed to be.

He idly watched Garvin as the clerk finished the rest of the mail, handed out a few packages. Jaansma opened the small envelope, pulled out what appeared to be a card. His face reddened, and he looked around to see if anyone noticed. Njangu was busy with his nails.

Garvin read the card once more, crumpled it, tossed it into a waste container, and went down the steps into the company area, bootheels thudding hard. A new troopie went by at the double, as required of all potential I&R recruits.

'Hold it, soldier,' Garvin snapped.

The striker broke stride, almost fell, froze at attention.

'Yessir!'

'There's this thing called saluting,' the officer said.

'Sorry, *Alt* Jaansma. Sorry, sir.'

He saluted, Jaansma returned it ill-temperedly.

'Carry on!'

'Yessir. Sorry, sir.'

The soldier watched Garvin pace away, his expression worried, as if this might be enough to get him returned to his parent formation, then ran on.

Njangu went to the waste can, took out the crumpled card Garvin had tossed away, unwrapped it:

LOY KOURO
&
JASITH MELLUSIN
REQUEST THE PLEASURE AND HONOR
OF
YOUR COMPANY
AT THEIR POST-NUPTIAL
BEACH BACCHANAL . . .

'Well, Jesus in lace,' Njangu muttered. 'There are some *evil* humpers out there a lot worse than I ever thought of being.' He wondered who sent the invitation – the worthless Kouro or his bride-to-be. Yoshitaro'd never had much of an opinion of Jasith, other than the general disdain anyone growing up without a pot to piss in or a window to throw it out of had for the rich.

He made a note to stay out of Garvin's way until some days after the reception.

At least, he thought, *they didn't invite him to the wedding. Probably afraid he'd strafe it with a flight of Griersons, which wasn't that bad an idea. Get rid of a whole* flock *of Rentiers . . .*

*

Two days later, an ebullient Ben Dill ricocheted into Garvin at the I&R Company's landing field.

'Kiss me,' he ordered.

Garvin gave him a hard look, which Ben was oblivious to.

'I just got my license ticked for deep space! I'se a real piloter! C'mon to the O Club and help me drink it in.'

'Sorry,' Garvin said shortly. 'I'm running late on the company report. Maybe another time.'

He nodded, walked away.

Dill stared after him.

'Well excuse the *hell* out of me,' he said in a hurt tone. 'And what's the matter with my perfume today?'

Jon Hedley considered the aircraft park, then the camouflage nets, which blocked infrared and heat signals as well as sight.

'We could have us,' he told *Mil* Angara, 'a flipping good shipping company if we wanted.'

Angara nodded.

'Six freighters, eight yachts, a skedaddle of lighters, six converted customs patrol craft, all the Griersons and Zhukovs tested for out-atmosphere deployment . . . what more could we need?' Hedley said.

'A destroyer, a cruiser, a battlewagon, a fighter-launcher for openers,' Angara said.

'You surely know how to rain on somebody's flipping parade. You'd think you were expecting, oh, say, the flipping Musth or maybe Alena Redruth.'

'I expect everything, I expect nothing,' Angara said. 'I am an open vessel.'

'But you gotta admit we're as ready as we're able to be.'

'We are,' Angara agreed. 'I just wish we had more stuff to get more ready. At least we're pretty well dispersed, so all there is to do is worry.'

'Not quite,' Hedley said. 'Considering it's a half hour back to Camp Mahan, and it's pretty near opening time, we'd better hurry.'

'I see you caught that about open vessels, didn't you,' Angara said.

'I always listen to my flipping superiors,' Hedley said piously.

'A word?' Njangu asked, sounding a bit formal.

Garvin put down his paperwork.

'Go ahead.'

'Has anybody suggested you're behaving a bit like an asshole lately?'

Garvin colored, got up from his desk in the I&R Company Headquarters.

'You know, I didn't need this shit from you, of all people.'

'Who else is gonna give it to you?' Yoshitaro pointed out. 'We happen to be friends, remember?'

'Just leave it alone,' Jaansma said. 'I'll be all right.'

'Sure you will. You'll get over being dumped on, sooner or later. Nobody I ever knew died of a busted heart. But you're sure playing hell with the company while you're getting better, growling at everybody so nobody knows whether to shit or go blind, ignoring people half the time, giving them a ration of crap the other half.'

Garvin stared out at the company street, at a team going through gun drill on a rocket launcher borrowed from an Artillery section – I&R trained on every weapon, every vehicle in RaoForce as a matter of routine.

'Whoever dumped that invite on you wasn't your friend,' Njangu pressed. 'And they sure succeeded in getting to you.'

'You know about that?'

'I know about it,' Njangu said. 'And probably half the frigging regiment's figured it out by now.'

'I thought I had all that business tucked away, forgotten,' Garvin said. 'And then whambo, it came bouncing right on back.'

'Yeah,' Njangu. 'Ngai surprises us like that, making us think we're human and all every now and again.'

'And where the hell did you get all this sudden wisdom?'

'Easy,' Njangu said. 'It ain't my problem.'

Garvin smiled wryly.

'So what do I do about it, o combat advisor and valued friend . . . for a dickhead.'

'Go bleed somewhere else.'

'What? Take leave? And what happens if something happens while I'm gone? No way,' Garvin said. 'I've got too much to do.'

'Wasn't suggesting you go piddle off,' Njangu said. 'The new fools we've got training are coming up for their graduation exercise.

'We're fat city, no more'n two percent understrength, and the way it looks we're gonna graduate about eleven of them, with only two, maybe three washouts. Things like that are liable to make Hedley think we're getting soft since he gave us the company.

'So take these clowns up in the hills, bust their nuts, see if you can't get five or six of 'em to go crying home to momma.'

'Like where?'

Njangu considered the wall map.

'Here's something that'd be a real killer. Take the virgins across to Dharma Island, maybe on the far side of Mount Najim, hike on up into the Highlands. It'll be nice and frozen, make 'em homesick for the tropics down here.

'Go completely tactical, no air unless it's an emer-gency . . .' Njangu looked at the map again, checked the legend. 'Yeh. Here we go. Insert here, where it's still fairly livable, then shamble on up into the Highlands to . . . here. That's the Musth base they abandoned.

'See if there's any interesting sou-ven-waars. Tell the little bastards that we'll come in with hot rats and cold beer, give them a nice ride back here for graduation, then put on your best sorrow-face and say, "The airlift didn't show, and we'll have to hike back".'

'That ought to get some people busting into tears and quitting.'

Garvin looked at the map, at Yoshitaro.

'That's an evil thought. How long ago was it you went through this shit?'

'Year or so. Which reminds me. You never did qualify, not formally. So this'll be your own final grad. How's that hang, my friend? Be a real shame if you start wheezing and quit on us. They'll have to give the company to me, and send you back to polishing Griersons.

'Give me a chance to give it some kind of sexy name, like all these steel-teeth units do in the holos. Screw Jaansma's Jewels, it'll be Yoshitaro's . . . um . . .

'Yoinks,' Jaansma said, a smile coming for the first time in he didn't remember how many days. 'Yerks. Yaahoos. Yobbos. Yoodles. Yackoffs.'

'Shut the hell up, *sir*. And go pack.'

'Thank you, *Aspirant*. I'll take your suggestion. God help those poor trainees. Take charge of the company 'til I get back.'

'I shall,' Njangu promised. 'And you'll not recognize it for the improvements.'

The Rentiers had built a great tabernacle, almost a fortress, overlooking the city of Leggett, just where the

ground rose into the Heights and the aristocrats'
estates.

Their religion was quiet, formal, full of exactitude,
and helped demarcate the established families from the
parvenus. A proper Rentier could maneuver easily
through the rituals, while still admiring or despising the
dress of a competitor or friend, considering whose turn it
was to invite a 'few friends' over for a postservice meal, or
the latest gossip from the night before's ball.

The Leader waited until the chorus's chanting died
away in the dim rafters of the temple, then walked forward, his white-and-black robes swishing as he moved.

'This is the second reading of the matrimony proposed
between Loy Kouro and Jasith Mellusin. Again, is there
any among us who knows of a reason these two should
not be joined in matrimony?'

He waited.

Someone, no one ever found out who, far in the back,
giggled.

A few necks stiffened, but no one turned to look.

'There are none,' the Leader said. 'Now, let us turn to
this day's lesson . . .'

The Grierson came in hot, skidding sideways and letting
its momentum smash down brush on the edge of the
clearing. Eleven women and men staggered out, anthro-
poidal under huge packs, blasters cradled in their arms,
lumbered to the far side of the clearing, and fell into a
defensive perimeter.

Inside the Grierson, Garvin started to unplug his
throat mike, hesitated, keyed a sensor.

'Vehicle Commander, this is Jaansma.'

'Yeh,' Ben Dill said flatly.

'Hey. Sorry I was a shit-for-brains.'

Without waiting for a reply, he lifted off the flight

helmet, pulled on a floppy patrol hat, and lurched out into the center of the perimeter, dropping to his knee beside the trainee named as that day's patrol leader and her com man.

She, like the other recruits, had been ground down to the point of emaciation by the long weeks of training in and around Camp Mahan, and her face, which might be pretty after a week's sleep, was pale in spite of the blazing sun. She was seventeen and, like the others, had her black hair shaved.

The Grierson's ramp snapped up, and the combat vehicle lifted away sharply. This was the second time it'd lowered into a jungle clearing, and in common with standard insertion tactics, would do a second false insertion before returning to Camp Mahan.

The trainee, a woman named Montagna, reflexively waited for Jaansma to tell her what to do, then realizing she was The Man now, recovered. She checked her map hastily, making sure, as best she could, they'd been landed where she'd asked to be put down.

The patrol order had been set before they lifted off. Montagna nodded to the point man, and he checked his primitive compass, got up, and, moving slowly, eased into the jungle. Jaansma had insisted compasses be used, rather than global positioning SatPos, both to increase the hassle factor and because it was possible for an enemy not only to use satellite positioning to give false locations, but to backplot and locate someone using the system.

Behind the point man came the woman picked for slack, then the rest of the patrol.

Jaansma walked behind Montana and the com man, moving in easy rhythm, as he'd done in many, many training patrols since taking over I&R, wondering why the hell he'd allowed himself to be talked out of being a nice quiet gunner on a Grierson, riding around high over this muck, letting his mind forget Mahan, Leggett, and people who were going to get married.

''Kay,' the wedding coordinator said briskly. 'Now, imagine music . . . bumpbumpadump, bumpbumpadump . . . and the bride, that's you, Jasith, will come through those doors, that's right, no, more slowly, dear, you'll lose your flower girls, and go to the center aisle, where Loy will be waiting.

'You'll hold the moment for the coms which'll be up there, remote from the rafters, another one in this pew, a third from behind you, at the main entrance.

'You bridesmaids, don't pay any attention to the cameras, don't wave, or play the fool, or you'll get no champagne at the reception.

'Now, let's run through it . . . bumpbumpadump, bumpbumpadump, pause, turn, now start up the aisle, bumpbumpadump, bumpbumpadump, and here comes little whatsisface holding your train and what the hell do you want?'

The portly red-faced woman was scowling at a slender woman with a com.

'Florist, ma'am. I need to go over just where you'll want the wreaths, and where the flowers from guests will go.'

'For the love of . . . all right, girls. Take a break.'

Jasith Mellusin slumped into a pew, wiped sweat. Mellusin was not quite the richest woman on C-Cumbre, heir to her murdered father's mining empire, but close. She was just twenty, medium height, with a slender model's body, black hair she kept long, and a pouty, provocative face.

'This rehearsing is hot and stupid,' she said.

'Not as hot and stupid as it's going to be on The Day,'

one of her bridesmaids, Karo Lonrod said. 'Aren't you glad you decided to get married, ha-ha-ha?'

Lonrod was a year younger and a few centimeters shorter than Jasith, red-haired, with a slight tendency to chubbiness that her fanaticism for sports kept under control. She, like all the other women in the huge temple, was a Rentier, wealthy, and most aware of it.

Jasith hesitated for a bare instant, then said, 'It's better than the alternatives. And I could use a drink.'

'Who said it's better?' Lonrod said. 'I don't plan on hitching to anyone 'til I'm an old maid, maybe twenty-five, no matter what Daddy wants or what rich prick he tries to shove down my throat.'

She giggled. 'I didn't mean what I said to come out like that.'

Jasith managed a smile, looked around, saw no one was in earshot.

'Karo, can I ask you something?'

'Surely. Perhaps I'll even give you an answer.'

'You went out with Loy.'

'I did.' There was sudden caution in the other woman's voice.

'What's he like in bed?'

Karo blinked at Jasith.

'You mean you don't know?'

'No,' Jasith said, not looking at her friend. 'I wanted to, but he said he wouldn't, not with the woman he was going to marry.'

'Oh boy.'

'What does that mean?'

'I don't know what it means,' Lonrod said. 'But I didn't know there was anybody in our group that won't screw anything that comes in range. Did he say why?'

'No. He just said it was real important to him.'

'That's weiiiird,' Karo said. 'But 'kay, if that's the way he thinks. He's 'kay in the rack. Isn't as creative as some, but he stays there 'til you go off, at least.

'But he isn't one of those go-all-night wonders like a couple you and I could remember.'

Jasith's serious expression dissolved, and she giggled.

'As long as you asked me,' Lonrod said. 'What was that soldier boy you were going out with like? And why'd you dump him?'

Jasith's laughter stopped suddenly.

'I don't really want to talk about him,' she said. 'But I'll tell you why I couldn't stay with Garvin. Just thinking about him reminded me of all that blood, and the shooting, and what happened to Daddy.'

'I don't track,' Karo said. 'He didn't start the war.'

'I don't know,' said Jasith. 'But I couldn't think of going to bed with him after that. I don't know why. Maybe . . .' she let her voice trail off.

Lonrod looked at Jasith closely.

'Are you sure this whole. thing is that good an idea?' Her hand swept the temple, the twenty people waiting for the rehearsal to resume.

'I've got to get married sometime, don't I? And Loy's surely the kind of man my father'd want me to marry, isn't he?'

'Oh, no question about that,' Lonrod said hastily. She was about to say more, caught herself.

'It's too hot to be serious,' she said. 'Let's go see if anybody's got anything cold in their lims.'

Three days out, the patrol reached the steep slopes that led to the Highlands. Already it was cooler than it had been in the lowlands, a chill wind blowing down from the heights.

So far, no one had quit, even though Garvin had been

pushing them hard, giving them only three hours of sleep, and running regular night exercises.

He pointed up and stepped out of the line, then motioned to that day's patrol leader, Abana Calafo, a small cheerful teenager who let nothing bother her, who – Garvin knew – would make it through the training. She came close.

'Straight up,' he whispered. 'Rope up.' A standing joke was you could tell an I&R troop because she'd follow SOP of no sound in the field, and whisper at her own wedding.

She nodded, went to the point man and whispered the procedure. Garvin waited, looking impatient, secretly glad for the chance to wheeze a little before further exertion, while the patrol unrolled the climbing rope each wore around his or her waist, tied in, and started the ascent, which was just steep enough to be interesting if the climber slipped.

Darod Montagna, next to last in line, moved past him, exhausted eyes sunk deeper in her gray face, but still determined, took a deep breath, and began climbing.

The last man was Baku al Sharif, a solid block of a 'Raum. Garvin saw him watching Montagna's buttocks with a mildly interested expression.

The combat knife flashed from Garvin's sheath, cut the rope linking al Sharif and Montagna.

'You've got too much energy, troop,' he whispered. 'It's too slick, and the rope broke. You get to solo on up . . . that way.'

'That way' was a steep, brush-choked ravine.

Al Sharif's lips pursed, and he glared at Jaansma.

'A little hard?' Garvin suggested. 'It gets to you. Yahweh knows I understand. You know, you don't have to put up with this crap. I could hit the com right now, get a Grierson inbound, and an hour from now you'd be in a nice hot shower back at Mahan, getting a real meal instead of this dried crud.

'Then sleep. Nice white sheets, quiet, and maybe a three-day pass on the beach to recover from this stupid shit.'

Al Sharif looked at Garvin coldly.

'Screw you. Boss.'

He pushed his way into the brush, started clambering up the face.

Jaansma laughed.

That'd be at least two that'd make it.

He grunted, and started up the slope. He looked up, saw Montagna climbing just above him, thought, *She does have sort of a cute butt, pity you can't socialize with anybody you're in charge of*. Then he realized he hadn't thought of Jasith at all that day.

'Y'see what you're gonna be missing?' the man shouted at Loy Kouro over the band's blare, waving at the three strippers onstage, who were down to scarves and smiles.

Kouro owled at them, picked up his glass, and upended it in the general area of his mouth, half of the contents making its way down his throat.

'Nup, nup, Jermy,' he said, weaving a bit in his seat. 'Th' time for that's pissed . . . passed . . . gone.'

'Not yet it isn't,' his friend said. 'Tomorrow, you stand up, take th' vows, an' you've got to become a good boy . . . or anyway not get caught bein' bad. Bad, bad, bad. Won't be able to do what we used to do with the girlies. Wouldn't want Jasith pissed at me, I wouldn't.'

He winked elaborately, sloppily refilled Kouro's glass with a mixture from three of the bottles on the table. Somebody wove past, grabbed the glass, disappeared with it. Jermy cursed, found another glass, dumped its contents out on the rug, and began rebuilding a drink.

'Look around, m'friend. Nothin' but your friends here.'

The club was, indeed, packed with young Rentiers: some actually Kouro's friends, the others wise enough to want to stay on the good side of the planet's biggest publisher.

'Th' girls finish up, an' they'll be over d'rectly,' Jermy promised. 'An' there's a room upstairs, an' you can go on up with any of 'em you want. Hell, all of 'em if you want. There's more ordered up, arrivin' in a bit.'

'Better make it a night to remember.'

'Nup, nup, nup,' Kouro said. 'That'd be dishonest, bein' untrue. I'd sure be pissed off if Jasith was runnin' around on me.

'Time I grew up, anyway. Got to be like Hank Sank.'

'Huh?'

'An old Earth play. By somebody or other. Couple plays, actually. Henry Vee, which stands for five in some old-timey language. This guy's a prince . . . that's next to a king . . . and he's a wild hair until he gets the throne, and then he becomes a great . . . greaaaat . . . warrior. Wins the Battle of Hastings or some-such. Long time since my father made me read it.

'He's gone, now, and I've got to do what he'd want me to do. Marry good, think about havin' kids, keep the dynasty going.'

'Gods, man, you're not gonna turn into a dreek, are you?'

'Got to grow up sometime.'

'Who says?'

Kouro didn't answer, but reached for the drink. He overbalanced, fell facefirst into a pool of liquor. After a moment, he began snoring loudly.

Jermy stared at him.

'Poops out at his own party. Hafta come up with some

stories about what really happened for tomorrow morning, when he's real hungover and needs some shame.' He
stood, waved at the stage.

'Hey, girls! Hey. The party boy's out, but there's somebody over here still able to show you a good time!'

A foot tapped Garvin's boot, and he forced himself
awake, ignored groaning muscles, and tried to look alert
and eager. The patrol lay in a large star formation, legs
almost touching.

This was the day they'd 'make contact,' or, in reality,
reach the abandoned Musth base.

Garvin tried to decide if the mist was coming down
hard enough to qualify as rain, decided it was, and that
he hadn't been this wet since the last time he went to the
field.

He was incredibly dirty – they'd been out . . . and he
had to count on his fingers . . . ten days now, and other
than streams or when the near-constant mist became a
drencher, nobody had bathed, and everybody wore the
same combat fatigues they had on when they came off
the Grierson. At least Jaansma had three pair of socks,
one pair on his feet, another pair tied to his backpack
being 'washed' by the rain, the third just in the top of his
pack supposedly drying.

This was the I&R way, and again he wondered why
the company never seemed to lack for volunteers, had an
even greater wonderment about why he remained in the
unit.

Darod Montagna was again patrol leader, and made
the mission briefing. Garvin had given her the data on
where the patrol was and the situation posited by the
exercise the night before, and now listened to her break
it down.

Everyone listened intently, fingers moving from point

to point on their maps. No one wrote anything down – a lost or captured map could doom them all if this were real.

'When we reach the target area,' Montagna went on, 'Alpha Element goes on line, and I'll indicate which way Bravo goes, left or right. Bravo will sweep the area, Alpha giving support fire. When the area's secured, Alpha moves across the area, and both elements reassemble.

'If there is contact, each of you fires one unit of ammo. If the enemy's stronger than we are, I'll give the order, and we break contact, go for the RP . . .'

She gave the map coordinates of the rendezvous point, went on, '. . . commo . . . support . . . chain of command.' She finished, looked at Garvin.

' 'Kay,' he said briskly. 'We eat, then move out. Now lemme give you the reality of what we're coming on. It's the old Musth headquarters, which'll most likely be boarded up.

'You're carrying live ammo, but pick a god to pray to if anybody rolls a ball out the muzzle for real and makes a hole in somebody else's real estate. We're not at war with the Musth, and it'd be real goddamned dumb for somebody to start it over a busted window when and if they come back.

'Same thing goes for souveniring, looting, or casual vandalism. The words are RTU if you do.'

RTU – Returned to Unit, the threat all of the trainees had been facing since they volunteered for Intelligence and Reconnaissance from their parent companies.

'Reality is we'll sweep around the buildings, as Montagna said, then form up on the other side, call for pickup, and go home to a nice, hot bath.'

He hid a grin, wondering what the reaction would be when he told them sorrowfully that the Grierson had been driven off by enemy fire, and aw, hell, they'd just have to walk back, and how many trainees would just go flat and say 'Screw it,' throwing away the last two Emonths of sweat, strain, and not a little blood, not realizing they hadn't come close to touching their last reserves, which was really what all the harassment and pressure of I&R training was supposed to teach.

Garvin reached in his pack, took out a block of something, put it in his mess tin, poured water from a canteen over it, and refilled the canteen from the rain trap he'd made with a small waterproof cloth. The block squiggled and became something moderately resembling a chunk of protein with something that might have been button fungi around it.

He doused the mixture with the hot sauce every experienced soldier carried, ate mechanically, scrubbed the small plate and his spoon with grass, and restowed everything in his pack.

'Any time you're ready,' and the patrol moved off, feet squidging through the ankle-high waterlogged mosses, past the trees that rose like sentinels from the mist, through the marshland of the Highlands.

Music swept through the great temple, swirling around the packed benches, then died, and the orchestra lowered its instruments.

The Leader rose, walked to the podium, and his voice rolled forth:

'Brethren, this is a day of joy and happiness, for on this day, we celebrate, with our own bodies, the mystical union between the Creator and Ourselves, a day of wedding, an estate to be entered into soberly and with considered judgment.

'If there is any among you who knows of a reason these two should not come together in holy matrimony, let him speak now . . .'

*

The Musth building rose out of the mist, strange poly-
gons apparently made of glass and onyx. They showed
few signs of abandonment, nor any measures by the
Musth to prevent damage. Here a panel was shattered
from some Cumbrian animal's curiosity, there a few
moss-vines had begun twining up the walls.

Montagna signaled, and Alpha flattened in firing
positions, weapons ready, even though the magazines
were still tucked into their pouches.

Bravo came up, on command, moved forward, slowly.
quietly.

Then one man went flat, flailed at the air with one
hand, palm down, and the others obediently dropped,
wondering what the hell was going on, if the goddamned
alt was pulling some crappy game. The man signaled
again, fist clenched, thumb pointing down.

Enemy in sight?

Garvin was about to start snarling, then a small box
spun through the air toward them, and Jaansma saw a
tawny paw disappear behind a building. The grenade hit,
and small insectlike creatures swarmed out and flashed
toward the nearest man. He screamed, clawed at himself,
and died.

'Musth!' Garvin shouted, fumbled a magazine from
his pouch, loaded his blaster.

'Load 'em up!' was his command. 'For real!'

A *devourer-weapon* chattered, and finger-sized bullets
thudded into the peat, close to a trooper.

'Stop shooting, you Musth!' Garvin shouted. 'We're
not attacking!'

Another blast came from another direction.

'Cease firing, goddamit! We're not your enemies,'
Garvin called again, even as his fingers found a blast
grenade. His thumb reflexively clicked its timer four
times, and he straight-armed it at the building.

Four seconds later, it went off, and most of a wall exploded inward.

A Musth appeared in the gap, spray-pistol hissing acid toward al Sharif, and the 'Raum blew the alien in half with his blaster.

'Go in for real,' Montagna called, and in shock, but ground-in reflexes taking over, Bravo Element started toward the complex, zigging, crouching, firing at the buildings.

Loy Kouro and Jasith Mellusin met at the rear of the temple, then moved toward the Leader, who stood below the podium, waiting, as the music rose once again.

A striker rose to throw a grenade, and a Musth came up, fired twice, and the man dropped as a round struck him, then began writhing as the *devourer-weapon*'s creatures came out of the cartridge and began eating the flesh around the wound.

The Musth was about to fire again. Garvin shot him down, then rolled twice as a grenade bounced and exploded a meter away from him. He waited for the stings, but the wasplike insectoids missed him.

'Wilt thou, Loy Kouro, have this woman to thy wedded wife, to live together after the Creator's ordinance in the holy state of matrimony?'

'I will.' Kouro's voice was firm.

'And wilt thou, Jasith Mellusin, have this man to thy husband, to live together after the Creator's ordinance in the holy state of matrimony.'

'Yes,' Jasith said, and no one noticed the brief hesitation.

Garvin blew another panel open, diving through the

ragged hole into the building. He heard shots from the next room, or bay, or whatever it was, ran through the door, past strange furniture, booted a doorway open, and the Musth turned, his pistol's mouth sweeping toward Jaansma.

Garvin pulled the trigger twice, and the Musth fell forward, lay silent.

He heard more shots, a volley of them, a blast of two grenades, one Musth, one human.

'They're down,' someone shouted, and another gunshot made him a liar, and more blaster rounds answered.

'He's dead!' someone shouted.

'Are there any more of the bastards?'

Silence, then:

'No! We've killed them all!'

'O Eternal Creator,' the Leader said, 'Creator and Preserver of all Mankind, send thy blessing upon these thy servants, and recognize the ring the man hath given the woman is a symbol of their eternal troth and the covenant between them.'

'What's the count?' Garvin said.

'Three of ours dead ... two more wounded,' Montagna said. 'We have six dead Musth. No wounded. We tried to help one of them, and he shot himself before we could get to his gun.'

Her control broke, now that it was over, and she tried to keep tears back.

'God *damn* it, why'd they shoot at us? What did they think we were doing? We aren't fighting them! What the hell's going on, anyway?'

'When you figure it out,' Garvin said grimly, 'be sure and let me know.'

*

'May the Creator preserve and keep you, look down upon you and fill you with all spiritual benediction and grace; that you may so live together in this life that in the world to come you may have life everlasting.'

'Lance, this is Sibyl Six Actual,' Garvin said into the mike, proud that his voice was calm, emotionless. 'I shackle XRAY VELDT RANGE, repeat, XRAY VELDT RANGE. Attacked by Musth. All aliens killed. Need immediate medic flight, request Grierson extraction, two heavy hitters and standby reaction company. Musth were evidently part of some spy operation — extensive com gear found.

'We're in very deep shit now.'

'Loy Kouro, you may kiss your bride.'

FOUR

'So here the Musth were, sending whatever reports they were sending,' *Caud* Rao said. 'Lord alone knows what data that was, since nobody's reported seeing any furry guys skulking around since the Musth officially pulled out.

'You come booming through the brush, and naturally, they think the worst and start shooting.'

'Yessir.' Garvin's eyelids were bouncing together. It was well past dark, and the I&R trainees were either in bed or hospital. 'My fault—'

'Bullshit your fault,' Angara said. 'I approved the exercise, and they fired the first shot. *Caud*, I think our *alt* needs sleep more than anything, and this is the fourth time we've put him through the wringer. Jaansma, get your ass out of here, and die until you wake up. Don't pay attention to anything but loud explosions.'

'But . . .'

'That's an order. Go. Yoshitaro's outside, and he'll point you toward your bunk, maybe hose you off a little first. Now get gone.'

Rao, Angara, and Hedley waited until Jaansma staggered out.

'Now what?' Angara asked.

'Hedley, that's your department,' Rao informed his Intelligence chief.

'We flipping disperse like we've never dispersed before, making as rotten a legion of targets as we can,' Hedley said. 'None of the offplanet warning stations detected any transmission from the Musth when the patrol hit them, but they never picked up anything before, either.

'So we've got to assume they punched a message through on some unmonitored freq, and if their fuzzy brothers weren't on their way back to Cumbre with a case of the ass like they promised to have after the 'Raum War, they surely must be by now.

'Plus let's not forget Our Friend Redruth has, or had anyway, somebody reporting to him that we've never tracked down. So that's another country to be heard from. Lord knows what the Kurans are going to do, but I think we should assume flipping unpleasantries.'

'Who knows if you're right,' Rao said, 'but we can't assume you're wrong, so we'll move this instant.

'Here's what we'll do: Keep Headquarters and Support, less the units I'm going to detach next, here at Mahan, along with I&R Company and their proprietary air. That'll have to be our reaction force, pissyass though it is. Mahan's almost completely underground and hardened against anything short of prolonged nuke bombardment, so we should be covered there.

'Pull one infantry company from a regiment and get it across to Mullion Island's airbase as their security element, plus all pilots who've been involved with our hideout fleet.

'First Regiment will disperse to Leggett, somewhere back of the Heights; Second to Aire; Third to Taman City; Fourth to Kerrier. Split up Artillery and Gunship Battalions, plus support, into the usual elements with each regiment so they're independent. Have them bivvy outside the cities, using what bunkers are available building more. We'll run showers and field kitchens out to the regiments. I'll have PlanGov commandeer some translifters to shuttle the troopies back and forth from the boonies to Mahan in a week or so for some time off.

'We're screwed if anybody hits us and we have to react quickly in force, but we'll have to take the chance. I'd rather be spread out than sitting in a big happy pile waiting to get massacreed.

'From now on, no passes, no leaves, one-third on alert. I can hear the troopies scream now.

'Oh yeh. How many of those Musth attack ships do we have flying?'

'Four *aksai* are at full readiness. Maybe five in a day or so. And we've got ten pilots trained on them fairly well. They probably'd get nailed in a dogfight with experienced Musth pilots, but I think they'd at least give the furry ones a tough way to go for a few minutes.'

'Good. Disperse those to Balar, with their pilots, and give the force one of the freighters for a mother ship. Offworld, they can maybe be a bit of a hole card, and give us an inch of the gravity well if we're attacked, or anyway some surprise. Put three or four Zhukovs, the patrol craft, and a couple of the yachts with 'em.'

'Yessir.'

'One more thing I should've taken care of – with all these extraneous aircraft, we're a bit short on pilots. Tell the regimental commanders to link up with the local flight schools for support – they can invoice PlanGov with their expenses – and get any of our soldiers who want to fly into training. Also, get our recruiters banging the drum for recruits who've got any sort of flight experience or who're interested in leaving a perfectly good planet behind.

'And we're going to have to figure out some way to start building a navy. But that's for PlanGov and me to figure out.

'That's all I can think of.'

'What about the civilians, sir?' Angara asked.

Rao thought for a moment. 'That's PlanGov's department, but I don't see what good we can do telling them the shit's going to come down maybe soon, except start a wave of hoarding and maybe panic. Plus I don't think . . . emphasis think . . . the Musth will start strafing the innocent. At least, not in the beginning.

'So wake up the hundering third, and get them rolling.'

'On my bike, sir.' *Mil* Angara hurried out, and a few seconds later alarms began to gong monotonously. Rao pictured soldiers tumbling out of bed, cursing and wondering where the hell their blasters and alert gear were.

'You know any prayers, Hedley?'

'Not a flippin' one, sir.'

'Me either. This may get interesting.'

Normally, graduation from Infantry and Reconnaissance Qualification was a private, verbal ceremony, followed by a three-day pass and extended drunkenness.

Six days after the fight with the Musth, *Caud* Rao ordered Headquarters onto the massive parade ground at Camp Mahan, plus representatives from the fielded regiments to return for the ceremony.

Five men and women stood at attention in front of *Caud* Rao, with Jaansma and Yoshitaro flanking him. All wore full-dress uniform: midnight blue trousers, belted tunic and kepi, yellow piping on trousers, cap, and epaulettes.

Next to the five were three blasters, stuck muzzle

down into the ground. Hung on their stocks were the dress kepis of the recruits who'd died in the Highlands, their highly-polished boots in front of the weapons.

There was a pickup, casting the ceremony to the two soldiers graduating long-distance and on their backs in the Force hospital.

'You made it,' Jaansma said. 'Things got a little grimmer than usual, but that's the way soldiering always seems to go. Congratulations. You did well, all of you. I'm proud to welcome you to the company.'

Yoshitaro just nodded, said nothing.

Rao's remarks were almost as brief.

'Striker Darod Montagna, for bravery and coolness when brought under fire by an element of the Musth race while on a training maneuver, you're given the Order of Merit, and promoted to *finf*. Striker Baku al Sherif, you're awarded the Combat Legion award. All of you are promoted Striker First Class, and your performance commended in dispatches. Those who died in the line of duty, Strikers Joanes, Zelen, Hathagar, and those who were wounded, Strikers Mahue and Seelam, are awarded wound stripes.

'I'm afraid this is just the beginning. I warn all of you, not just the men and women honored in this ceremony, to soldier well and carefully in the days, weeks, and months to come.

'Never forget. You serve the Confederation as well as Cumbre, and the honor of the Strike Force depends on you, and only you. Serve as bravely as these eleven did, and we shall never have cause to be ashamed.

'Thank you again. *Alt* Jaansma, take charge of your soldiers and dismiss them.'

The Kouros, Matin's society section reported, were

spending a protracted honeymoon on one of the family's private islands.

'I remember,' Jaansma said thoughtfully, 'I went with my parents on an animal-buying expedition once. Don't remember what world it was, but it was pretty desert-y. We were buying flying reptiles.'

He and Yoshitaro'd been invited to the noncommissioned officers' club at Camp Mahan by First Tweg Monique Lir. Normally thronged with noncoms from the ten-thousand-man unit, now it was cavernous, almost echoing.

At least, Lir'd told them, they didn't have to worry about rationed suds, like the dispersed regiments had to until they'd made their own quiet arrangements. There was the whole Legion's allotment to swill down, unless they wanted to shame I&R. But Yoshitaro noticed that none of the warrants were drinking heavily, any more than the two officers. If it came down right now, nobody wanted to get bombed while bombed.

'Somebody actually *wanted* flying snakes?' Lir said. 'As if the bastards aren't enough just crawling up your legs.'

'People want thrills,' Garvin said. 'The circus delivers.'

'Now I know why my folks never took me to one,' Monique said. 'Brragh!'

'Second that emotion,' Njangu said. 'But go on. Here you were, cute'n'cuddly little Garvin, toddlin' around with all these writhers writhin' at you from the skies.'

'Actually,' Garvin said, having patiently ignored the backchatter, 'it wasn't the snakes that got my eye, but some of the local furry rodents the snakes fed on. I remember watching these little bitty sorts, all furry and friendly, and how they'd scurry from bush to bush, always with one eye cocked up, to keep from becoming somebody's dinner.'

He sipped at his beer, seemed finished with his story.

'So?' Monique demanded.

'So ... the way things have been, I'm starting to understand those cute little buggers real well.'

'Got the moral,' Njangu said. 'But you don't look very cute and cuddly.'

'Nope,' Garvin said. 'But I sure feel like an amblin' target.'

'Question?' Njangu asked quietly.

'Yeh?'

'You feel better?'

'About what?'

'Shit me nix, little brown brother,' Yoshitaro said. 'About your former flame.'

'Her?'

'Her.'

'Have I ripped anybody's lungs out lately?'

'Who didn't need it? No,' Njangu said.

'Answers your question, doesn't it?'

Njangu eyed his friend, decided that was enough answer for him.

It was another week before the alarms went off, first from one of the innermost ice giants, F-Cumbre, then echoed, within the hour, by other automated posts closer to D-Cumbre.

One ship, medium-sized, inbound.

More sophisticated if shorter-ranged sensors 'saw' four patrol craft accompanying it.

The bigger ship was identified as an obsolescent Confederation *Remora*-class destroyer leader, the three patrol ships types unknown.

Shortly thereafter, coms set on the standard Confederation frequency clicked on:

'C-Cumbre Control, this is the *Corfe*, inbound from

Larix and Kura, Protector Alena Redruth aboard. Request landing instructions for Confederation Base Camp Mahan.

'Members of the current Planetary Government are requested to attend Protector Redruth on his arrival.'

The voice, even filtered through com speakers, wasn't asking, but demanding.

Fifteen Council members and *Caud* Rao nervously waited outside the still-sealed airlock of the *Corfe*. Behind them were thirty volunteers from the Legion, ostensibly an honor guard since Redruth was still a Confederation member, actually as much of a bodyguard for the Council as Rao could devise.

Each woman or man had, concealed under their dress uniforms, two magazines for their blasters, and small handguns hastily grabbed from Hedley's 'contingency' armory. They were also well trained in unarmed combat and knife fighting.

Hidden inside a hangar, its doors open a slit, a warrant ready to hit the door-lifter control, were two autocannon-armed Cookes. Garvin commanded one, Njangu the other. Garvin's pilot was Rao's driver, *Dec* Running Bear, his gunner *Finf* Ho Kang, the former ECM specialist with Ben Dill's Grierson.

Yoshitaro had an equally skilled crew of hastily-picked volunteers.

The autocannons were fully loaded, and the gunners ready.

Garvin watched the *Corfe*. Its chaingun turrets were lifted, guns ready, and missile launch tubes unmasked.

'Stand by,' Garvin said. 'Their hatch is coming open.'

The gangway hissed down, touched the tarmac. Four soldiers in dark green dropped down it, stood at attention, blasters ready.

A speaker crackled.

'I'd like to extend an invitation for you men and women of Cumbre's government to board my flagship, so we may discuss matters of great urgency.'

Even through electronic filters, the invitation was, again, clearly a command.

The Council members exchanged looks, then slowly went up the gangway into the ship.

Waiting inside the lock was Protector Redruth, who still looked more like a stocky, balding low-level bureaucrat than the dictator of two systems.

'I welcome you,' he said, tone not at all friendly. 'We have matters of great import to discuss. If you'll accompany me to the conference room?'

A green-uniformed man came out with a detector and swept each of the Council members, in spite of protests. *Caud* Rao made none. Nothing he had hidden on him would respond to any detector he was aware of.

'None of them are armed, Protector.'

'Good. This way, then?'

The men and women followed Redruth. Rao tried to take in everything, trying to reach an estimate of Redruth's military. The *Corfe* was spotlessly kept, even if it was obsolescent, and the two weapons stations he peered into were manned by alert-looking soldiers, clean-cut and sharply dressed.

The conference room was paneled with false wood, old prints on the walls. It could have served any Rentier corporation well.

'If you'll be seated,' Redruth said.

A door slid open, and a man Rao recognized as Celidon, Redruth's military leader, came in. He wore dark green, as his soldiery, glittering with decorations, and a Sam Browne belt with pistol holstered on one side, dagger on the other. He was tall, muscled, with a scar along his forehead. He gave Rao a slight nod, looked at the Council members with chill amusement, but said nothing.

'I know all of you are busy with your normal duties,' Redruth said. 'So I'll keep this very brief.

'I'm sure you know that some time ago, I offered to place the Cumbre system under my protection. The offer was refused by your Planetary Government.

'That was then, and we'd just lost contact with the Confederation. I was most concerned about inroads the Musth would most likely make on Cumbre, up to and including trying to seize the system for their own.

'My offer was foolishly rejected.

'Nothing has changed to improve your situation, and it's inconceivable that I would allow my own people to be endangered if the Musth carry out the plans I consider inevitable.

'Therefore, although I would always rather rule by consent rather than fiat, I have decided Cumbre is to be placed under my protection immediately.'

There were gasps, protests. Redruth waited, his expression calm, as if nothing was being said.

'This is not a debatable matter,' he said. 'Of course, I want our liaison to be as painless as possible. I see no reason why this Council cannot continue to handle matters as before, although, of course, I'll appoint a regent to moderate the Council, report to me, and present my views on pertinent matters so you may help me implement them.'

Now there was a yammer – 'can't do this,' 'sovereign state,' 'violation of Confederation laws,' 'goddamned pirate,' and so forth. One woman stayed silent, Rao noticed, Jo Poynton, who had a smile of tight amusement on her face.

Redruth waited for a moment, then rapped sharply with his knuckles on the table.

'As I said,' and now his voice was steely, 'this is not a

matter for debate, but for you to implement as rapidly as possible, or face severe consequences.

'My plans are—'

'Excuse me,' *Caud* Rao said. 'As you know, my Strike Force is part of the Confederation military, and is sworn to defend Cumbre's *present* government. Are you declaring war against the Confederation?'

Celidon smiled thinly. 'I hardly think the matter is important enough to be called war.'

'What Celidon means,' Redruth said, 'is we have no intention of interfering with your Force. However, since you lack a naval element, we shall be providing that. I see no reason that my security forces and yours cannot coexist comfortably in keeping order.'

'Unfortunately, I do,' Rao said. 'You've announced plans to usurp authority. We must stand against it.'

'I don't think things will come to a confrontation,' Redruth said. 'Particularly if the Council welcomes my presence, realizing the choice is very simple: either my protectorate or conquest by the Musth. That would make the slight change I propose within legal boundaries, and therefore not the concern of you or your Strike Force.

'Don't lose your temper, *Caud* Rao. Consider this. The Cumbre system is on the edge of nowhere, barely self-sustaining. Allied with Larix and Kura, there'll be not only safety, but increased trade, increased wealth flowing into this system.'

'And what will be flowing out?' Poynton asked.

'Certain exports,' Redruth said. 'But we'll hardly be appropriating them. We'll pay an honest price.'

'Starting with the mines,' a Councilman said cynically.

'That is one of the most important areas of concern,' Redruth said. 'Is there a representative of Mellusin Mining present?'

'Jasith Mellusin,' a man said, 'has recently married.

She and her husband are honeymooning. A message was sent to their island as soon as you summoned us for this meeting. I don't know if it was received, but I'd assume it was, and she is on the way now.'

'Good,' Redruth said. 'We can begin with the ores on C-Cumbre, then discuss other matters, such as the minor increase in your present taxes necessary to support my garrison here.'

'Which will be of what size?' Rao asked.

'That's still undecided,' Celidon said. 'It'll depend on how easily these meetings go, won't it?'

'I see,' Rao said, hand unobtrusively pressing a transmitter taped to his side under his tunic. The transmitter sent a one-second beep.

'How much,' a Councilwoman asked, 'will you be increasing our taxes?'

'Initially, no more than one percent on all products, although you might choose to increase the present income tax instead. I have no interest, by the way, in what method of taxation you choose, or the percentage called for from any particular income group.'

'In other words,' Poynton said, 'if we decide to soak the poor, you could give a damn.'

A man turned and scowled at her.

'Dammit, this is hard enough, without your 'Raum bullshit!'

'Excuse me,' Redruth said. 'I understand your recent problems, but I see no reason to bring them into this matter. Now, let's consider just what of Cumbre's products are most important to the continued security and welfare of our mutual systems . . .'

All commanders in the Legion, and all combat aerial and ground vehicles had secondary receivers tuned to Rao's transmitter.

'That's it,' Garvin said. 'Crank 'em up, and get ready to move.'

The drives on the two Cookes whined to life.

The speedster drove hard past Lanbay Island, into Dharma Bay. Loy Kouro was at the controls, Jasith Mellusin beside him. They were barely fifty meters above the water, at full speed.

Kouro was furious. 'The biggest damned thing since the war, and I'm off playing with you!'

'Loy,' Jasith pointed out, 'taking an extra two weeks for our honeymoon was your idea.'

'Whatever,' Kouro said. 'What the hell do you think these people want, anyway?'

'I'm pretty sure it won't be good,' Jasith said.

'In ten minutes,' Kouro said. 'We should be able to see Chance Island.'

'This is Scimitar Alpha,' Ben Dill said. 'Inbound from Balar. ETA Mahan three zero. Scimitars Beta and Gamma monitoring transmission. Over.'

The three *aksai*, at three-quarters drive, saw D-Cumbre growing large ahead.

'This is Control,' *Mil* Angara said into a mike, and the scrambled signal spat from a bunker below Camp Mahan into space. 'No change to orders. You're cleared to respond to any hostile action. If none is made, remain out-atmosphere for further instructions.'

'Clear.' Dill switched frequencies. 'You heard the man. Let's go kill some Larries or Kurans or whatever they're calling themselves these days. Out.'

He touched sensors, and missiles armed themselves.

Across D-Cumbre, the scattered soldiers of the Force went to full combat readiness.

In the chatter, no one noted a remote sensor, off the small planetoid of L-Cumbre, as it began reporting:

SIX OBJECTS ENTERING SYSTEM . . . ANALYSIS SUGGESTS NOT NATURAL . . . NONE CONFORM TO KNOWN STARSHIP CONFIGURATION . . . ORBIT PROJECTED TO INTERSECT D-CUMBRE WITHIN THREE HOURS . . . SIX OBJECTS ENTERING SYSTEM . . . ANALYSIS SUGGESTS . . .

Redruth had opened a folder, was going through exactly what tribute Cumbre would be expected to pay when a man in green entered. went to Celidon.

He whispered hastily. Celidon's cool gaze flashed into an angry frown.

'Excuse me, Protector,' he said. 'But the bridge reports increased signals around the planet, and unknown signals from the moon.'

'What is it? *Caud* Rao, what's going on?' Redruth demanded.

Rao shook his head.

'I don't know,' he lied. 'I've been in this room for two hours now. Possibly my executive officer has decided to increase the ready status of my Force.'

'Celidon!' Redruth snapped.

'No problem,' the big man said. 'If they're getting cute, we can do the same.'

He went out the door, toward the bridge.

Redruth got to his feet, backed toward the door.

'I don't know what's going on,' he said. 'But if any of you have any ideas——'

Caud Rao had a small ceramic tube, the weapon no metal detector could pick up, leveled.

'You can stand quite still,' he said calmly. 'This has only one round, an old-fashioned pottery ball that'll shatter quite messily when it hits something, so perhaps you don't want to breathe heavily.'

Redruth's face reddened, but he froze.

'Now, we're going back out the corridor to the air-lock,' Rao said. 'You Council people, move first, and quick. We're leaving the ship.'

He palmed the door open, motioned the stunned Council out.

A crewman came toward them, saw the tiny weapon, and grabbed for his sidearm. Jo Poynton was on him, a palm striking hard into his face, an elbow smashing his throat, and she had his pistol out of its holster before he fell, gurgling, twisting in pain.

She hefted it, grinned. 'Just like the old days. I'll meet you at the airlock,' and she trotted away.

'Now you,' Rao said, motioning Redruth out of the conference room. 'Think of me as protecting the Protector.'

'My men'll never allow this!'

'Possibly,' Rao said cheerfully. 'But you'll reap extremely negative benefits from their faithfulness.'

Rao looked at the gun, grimaced, and went down the corridor.

'All right,' Celidon said as he came on the bridge of the *Corfe*. 'I have the deck, Mister. What's going on?'

'Sir,' the ship's captain reported, 'we have at least fifty, maybe more, ships in the air. Everything from yachts to aerial combat vehicles.'

'What the hell set them off?'

The officer shook his head.

'Well, find out, Mister! We can't take action until we know what's going on for certain!'

The captain, remembering he'd been promoted per Celidon's anger at his vacillating predecessor and a firing squad, shouted for silence, then told all stations to report.

Celidon waited, listening, not realizing one hand kept touching the haft of his dagger, then moving away.

'This is *Corfe-Two*,' one of the *Nirvana*-class patrol boats reported. 'Three ships inbound from Balar . . .' the toneless voice changed, '. . . *Jane's* IDs them as Musth fighting ships!'

Almost simultaneously:

'This *is Corfe-Four*,' another patrol boat called. 'Six large ships on course toward D-Cumbre, unknown origin, no *Jane's* ID! Request instructions.'

The bridge of the *Corfe* buzzed in confusion, and Celidon shouted silence.

A speaker turned, reported as ordered:

'Sir, Eleven Weapons Bay reports hearing a shot within the ship!'

'What?'

The speaker repeated the message.

'Get the landing squad out,' Celidon snapped. 'Find out what the hell that was! Get a security element to the conference compartment, make sure the Protector's all right!'

A tech reported:

'Sir, we have an incoming, low-level flight, from the east, approximate speed two fifty kph, did not answer challenge on standard guard frequency. Three gun stations are tracking it.'

'Knock it down!'

'Yessir,' a weapons officer said. 'Three Weapons Position, fire!'

The bridge jarred as the nearby chaingun blasted.

*

Cannon fire slashed into the water less than twenty meters short of Loy Kouro's speedster. He gaped, jerked at the controls, smashed into the waterspout.

The speedster skidded, went sideways.

Kouro fought for control, had it for an instant. Then the speedster snaprolled twice. Kouro slid the control back, and for an instant the speedster stabilized. He tried to climb for altitude, then the drive died, and the speedster stalled.

It nosed into a dive, Kouro fighting it. He brought the speedster level, then ran out of altitude. At just under 100kph, it hit the water, skipping like a spun stone.

The hangar door slid open, as the *Corfe* fired across the parade ground, at some distant target in the ocean.

'Gunner!' Garvin shouted. 'That weapons station.'

'Acquired,' Ho said calmly, and touched the firing studs of her autocannon.

The 20mm cannon roared like a primeval beast, and collapsed-uranium rounds smashed into the exposed Kuran guns.

Two ammo drums exploded, and a ball of flame swept the compartment, killing the gunners before they had a chance to realize they were dead.

A panel slid shut, sealing the station, as the *Corfe* rocked from side to side.

'Evasive action!' Jaansma called, and the two Cookes skidded out of the hangar, zigged out of sight as another cannon blasted holes in the tarmac.

'No shiteedah,' Running Bear managed, hands blurring across controls as the Cooke banked, almost smashing into a shed.

Rao found three sprawled bodies in the corridor, and pushed Redruth harder. They ran into the airlock's suiting chamber, found the Council, and Poynton with a pistol in each hand. A Councilman held the third weapon.

'How're we going to get out of the ship without getting gunned down?' Poynton said.

'Give me one of those,' Rao said, and Poynton tossed him a pistol.

'Your honor guard took care of the sentries,' Poynton said. 'They scattered, got to shelter before the ship could retaliate, and we've got some support fire from them.'

'They keep trying to close the lock,' another man said. 'I'm holding down EMERGENCY OVERRIDE.'

'Next?' Poynton said.

'You can't run,' Redruth said smugly. 'My gunners'll drop you before you make ten meters.'

'Then we'd better kill you now,' Poynton said.

Redruth paled as Rao leveled the pistol.

'I have you, I have you, oh Lordy lord now I have you,' Ben Dill crooned as the *aksai* swooped on a Kuran patrol boat. He thumbed the firing button three times, and missiles hissed away.

The patrol boat went to full power. tried to jump into stardrive, didn't make it as one missile blew its nose off, then the second homed on the engine room, and the ship. became a geometrically perfect ball of flaming gas.

'Ho-ho.' Dill shouted into his mike. 'First blood for Ben!'

'*Corfe, Corfe*, this *is Corfe-Two*,' the panicked patrol boat's commander broadcast. '*Corfe-Three* destroyed by Musth . . . there's too many of 'em, all attacking! *Corfe-Four* under attack as well!'

A missile launched by one of Dill's wingmen blew up

half a kilometer away, and the man flinched, reflexively slamming his ship into stardrive.

Rao heard movement, stuck his pistol around, and slammed half a dozen rounds down the corridor without looking to see who it was.

'We're dead if we stay here,' Rao decided. 'Out of here, and run for that hangar! Stay spread out!'

Fearful faces peered at him, then obediently clattered down the gangway.

Rao's eyes were on them, and Redruth seized the moment, knocking the *caud* sideways, then darting back into the corridor, into a compartment, and sliding the door shut.

'Bastard!' and Rao went after the others.

A Kuran gunner saw the running men and women, switched his target acquisition to manual, and swiveled the guns down toward them.

Yoshitaro's Cooke popped up above a transport lifter, and his gunner sent 150 rounds into the position before the man could open fire.

Moments later the Council members ran into the hangar, through it, and out the other side. *Caud* Rao was last. He crouched, blew the rest of his pistol magazine into the open lock of the *Corfe,* doing no good but no harm either.

Then he was gone, after the others, as cannon shells ripped through the tarmac where he'd been.

'Close the lock,' Celidon ordered. 'Why was this not done—'

He broke off, realizing the stupidity of blame-finding until later.

Another com clicked.

'Bridge, this is Gunnery Compartment Thirteen. We have the Protector safely . . .' There was a clatter of static, then Redruth's voice: 'Celidon! Lift the ship out of here! They've trapped us!'

Celidon forced calm.

'Captain, prepare for lift. Take it straight out over the ocean, then into stardrive as soon as we clear atmosphere.'

'Yessir.'

'Have all patrol ships pull in to support us.'

'Yessir.'

Celidon noted pressure in his ears, realized the lock was . . . finally . . . shut.

'You . . . Section Leader . . . three men to Gunnery Thirteen, and escort the Protector to the bridge!'

'Sir!'

Celidon felt the flagship come clear of the ground, heard the subdued whine of the antigravs.

Ben Dill flashed through the outer atmosphere, his screens showing Camp Mahan far below. He held the zoom sensor in, saw the *Corfe* as it started to move.

He punched the missile firing button as he plunged down, through thirty-thousand meters at some impossible Mach number, felt the *aksai* wiggle as all his missiles ripple-fired, and realized he was about to make a crescent-sized hole in D-Cumbre, slid sensors back, cut power, and the Musth fighting ship bucked, shuddered, began trying to pull out of its dive, fighting compressibility, barely on the edge of control.

The missiles, intended for air-to-air or space use, lost the target in ground clutter and smashed into the tarmac, not one hundred meters from the *Corfe*.

Two seconds later, Dill's *aksai* whipped past, not thirty meters above the *Corfe*.

*

On the bridge of the Musth flagship, a huge, new, heavily armed mother ship, Wlencing considered screens. Beside him was a slightly smaller Musth, with much the same markings as Wlencing.

'So they are fighting,' he told Aesc. 'Each other, I assume. But where did those *aksai* come from? We know of no other Musth having interest in this region this matter, do we?'

'No,' Aesc said. 'A puzzlement. The humans must have found some of those ships under repair we did not have time to load.'

'Leader,' a weapons-firer reported. 'One of the human ships, a ship-of-patrol, has launched at us. A counter-missile has already been released. It has acquired and is about to destroy their weapon. Shall I return fire on the ship-of-patrol?'

Wlencing looked at the Musth beside him.

'Alikhan, I assume you would like to launch in your own fighting craft and deal properly with these enemies, no doubt, wanting to be a young hero?'

His eldest offspring lifted a paw.

'I am not foolish enough to believe I could reach him before a missile, Progenitor.'

'Good,' Wlencing approved. 'Never forget a gun's reach far exceeds a knife's. Destroy the ship.'

The weapons-firer swept a hand over a bank of sensors.

Ten missiles spat toward *Corfe-Four*. It evaded two then the third smashed into its midsection and the ship vanished.

'Good,' Aesc said. 'Recall the other missiles and proceed with the landing.'

'Those are Musth ships,' Celidon said. 'Some kind of mother craft. We were too late taking over the planet, and—'

Redruth burst onto the bridge, panting, eyes half-glazed.

'Get us into space,' he snapped. 'This was a trap!'

'Perhaps not a trap,' Celidon said calmly. 'But we certainly didn't credit these Cumbrians with enough brains. And no one could predict the convenient arrival of the Musth. We're already lifting for space. Calm yourself, Protector.

'We'll fight them . . . destroy them . . . another day.'

The *Corfe* cleared Chance Island, never noticing two tiny Cookes at full drive after it. Garvin Jaansma was in the first Cooke, Njangu Yoshitaro in the second, somewhat to the rear.

'Can you hit it?' Garvin demanded. He was half-standing, crouched behind the windscreen.

'Doubt it, sir,' Ho Kang said.

'We're losing ground,' Running Bear reported. 'They've got legs on us.'

The com crackled.

'What the hell are you doing? That bastard's gonna turn around and swat you like a fly,' Yoshitaro snapped.

Garvin paid no mind.

'Give 'em a burst.'

'Yessir.'

Ho Kang pushed her firing stud, and tracers sailed out, fell hundreds of meters short of the fleeing *Corfe*. The Cooke shuddered, slowed in reaction.

'Shit, shit, shit. Can you lob it over 'em?'

'Not a chance, sir.'

Garvin came back to reality a little as the *Corfe* went vertical and flashed away, a dot, then a tiny flare from its drive. Seconds later, just out-atmosphere, it entered stardrive and was gone.

Jaansma sat down in his seat as the Cooke slowed.

'Crud.' He brightened. 'At least we gave it the good old try.'

Running Bear eyed him oddly, said nothing. Ho looked as disappointed as Jaansma.

' 'Kay,' Garvin said, suddenly tired. 'Take it back home, and don't call me a crazed sort too loudly.'

'Nossir.'

The Cooke banked, turned, and Yoshitaro's ACV caught up, closed alongside.

'Might I ask what the hell you were trying?' Njangu shouted.

'Kind of lost my temper.'

'Yeesh,' Yoshitaro said. 'You are, without question, either going to die a Sky Marshal with a double Confederation Cross, or I'm going to strangle you for sheer—'

'Uh, sir,' Running Bear interrupted. 'We've got a Mayday beacon. Just ahead of us. In the water, I think.'

Garvin puzzled, then remembered that strange burst of fire from the *Corfe*.

'Let's see if there's anything to pick up.'

Running Bear cut speed further and shed altitude until he was just above the ocean.

'There it is,' he said.

The speedster bobbed, two halves, one nearly submerged, in the small waves.

'Doesn't look like we need bother stopping.'

'Negative,' Jaansma said. 'I see a hand waving. Bring it on down.'

The Cooke hovered in, close to the wreckage. The speedster was a shambles, but spread across the instrument panel were the fully deployed impact bags. A man was sprawled across one, facedown, behind the controls.

Jasith Mellusin was looking at him, eyes bleared in shock.

'Garvin?'

'Yeh. Me.' Garvin jumped down into the sinking speedster, almost fell as waves rocked it.

Loy Kouro, his face bloody, staggered up from the control seat.

'I'm hurt,' he mumbled. 'Help me. Get me to a hospital.'

He started forward, and Garvin neatly pushed him back.

'Wait your turn,' he said. 'Ladies go first.'

He picked up Jasith, remembering other times smelled her familiar perfume over burnt insulation and spilled fuel. He felt tears come, pushed them away handed her up to his gunner.

'All right, you sorry bastard,' he said, turning back. 'It's your turn.'

And then the Musth smashed in-atmosphere.

FIVE

There were nineteen Council members in the chamber with their assistants; *Caud* Rao with his exec and intelligence officer; System-Leader Aesc and War Leader Wlencing.

'Firssst,' Aesc said, in Terran, sibilants hissing as almost all Musth did when they spoke Basic, 'I must assssure you of one thing. While our raccce is angered by the deathsss of our people, we have decccided to offer another chanccce.'

The Council members mostly looked skeptical.

'We would like to live in peaccce with Man,' Aesc insisted. 'Perhapsss one of our problemsss before wasss we chossse to live apart from each other.

'Thisss matter hasss been consssidered, and we sshall attempt to conjoin with you.'

'What, precisely, does that mean?' Jo Poynton asked.

'Firssst,' Wlencing said, 'we sshall not dwell on mattersss such as the deathsss of our people in the recccent uprisssing, nor even on the recccent deathsss of our caretakersss in the headquartersss on the high flatland, ignoring even the posssibility that our fellows were ssset upon and murdered in a mossst unwarrior-like manner.'

'We sshall offer positions in our minesss on Sssilitric, in every capacity from sssupervisor to rock-worker,' Aesc said. 'Payment ssshall be made in gold, which I asssume can be converted into your creditsss.

'Perhapsss, also, sssome of our mining expertsss might benefit from working with their human counterpartsss, working or at leassst obssserving your methodsss.

'Alssso, while our main headquartersss ssshall be where they were before on the high flatland and on Sssilitric, after we have purified them from the deathsss of our caretak-ersss, we ssshall open . . . consssulshipsss, I believe is your word, in mossst of the cccitiesss on this world.'

'To what purpose?' a Councilman asked.

'Asss I sssaid before, dissstance, unfamiliarnessss, can breed hatred,' Aesc said. 'With our people in closssse-nessss to each other, we can grow to know the other, and perhapsss regrettable instancesss of the passst ssshall not recur. Perhapsss, even, in the future, we might be able to offer visssitsss to sssome of our worldsss to further bring our peoplesss together.'

'It appears,' *Caud* Rao said, 'you've returned with far more of your people than before, and it also appears from our analyses that your ships are for war, not merchant or mining.'

'Sssuch isss the truth,' Wlencing said. 'We are a cau-tiousss raccce. And perhapsss it is well that they are, for we were able to drive away the one you sssaid was trying to take over thesse worldsss.'

'True,' Rao admitted. 'But what, specifically, is your military intent, remembering this system is still part of the Confederation?'

'Only a fool comesss to a place and immediately sssays what ssshould be done here, there, and everywhere,' Wlencing said. 'We would like to take a few cyclesss to ssstudy the matter, jussst obssserving, and work with your warriorsss.

'I am cccertain sssome sssort of equitable matter

might be achieved. Perhapsss we could sshare the tasssk of defenssse, with our warriorsss taking responsssibility for aerial and ssspace defensse, and you deal with mattersss here on the ground.

'Or perhapsss cccertain unitsss might be combined, asss an interesssting experiment.'

'With which race in command?' *Caud* Rao said.

Wlencing pushed a paw against the air, signifying lack of concern. 'That decisssion might be reached at the correct time, not thisss one. I noticcce, by the way, you disssperssssed your forcesss from the manner they were when we were here before. It would be a good gesssture if they would be returned to their peacccetime dutiesss and barracksss.

'One thing we mussst insssissst on. You cleverly were able to put a sssscattering of *aksai* into combat with the intrudersss. We asssssume you plan the return of thossse fighting ssshipsss at your bessst convenience.'

Rao hesitated, then nodded. 'We shall.'

'That iss good,' Wlencing said, inclined his head to Aesc. 'I am sssorry to have intruded on your ssspeech, but there were mattersss of my expertnessss to be ansssswered.'

'I have little elssse to sssay,' Aesc said, 'other than we ssshall remain in clossse contact with thisss Counccccil, and asss other mattersss presssent themsssselves, no doubt other meetingsss will be ssscheduled, with hope that they are asss congenial as thisss one.'

Without waiting for a response, he turned and moved lithely away, Wlencing following him. The war leader paused beside *Caud* Rao.

'Isss it not good that my belief that we would be fighting when next we met hasss not come true?'

'War is never good,' Rao said.

Wlencing moved a paw across his chest, then turned and followed Aesc out of the chamber.

'What did that last gesture mean?' Angara asked.

Rao shrugged, Hedley shook his head.

'Maybe that he thinks you're a flippin' pacifist, which the Musth don't have much use for?'

'I surely don't like the idea,' Angara said, 'that the Musth run around with all the air power, and we pound the ground. That isn't exactly cutting the pie in half. Nor am I bouncing up and down about the idea that we have to pull everybody back to Mahan and go back to being a big fat target.

'But I can't think of a damned thing we can do to change that.'

'And I'm not very fond of giving those hot little *aksai* back,' Hedley said. 'But like you said, we seem to have a shortage of flipping options.'

'What's your appreciation?' Rao asked his intelligence officer.

'Specifically, that the Musth have too many of those big mother . . . in two senses of the flipping word . . . ships, that every one of them I see looks and acts like a fighter, not a miner, that I'd guess the Force is outnumbered two or three to one, most likely more.

'Overall . . . the Musth are almost as flipping good at lying as I am,' Hedley said.

'That's what I'm thinking,' Rao said.

'*More* flowers?' Jasith asked.

'Indeed,' the nurse said, and examined them critically. 'I quite think they're the loveliest yet. No doubt encouraging you to get off your cute little heinie, pay your bill, go home, and leave us alone.'

'Merle, that isn't very nursely.'

'And what made you the judge of nurseliness?' the young man asked.

Jasith grinned. 'Like you said, I'm paying the bills.'

'If you want to be *that* way about it . . . your husband called, and he'll be about an hour late. Council meeting with our furry friends from beyond.'

'Only an hour. Practically early for Loy,' Jasith said.

'Now, now,' Merle said. 'By the way, a bit of under-the-stretcher information. Your doctor thinks the infection's finally been knocked down, so you should get out of here in the next day or two.'

'If you want a kiss,' Jasith said fervently, 'you have only to ask.'

'Not quite my style,' Merle said. 'Besides, I don't believe him. Whatever strange rot you picked up going swimming out there's probably still with you. And I watch my health.'

'Why don't you go find me some fruit juice,' Jasith said. 'And slip about three fingers of alk in it?'

'And then drink it myself,' the nurse said. put the elaborate arrangement on one of the long tables in the suite, already looking like a botanical garden, and walked out.

Jasith looked at the arrangement, decided Merle was possibly right and it was the prettiest, and opened the card.

BEST,
    GARVIN

Jasith Mellusin grimaced, crumpled the card, and tossed it into the trash.

She went to the window, looked down at Leggett, then across the bay to Chance Island, dim in the morning mist.

Two of the strange, frightening Musth fighting ships smashed over the city, then climbed sharply toward a mother ship hovering high overhead. Even through the insulated windows Jasith heard the *snap-crack* of the sonic booms.

She stayed at the window for a long time, then came back, picked Garvin's card from the trash, carefully smoothed it, and put it in a safe place.

Alikhan, Wlencing's cub, eyed the three *aksai* parked beside one of the taxiways at Camp Mahan's landing field.

'All three of these can fly?' he asked the officer beside him, a human almost as big as the Musth.

'Yes. Two fly well, the other's a limper . . . sorry, a cripple,' *Alt* Dill said.

'I see.' Again, Alikhan looked at the *aksai*. 'These are the ones that were flown against the invaders?'

'That's right,' Ben said, hoping the Musth weren't able to see through a liar as transparent as he was.

'That is remarkable,' Alikhan said. 'I would never have expected aircraft in such condition to be capable of fighting, maneuvering.'

'It was interesting,' Dill said, for once telling the truth.

'You were one of the pilots?'

'I was.'

'Who was the one who killed the patrol ships?'

'I hit one, my wingman . . . that's one of the men who flies beside me and keeps me being attacked from the rear . . . got another.

'I missed the *Corfe* . . . that's Alena Redruth's flagship.' Dill knew he was talking too much.

'So you have a kill,' Alikhan said. 'I have not been that fortunate.'

'I hope,' Dill said, 'you remain unfortunate, as long as you stay in this system.'

Alikhan's mouth came open, and he hissed from the back of his throat, sounding like an enraged cat, and Dill stepped back, hand touching his pistol, then realized the sound must denote amusement.

'You are most clever,' the Musth said.

'Thanks. Sorry for misunderstanding . . . I haven't been around you people very much.'

'Nor have I.'

'How did you learn to speak our Common Speech so well?' Dill asked. 'The few Musth I've been around sometimes are hard to understand.'

'You mean we sound like an air leak?'

'I wouldn't put it quite like that.'

'The one who taught me to speak Basic, a most harsh taskmaster, did.'

Dill grinned. 'What do *we* sound like, talking Musth?'

'No one knows,' Alikhan said. 'None of you have ever succeeded in learning the language.'

Dill, laughing, didn't see Alikhan's hand touch his projector, waiting for the reaction. Alikhan took his hand away, allowing his own amusement to show.

'I'd ask you back to the officers' club for a drink.' Dill said. 'But I don't think you drink alcohol.'

'We do not,' Alikhan said. 'I learned about your habits, shudder to think of some. Nor would you like what we consume for relaxation.'

'Which is?'

'Meat that has been allowed to decay for a time, with various spices.'

'Mmmh,' Dill said. 'We do that, but cook it first.'

'Thus ruining all the savor.'

'It's a pity,' Dill said, changing the subject, 'your leaders wouldn't let us keep these ships. It would be interesting to fight mock-war against each other, with the same equipment.'

'It would,' Alikhan agreed. 'But perhaps it would be inappropriate for such a rehearsal.'

Dill looked at him carefully.

'Are you sure that was the word you meant to use?'
'Certainly,' Alikhan said. 'For what else can happen but war? Whether you or I wish it is immaterial.'

Dill considered him thoughtfully.

'I've noticed that people who decide there's gonna be a fight generally produce one. The problem is, it doesn't come out the way they've figured, all the time.'

Caud Rao decided to wait to bring the regiments back to Chance Island until the Musth brought it up again.

But they didn't for more than two weeks, and Rao couldn't decide if that was good or bad. Were the Musth forgetful, or didn't they take RaoForce that seriously?

Garvin whistled cheerily into the BOQ suite he shared with Njangu, took a moment to realize Yoshitaro was staring, as if hypnotized, at the com screen. There was an image frozen on it.

'Whassup?'

'Look,' Njangu managed.

Garvin looked at the screen.

'Who they?'

'You uneddicated oaf, that's the Planetary Council.'

'I would've guessed a bunch of fat thieves.'

'That too.'

'So what?'

Njangu manipulated controls, came in on one person. Garvin looked closely at it.

'Hey! That's . . . what the hell was her name? The 'Raum who was The Movement's intel chief when we were playing covert? The one you cut a skate on at the end and told her to get lost?'

'Jo Poynton,' Njangu said. 'That's her. I thought it

was a cover name, like most of them used. But if it was, she's using the same one now.'

'And she's on the Council?' Garvin was incredulous.

'Why not? The war's over,' Yoshitaro said cynically 'and all wounds are healed up ickle and pretty.'

'But she was their main spymaster, part of the main rebel command, what'd they call it, the Planning Group!'

'Guess that proves cream rises to the top.'

'But how come nobody tattled her to the journohs? That idiot Kouro'd be happy to call her all kinds of sons of bitches if he knew.'

'Maybe,' Njangu said, 'the only entry that's still around is in our archives. I'd guess that when PlanGov got blown up, all of Policy and Analysis files got naturally shredded, along with the shitheads that tortured the info out of people.'

'So what are we going to do about it?'

Njangu shrugged. 'I guess nothing.'

Garvin looked carefully at his executive officer.

'Weren't you and her, uh . . .'

'Uh is the way to put it.'

'You gonna ring her up?'

'And say what?'

'Hell if I know,' Garvin said. 'I got my own problems.'

Njangu eyed Jaansma.

'I didn't get it before, but you *are* a little too god-damned happy. For why?'

'Well,' Garvin said, sounding a little guilty, 'I just sent some flowers out.'

'Ali with his beard on fire,' Njangu swore. 'Don't you ever give up? She's a married woman, remember?'

'I know,' Garvin said, and Njangu realized the conversation had just come to an end.

' 'Kay,' he said. 'Forget it.' He picked up a message

slip from his desk, sailed it across to Garvin. 'Better you think about this.'

'What is it?'

'The Leeat Islands,' Njangu said. 'Bunch of little islands way to hell and gone. They got problems with pirates.'

'Yeh, right, pirates.'

'Truth, or anyway they swear to it,' Njangu said. 'Ex-'Raum that didn't want to go back to making a semihonest living, so they're out there poaching on the local fisher folk. Not a very nice bunch of people, it looks like, since nobody's come back with details.

'The cops can't seem to do anything, since the baddies have good skinny from the locals. Every time they go out looking, there's nobody but innocents.'

'So, naturally,' Garvin said, 'they want us to handle the rough work.'

'You rather sit around here and worry about the Musth?'

'Good point,' Garvin agreed. 'What do we know about these pirates?'

'Not a whole helluva lot. Boats just flat disappear. No bodies, nothing. The best intel is from little bits somebody hollers on the Mayday freq before they vanish.

'I'd guess they kill the fishermen, shake the boats for anything valuable, then either sink them or maybe run them back to wherever they're based. A quick paint job and back to sea as Fishing Boat *Justlaunched*. I wouldn't be surprised if they've got spies out in some of the fishing villages to tip 'em to the best cargoes to grab. And that's the sum total of what I've got. Somewhat less than nothing.'

'You got maps and such so we can at least start figuring how we're going to flounder around?' Garvin asked.

'Would I be the evil genius of the Legion if I didn't?'

'Well I shall be dipped,' Njangu said. 'I thought you were frigging dead!'

'I was,' *Finf* Ton Milot said wryly. 'But then I realized I was hurting too bad. The bastards clipped me the arm, leg. Damned near lost the leg, and I've got about a meter of synthbone in it.'

'You know they gave Hank Faull the Star of Gallantry,' Yoshitaro said. Milot had been wounded, Hank Faull killed in the final battle of the 'Raum uprising, securing the Eckmuhl.

'Yeh,' Milot said flatly. 'Bet that made his widow feel real good and puts lots of rations on his kids' plates.'

'So what're you doing still in uniform?'

Milot looked away.

'Goddamned if I know,' he said. 'If I'd had a brain, I would've taken the wound pension and gone fishing. Instead . . .' He let his voice trail off.

'Hey,' he went on. 'Aren't I supposed to salute you or something now you're a highborn *aspirant*?'

'Bite me,' Njangu said. 'A proper banging of the head on the floor's enough.'

'Wish in one hand, shit in the other, see which one fills up first,' Milot said.

'Nice to see you haven't changed. Welcome back to I&R. I assume you can still carry the load.'

'Either that or whip up on some 'cruit to do it for me,' Milot said. 'By the way, did you know Lupul and I got married?'

'Congrats,' Njangu said. 'Whyn't you invite me to the wedding?'

'It was sort of a flash idea,' Milot said. 'Fact was, well, I was sort of talking to Deira. You remember her?'

Njangu did. He'd taken a pass with Milot to the small

fishing village of Issus after they'd graduated from I&R training, and ended up in a threesome with fellow striker Angie Rada and the sixteen-year-old girl.

'Well, Lupul got the wrong idea.' Milot grinned thoughtfully. 'Or maybe the right idea. So she said it was time for me to either stay a merry bachelor and she hoped my cock rotted off, or else.

'I thought about it for, oh, a second and a half, realized I couldn't do any better than Lupul, and so we just up and did it. Colorful fisherman's custom on a boat and that kind of thing.

'Deira asked about you, by the way.'

'It never rains . . .' Njangu muttered, thinking of Jo Poynton.

'Maybe you want to come over to Issus with me sometime,' Milot offered. 'That is, if it's not illegal for an officer to do something with one of us enlisted swine.'

'We'll do it,' Njangu promised absently. An idea was pulling at him. 'Ton, do you suppose you could borrow a fishing boat from one of your friends?'

'Not borrow, but rent. Fishermen gotta make a credit somewhere. And if you want it officially, I'd guess there might be some bullet holes to patch up when it comes back. Plus we could hire my brother to help run it. You remember Alei . . . that was his boat you fell off of, the time we went fishing and you ended up as bait.'

'Let me ask you something,' Njangu said. 'First, you can forget about that fishing trip we went on anytime you want to. You know of the Leeat Islands?'

'A little bit,' Milot said. 'A bunch of islands way to hell and gone other side of Cumbre, isn't it? Never fished there, but I know some people who did. Contract work. Fly over, work a season, come back. They did 'kay. Didn't get rich, but had some good stories to tell. Big fish in those parts.'

'I'll want to talk to them,' Yoshitaro said. 'Because we're thinking about going for the biggest fish on the planet.'

Milot flickered his eyebrows.

'Good, boss. Very good story. Glad there's no other reason you want to visit my village.'

'Goddammit, I'm telling the truth.'

'No question about that, boss. Good truth, too, huh?'

'I think,' Njangu said comfortably, 'this is the sneakiest plan I've ever come up with.'

'Possibly,' Garvin agreed. 'And don't get a swole head, but it might even accidentally work.'

'So reward your fearless, peerless executive officer and open me a beer. I'm the poor sod who had to go spend the last two days in that backwater of Issus talking to fishermen to make sure my idea'd work.'

'I don't guess,' Garvin said, 'busy as you were, you found time to talk a walk in the moonlight with anybody?'

'Goddammit,' Njangu snarled, 'does everybody know everything about my love life? And whether or not I did is none of your bidness. Now, boss, can I have my frigging beer?'

Garvin obliged, got another for himself, and examined the holo-projection table again.

'Lift the sucker in here,' he muttered. 'A day's sail from most of the activity . . . fish our way to here . . . and the py-rates hopefully jump out at us somewhere along the way and get shortened by a neck. Yer right, Yoshitaro. I don't see anything that can go wrong.'

There was a tap at the door.

'Whozat?'

'Lir,' the first *tweg* said. 'With a guest.'

'What kind of security clearance he or she got?'

'Higher one than you flipping do,' Hedley said, pushing his way into the company commander's office. 'Are you two through plotting your villainy?'

'Pretty close, Jon,' Hedley said. 'You want a quick brief?'

'After I give you a small addition. Nothing that'll worry you.'

'Uh-oh,' Njangu said.

'We're listening,' Jaansma said suspiciously.

'Some observers want to come along.'

'Boss,' Garvin said, 'come on! This is a for-real covert operation, dammit! We aren't gonna have any place for a straphanger who maybe wants to see what a loud bang looks like up close.'

'Three straphangers to be precise,' Hedley said.

'Goddamned wonderful,' Njangu said. 'Can't you tell 'em to pack their asses with salt and piss up a rope?'

'Nope,' Hedley said, holding back a grin.

'Ho-kay,' Garvin said. 'So which one of the PlanGov twits has enough clout to shove themselves down our throats, and why?'

'Why is easiest,' Hedley said. 'Our observers want to see the way we operate for real, not some kind of training exercise, and I&R's currently the only game in town. As for the who . . . it ain't flipping PlanGov.'

'Uh-oh twice,' Njangu said again.

'Make it thrice,' Hedley said. 'Your observers, who as you correctly guessed, didn't ask but told, are a being named Wlencing and two of his aides.'

'Aw fiddle,' Njangu said, collapsing back into his chair. 'Howinhell are we gonna pack three frigging Musth on a fishing boat and look inconspicuous?'

'Damfino,' Garvin said. 'But you're the specialist in being sneaky.'

'Maybe one of them could be a figurehead on your

boat?' Hedley suggested, and Njangu gave him a look of pure hatred.

The dockyard heavy lifter had been beefed up with extra fuel cells, its antigrav units carefully inspected. Predawn, with a two-person crew from the Legion, it slid out of Leggett's commercial dockyards into the bay, then headed east, toward the end of the peninsula. Around midday, it rounded the point, and just before dusk landed at a beach beyond Issus.

Waiting was a careened twenty-meter fishing craft, the *Urumchi Darling*, less lifter than a boat, intended for long sea trips, where constant use of the antigravs would be cost-prohibitive. It pretty much matched the lines of the Leeat Islanders' boats. It'd been rented from one of the Issus fishermen. With it went Ton Milot's brother, Alei, as promised. He was only slightly more expensive to rent than the boat.

Alei had been warned it could get dangerous, but he shrugged and said no more so than a good typhoon, and wouldn't last as long, either.

Ton had asked if perhaps Yoshitaro would like to ask Deira along, for more authenticity – a lot of fishing types took out families with them. Njangu declined, considering the wide range of dirty jobs he'd find for Milot when all this was over.

After beaching, the *Urumchi* was modified to look even more like one of the Leeat Island fishers, with a small steadying sail on its stern, twin trawl booms on its mainmast, and the harpooner's pulpit removed. Then it had been given a characteristic paint job – a red stripe along the waterline matching the double exhaust pipes, and blue railings – and refloated on the rising tide. The work had been done by the two I&R teams chosen for the operation, with *Dec* Deb Irthing as senior noncom.

Garvin hadn't mentioned that before they got to play they'd have to do a little scut work with hammer and brush, but nobody objected, since that was a lot better than normal garrison duties around their barracks.

They'd arrived from Camp Mahan in three Griersons, Ben Dill commanding. The Aerial Combat Vehicles were hidden back under the trees, and the troops pitched hasty-domes around them. All wore plain civilian coveralls, like most fishermen did.

At dawn the next morning, while the team was waiting for high tide to refloat the *Urumchi*, a Grierson electronic warfare specialist gave the alarm as the troops were eating their rations after calisthenics. Her radar had picked up a large spacecraft, in-atmosphere from space, due east. She lost the ship behind the dumbbell-shaped island off Issus, then picked it up again as it lifted over the uninhabited island and sped toward them, just above the water.

Five minutes later, they had it on visual, and IDd the ship as one of the Musth armed transports they called mother ships.

The ship slowed, approached the beach, and hovered at the shoreline, spray created by the ship's drive clouding the air.

A lock opened, and a gangway pushed out. Down came Wlencing and two other Musth, wearing combat harness and carrying, clipped to their harness, tubular duffles. One also carried a small contoured box high on his back that looked like a com.

Garvin and Njangu met the three, Garvin saluting. The two teams were behind him, at attention. Wlencing raised a forearm, bowed his head, stood motionless in return.

'You are welcome.'

'I doubt that,' Wlencing said.

'Oh?' Garvin said neutrally.

'I would not like it if I were about to fight, and otherss who look ssso very different insssisssted on joining me,' he said.

'You're right. I don't, particularly,' Garvin said. 'But I have my orders, and I'll obey them.'

'We ssshall attempt to remain out of the way, although if killing developsss, we would be delighted to help.'

Njangu heard somebody mutter 'no shit,' from behind him, recognized the voice, promised retribution.

'That's as may be,' Jaansma said. 'If . . . or rather when we fight, any soldier is welcome. But one thing that's got to be clear – there's only one commander.'

'Sssuch is only logical, and our policccy asss well. We ssshall follow your insssstructionsss when fighting.'

Garvin led them up the beach.

'I think I remember you,' Wlencing said. 'Have not we met?'

'We did,' Garvin said.

'You were . . . a gunner, then. Learning how to be a warrior.'

'Yes. You've got a good memory.'

'And now you are a leader, commanding thossse who go forward of the linesss?'

'Yes.'

'You mussst have ssstudied well.'

Garvin shrugged.

'I ssshall be interesssted in ssseeing your patternsss, your ssskills,' Wlencing said.

'Then let's get about it,' Garvin said. 'We'll lift in the Griersons, transfer to the boat when we arrive off the Leeats,' Garvin said. '*Dec* Irthing, load 'em up!'

The yard lighter's drive whined to life, and it lifted, hovering above the beached *Urumchi*. Gyro-stabilized, the lighter's hull split lengthwise, each part separately controlled. S slings were lowered from each half, forced under the *Urumchi*'s hull, and the boat lifted. As soon as it cleared the sand, other slings were installed equidistant from the *Urumchi*'s center of gravity.

The lighter's skipper signaled to her mate in the other half, and the lighter closed up into a single ship, and the *Urumchi* was secured in the slings.

Escorted by the Griersons, the lighter flew out to sea, first due east to clear land, then slightly east by northeast, toward the Leeats.

Striker Mar Henschley was fresh from her I&R training as a Shrike gunner. But she was learning that everyone in I&R was basically infantry when anyone shouted. She sat cramped on a Grierson bench, wishing she had her missile launcher instead of just a paltry blaster. Just opposite her, next to the ECM ball turret, a Musth sat. She *thought* it was sitting anyway, although not sure how to describe someone braced on its tripod tail and two legs. The Musth was cramped, half-bent over, head brushing the armored roof of the Aerial Combat Vehicle.

It looked as uncomfortable as she was.

The striker chanced a sympathetic grin, got nothing but a curious look in return. Then his ears cocked toward her, and the snakelike head bobbed. She hoped that was a friendly response, not an invitation to fight to the death.

The yard lifter settled down in the water, the *Urumchi* cradled below. Just above and behind it, the three Griersons hovered.

They were far at sea, off the Leeats, and there was nothing on the horizon.

The lifter lowered, and the boat touched the water,

then floated. The two Milots slid down from the lifter onto the *Urumchi*. Alei ran to the controls, started the engines as the Griersons closed on the stern, and the I&R teams dropped down. Njangu and Garvin stood ready to give the Musth a hand, but they jumped lithely onto the *Urumchi*, ignoring the offered assistance.

The Griersons' drives hummed, and they lifted away.

'They'll stand by on one of the uninhabited islands,' Garvin told Wlencing. 'We'll have them plus a flight of Zhukovs . . . those are our heavy support vehicles . . . and a reaction force of infantry on standby if we need them.'

Wlencing bobbed his head, but didn't answer.

'All right, people,' Garvin shouted. 'Get inside, and keep out of sight. *Finf* Milot, let's go fishing.'

'Aye, skipper,' Milot said, and the *Urumchi*'s engines hummed to half speed.

An hour later, Alei Milot called, 'Let's get authentic . . . we've got fish on the sonar. Get those nets down!'

The decks of the *Urumchi* suddenly got more crowded as inexperienced soldiers helped muscle the nets from their piled storage on the deck to the railings. Ton secured them to the booms, and the nets were shot overboard.

'What the hell happens if we catch anything?' a soldier wondered.

'We sell it,' Njangu said. 'Put the money in the beer fund.'

'Better,' Wlencing said from the boat deck, watching with possible amusement. 'We dine on them.'

'How many fish can you eat?'

'Many, many,' Wlencing said. 'Perhapsss we ssshall have luck.'

'Haul out,' Alei shouted, and the laborious work of

bringing the two nets up began. As the bunts surfaced, booms were secured to them, and, one at a time, lifted the nets on board. Irthing muttered, 'Keeripus, but there's some ugly-looking things come up from the sea.'

'With a yo and a ho and a heave and a ho,' Alei called, and the soldiers muscled the first bunt, the fish-carrying end of the net, onto the deck, and fish spilled everywhere.

'Now what?'

'Gut 'em and throw 'em in the cooling pen,' Ton called cheerily, brandishing a knife that could serve as a cutlass.

'I'm thinking,' a soldier said, 'there's people who work a *lot* harder than we do.'

Mar Henschley had a plate of fresh fillets on her knees, nicely rolled in meal and fried. But she was staring in distressed fascination at a Musth – she thought it was the same one who'd been in her Grierson.

He had a plate of fish as well, still moving slightly after being gutted. Henschley held a forgotten bite on her fork, watching the Musth as razor claws slid out of his paws. He cut a fish apart along its spine, delicately lifted one half to his mouth, chewed two or three times, then swallowed.

The Musth saw her watching, extended the other half of the fish, tossed the skeleton overboard.

She hesitated.

'Go ahead,' Njangu Yoshitaro said, chewing, and Mar realized with a bit of horror his plate was also full of raw creatures. 'Good.'

Reluctantly she tried, closing her eyes, chewing, not thinking about what she was eating until her tastebuds told her it was good. Very good.

She offered some of her cooked fish in return, but the Musth held up a rejecting paw.

Feeling a bit superior, she pointed at and got another piece of raw fish, and chewed vigorously.

Njangu turned his head, hiding a smile.

The next day, they came on a fishing fleet. The troops hid behind the *Urumchi's* high bulwarks or crowded into the small cabins.

Alei Milot, on the bridge, scanned the boats ahead with stabilized binoculars. 'All I can see is flashing signals from people watching us,' he said to Njangu. 'They're trying to figure out if we're the pirates. Pretty soon, somebody'll call us, on a voice channel. Fishermen don't use video much . . . too easy to tell when you're lying.'

Ton, at the *Urumchi's* controls, said, 'I'll beat them to it,' picked up the boat's com, keyed a sensor.

'Anybody catching anything?'

'Who're you?' came a voice.

'The *Urumchi*, out of Teku.' Teku was the farthest-distant settled island of the Leeats.

'Long haul from your waters.'

'Which means the catching better be good,' Milot said.

'Who's skipper aboard?' another voice asked, and Njangu could hear suspicion.

'The Milot brothers. We're from Issus, decided to try fishing some distant waters. Got a contract to run this scow.'

Silence for a bit, then, another voice:

'I know one of you. Alei, that's the name. You an' me got drunk, once. This is Juba Nushki. I came to Dharma Island, was mate on the *Ayalew*.'

'Sure,' Alei said, taking the com. 'You were drinking

wine and chewing herbs, chasin' whores like they wanted
to pay you.'

'That's me. Caught one, too. Too trashed to do anything, though. And I had a head the size of a fish trap the
next morning. Learned my lesson about you wild city
people, so I came back where I belong.'

The region around Issus had a population of about five
hundred.

'So what's the catch like?'

'Eh,' Nushki said. 'There's big runs of flatters, catch
'em at dusk, some say. But we're doing crappy. Nothing
out here at all for us.'

'That means,' Ton told Njangu, 'he's fishing his nose
off. There's never been a fisherman'd claim luck to anybody else with a net who might bust in.'

'Nothin' but nothin', like Juba said,' another voice
came, trying to sound gloomy, 'Nothin' much but trash
fish and waitin' to get hit by pirates.'

'We heard about them,' Ton said. 'Is it for real?'

'You best know,' another voice came. 'Lost two ships
from our island a month ago. Nothing this trip. We was
thinking maybe you was one of them, not bein' able to
spot your paint job.'

'Times don't improve,' Ton said, 'we might think
about joinin' 'em.'

'Me too,' Nushki said. 'Best you fish right around
here, stay not far from the rest of us. Strength in numbers.'

'And let you fools sniff around my nets when I shoot
'em? I'm dumb, but I'm not that dumb.' Ton hung the
com up. 'So now everybody knows who we are. Nice
greedy fishermen, like everybody else out here.'

'Let's hope the pirates are listening.'

Two days later, after having seen nothing but fish and the

occasional lone fishing lifter, which generally skittered away without closing, Wlencing had a suggestion for Garvin:

'Isss it not posssible that thessse fissshermen have not the truth?'

'Hell yes.' Alei Milot said. The two humans and Wlencing were the only ones on the *Urumchi*'s bridge. 'A fisherman isn't happy unless he can get off one, maybe two lies a day.'

'Do you humans not have firmsss who ssspread the risssk for creditsss, so if sssomething happensss it's easssier on the many than the few?'

'Insurance companies? We have them,' Milot said.

'A fissshing vehicle could vanisssh, then, and whoever paid the . . . insssurance companies . . . could collect the creditsss, and the vehicle be sssold in sssome faraway placcce?'

'What about the distress calls?' Garvin asked.

'Sssseasoning on the disssh,' Wlencing said. 'To make it appear more real.'

'Could be,' Garvin said. 'But you'd think the police would've followed up on whoever got paid off for losing a boat, and found out that the people who're supposed to be drowned are spending money somewhere.'

'Why?' Wlencing asked reasonably, 'Would not the fisssher persssson's brothersss, who know about thisss dec- cceit, protect him or her? What do they owe sssome disssstant group of people they do not know? And are your human policcce infallible, are they without thossse who would take creditsss to keep sssilent?'

Garvin considered.

'That's not that bad a thought,' he said. 'And it'll get better in a few days if nothing happens. This frigging about is not only duller than watching rocks change into sand, but it's playing hell with the Legion's budget.'

Two days later, the pirates attacked.

The *Urumchi* was passing through a long curving archi-
pelago, almost an atoll. Its antigrav was on just enough
to keep it skimming the almost waveless water, and it
was moving at half drive.

Njangu had the bridge watch, Alei at the controls
beside him, staring dreamily at the small tropical islands
on either side of the fisher and considering the possibility of deserting to one of them. Sunny, nice, soft breeze,
no problems. Live on fruit and fish . . . maybe bring a few
giptel with him. Chasing them down for roasts would
give him exercise.

Swim, lie in the sun, forget this goddamned army . . .

Being alone could get boring. Bring a holo?
Njangu shuddered, thinking what Cumbre considered
great entertainment. Disks? Njangu wasn't that much
of a reader unless there was something he needed to
know.

Company? Well, there was Deira . . . or maybe Jo
Poynton. Or maybe . . .

Njangu sighed, began constructing a partner from
women he'd known or wished he'd known, trying not to
remind himself what a city rat he really was and how
he'd go berserk after a week by himself, when a lookout
shouted.

'Boss! Got some lifters coming hard on our right.'

Yoshitaro grabbed binocs, saw five small vehicles,
about ten feet above the water, coming out of a hidden
bay, coming fast.

'Turn 'em out,' he said, and the alert team started
booting drowsy soldiers into readiness.

Jaansma clattered up the bridge ladder, Wlencing just
behind him.

The dots got closer.

Njangu was about to tell Wlencing to get under cover when he IDd the lead vehicle.

'Shit, it's a Cooke . . . and it's armed!'

All five were Cookes, he realized, the borderline obsolescent small combat lifters the Legion was trying to retire as quickly as possible, and Njangu wondered where these outbackers had been able to acquire them.

'Lead Cooke's got a cannon mounted,' a lookout reported. 'So does number three.'

'We've got a party,' Jaansma called. 'Cannon team, get ready. The rest of you clowns, load and lock, but stay down. I'll have the first one who shoots without orders grilled.'

One of I&R's 20mm autocannon had been set on a folding mount and was ready in the bows of the *Urumchi*. Its team crawled to it, pulled the operating handle back, chambering a round from the drum magazine.

Other I&R soldiers crouched, blasters ready, behind the bulwarks.

'Deb,' Njangu said, 'honk up our air support, get the whole lot of 'em inbound. This is a little bit stronger than one lousy little putt-putt.'

Wlencing went back down the ladder from the bridge and called to one of his men, the one with the small pack. The Musth gave Wlencing a curved piece of metal, like a large bracelet. Wlencing clipped it to his throat, began speaking in Musth.

It was very quiet then. Njangu could hear the whine of the *Urumchi*'s drive, the pat of waves against the hull, even the distant hum of the incoming raiders' combat vehicles.

Sirens howled from the incoming Cookes, no doubt intended to paralyze their targets.

'Guess we know why there haven't been any survivors coming back with tales of woe,' Njangu said.

'Guess so,' Garvin said. 'Listen up, people! Don't shoot the last bugger up too bad. We want to be able to track 'em to their home. I'd just as soon not have to come back here again.'

'You're assuming they aren't gonna shoot *us* up too bad,' Njangu murmured.

'Of course,' Garvin said. 'We're the good guys, right? Good guys always win, right? Bad guys can't shoot, right?'

'As an ex-bad guy, I resent that,' Njangu said. 'They're down to about two hundred meters, so I think—'

Njangu's suggestion was interrupted by a roar from the cannon in the lead Cooke. It churned blue water into spray about five meters in front of the *Urumchi*, and a speaker blared:

'Cut your engines! Cut your engines! Stand by to be boarded!'

'Cannon up,' Garvin called calmly, and the two assistant gunners muscled the two-meter-long weapon into firing position.

'Gunner! Lead incoming Cooke! One seven five meters!'

'Target!' the gunner shouted.

'Five rounds!'

The cannon roared for an instant. The first round was short, the rest blew the bow off the ACV. It pinwheeled, dug into the water, and spat cannon and crew into the sun-dappled waves.

'I&R . . . up! Fire when you've got a target!'

Individual blasters and Squad Support Weapons crashed, and Njangu saw raiders scream, fall, Cookes zig back and forth.

The raiders' second cannon chattered, and tracers came toward Njangu very slowly, lazily, then whipped past, thudded into the boat's superstructure. Someone shouted in pain, and Njangu brought his blaster up, aimed, adjusted for the boat's rise, fall, touched the firing stud.

Across the water, the gunner on the autocannon spasmed, arms going wide, rolled into the water.

Njangu switched the selector switch, let a quarter of the drum magazine's one hundred rounds chatter across the Cooke.

'I have Sibyl Scythe Six Actual,' a com man intoned, as calmly as if he was on a field exercise, and passed the com to Garvin.

'This is Sibyl Six Actual. Go.'

'This is Sibyl Scythe,' the voice said – Ben Dill. 'Golan Flight in support. You got something juicy?'

'This is Sibyl Six, Ben,' Garvin said. 'Got four Cookes playing bad. Careful, they've got 20mammamamma breath.'

'Affirm. Have you under visual. About, oh, one five angels, inbound hot. Duck yo' little heads, sisters.'

'Air coming in,' Garvin shouted, and saw three Griersons swooping down. Behind and above them were three of the massive Zhukov weapons ships. Smoke plumed from the Griersons, and missiles smashed down.

One missile hit a pirate Cooke, and it vanished in iridescent spray, others splashing around it, a chain of explosions rolling across the water.

Someone was behind the autocannon on the Cooke again, and shooting. Tracers climbed high, intersected with an incoming Grierson. It bucked, volleyed its missiles wide, rolled, and black smoke poured from its fuselage.

'Shit!' somebody said into an open com.

The Grierson rolled, straightened, then climbed.

'This is Sibyl Scythe Beta,' a voice came. 'Hit, ECM wounded . . . losing power . . . breaking off. Returning to base. Should be 'kay.'

'Sibyl Gamma,' Dill said. 'This is Sibyl Scythe Six . . . Break off and accompany Beta home. I don't want either of you getting your feet wet.'

'Beta, understood, clear.'

A Zhukov dived past, 150mm autocannon churning, and the ocean geysered around the Cookes.

'This is Scythe Six . . . coming in again,' Dill said. and the Grierson dived down.

Sunlight flashed from the right, and Njangu saw a crescent-shaped spaceship, maybe three meters above the ocean. Dill, in the Grierson, saw it, snaprolled away, almost losing control.

An instant of green haze flashed at the *aksai*'s wing, another Cooke exploded, and the *aksai* climbed at speed. Two others flanked it.

'Son of a bitch,' somebody beside Garvin said. 'Where'd *that* come from?'

'Are you in contact with him?' Garvin shouted to Wlencing.

'I am.'

'We want at least one boat intact to follow.'

'I ssshall sssend to him.'

Wlencing touched a paw to the mike as the lead *aksai* rolled inverted, came down again, fired, and the next to the last Cooke blew up. The Musth fighting ship flashed over the *Urunzchi,* and Njangu thought he could've touched the pilot in his sealed canopy.

He climbed, came back, and Ben Dill's Grierson was between him and the last Cooke as the ACV scrambled back toward land. The *aksai* banked, tried to clear the Grierson, and Dill flat-spun, went out of control for an instant, then recovered, and at full power flew between the *aksai* and the Cooke, blocking its attack.

Wlencing was talking loudly into his com.

The Musth fighting ship skidded through a turn, then

shot skyward and began orbiting overhead. high above the Grierson and the flight of Zhukovs.

Garvin turned to Alei.

'Stay on that goddamned Cooke, and . . . aw hell, medic!'

Alei, still at the helm, was looking interestedly at a long sliver of plas from the cabin wall sticking entirely through his upper arm.

'You know, what I'm charging you just got real expensive,' he said calmly, then pain took him, and Garvin eased him away from the controls.

Ton Milot was on the bridge, had the controls, as a medical tech and Njangu helped Alei down the ladder to the deck.

He hurried back to the bridge. The *Urumchi* was at full power and antigrav, clear of the water, about an eighth the speed of the last pirate Cooke.

'This is Sibyl Six Actual,' Garvin said quietly into his com. 'Ben, I want you just behind and above me. Jinking . . . the bastards might have AA capability. Don't kill him until we know where he's going. Bring your Zooks in just in front of me as soon as the Cooke hits land, wherever it's going, and hit anything that looks like a target.'

'Affirm,' Dill said.

'Wlencing, keep your fliers out of it!' Garvin said. 'I don't want them to slip a little, and we're suddenly the target. Njangu, get downstairs and get the troops ready. Ton, look for something expensive to plow this heap into. Njangu, when the crashing stops, disembark everybody off the stern, and get 'em shooting.'

'You hear that, troopies?' Njangu shouted, and there were rounds slashing overhead from Dill's Grierson.

'When we hit, get away from the boat, form up, and go in,' he ordered. 'Anybody shooting's a target; try to keep from hitting anybody real civilian.'

He was pleased his voice was as calm as anyone else's.

Njangu had an instant to look around, saw two casualties besides Alei Milot. Soldiers' faces were white, tense, scared, but determined.

Ahead was the fleeing Cooke, just off the water, steadily pulling away from the fisher. It was heading for a cove with a boulder-lined inlet carved into it, and scattered buildings, mostly shacks or prefabs spreading under the trees. Fire was coming at the *Urumchi* from the buildings, from the Cooke.

'We don't need the Cooke anymore,' he called to Garvin.

'Kill it for me.'

'Cannon! Target that last bugger.'

'Got it, boss,' and the cannon roared. Flame flickered from the Cooke's rear, and it wobbled, then smashed into the beach just at water's edge, flipped high into the air, crashed into the middle of the inlet, and exploded.

The *Urumchi* came up the beach, and Garvin was shouting to cut the power. The fisher smashed into a building, spun sideways, and the soldiers were jumping, falling off its sides.

Somebody shot at Njangu and he shot back, without seeing whether he hit anyone. A soldier bumped him aside, ran down an alleyway. A blaster cracked, and part of a wall fell away. Njangu sprayed rounds in the blaster's direction, and somebody screamed, then was silent.

A man, big, bearded, came out of a hut, weapon lifting. His chest exploded, and white worms writhed in the gaping wound, and Wlencing went past, hurling a waspgrenade into the hut, shooting someone else as he did.

Garvin was there, flanked by a com man and Irthing.

'I'll take Gamma around the side. You keep on pushing the way you're going.'

'Take the easy part, why don't you,' Njangu said, but Garvin was gone, shouting for Gamma to follow him.

Njangu ran after Wlencing, came into a small square, saw a store; somebody was crouched behind a wooden counter.

Njangu let a burst go through the counter, proving it to he rotten cover, and the woman dropped, her long sporting rifle clattering against the floor. A man appeared behind her. Njangu didn't have time to see if he was armed or not, shot him, ran on.

He thumbed a grenade into a doorway and heard screams after it exploded. Suddenly there was a large hole in the wall beside him, and Njangu dived for the dirt, landing in muck and something that smelled like a latrine, rolled, sprayed rounds, came up, ran on.

At the end of the winding lane was a largish building, and men and women were coming out. Njangu started to shoot, saw most waving white – clothes, towels, undergarments, heard a blaster go off, and one of them went down.

'Cease fire, cease fire,' he was shouting, and slowly the shooting died away, and it was quiet except for someone sobbing, and a man somewhere calling for his mother as life bubbled away.

An hour later, I&R was assembled in the square. In front of them were thirty-eight sullen, frightened men and women, plus five very young children.

I&R had taken five casualties, one killed.

Dill's Grierson was landed on the beach, the flight of Zhukovs orbited overhead. The *aksai* had vanished as thoroughly as it had arrived.

Wlencing and his two aides were looking at the prisoners interestedly.

'Now there ssshall come a trial?'

'Yeh,' Garvin said. 'The lifters are inbound for them now.'

'And what will the ressssult be?'

'Guilty,' Garvin said.

'And the punissshment?'

'They still kill people for doing things like this,' Jaansma said, and the taste of victory was suddenly flat. 'I guess that'll be what'll happen to anybody who doesn't have some kind of reasonable explanation for what he's been doing.'

'That isss good,' Wlencing said. 'A failed brigand isss worthless.'

'But a successful one?' Njangu asked. Unlike Garvin, he considered the captured raiders, and their probable fate, as coldly as Wlencing.

'That one,' Wlencing said, 'will become a lord of the universsse, if he or ssshe is not caught.'

'There isn't that much difference between us, is there?' Njangu said. 'You're just more open about things.'

Ben Dill trotted toward them.

'Good going, folks,' he said. 'My wingmen made it back to Mahan, no problems. All I want now is the pilot of that goddamned *aksai* who kept me from getting more.'

'That *wasss* interesssting,' Wlencing said. 'I did not think it wasss posssible for one of thossse aerial beassts you fly to outmaneuver an *aksai*.'

'It isn't,' Dill said. 'I just got hot.'

'My cub will not be pleassed,' Wlencing said. 'I ssshall jape at him, even though he did well. He ssspent too much time ssstudying peaccce, rather than war.'

'Your cub, I mean child?' Dill asked. 'Alikhan?'

'You have knowledge of him?'

'Yeh,' Dill said. 'Tell him from me that the only reason I kicked his butt is he was surprised. I'll give him a rematch anytime he wants.'

'I ssshall give him that messsage sssometime,' Wlencing said. 'When he isss adequately humble.'

'Why,' Garvin said, 'didn't you tell us you had your own air support? Didn't your Leader say something about interspecies cooperation?'

'Becaussse,' Wlencing said, 'you did not asssk.'

SIX

'It looks like we'll be fighting the Musth pretty soon, boss?' *Dec* Ho Kang, formerly an electronic counter-measure specialist on Garvin's Grierson, now an aircraft commander, said the last word a bit tentatively. She still wasn't used to the I&R customs.

'No secrets around here,' Haut Hedley sighed. 'It's got a good probability to it.'

'And we know not very much about 'em?'

'Slightly less than bubkus.'

'Would it help any to know something about their empire? Like where their worlds are?' Ho persisted.

'Hell yes,' Hedley said. 'Give us a chance to think about raiding them, if we ever score any flipping war-ships.'

Ho came to attention.

'Request two weeks detached service, and permission to visit C-Cumbre, sir.'

'You want to tell me why?'

'Nossir.'

'You got permission from Garvin or Njangu?'

'Nossir. If I'm gonna hang my ass out, I'd like as few witnesses as possible.'

'Problem with I&R,' Hedley grumbled. 'Too many

primas, not enough donnas. You look like you're on to something. Go.'

Even spiced and four meters away, the decaying meat that was the Musth equivalent of a stiff drink stank to the heavens.

Garvin Jaansma tried to ignore it, concentrating on his plight and his ship's unfamiliar controls.

Ahead of him, no more than two planetary diameters off their homeworld, fourteen bulbous Musth deep-space attack craft came toward him. Garvin's alarm systems were screaming that he was targeted by all of them.

'I don't like this.'

'Who does?' Njangu Yoshitaro said. His ship, along with two other Confederation small corvettes, were behind and above him.

All four Confederation ships had just emerged from hyperspace to find the Musth fleet mounting their attack.

'Options?' Njangu suggested.

'Flash and flurry, I guess,' Garvin said. 'Try not to give them too good a target.'

His hands swept the controls, and his ship flashed back into hyperspace for an instant, came out between the Musth and their planet.

'Target . . . nearest starship, set for auto-home as soon as possible,' he commanded.

'Acquired,' the robot system told him.

'Two missiles . . . fan spread . . . fire.'

'Launched . . . evasion impossible.'

Garvin 'jumped' a second time, emerged outside one flank of the Musth formation.

'Nearest starship . . . same procedure . . . two missiles . . . fan spread . . . fire.'

'Launched . . . tracking . . .'

An alarm gonged.

' I have a three-missile launch inbound . . . impact three zero seconds.'

Garvin dimly noted a ball of gas half a PD away, realized his first launch had impacted, jumped a third time, to the far side of the Musth formation, set up for another launch, saw on-screen that his other ships were engaged, and then the world spun, went black.

He took the helmet off, and a moment later, Njangu. sitting at the next panel, did the same.

'You're dead, too?'

'Guess so.'

Wlencing and half a dozen other Musth got up from their consoles, came toward him. One was Wlencing's cub, Alikhan.

'That wasss not a predictable, logical ressssponsssse.'

Garvin blinked, stood, stretched, not used to being killed.

'Whose logic?' he asked, maybe a little snappily.

Wlencing stopped.

'Why . . . the obviousss, the way a warrior ssshould fight, ssshould be trained to fight.'

' 'Kay,' Njangu said. 'What *should* we have done?'

He walked to a long table along one wall of the room, opened one of the bottles of the beer that sat in an ice-filled tub that the Musth had provided specially, drank. There were simulator consoles in a ring around the room, then, in its center, a lowered area. Soft pads had been stacked in two places as improvised seats for the humans.

'You want one?'

Garvin nodded and Njangu brought him one.

'What you ssshould have done,' Wlencing said, 'was consssider the oddsss, and then take flight.'

'Couldn't your ships have caught us?' Garvin asked.

'Probably, but that isss not for cccertain.'

'Was this a real battle?' Njangu asked.

Another Musth, Argolis, answered: 'It wasss. It wasss one of the early encountersss when Man and Musssth fought, yearsss ago.'

'What happened then?'

Neither Wlencing nor Argolis seemed to want to answer.

'Your ships entered combat,' Alikhan said. 'The lead scout attacked our flagship with missiles, which were engaged and destroyed before they struck. It then dived into the flagship, destroying it. Another of your ships did the same to one of our flanking attack craft, giving the other two chance to escape.'

'So I got killed,' Garvin said. 'Just like happened in the olden days. But this time I took three of your ships with me.' He shrugged. 'If you've got to go, that's not the worst way.'

Njangu looked skeptical. 'So you say.'

'Hell, you got dead, too,' Garvin said.

'But not out of any desire to play hero. I just screwed up and zigged when I should've zagged.'

Garvin grinned.

'Yet another thing not to understand,' Wlencing said. 'You two are commander and underling, but you do not ssshow the ressspect to each other you ssshould.'

'I hope to hell not,' Garvin said. 'We're friends.'

'A word I know only the definition of,' Wlencing said. 'Poorly defined, not meaning battle-allied, sssubordi-nate/ssssuperior, breeding partner.'

'Try someone you don't mind being around,' Njangu said. 'Even if you can't breed with them.'

'Outside of the parameters my father just gave,' Alikhan said, 'the concept remains alien to us Musth.'

'What about fun?' Njangu asked. 'Is there a working definition of that? Don't you have any more relaxing way to spend off-duty time than playing war games?'

'Cccertainly,' Wlencing said. 'We eat, we hunt, which isss not possssible on this world, we sssleep, we intermingle.'

'What's that last?'

'We sit and share experiences,' Alikhan said.

'About goddamned time,' Njangu said. 'Let's try that for a change, although I don't mean to be rude, since you invited us here to the Highlands.'

'It wasss a reccciprocal event,' Wlencing said. 'In ressponssse to your allowing usss to particcccipate in one of your actionsss.'

'So break out some more dead whatever it was,' Garvin said. 'I'll drag the beer closer, you guys get comfortable, and let's start the bullshit session.'

'I do not undersssstand the referencccce to excrement,' Wlencing said.

'I do, I think,' Alikhan said, and spoke rapidly in Musth.

Njangu moved closer to Garvin.

'This shows every sign of being a *long* goddamned evening.'

'Shaddup and be civil. We're showing the flag, and exchanging courtesies.'

'Which is why I never wanted to be a diplomat,' Njangu grumbled, but painted on a cheerful smile.

The Musth mining base on C-Cumbre was silent, shattered in the hot, dry sun. Wind whispered dust across the ruins.

The base had been destroyed by a 'Raum suicide mission and abandoned within days by the aliens.

Ho Kang pushed through the broken oreship, past the desiccated corpse of a Musth, head back, fangs gleaming in a final snarl against the flames that had killed him. She refused to let the corpse, or the three others in the wreckage, bother her, other than to wonder what Musth death ceremonies were, and went into the control room she'd been able to cut her way into the previous day, just at dusk.

Ho oriented herself ... control chair there ... there ... pilot ... copilot, maybe. A bank of charred instruments ... ship's engineer?

One seat was to the side, below a ruptured screen. Behind it was a panel, unscathed by fire.

'I don't understand what I'm looking at, but I think I understand I'm looking at what I hope I'm looking at, I think,' she muttered to herself. She used her thumb to depress and unlatch two of the convex buttons the Musth used for screws, pulled away the panel cover.

Inside was a single half cylinder. In a cabinet below were others. Ho collected them all.

'Now for wiser heads,' she muttered. 'Assuming any have the proper clearance.'

'So what's your opinion of those furry folks?' Njangu asked, as he piloted the Cooke down from the Highlands toward Leggett and the bay. It was a couple of hours past midnight.

'Interesting,' Garvin yawned. 'Not the best cocktail chitchat I've ever had, though.'

'Kinda limited,' Njangu agreed. 'If it isn't about conquest or killing, it doesn't seem to matter much to them.

'Although Wlencing's kid, Alikhan, acted like he wouldn't mind talking about other things. But I guess baby Musth don't interrupt.'

'We ought to have sent a couple of old-timey warrants up there,' Garvin said. 'The ones who never get tired of telling war stories.'

'Am I being horseshit,' Njangu wondered, 'or do I detect a certain lack of humor in our invaders?'

'Couldn't prove they've got any by me,' Garvin said. 'Although that Alikhan might be able to develop one in half a dozen centuries or so.'

'So why'd they ask us up there? I sure don't believe it was just because we took them out banging heads.'

'Probably,' Garvin said, 'because most of them haven't spent any time with one of us, any more than we have. I'd guess those others were Wlencing's staff or something like that.'

'Get to know your enemy before war breaks out?'

'Something like that.'

'Which works both ways,' Njangu said. 'I think I got more out of them, starting with the way they think war should be fought, than I gave back.'

'Let's hope so,' Garvin said. 'And let's hope they weren't playing downy naive chicks for our benefit.'

'You're always such a *cheerful* son of a bitch.'

'Ain't I, though.'

Ho Kang was more than a little disappointed. She'd expected the 'greatest physicist in the Cumbre system' to be a little on the short side, a little heavy, straight hair, probably not tended as carefully as it should, dress clean if a little rumpled – in short, something like Ho Kang.

Instead, the woman, Ann Heiser, was slender, hair waved in the very trendy brushover style, vivacious, dressed as if she were a Rentier or an executive – even, Ho grudged, pretty.

At least her colleague, Danfin Froude, looked like a mathematician – hair in a stook like he'd been electro-shocked, old-fashioned coat seemingly never pressed pants baggy, and his expression kindly and vague. He even wore archaic glasses. He was one of the few humans who had a reading knowledge of Musth.

The two had been suggested and vetted for security

purposes by Hedley and their presence requested at Camp Mahan.

One of the small half cylinders Ho had taken from the wrecked transport was in front of Hedley. He introduced Ho, then explained where the cylinder had come from.

'A chart,' Heiser said.

'I thought,' Ho said, 'if we could translate it, that might give us some information on the Musth worlds, so we could—'

'Put it to the appropriate use,' Hedley interrupted. 'Which doesn't have to be your concern at this point.'

Froude picked up the cylinder. 'This could be a long long investigation. And I'm hardly naive enough to think we have much time. 'Twould be nice if we had at least one known point to work from.'

'Maybe we do,' Ho said. 'I got interested because I noticed that almost all Musth entries into this system were reported by one or another of the stations on the outer worlds. Most were reported at roughly the same coordinates.'

She handed a microfiche across.

'This is the transcription of twenty-five reports, all ships tracked to C-Cumbre. I thought most of them would be ore transports.'

'Seems within the bounds of supposition,' Heiser agreed.

'Then I wondered if I could find one of those ships, and one of their charts, if that's what this is, that would have either as a start or end point, depending on whether they were coming into or exiting the Cumbre system, congruent with the places our sensors discovered the ships.'

Froude's face was flushed with excitement. 'One plot,' he said. 'A beginning. A very definite beginning.

'We have computers, secure facilities set aside,' Hedley

said. 'We'd like for you to begin your investigation at once. If you need anything ... assistants, apparatus, whatever, you have the highest priority, for reasons I'm sure you can figure out.

'Again, I must insist, though, that you discuss this matter with no one who hasn't been cleared by us, for obvious reasons. I've detached *Dec* Ho Kang to work with you on this.'

Ho and Heiser got up, and Hedley summoned a guard to take them to their assigned offices. Froude lingered behind.

'I do want to thank you, *Haut* Hedley, for letting me possibly help. But I was, well, hoping you wanted me for something else,' Froude said, a trifle wistfully.

'Such as?'

Froude looked behind him, closed the door.

'One thing your Force lacks,' he said, 'is scientists.'

'We're soldiers, in case you haven't noticed.'

'Which means you're full of strange oaths, jealous in honor, sudden and quick in quarrel.'

Hedley grinned. 'Maybe. But I'm not bearded like a pard, whatever a flippin' pard is. So what do you think you could help us with?'

'I'll give you a quick example. You're the former Commanding Officer of Intelligence and Reconnaissance. Don't look startled, I'm a bit of a military buff, and keep up with things. You take young soldiers, give them some very intensive training in scouting and such, wash out at least half of all applicants. Is it worth the effort?'

'Hell yes,' Hedley said.

'Can you quantify that? How many missions, tasks, can one of your highly trained soldiers perform before he becomes a casualty, physical or psychological? How much more, or less, functional would an average infantryman be, given the same tasks and, possibly, accepting a casualty rate somewhat higher, compensated by the ease of replacement? And we'll ignore the problem that an I&R soldier might remain a striker for quite a time, given the general excellence of those around him, and thus contributing less to the Force's needs, whereas in a normal unit he'd quickly be promoted to warrant rank?'

'Allah-be-damned if I know.'

'I do,' Froude said, a bit smugly. 'By my figures, he's good for perhaps a dozen missions, whereas the average soldier, without the stiffening your rigorous selection puts him through, would probably break after four, perhaps five. As for promotion, that's not really a factor, given I&R's greater casualty rate, so even with restriction in ranks, a good . . . and lucky . . . trooper will probably be promoted as rapidly as if he'd remained in a normal unit.

'That is the sort of thing I hoped you'd be interested in.'

Hedley ran a hand over his head, surreptitiously glanced at his fingers to see if any more hair was falling out.

'Dr. Froude, I'm damned if I know any of the answers, and maybe we *should* pay more attention to scientists. But can we bring this up later?'

'Of course. I merely wished to give you something for future consideration,' Froude said.

Garvin, immaculate in officer's dress whites, sat at the long, curving and deserted bar of the Shelburne, looking out at the yachts moored offshore, lined by the setting sun. He sipped again at his drink, a smooth tropical concoction he knew better than to have three of, and wondered how he'd pass the evening.

Hedley'd grabbed him, asked how long it'd been since

he'd taken a pass, then, when Garvin had to think for a minute, told him to get offpost and away from the flippin' military before he rotted.

Njangu had agreed, told him to get gone, and, besides, Njangu might have something interesting to talk about when he got back, and so Garvin had gotten spiffed, and gone across the bay into Leggett, looking for trouble.

He remembered, a long, long time ago, when he'd just graduated from his basic training, spending an evening here, getting sleazed on by the band's singer and landing in more trouble than he knew how to handle.

Garvin smiled, thinking of how long ago and far away *that* was. Not quite three years. Ancient history. He wondered what'd happened to the singer, Marya, that was her name, and hoped she still wasn't singing here. Even as disgustingly celibate as he was, he didn't think he'd ever be ready for someone like her again.

Someone came in the bar, sat on the other side of the waiter's station, and ordered, in a rather nice contralto, a white cordial.

He glanced over as the bartender poured, and the quiet late afternoon shattered like broken crystal.

A moment later, Jasith Kouro recognized him as well.

'Uh . . . hello,' he managed.

'Hello,' she said.

The two stared at each other, the silence pyramiding.

'Thank you for the flowers,' she said. 'And for rescuing me . . . us.'

Garvin tried to think of something clever, failed.

'It's all right,' he managed. 'You're all right now?'

'Fine. The only reason I was in the hospital that long is I picked up some kind of infection.'

'Yeh,' Garvin said, knowing he was sounding very

much a fool, wondering where his vaunted silver tongue had gone to. 'Infections can be dangerous.'

'You look very good,' Jasith said, equally knockwittedly.

'Thanks. And so do you,' Garvin said. 'So what brings you out here,' he tried feebly. 'Don't you have everything delivered up on the Heights?'

Jasith looked at him, decided he wasn't trying to be offensive.

'I'm meeting Loy here for dinner,' she said. 'With some of his editors. They're going to talk about how we should deal with the Musth. I think it's going to be pretty dull, so I decided to show up early and fortify myself a little bit.'

'You're probably right,' Garvin said. 'In which case, you need what I'm drinking.' He nodded to the waiter, gave the order.

Jasith sipped at her drink when it arrived.

'Uhh . . . Garvin? You could run a speedster on this. I don't want to be doing a strip show to keep everybody interested!'

'Why not? Or maybe, a better thing for you to do to make matters really interesting might be to ask the journohs how they think the Musth is going to deal with *us*.'

'What do you mean? So far there's been no trouble.'

'As the man said as he passed the forty-fifth floor of the fifty-floor building he'd fallen off.'

Jasith looked around, saw no one, moved to the stool beside Garvin.

'Frankly, I *am* a little worried,' she said. 'Loy tells me I'm being foolish, but the Musth were always miners, and my father always thought they wished they could control all of C-Cumbre's mines.'

'I don't think you're being foolish at all,' Garvin said.

'And I wish I could give you some hints. All I know, and you did not hear this from me, when the Musth left, they promised they'd be back, and not peacefully.'

'But they didn't attack us when they did come back.'

'They also happened to get here at just the right time, too. Ran off Redruth and crew and looked a little bit like heroes. Maybe they're biding their time for a bit.'

'So what are they going to do, and when?'

'Again, no answers. But I'd bet they're looking for some reason, maybe just an excuse, to have a lot more to do with the way Cumbre's run than they do now.'

'And if they do get more power, the first thing they'll go after is me.'

'Your properties, anyway,' Garvin agreed. 'You, I don't think so. You're not furry enough.'

Jasith giggled, then looked hastily away and concentrated on the sunset. After a time, without looking at Garvin, she said, in a low voice, 'I guess I treated you pretty badly, didn't I?'

Garvin thought of being polite, then of being honest, decided to say nothing.

'Everything just happened too quickly,' she said. 'I wanted to run away, wanted to hide, didn't know what to do.'

'So you married Loy Kouro,' Garvin said, unable to resist the jab.

Jasith took a deep breath, then said nothing, but nodded jerkily.

'You know,' she said, 'sometimes I wish—'

'Don't,' Garvin said, voice harsh. 'It's hard enough already.'

Jasith lifted her drink, then set it down.

'I'm sorry,' she said, hastily got up, and went out.

Garvin stared at her barely tasted drink, then swiveled on his stool and looked at the exit.

'Son of a *bitch*,' he said in a low voice to nobody in particular.

'I think,' Doctor Froude said deliberately, 'we might allow ourselves a glass of sherry.'

'Which is what?' Ho asked.

'Some sort of ancient wine, I think, that great thinkers allowed themselves when they accomplished something.'

'I think I'm going to have a straight shot of pure quill alcohol and dance naked on a tabletop,' Heiser said. 'We're getting very close, aren't we?'

'Three of the last four permutations gave us range-on-range to J-Cumbre, to our moon Fowey, and to C-Cumbre. I'd call that close,' Froude said.

'What about number four?' Ho asked.

'I think you're lost as a soldier, Ho,' Heiser said. 'You've got such a grievously suspicious mind you ought to be a scientist.'

'Didn't have the money for an education,' Ho said, uncomfortably.

'You will when this is finished,' Heiser said.

'What do you mean?'

'Never mind. Shut down. It is indeed, time for a drink.'

'I still wish we had an idea where that fourth range goes to,' Ho said. 'If I projected it right, like you told me, it just ends up about half a diameter beyond M-Cumbre, and you said there's nothing out there, right?'

'Right,' Froude said. 'Wrong. I'm an idiot. When you take off from Camp Mahan in your Grierson, don't you have some common departure point if you're flying with other aircraft?'

Ho nodded. 'Of course, we always set a Rendezvous Point on any mission. Why should the Musth be different? Which gives us our fourth point of congruence, and a place to start translating the charts' other figures from.'

Froude smiled happily. 'Now do we get our drink?'

'We do,' Ho said. 'And I'm buying.' She bounced up from her desk, sending a keyboard and papers flying. 'We Are Almost There!'

'Are you going to live?' Njangu asked solicitously.

'Doubtful,' Garvin moaned.

'So where'd you end up?'

'The last thing that's clear,' Garvin said, 'is being in one of those goddamned waterfront clip joints.'

'Were you with someone?'

'I don't think so, but I sort of remember being with somebody a couple of hours earlier. I think I kept comparing them to ... to somebody, and I think they got pissed and dumped me.'

'That's all?'

'That's all,' Garvin said. 'Except this.'

He dug in his fatigue pocket, took out a huge roll of bills.

'I woke up with all these goddamned credits in every pocket.'

'Only you,' Njangu admired. 'Any of the rest of us get shitfaced, and we wake up jackrolled in an alley. You make a profit on the deal.'

'Yeh, but I'd sure like to know why,' Garvin said. 'Just about as much as I'd like a cold beer.'

'Tut,' Njangu said. 'You're on duty, and you don't want to give a bad example.'

'I *am* a bad example.'

'Well, let me make life a little worse for you,' Njangu said unsympathetically. 'After you left, Hedley called, and wanted to go play in the bushes. Seems SigInt picked up transmissions from way the hell out the end of Dharma Island. Very, very tight beam, punched straight on out to the edge of the system.

'About the same time, one of the remotes off L-

Cumbre picked up an incoming. It held an orbit, and did a blurt-transmission in some code we don't have on our books toward Leggett. The blurt-transmission, in turn, was responded to from that transmitter in the tules.

'Hedley said there was no way we could scramble anything but the *aksai* out to L-Cumbre in time to make an interception, and we're keeping the lid on those suckers for the moment. But we could take the alert crew and jump on top of that transmitter.

'Which we did, about midnight last night, just about the time you were shifting into full drive.

'Dunno what gave us away, but we bashed on down, and found a little temp shelter, rations stacked up for a few days, and a beeeg mother transmitter, big enough to punch way beyond this system if it wanted.

'But nobody was home.'

'What's Hedley's explanation?'

'He got one about dawn,' Njangu said. 'Seems the frequency is one that's on the old books as common to Larix and Kura's military.'

'Urgh.'

'Just that,' Njangu agreed. 'Somebody, one of Redruth's messenger boys, probably slid into the Cumbre system, got a report from an agent, or maybe gave an agent instructions, and headed out again. With a blurter, there would have been time enough to transmit a whole goddamned order of battle, either way.

'You remember we never did nail whoever was on Dharma smuggling guns to the 'Raum from Larix/Kura during the uprising.'

'I remember very well,' Garvin said sourly. 'So we know something, but we don't know what it means.'

'Welcome to military intelligence. Now, doesn't that make your hangover worse?'

*

'I've got something interesting,' *Mil* Angara told *Caud* Rao, 'which I don't have the slightest explanation for. Nor does Hedley.'

'Which means there might be something honorable or decent about the matter if neither of you can understand it,' Rao said.

'The Musth have started opening their consulates, which they're calling places of information,' Angara said.

'I've already gotten reports on that.'

'Did anybody point out where these offices are being located?'

'Just in various city centers.'

'Where in the city centers is what's maybe the problem,' Angara said. 'I could bring up a projection if you want, but all that you really need to know is those places of information are in really cruddy parts of town.'

'All of them?'

'All of them.'

'Maybe the Musth look for cheap real estate,' Rao offered. His executive officer didn't laugh. Rao thought for a moment.

'You know,' he offered, 'if I were looking to create an incident, I might want to have my people right out in the open, where any asshole with a grudge could take a shot, which would account for the Musth wanting thessse counsssulssshipsss,' Rao mimicked. 'What batsssshit.'

'Yeh.'

'And if I didn't give a damn about taking a casualty or two, to make sure it was a real proper incident, I might suggest my people take walks through skid rows, wiggling their little heinies with bells on. I'd assume a secretary, or whatever the hell the Musth equivalent is getting hisslashher ass in a crack would get things nice and stirred up.'

'Shit,' Angara said. 'Not unlikely if that secretary's office happens to be right next to Vagrant Central.'

'Exactly.'

Angara sighed. 'So what are we going to do about it?'

'As if we don't have enough already on the plate,' Rao said. ' 'Kay. What we'll have to do is put more troops on provost duty, making sure they "just happen" to wander past the Musth areas around, say, dusk.'

'Boss,' Lir called. 'Line three. Some muckety named Glenn. Wouldn't say what he wants.'

Garvin glared at the two screens in front of him, minimized them, touched a sensor. The face of a used-up cherub appeared.

'This is *Alt* Jaansma,' Garvin said.

'*Gy* Glenn here,' the man said. 'I'm senior partner with Glenn & Lansky, Attorneys-at-Law.'

'How may I be of service?'

'One of my clients, who wishes to remain anonymous, is quite patriotic,' the lawyer said. 'The client feels that RaoForce isn't sufficiently funded by the Planetary Government.'

'I couldn't argue with him on that.'

'Because of this, my client is making a donation directly to the Force, in the sum of one million credits.'

Garvin blinked, scrabbled for his poker face.

'Pardon?'

'You heard me correctly.'

'That's . . . well, that's very nice, I guess, anyway,' Garvin said. 'But I'm not the commander of the Force, Mister Glenn. *Mil* Prakash Rao—'

'I'm aware of who your CO is,' Glenn said. 'I should have been more specific. My client's donation is specific-ally tagged to Intelligence and Reconnaissance Company, RaoForce Headquarters.'

'What the hell . . . sorry, who the hell is your client?'

'As I said before, the client wishes to remain anonymous.'

'A million . . . what the blazes would I&R do with a million credits? Perhaps your client doesn't know Infantry and Reconnaissance has only one hundred thirty-four men and women.'

'My client is familiar with your personnel roster.'

'Uh, Counselor, what is this money to be used for?'

'My client said it was to go to, and I quote directly, "the betterment of the men and women of the I&R unit to perform their duties and living conditions, in any way the commander of that unit deems appropriate" end quote.'

'You mean, I could build a brand-new barracks for the company with the money, if *Mil* Rao approves?'

'You could.'

'Or I could divvy it out to my troops, which'd give each of them, what, eight grand, let them blow it on whoopee, and your client wouldn't give a damn?'

'My client might think that was somewhat unusual, but no, there would be no objections.'

'This is real irregular,' Garvin said.

Glenn nodded. 'Exactly my comment when my client proposed the matter.'

'Obviously,' Garvin said, 'I can't make any comment about this right now, certainly not until I talk to my superiors.'

'That was anticipated,' the lawyer said.

'I'll call you back after I do,' Garvin said.

'I'll be expecting your call.'

'Wait!' Garvin said. 'Is one of your firm's clients Mellusin Mining, by any chance?'

A rather wintry smile touched the lawyer's lips.

'We have represented that conglomerate in certain matters. Good day, *Alt* Jaansma.'

The screen blanked.

'Well toss me in the shitter and call me a chocolate bar,' Garvin muttered, as the door banged open, and Njangu wheezed in, wearing running shoes, shorts, and a sweaty undershirt, and slumped into a chair.

'Phys conditioning's nothing more than stobor poop. Set an example my left testicle! Give me a nice lazy fellow who lets the other clown bust his ass running and jumping, then backshoots him while he's puking! Glad to get in here out of sight, where the troops can't see my lungs bleed out my nose.'

'Brace yourself,' Garvin said. 'I've got a *real* surprise.'

Two hours later, Garvin's shock wasn't any less. After consultation with *Mil* Rao and the Force's judge advocates, the grant was deemed perfectly legitimate.

'So what are we gonna do with Jasith's money?' Garvin asked plaintively.

Njangu shrugged.

'Throw one *big* motherin' party,' he suggested. 'Better question: What are you going to do about Jasith, since it looks like she's maybe trying to say she's sorry the only way she knows how?'

The sea was phosphorescent, small waves of pure light hissing up the beach. Two Musth walked just at the water's edge, talking quietly.

Camp Mahan glowed dimly in the center of the bay to their right, Leggett's boardwalk to the left, and Shelburne pushed a gleaming finger into the ocean ahead.

Behind the Musth darkness moved, became four men, moving quickly if unsteadily. One slipped, went flat in the sand, and swore.

The Musth turned, saw the intruders.

'Who isss your busssiness?' one demanded.

A raucous laugh came, and a hurled bottle thudded into one Musth's side. Her head darted, ears cocked, eyes reddening in anger.

'Leave usss,' her companion ordered, 'or be killed.'

Another one of the four laughed.

'Yer bluffin', not carryin yer weapons belts. We been watchin', waitin' to take our chance.'

'Get in wi' 'em, Sayid,' a man shouted, and one man sprang forward, a belt knife in his hand.

The female Musth went to the side, her claws out, and she slashed, ripping Sayid's shoulder open. He screeched, stumbled, and fell, rolling. The other Musth kicked at him, missed, and he came back to his feet.

Two men were on the female, one swinging a club, the other looking for an opening with a broken bottle.

The phosphorescence came alive, and a monster wearing only swimming trunks, came out of the ocean, growling, and, moving very fast, was on the threesome.

The man with the bottle screamed as his arm snapped, then his breath died as a massive fist smashed ribs like twigs. The one with the club didn't have his club anymore, and the end of it went into his face. He clawed at it, fell.

The fourth man pulled a small pistol from his waistband, aimed, and the monster Ben Dill spun inside his reach, pulled his gun arm hard, yanking it out of its socket, then head-butted the gunman in the face.

Sayid still stood there, knife ready, waving it back and forth.

'Don't get any closer, or—'

Dill didn't waste energy talking, but snapkicked up. His hoof caught Sayid just short of the elbow, and the knife was gone. Sayid turned, trying to run, but Dill's huge hand had him by the hair, jerked him backward across his knee, and Sayid's spine snapped.

The man who'd had a club and a face was on his knees, whining, as four men and women in civilian clothes ran up. All four of them had pistols.

'Stop!' one shouted. 'Confederation Military!'

'Confederation goddamned late!' Dill roared back. 'Ben's playtime now!'

He kicked the man on his knees in the chest, knocking him flat, then deliberately high-stepped forward, foot turning, and stamp-kicked down, into the man's throat, crushing his hyoid.

Dill turned, saw the four holding guns on him, sneered.

'Little late, like I said.'

'What the hell are you doing here?' Stef Bassas, I&R, RaoForce demanded, recognizing the hulking officer.

'Going for a swim before a nice off-duty dinner, not that it's any of your business,' Dill growled. 'And aren't you forgetting something?'

'Sorry,' Bassas said, 'sir.'

'Better,' Dill said, recognized another of the I&R team. 'Mahim, isn't it?'

'Yessir,' the woman said, putting her pistol away.

'What's the excuse?'

'Half a dozen left their consulate at the same time,' the woman said. 'We picked the wrong ones to fly cover on, not figuring anybody'd try to drygulch someone around the Shelburne. Obviously, we were wrong.'

'You're a medic, aren't you?'

'Yessir.'

'You interested in tending to any of these casualties?'

'Don't know, sir,' Mahim said. 'Are any of them still alive?'

Dill looked around. 'He's gone . . . he's gone . . . he's a lunger and probably gone, but you could mess with him if you wanted . . . the guy I head-butted'll probably be okay, even if his mommy won't recognize him.'

'Not really that interested, sir, thanks for the offer.'

'Tell you what,' Dill went on. 'You people go on about your business ... which I assume is protecting Musth ... and I won't snitch you off for being a little on the laggard side, 'kay?'

'What about them?' Bassas asked, pointing a thumb at the two Musth.

'You let me worry about my friends,' Dill said. 'And next time, do a better job of bodyguarding, or I'll do something about it after I get through personally wringing your necks.'

'Yessir,' Bassas said, and the four faded into the night.

'Sorry for what happened,' Ben Dill said. 'This is generally a pretty safe place to be.'

'You came in,' one Musth said. 'Helping usss.'

'Good eyes,' Dill said. 'Yeh. So what?'

'I do not know we would do that for you.'

'Wouldn't expect you to.'

'And, if I heard your wordsss correct, thossse othersss are sssoldiers, too, and asssigned to protect us? Without our knowing about it? Without telling our warrior leadersss?'

'That's an interesting guess,' Dill said.

'We are in your debt.'

' 'At's right,' Dill said cheerfully.

'How may we charge that debt?'

'You mean discharge, I hope.'

'Repay isss the word I sssought.'

'You have any Confederation money?'

One Musth fished in a belt pouch.

'We have been given sssome.'

'It better be enough to buy me a drink. C'mon, you two. Let's go slumming.'

The Musth looked at each other in what might have been puzzlement, then followed the enormous human toward the beckoning hotel.

'Gentlemen,' *Mil* Rao said. 'Have a seat.'

'This is Dr. Froude,' Hedley said.

'Doctor,' Rao said, 'I'm sorry I haven't taken the opportunity to meet you, but things've been very hectic.'

'On my front as well,' the mathematician said.

'I assume this has something to do with the navigation cylinder that was found?'

'Unfortunately not, sir,' Hedley said. 'That matter's proceeding apace. This is something else, and something a lot worse.'

Rao's congeniality vanished.

'Go ahead.'

'Dr. Froude told me, just after he volunteered to help us with the charts Ho Kang acquired, he wished the Force would use science more than we do, that we should analyze things more systematically. Something came up, and I decided to take advantage of his offer.' Hedley was watching his language around his CO with a civilian witness.

'I happened to notice something, going over an I&R training-mission report I thought was a bit strange. I checked other reports back as far as the initial Musth arrival. Most of them reported the same thing as the first one: when I&R teams went out, at some point they saw a Musth *aksai* nearby.

'No interference or contact was made with our soldiers at any time by the Musth, incidentally.

'However,' Hedley said, face most grim, 'two things became apparent: These *aksai* only materialized after the unit had operated its com.

'Dr. Froude, what is the probability of those appearances being purely by chance?' Rao asked.

'So close to zero the difference is immaterial.'

'The Musth have broken our standard code,' Rao said. 'That is just the sort of intel I needed before midday meal.'

'Worse, sir,' Hedley said. 'I ordered I&R to use other codes, which they did. And for two weeks, the Musth still showed up, just like clockwork mice. Then they stopped coming at all. Obviously they've got somebody on their intelligence staff who got worried we might be on to them, and changed the rules.'

'How many of our codes are they reading?'

'Most of the normal low-level ones,' Hedley said. 'Plus our emergency code . . . *and* the code used between this headquarters and PlanGov for emergencies.'

'This is not good,' Rao said. 'Not good at all. I wonder how long they've been reading our mail?'

'Since the rebellion, at least, sir,' Hedley said. 'I've taken a hard look at some of their miraculous appearances, which get a lot less miraculous with what we have now.'

'All right,' Rao said. 'So we've got to change the codes from top to bottom.'

'Yes and no,' Hedley said. 'Doctor Froude presented an option, and I think we ought to consider it.'

The man who used the name Ab Yohns sat in a nondescript lifter down the street from the Musth embassy in Leggett. He could just as easily have surveilled the waterfront building with a planted camera from his comfortable house in the mountain villa of Tungi, outside Leggett, to do his thinking. His campaign was still nowhere near action phase.

But he found it helped if he could see the enemy, or at any rate have some reminder of who they were.

He considered the possibilities he'd uncovered, and of Protector Redruth's orders.

He frankly thought Redruth, if not mad, to be deluded and certainly egomaniacal, even though he'd never met the man. So the Musth had spoiled Redruth's plans for the moment. So? There were other moments.

And as for his latest orders . . . the operator thought that would more likely worsen the situation, possibly irretrievably, rather than improve it for Redruth.

But that was none of Yohns' concerns. He prided himself that he always carried out an assignment, assuming it wasn't suicidal and the credits were good.

He'd done many well-paying jobs for Redruth, from the Confederation to this Cumbre system, and thought it somewhat amusing he'd never had a face-to-face with the man who'd made him fairly rich.

So he'd continue to serve, as long as the credits flowed, and the danger wasn't suicidal.

If the worst case did happen, as had so nearly occurred when he'd nearly been caught making his last transmission, Yohns had a small yacht in a hidden bunker deep in the jungle, and Redruth would send a ship to pick him up once he exited the Cumbre system.

So if what Redruth had ordered ruined Cumbre . . . Yohns mentally shrugged, without ever moving. The only sign of life the napping rustic showed was the flicker of his eyes, watching the consulate in the lifter's rearview scope.

The problem was, he decided, there wasn't a target he could reach yet that was big enough to fulfill Redruth's needs.

But there would be, he knew.

'Sir,' the technician reported, 'one of our remote sensors on M-Cumbre reports ships in-system.'

'What's the ID?' Rao asked.

'Musth, sir. They match the profile of the mother

ships they came back in. Except that one is big. Really big.'

'Do you have an orbital prediction?'

'Affirm, sir. Destination is suggested to be E-Cumbre.'

The Musth headquarter world.

'Continue observation,' Rao ordered, and touched the red sensor.

Alarms shrilled across D-Cumbre, and the Force scrambled to full alert.

SEVEN

The Musth ship was monstrous, dwarfing its escorts. It looked like an archaic artillery shell, with flying buttress-like 'wings' tipped with smaller, manned 'bullets' supporting, along with antigravity, the ship's bulk. The Musth called it a *striking-point-commander*; humans might've typed it a command flagship. Since the Musth were never sentimental about machinery, it had only a number, not a name. It was Clanmaster Paumoto's mobile headquarters.

It sat on one of the great landing fields of E-Cumbre, which the Musth called Silitric.

Silitric was E-normal, if a bit chilly for human comfort, with small oceans dotting the rolling tundra and low mountains. Virgin forest covered the heights. The Musth had only built three bases close to the mountains, half-underground, and only half-occupied at the busiest of times. Thus far, few Musth had found their interests leading them toward Cumbre.

In one of the ship's conference places, Clanmaster Paumoto listened to Aesc and Wlencing. When they finished, he rose from his tail-brace and went to a viewscreen, looking out at the subarctic landscape without seeing it, head darting back and forth as he thought.

Finally, he said, 'I thank you for sharing this with me, even though I have no immediate interest in your actions.'

'Would you care to give us your opinions?' Aesc answered.

'Perhaps,' Paumoto said. 'It might be of value if I make you aware of what is currently the thinking on our own worlds.

'Your actions in returning to Cumbre have been hailed by many. Keffa and his clique in particular are saying you are building the crossing to the inevitable future.

'Of course Senza and those of his ilk think you are bringing disaster on us, returning us to our barbaric past. You'll probably be the cause of interstellar war between us and Man, and so on and so forth, and they want immediate withdrawal. None of which makes the slightest sense, but there are other Musth, motivated by their own concerns which follow different trails than yours, who agree with them.'

'Which side is growing stronger?' Aesc asked.

'I would hate to be held to an opinion,' Paumoto said. 'But I would hazard a guess that there have been some of the 113 masters who favored your action who've retreated to the side of neutrality, and perhaps a few of the neutrals have decided to favor Senza's course.'

'Then we are losing,' Wlencing said.

'Not necessarily,' Paumoto said. 'But that is why I wished this conference to be on my ship, for I am assured it is completely sealed, and, while I'm confident you two share my views, I'm not so confident about other Musth, who might well be a link to Senza and his faction.'

'We are very interested in any help you might offer,' Aesc said.

'If something were to happen, some sort of incident,' Paumoto said carefully. 'Something that shows the true depths of Man, something that would horrify our race to its base—'

He broke off. Both Aesc and Wlencing had their mouths open, hissing from the backs of their throat, indicating amusement.

His ears cocked for an instant, then he understood.

'Ah. I am bringing salt to the ocean?'

'We have had exactly that idea,' Aesc said. 'And since the men are being most uncooperative, we are trying to increase the possibilities of such an event.'

'We have moved down among them, establishing what they call consulates, as you suggested some time ago.' Wlencing explained. 'We deliberately emplaced these in parts of their cities where we know, from our studies of Man's patterns before the uprising, crime is most likely to occur, and the lower classes congregate.'

'Very clever,' Paumoto said. 'Something happening to an underling, while unpleasant for them, could be most helpful to the rest of us.'

'Just so.' Wlencing said. 'Unfortunately, we face a rather clever foe. Our idea seems to have been found out. and their soldiers are providing unobtrusive security to our people.'

It was Paumoto's turn to be amused.

'So the leaper dances back and forth with his enemy,' he said, referring to a popular board game, 'and larger pieces are stymied, and the game is in impasse.'

'I'm not sure it is that knotted,' Wlencing said. 'Hardly beyond resolution.'

'We are moving very carefully,' Aesc said. 'We want to make sure that, whatever incident occurs, there is no chance of it being, let us say, misinterpreted by Senza and his milk-drinkers.'

'Good,' Paumoto said. 'Again, I appreciate your sub-tlety, System-Leader Aesc.'

'We could remain here all the planetary day,' Wlencing said, 'using nice words to each other, while nothing happens except the sun moves. I have a question, Clan Leader. You say you have no immediate interest in the Cumbre system, yet you have visited us, without notice.

'I am hardly a cub, to assume you have done this merely from your innate desire to assist us.'

Again, Paumoto showed amusement.

'Of course not,' he agreed. 'There are several contributing factors to my decision to visit Cumbre. I had already planned a periodic visit to some of the worlds I am involved with, and the jumps to Cumbre were not all that difficult to make. Another reason is that I have found the extraction of minerals of interest from time to time, and the geological reports on the riches of Cumbre are interesting.

'But there is a more pressing reason. Like you, I despise the direction Senza wishes for the Musth to take. He is an utter fool, who doesn't realize a race, like a being, is either growing or dying.

'Only in expansion, continued expansion, to the limits of the universe, can the Musth fulfill their destiny, not to mention achieving the greatest personal benefits and satisfactions.

'The Cumbre system is but a beginning. If we hold here, if we reduce Man to his proper role of a humble servitor, the way lies open for us to expand into the worlds Man formerly held. We can follow the Confederation's steps, avoiding worlds or systems that were not beneficial to them, and be handed golden world after world as our reward.

'No, I am hardly a fool who believes helping others without self-interest is sane.'

'Then,' Aesc said, 'I have a suggestion, Clan Leader, on how you might assist us.'

'Short of murdering one of our own minorlings with a man-gun, I would be delighted,' Paumoto said.

'This ship is impressive. Perhaps we should announce a receiving on Man's world for you, a well-known member of our "government," Wlencing said, putting the last word in Standard.

'I do not speak the tongue of Man,' Paumoto said.

'A government consists of an agreement they make among themselves, or else something another one imposes by force of arms, for all to behave in a certain manner for a prolonged period of time, supposedly for each other's mutual good. The ultimate example is what they call the Confederation.'

'An absurd conceit.'

'True. But this is the way they claim to think.'

'That is not thinking, but dreaming,' Paumoto said. 'But I veer with the surprise of that thought. Of course we should do some sort of showing of our potential force. I do not see how that will accelerate the time of reckoning, but when it does come, as I agree it must, the memory of our strength will certainly make them quail, and a cautious foe is already half-defeated.'

'Mighty big ship up there,' Garvin drawled. 'Intimidating and all.'

'You're right, boss,' his first *tweg* said. 'If somebody put, oh, eighty kilos of Blok, nicely shaped, right on the edge of that fin there, which'd most likely cut right through its structural integrity, and maybe dump a Shrike right in the middle of their antigravs, that ship'd make a mighty big splash when it went down.'

'If you two clowns can stop parading your testosterone,' Njangu said, 'you've got to admit the bad guys have a pretty healthy mother over there.'

Everyone on Leggett – and across a good-sized piece of Dharma Island – had to agree. The Musth ship towered almost as high as the Heights the Rentiers lived on, and could be seen not only on Chance Island but across the bay to the far peninsula. Three of the mother ships flanked it, almost filling Leggett's main port.

'The thing that gets me,' he continued, 'is their *escorts* are bigger than anything we've got to play with.'

'If they're trying to impress us,' Garvin reluctantly agreed, 'they sure succeeded.'

'And you, boss, you lucky little *felmet*,' Njangu said, 'will get to be really impressed, by the way. The Musth are having a reception aboard, and the old man decided I&R'll be a nifty honor guard, white gloves, spit-shined heinies, and all.'

'Buddha's illegitimate mother!' Lir swore. 'We're not a bunch of parade-ground fakers!'

'At least we can afford the white gloves,' Njangu snickered.

'What?' Monique puzzled. Garvin hadn't told anyone in I&R besides Njangu about Jasith's gift, and gave Yoshitaro a somewhat dirty look.

'Never mind,' Njangu said. 'Rao wants us to wave the sabers around because he thinks he might need a bunch of thugs looking innocent within easy reach, like happened with Redruth. Just in case this grand party turns into a big nasty.'

'Oh,' Monique said, relaxing. 'Not bad. Boss, shall I fall the troops out and start helping them remember their ceremonials?'

'Couldn't hurt.' Garvin said. 'They're really gonna love this one.'

'We've flipping got it,' Hedley said. Beside him, Ho,

Froude, and Heiser beamed exhaustedly at Rao and Angara. 'Every point checks between our charts and the Musth. We can . . . I already had one of the patrol ships try it . . . use their coordinates to jump around the system.'

'Congratulations,' Rao said. 'Now, what do we do with it?'

'Why,' Froude said, a touch indignantly, 'we'll use that information to decipher other Musth charts, which will give us kilotons of data about their planets.'

'And where do we get said other charts?' Angara asked.

'Why, steal them,' Heiser said. 'Just like Ho got the first one.'

'Which'll be simple,' Rao said, 'once we bell the tiger . . . or rather, find the tiger to bell.'

'That's the simplest thing,' Froude said. 'Just get inside that great bloat of a ship of theirs and grab half a dozen.'

'All you'll need is a good thief,' Heiser said.

Rao looked at them, started laughing. Ho, a bit more familiar with life as it was lived, looked a bit embarrassed.

But Hedley was thoughtful.

'Not that bad an idea,' he mused. 'And I think I know just the flippin' thief we might want.'

'Yeep,' Njangu said. 'You never ask me to volunteer for the easy ones.'

'Those aren't any fun,' Hedley said.

'Neither is getting dead,' Njangu said. He considered the holograph of the Musth command ship on the desk between them. 'This is a real stinker,' he went on. 'I was a pretty good heist artist, back before the Confederation civilized me. But breaking into an alien ship, when I don't know zip from zap . . . I think my insurance rates went up.'

'Let's assume you could get inside that dinosaur of theirs, just for the sake of argument,' Hedley said. 'Make your way to the control room—'

'Which would be where?'

'I'd assume at the pointy end, to use technonaval jargon.'

'Probably,' Njangu said.

'So all you'd have to do is slide in,' Hedley said enthusiastically, 'grab the flipping charts, and then slide back out.'

'And if I get caught?'

'Can't allow that to happen,' Hedley said. 'That'd be a real embarrassment for RaoForce and Cumbre.'

'Not to mention me, as those goddamned pussycats slice me raw for breakfast.'

'What's life without a few risks? Besides, Njangu, can you think of anybody else in the system who *might* . . . just *might* . . . be able to pull it off?

'No,' Hedley continued, changing his mind midstream. 'I was wrong. Cancel the whole idea. It's just too flippin' risky, and there's zero chance of getting away with it.'

'I'm on to your ploy, boss,' Yoshitaro said. 'Now I'm supposed to bristle and say hang on a goddamned second, I haven't said I wouldn't do it, and you'd reluctantly allow yourself to be talked into letting me suicide.'

'Very good,' Hedley said. 'I think it's about time to promote you to *alt*. You're getting smarter the longer you hang around me.'

'Bastard,' Njangu said, turning away from the projection and looking out the window, across the bay, at the Musth ship and its escorts. 'Sweet-talking me isn't going to make it any more possible to get in that pig.

'But,' he said, after a few moments, 'I do have an idea. It's just not *your* idea.'

'I'm quite looking forward to tonight,' Loy Kouro said. 'Dear, is my cummerbund straight? It feels twisted in the back.'

'You're fine,' Jasith said, glancing at her husband's reflection in the great mirror. 'But I don't see why you think this is going to be such a thrill. I'm expecting this Paumoto to announce the Musth are finally through fooling around, and are simply taking over. Otherwise, why that monstrosity of a ship?'

'Come on, Jasith. You're being paranoid. You ought to know important people travel in important ways. This is just a way of showing us how significant Cumbre can be to the Musth.'

Jasith put down the tiny spray of blush, swiveled to face Loy.

'So what are *you* expecting to happen?'

'Not much,' Kouro said. 'At least, not much tonight. I'll bet Paumoto just wants to meet the high-level people of Cumbre and figure out those he might be able to make whatever business arrangements he wants to with.

'You and I do the same thing. Something like this'll winnow out the chaff, as the cliché goes. I predict the Musth and ourselves, now that the Confederation appears to be out of the picture for a time, can form significant, profitable alliances.

'That's what I believe, and that's the position my leader writers are holding to.'

'Which'll make sure it comes true,' Jasith murmured. 'I hope you're right, my love.'

Loy grinned, came over and kissed the top of her head, rubbed her shoulders.

'I don't see any reason I won't be.'

Jasith moved against his hands like a cat. 'That feels good,' she said, her voice lowering a bit. 'Take a look at the night. Two moons out, how clear it is.'

'It certainly is.'

'Maybe, after the rubber *giptel*'s gone, we can make our excuses . . . maybe jaunt out toward the mouth of the bay, see if we can see Kailas rising? Or anything else that comes up?'

'That's a nice thought,' Kouro said. 'But I've got to stop at *Matin* and brief the night staff on what happened. Maybe after I finish, if there's time.'

'If there's time,' Jasith agreed, voice flat, and went back to her makeup.

Multicolored lights flickered up and down the hull of the command ship, kaleidoscoping light over Leggett and out across the dancing waters of the bay.

Around the ship was a swarm of lims and sporters as the elite of D-Cumbre arrived, to decide if they were meeting new masters, allies, or partners.

The command ship's port was open, and Musth lined either side of the ramp to the ground. Their weapons belts were burnished, and they wore multicolored scarves that matched the lights from the ship.

At the ramp's base, extending out onto the tarmac, a hundred I&R men and women were drawn up at rigid attention. They wore dress uniform – midnight blue trousers bloused into black mid-thigh boots, waist-length belted tunic, service kepi. There was yellow piping on the legs, cap, and epaulettes, and each trooper wore a Sam Browne belt, with dagger sheathed on one side, pistol holstered on the other.

They carried other weapons not generally used at cere-monial occasions – blast grenades, hideout guns. throwing knives – hidden around their uniforms.

Garvin stood at the beginning of one rank, First *Tweg* Monique Lir on the other.

Caud Prakash Rao approached, accompanied by his Second Regiment Commanding Officer, *Mil* Ceil Fitzgerald, and was saluted. He returned the salute and went up the ramp into the ship, seemingly a little ill at ease, repeatedly adjusting his uniform's lapels.

Civilian and governmental dignitaries in turn flocked toward the honor guard, passing between the lines to the ramp.

Garvin saw Loy Kouro, in old-fashioned evening black, and Jasith Mellusin, wearing what looked to be black at first, but somehow the fabric caught the lights from the ship, mirrored and then flung them back.

Kouro looked Garvin up and down, half smiled superciliously, went on.

Jasith, lagging a bit behind her husband, seemed to stumble. She steadied herself on Garvin's arm for an instant and adjusted her shoe.

'Thanks for the goodies,' he said out of the corner of his mouth.

'I'll call you,' she whispered back. 'We should meet somewhere.'

'With or without *him?*' he said, a little bitterly.

Jasith Mellusin straightened, looked at him, didn't answer, but went on. Garvin's eyes followed her, then came back to the front.

Monique Lir was looking at him speculatively, but then her face smoothed, blanked like the perfect soldier she was.

Njangu Yoshitaro was a shadow in shadows. He wore close-fitting black from head to toe, soft running boots, and had a small cutting laser, two gas grenades, a multi-bladed knife, and a heatsniffer in a pouch at his waist. He ignored the great ship in the center of the field, concentrated on one of the mother ships beside it.

Like the other Musth starships, its lock yawned open, occasional Musth coming and going, and inviting light beamed into the darkness.

Two guards stood at the foot of its ramp, but neither was paying much attention to his watch, instead watching the glittering aliens entering the other ship. Periodically they left the ramp, made a cursory sweep around the ship, returned to their main post and the spectacle there.

Njangu moved through the darkness, watching just beyond the guards, never letting his mind or eyes fix on the sentries. Superstitious perhaps, but how often had a watched cop turned for no visible reason . . .

He counted how long it took for them to march around the ship. *Thirty or so seconds. Time enough.*

Njangu got as close as he dared, and crouched, just a crumple in the darkness. The glare from the ships blinded everyone beyond the pool of light around them.

He waited, saw the guards move, came to his feet, then something warned him, and he collapsed.

One guard said something to his fellow, and they came back to the ramp. Njangu braced to run, then saw a guard pointing to a group of humans approaching the mother ship. He wondered what was particularly fascinating, then blanked his mind, became part of the tarmac.

The humans entered the command ship, and again the guards paced away into the night.

Njangu was up, moving fast, silent. a dark mote scuddering up the ramp, into the Musth mother ship.

He stopped just inside the lock as the antigrav took him, confusing his senses. The ramps now wound away on the level, not upward. He chose one, followed it.

*

In the heart of the command ship, dark gray metalloid bulkheads were broken with pictures, three-dee projections hanging unsupported. Some of the guests breezed past these exhibits without paying much attention, more studied them closely, wondering just what the Musth worlds were like.

There were unknown mountains; towering buildings in the middle of wildernesses; huge ships even greater than the one they were aboard; somewhat grisly pictos of Musth at play with their bloodied trophies of game animals; strange and beautiful star clusters no human eye had ever seen; stern-looking Musth intent on some unknown duty or cause; and, incongruously, three or four holos of Musth cubs, three or four in a group, rolling about like so many kittens.

Caud Rao paused by each, looked, adjusted his lapel. *Mil* Fitzgerald cocked her eye.

'If I was your tailor, I think I'd commit suicide,' she said.

'Stop trying to be clever,' Rao growled. 'So I'm a crappy spy. Hedley said to get pics of everything.' He touched his lapel again, triggering the tiny camera, and they went on.

Ramps spidered onward, and Njangu followed them. There were no safety rails, he guessed not necessary for a race with a comfortably stabilizing tail.

He felt the heatsniffer vibrate against his hipbone, remembered an alcove and went back into it, pressed against the bulkhead.

He saw the flicker of a Musth coming along the ramp, heard a hatch slide open, closed. *They're quieter moving than I am*, he thought, disgruntled.

Like Rao, Njangu had a minicamera, set to relay any pictures shot on a hopefully unmonitored frequency to a pickup in a civilian speedster parked not far away. *The Suicidal Spy*, Njangu wryly titled the saga to come.

The ship was huge, but lightly manned. A few hatches yawned, with silent machinery inside, or compartments that looked like troop bays, but with padded floors instead of bunks.

Njangu wondered about the emptiness, guessed the Musth had other duties when the ship made planetfall. Probably some were dancing attendance on the state dinner.

Several times he heard hissed sibilances from compartments, but managed to slip past without being seen.

There was a low humming in the corridor ahead, and he ducked into another empty bay.

The humming grew louder, and Njangu, gun ready, chanced looking.

Two Musth passed the open hatch, each pushing a pole with a softly buzzing bar at its base.

Even aliens have to sweep the deck, Njangu thought, and swore the two deck sweepers looked sullen, like they were on punishment detail.

He waited until the humming faded, continued towards the ship's nose.

The food at the Musth banquet was unusual, but tasty, Jasith thought. She thought she recognized some of the flavors, couldn't quite identify the foods, hidden as they were under strange spices.

Halfway through the meal, she remembered what they reminded her of, and giggled.

She leaned close to her husband.

'This is like when I was a Girl Guide,' she whispered, 'and we'd go out into the wilderness . . . we thought it was a wilderness, anyway . . . and cook like we were primitives.'

'So?'

'Since none of us knew how to cook. we mostly did everything about half-raw. I think the Musth used our manuals for this meal.'

Loy muttered something, chewed on methodically, as if what he had in his mouth was growing as he did.

Njangu came to a closed hatch. He pushed at it, touched everything that looked touchable, and it remained closed. *Now how do you pick an alien lock when you don't know if it's got tumblers, slides, beams, or little bitty mice running around inside? Especially if you can't see anything that looks even vaguely like a lock at all?*

He saw a tiny vertical slit at rib level, puzzled over it for an instant. Then he took out his knife, opened the thinnest blade, slid it through the slit. Obediently, the hatch slid open. *Of course. Just right for a Musth claw.*

He entered a room that was quite large, with a slowly rotating ball of a light gray metal in its center. Again he puzzled. It was just about big enough for a Musth, but he couldn't see an entrance. A pilot cage for zero gee? He didn't know. A ramp led onward, holding close to the curving wall.

Wishing he'd brought a blaster just for comfort, he inched his way, close to the wall, thinking invisible thoughts.

'. . . two great peoples,' Wlencing's son, Alikhan, translated Paumoto words as he spoke, 'meeting across a great . . . mmmh . . . distance, each with common things, each with differences . . .'

Caud Rao relaxed, stomach comfortably full, if of unfamiliar substances. He began to shut his mind off, thinking that, in the end, all beings were the same, their leaders giving the same meaningless speeches . . . and then he caught himself.

Very few politicians of the human variety carried weapons belts with pistols throwing rounds that ate holes in you . . . and seemed quite experienced in their use. Nor did they generally arrive in battleships if they intended peace.

Suddenly, he was very awake.

The corridor widened, with alcoves on either side. Ahead was an archway, and Njangu saw screens, control panels, and a low couch. Then he heard Musth speech, and went flat. Another voice came, then silence except for the contented clucking of machinery.

Hoping that Musth didn't look up or down any more than cops do, Njangu crawled to the end of the corridor, peered into the ship's bridge.

There were screens, more couches, panels that occasionally blinked inscrutably, and two Musth.

Only a dreamer would have hoped nobody stands bridge watch.

One Musth was running his paws across a featureless panel, watching symbols scroll on a screen above him.

Ship's log?

The other was intent on a holo display of large machines.

Drive room watch?

To one side was a couch, and a screen showing an abstract of a planet. One of the half-cylinder charts was in a slot below the display.

Now, if these clowns would only go out for a beer . . .

Neither Musth showed signs of thirst.

Njangu thought of shooting them, rifling the room, and running like hell, discarded that as bloodthirsty stupidity that wouldn't work anyway without a gun, and decided to check the alcoves.

The third he tried was gold.

Unlike humans, with their stupid insistence on tidiness, the Musth used doorless cabinets. Items inside stuck to the shelves, needing no retainers to keep their places.

This alcove held hundreds of the charts. Njangu was wondering which to steal when he saw a wall panel next to him. A dozen or so charts clung at random to it.

Theory – these are the most frequently used buggers?

Cursing himself for probable anthropomorphism, Njangu scooped those charts into his small pack.

If these don't help, they can goddamned well come back and play Raffles by themselves. Now let's see if I can sleaze out of this dump before somebody puts a wasp-grenade up me arse.

He went swiftly back the way he came, hoping there'd be nothing in the way of surprises.

Twice he had to retreat, duck back into a compartment as Musth passed. He crept past another compartment, hearing wailing that he hoped was music.

Njangu reached the lock compartment, and it still yawned open into the night. *Praise several gods*, he thought, *they're running late tonight*. He checked his watch finger, and realized with a shock he'd been aboard the Musth mother ship less than half an E-hour, not half the night as he'd thought.

He crept forward, saw no sign of the guards. He wanted to pelt down the ramp into the night, but forced calm. Njangu slipped back, waiting until the guards came back into view at the ramp's end, waited longer, nerves screaming, until they made another round, then, forcing coolness, almost sauntered down the ramp and back into the lovely velvet night.

A planetary week later, inside the central dome on Silitric, Aesc and Wlencing watched Paumoto's ship lift clear of the surface, climb slowly at first, then increasingly more quickly into the high cover. Just before the clouds swallowed the ship, it went to secondary drive and vanished.

The dull plop of air rushing into the suddenly vacant space could be heard through the insulation.

'I think Paumoto's appearance advanced our plans more than somewhat,' Aesc said.

'I suspect so,' Wlencing said cautiously. 'Although I'm not sure I like someone as important as he becoming interested in our endeavor. I would hate, after all this time, to be cut out of the spoils.'

'Do not worry,' Aesc said. 'If Paumoto isn't satisfied with the small percentage he may be entitled to, once Cumbre is ours, we can deal with the matter as we must.' He dipped his head. 'In the meantime, our plans are fully prepared. We must apply further pressure to the situation, to ensure we have the proper incident we need before moving to the final stage.'

EIGHT

From *Matin.* Loy's Kourner:

As we predicted after the most amiable and pro-
ductive reception given by Paumoto of the Musth
for Leggett and the Cumbre system's most cele-
brated citizens (which we are proud to be
considered one of), further meetings have been set
by Aesc of the Musth and various cultural, commercial, and military leaders, including the
above-signed, to tighten the bonds between Man
and his newest Ally, although the Musth have not,
as yet, been specific as to the agendas.

These meetings will begin Third Day, at the
system-famous Shelburne Hotel, and are expected
to continue for at least a week of not only highlevel
business matters, but social and cultural events as
well.

Your humble publisher is honored to be chosen
by the members of the community to host the first
day's orientation, which will begin at . . .

Njangu blanked the screen. 'Y'know, Monique, the boss's
ex-girlfriend's husband can't write his way out of a

busted jockstrap. Loy's Kourner my kurled frigging klav-
icle! Wonder what she sees in him?'

'He's good-looking and has money,' Monique
answered. 'Better question . . . what does *he* see in *her*? I
think she's about as brain-dead a twonk as I've ever seen.'

'She's a looker, and richer'n snot,' Njangu said.
'Richer'n he is, even. I just wonder why some other . . .'
His voice trailed off.

'Wonder what other . . . sir?'

'Wonder when I'll learn to keep my goddamned
mouth shut about shit that's none of my business,'
Njangu said. getting up from the desk in the orderly
room and grabbing his kepi. 'Tell the boss when he
comes in I'm up at the Headshed if he needs me.'

Half an hour later. the com buzzed.

'RaoForce, Intelligence and Reconnaissance Company,
First *Tweg* Lir speaking.'

No picture came.

A woman's voice said, '*Alt* Garvin Jaansma, please.'

'I'm sorry, he's in the field, and not expected for at
least an hour,' Lir said. 'May I take a message?'

'I'll call back.' The connection blanked.

First *Tweg* Lir considered the brief encounter between
Garvin and Jasith at the Musth reception, thought she
might recognize the voice, and decided Njangu's formula
would work well for her, too.

'Cityside,' the bored editor said. 'This is Ted Vollmer.'

'Er, yes,' the man onscreen said, his face as nondescript
as his voice. 'I'm an amateur photographer . . . hope to be
able to become a pro one of these days, maybe sell something to you . . . and I'd like to see if I couldn't get a
really spectacular shot of that Musth leader . . . don't
remember his name . . . arriving at that hotel whatsit.
Where'd be the best angle?'

Vollmer started to growl, decided on civility as a change of pace.

'Word we have is the Musth'll be coming in by air, and landing directly on the bay side of the Shelburne. most likely at the normal boat ladder.'

'Thanks.' The connection was broken.

'Goddamned photogs.' Vollmer swore. 'Musth whoosit, hotel whatsit . . . they're always such veritable founts of hard data.'

'Whyn't you tell him we'll have the staffers covering things like white on rice since this is our fearless leader's show, and he'll play hell trying to sell us anything we don't already have in the can?' his amused assistant said.

'Because the day I tell a freelancer something like that, every goddamned lenser on the staff'll have leprosy with his camera up his ass with the lens cover on,' Vollmer grunted. 'Goddamned photogs,' he said once more.

'That's what I like about you,' his assistant said. 'Last of the altruists.'

'Interesting minds these Musth have,' Dr. Heiser observed. 'Math to the base eight.'

'Why should that matter?' Dr. Froude asked. 'A number system is a number system is a number system.'

'For you, maybe,' Heiser said. 'I'd keep forgetting I have a couple of extra fingers to count on. But here's something interesting. All these charts we acquired have a base point.'

'All charts have that,' Froude said gently. 'True north, magnetic north, distance from Capella/Centrum or whatever base point a system or government chooses.'

'But the Musth use a single point as the center of their universe.'

'And that is?'

'I don't know for sure yet . . . none of the charts we

had stolen go that deep into their empire. But I ran a tentative projection, and home base is way the blazes out there. The only plotting system that gives a hint is the old Langnes listings. I'd guesstimate,' Heiser said, 'the 37420 sequence.'

'I'm not familiar with the Langnes plots.'

'You needn't be,' Heiser said. 'It's one of those hellish primitive ones that just happens to be about the most thoroughly compiled. The only reason I remember it is I had a bastard of an astronomy teacher way back at the university.'

An increasingly irritated Hedley had been listening to the interchange, head moving back and forth like he was at a racquetball tournament. He was already angry enough that he had only the maps, plus Rao's happysnaps and the transcript of Paumoto's speech, which didn't give him enough for an intelligence estimate as to what the Musth visit might've meant.

'Excuse me, and I hate to be flipping mundane and all,' he said. 'But were you able to translate the charts we gave you like you can the other charts?'

'Certainly,' Froude said with a bit of indignation. 'I said we'd have no trouble, didn't I?'

' And the charts give us?'

'Oh, sixteen, twenty, maybe more of the Musth settled systems. Pity none of the worlds are particularly close to us,' Heiser said. 'It's also interesting the way they appear to have expanded their empire, assuming Dr. Froude's translations are correct.

'They jump from cluster to cluster, with no apparent logic in their exploration, as if they just punted expeditions out after picking a destination by spinning a coin. Or using a star chart for a dartboard.'

'Regardless of that,' Hedley said. 'With the charts, we could have potential targets to hit, if or when war starts?'

'*When* war comes . . . easily,' Froude said. Hedley noted, uneasily, the emphasis.

'All we'd need would be some kind of starship to make the jumps,' Hedley said. 'Something better than the rustbuckets we've got hidden in the bushes.'

'I don't see a major problem,' Froude said confidently. 'You do have a thief, a rather good one, at your disposal, don't you'?'

Hedley thought of saying several things. decided none of them was quite appropriate.

And the gods bless Majormunroe, the man who called himself Ab Yohns thought, admiring his handiwork, and giving a moment of appreciation to the man, epochs ago, who'd made an interesting discovery about the direction explosions could be made to take.

His device appeared to be no more than a chunk of driftwood that'd been trapped between two pilings of the overhead pier.

Very pretty indeed, Yohns thought. *Virtually undetectable. You're not a bad craftsman, if I do say so myself.* He closed his helmet's faceplate, submerged, and swam away, underwater, back toward his boat moored in a nearby marina.

'*Alt* Jaansma speaking,' Garvin said.

The screen cleared, showing Jasith. Garvin felt, not for the first time, that he was in free fall for the first time in his life.

'Hi.'

'Hello,' he said, trying to sound neutral, businesslike.

'I tried to call you yesterday, but you were out,' Jasith said. 'I didn't leave a message.'

'My first *tweg* said a woman had commed,' Garvin said. 'I don't have that many admirers, so I guessed it might've been you.'

'Can we meet somewhere . . . sometime?' she said. 'I think I need to talk to you.'

'Didn't know we had anything in common anymore,' Garvin said.

Jasith flushed.

'Aren't you being a little goddamned self-righteous?' she snapped. 'Some of us don't always know what we're doing, and when things get a little too much we sometimes do things we maybe shouldn't. Haven't you ever done that?'

Garvin started to lose his temper in return, then caught himself. He had. And he remembered, guiltily, back when he'd been covert against the 'Raum, once he hadn't been all that faithful, either . . . and without more than a twitch at the time.

He took a very deep breath. 'You're right, Jasith. I'm sorry. I have been kind of a son of a bitch.'

Jasith licked her lips.

'I'd really like to see you . . . like to talk to you, whenever you can get free.'

Garvin thought. 'I can take off in the morning tomorrow, or is that too early?'

'No,' Jasith said. 'That's fine. Loy'll be tied up with that Musth conference all day.'

'Name the place,' Garvin said, feeling his body stir a little.

'I don't need anyone talking about what I do,' she said. 'Even though . . . I just want to talk to you, I think. Maybe explain something or somethings.'

'As I said, pick the place.'

'Remember that beach we used to go to?' Jasith said. 'The one far down, past the spaceport?'

'Sure.'

'How about there? Maybe in that little restaurant?'

Garvin remembered the bar very well. They'd spent

an evening there, just sitting, staring at each other, their wine barely touched, but half-drunk just the same.

'I'll be there.' he said. 'When?'

'At nine . . . no, make it ten. After the conference has started.'

Without waiting for a reply, Jasith blanked the screen.

Garvin stared at it for a long time, then keyed his com.

'Monique, track down Njangu and tell him he's got the watch tomorrow. I've got business in Leggett, early.'

The Musth speedster came in low over the Heights. with two *aksai* escorting it. flying high cover. It looked a bit like a standard human speedster, but was sleeker, wider, its windscreen set at more of an angle, with armor curving up on the sides and rear from the body and four gun positions. There were five Musth aboard: Aesc, his chief aide. two bodyguards, and the lifter's pilot.

It dove to wave level when it was over the water, and the *aksai* turned back to the Musth base in the Highlands.

The day was bright with promise, the incoming tide washing gently on the white beach sands.

The lifter followed the beach until it closed on the Shelburne, slowed, and hovered slowly toward the over-water deck at the hotel's rear.

Waiting, just inside an entrance, was a handful of dignitaries. Others were seated in the restaurant inside.

The lifter came to a halt beside the gap in the railing, was bumped against the deck by the morning breeze.

One of the bodyguards slid a short gangplank out from the lifter's fuselage, and Aesc stepped onto it.

He was halfway between the lifter and the Shelburne when Ab Yohns, watching through a high-power spotting scope from a high rooftop farther down the waterfront, touched a sensor.

The bomb, almost ten kilos of Telex, hidden in that innocuous chunk of driftwood just below the landing, blew straight up, as its charge had been shaped to do.

It caught Aesc, shredding his body, and the lifter was rolled away, the pilot fighting for control until the craft smashed into the water. Aesc's aide and one bodyguard were killed in the shock wave.

Ab Yohns dropped the scope and the sensor into a padded bag, pulled the fastener shut, and twisted the handle. The blast would go off in a dozen minutes, and completely destroy all of the electronics.

He walked briskly toward the stairs, down them, no more than a businessman thinking about his day. He would be safely back at his villa within an hour and a half.

Yohns hadn't built his bomb perfectly – there was enough of a blast to shatter a window, and scatter glass through the crowd. Half a dozen people required minor medical treatment.

Loy Kouro was behind a curtain, which caught the spattered glass and cushioned him against the blast.

He dropped, stayed flat until he realized whatever had happened was over, then jumped up.

Ignoring the moaning casualties around him, he started shouting for the journohs he'd assigned to cover the conference.

Matin must be the first to 'cast the atrocity.

Jasith Mellusin was airborne at the controls of her speedster when she saw a greasy cloud of smoke from the ocean, heard, through open side windows, the echoing blast.

She saw the curve of the Shelburne, and Garvin was forgotten. Loy was there. She whimpered once, forced herself to change course toward the hotel.

Garvin, too, heard the explosion, craned and saw, far down the waterfront, the blast cloud.

He hesitated for an instant, knew something at the conference with the Musth had gone badly wrong and there was no time for Jasith now, and ran hard for the Shelburne.

The *aksai* must have been in contact with the Musth lifter, because moments later, they banked back over the city, then dived down on the hotel.

Some men and women saw the ships, and thought they were attacking, but the two Musth fighting ships banked low over the wrecked lifter, then climbed and began orbiting the area, in shock, in grief . . . no one knew.

War Leader Wlencing. on distant Silitric, heard about the catastrophe within minutes. He ordered all Musth in the system to the alert, and a mother ship to transport him to C-Cumbre.

He allowed himself one moment of ironic appreciation for what had happened, then turned his mind to business.

The Musth had their incident and better.

NINE

The Musth swept the Cumbre system like a tsunami.

Now – far too late – Force Intelligence found out what the mother ships had carried.

There were the already-familiar *aksai*, flitting like swallows in the skies; larger, sharklike destroyers called *velv*; and flat, heavily armed aerial troop transports, like a large Grierson, armed almost as heavily as a Zhukov, *wynt*.

They swarmed the airspace over the major cities of D-Cumbre, over the mining companies' headquarters on C-Cumbre, and *velv* systematically took the surveillance stations on D-Cumbre's moons.

Wlencing's plans had been perfectly laid.

The Cumbre system passed into Musth hands without a battle.

The men and women of the Legion could do little but gape at the Musth aircraft orbiting Camp Mahan. One AA missile station was hastily manned, but as its launchers popped up from their underground sites, air-to-ground missiles slammed down, and the site, and its soldiers, vanished in rolling explosions.

Wlencing's mother ship landed in the park near the new

Planetary Government building, crushing brush, trees, and the freshly dedicated monument to the dead of the 'Raum uprising.

Aksai in close formation orbited the building as *wynt* skidded down on the driveway, and Musth warriors boiled out, weapons ready.

The lock on the mother ship opened, and Wlencing and his aides marched out in the odd vee-phalanx they used, strode into the PlanGov building. He paid no attention to the scatter of bodies around the building, security guards who'd obeyed their orders and died.

Wlencing entered the main chamber, where about fifteen of the Council were meeting to discuss the crisis of Aesc's death. They were milling about, faces white.

Wlencing started for the podium. A heavyset man growled an objection, came toward him. Two Musth pistols slid from holsters, and the man stepped back. raising his hands. Wlencing acted as if nothing had happened, continuing on to the podium.

'In the name of my raccce, our dessstiny, our fate, I claim the Cumbre sssysssstem, and all in it the sssub-jectsss of my people. All formsss of government, organization, are declared not lawful until otherwissse allowed.

'You humansss are ordered to obey all commandsss from me, or from my warriorsss absssolutely. The penalty for nonobedienccce or resssissstanccce is death.'

Jo Poynton, in the back of the chamber, slipped quietly out an exit and headed rapidly, unobtrusively, to the remains of the 'Raum ghetto, the Eckmuhl.

She'd fought from it once, and now it appeared she'd have to do it again.

There were other 'Raum she knew who hadn't been killed when the Eckmuhl was put to the torch and sword.

Nor had they surrendered their arms, but dumped them in secret locations. They would be ready.

Two *wynt* hovered down to the roof of *Matin*, and two fighting formations of Musth came out of the side ramp of each. They doubled through the roof door, down two flights of stairs, and burst into the executive offices of the publishing/broadcast conglomerate.

Someone stammered a question to which the Musth leader paid no mind.

'Loy Kouro,' he ordered, and a quaking editor took him to Kouro's huge office. The publisher came out slowly, empty hands spread in front of him, clearly expecting to be cut down where he stood.

'You have transsssmissssion capabilitiesss in the event of the emergencccy?'

Kouro took a moment to understand.

'Yes.'

'Other holosss have the technology to link with you?'

'We have a command linkup.' Kouro said reluctantly. 'But its use has to be coordinated and approved by the government.'

'We are now the government,' the Musth said. 'Take usss there.'

Kouro hesitated, and the Musth lifted his pistol.

'Follow me.'

'Bring technicalsss to work the apparatusss.'

Most of the coms across D-Cumbre were on, from villages to the Heights, people waiting to be told what had happened. But all that was seen was the normal entertainment channels. The news holos were blank, or playing music.

Simultaneously, all of them cleared, then showed the image of the slain Aesc.

A clear, metallic voice began:

'People of Cumbre. You have offended against us grievously. We, the Musth, have borne many wrongs, from slander to robbery to murder. In spite of repeated warnings, both to your citizens and your government, these offenses have continued.

'Now is the day of reckoning. From this moment forward, all planets in the Cumbre system are taken under the stewardship of the Musth.

'We urge all humans to remain calm. to take no action of stupidity against us. Any such measures of banditry will be met with the most severe penalties. The perpetrator will face death, as will his accomplices. Anyone found to support any action against us will also be sentenced to an immediate death, their properties and goods subject to immediate confiscation.

'We order all humans to continue with their daily routine. Report to your places of work as if the situation was normal.

'There are other emergency rules which must be obeyed: There shall be a curfew of all humans from dusk to dawn. No humans are permitted to gather in groups of more than ten, except as their work requires.

'All private weapons are to be surrendered at your local police station. All policemen are ordered to put themselves under the command of the Musth, and obey whatever instructions received without objection.

'All members of the military are to report to their barracks, where they are confined until we determine the disposition of these forces.

'All aircraft and spaceships are to return immediately to their home bases, land, and await further orders.

'Remember, we Musth wish only peace. Obey our orders, and find your place in a greater future.'

*

There were four faces on the split screen in Caud Rao's office – his regimental commanders.

'What do we do, sir?' *Mil* Fitzgerald asked.

Rao took a deep breath.

'There's nothing we *can* do. Not right now,' he said glumly. 'We've been ordered to surrender. We'll haul down the colors, and do like they told us to. Confine everyone to barracks, march them to chow, no leave. no passes, and keep your noncoms circulating so nobody's got a chance to consider starting a private war.

'Maintain discipline, keep your troops in hand, and don't give the bastards the slightest excuse to take any further action. Especially watch your hotheads. You know who they are. Don't punish them, but don't let them start something the Force won't be able to finish.'

Mil Chel Reese, CO, First Regiment, grimaced.

'Aren't there any options?'

Rao sadly shook his head.

'What should we do?' Dr. Froude asked *Dec* Ho Kang.

She thought a moment.

'We sure don't want all this work to get swept up by the Musth. We better get all of the charts together, all the disks. Right now. We'll hide you two somewhere, probably over on Mullion Island.'

The two scientists hurried to obey. Ho Kang touched numbers on a com.

'Regimental laundry.' a worried voice said.

'This *is Dec* Ho Kang, II Section,' Ho Kang said. 'Three of us are coming over. We have some material we don't want anyone to know about for a while.'

'Anyone,' the voice said, coming alive, 'like furry any-ones?'

'This com could be tapped,' Ho warned. 'But you're thinking right.'

'We can do that,' the voice promised. 'Allee time hidee hooch in it, since this ain't a clean line. Nevah nobody lookee, get to glow in dark if they dumb enough to do, trefoil signs all over. Whatever you've got, if it's smaller'n a Grierson, nobody'll think of there.'

'Screw this noise!' *Cent* Elles said angrily. 'We're just supposed to sit here and let them run over us?'

'We're already run over,' Ben Dill said calmly. 'And those were our orders.'

'Screw them, too!' Elles looked around the ready room, out the window at the hidden jungle base on Mullion Island. 'I say we go after the goddamned Musth! Maybe they'll take us out, but at least we'll have taken some with us!'

'That's not what *Caud* Rao ordered,' an *alt* said.

'I'm base commander here, dammit!' Elles said. 'Here's what we're going to do. Man your ships, take off, find targets, any Musth force or aircraft, and kill them. Shake off any pursuers, then return here for fuel, rearming, another mission.'

'And if we've got too many on our butts to shake, what're we supposed to do?' Dill asked. 'Let them find this base, or should we just bail out and take our chances?'

'Under no circumstances are you to reveal the existence of this base,' Elles snapped. 'Take whatever actions are necessary!'

He picked up a mike, touched the red sensor that turned on PAs around the field.

'Uh, sir,' Ben Dill said. 'One other thing?'

'What?' Elles said irritably.

Dill's snapped punch took him in the diaphragm, and Elles whuffed, folded. Ben thumped a fist on the back of his exposed neck, and the officer collapsed. The huge *alt* shut the microphone off and looked down at the base commander, shaking his head sadly.

'I think that's a court-martial offense,' he said. 'Maybe Ben loses his sash over this.'

'Being busted's better'n pointless suicide,' another pilot said. 'Especially 'cause I don't see any way we could get more'n five meters off the ground without getting wiped out.'

'Maybe so,' Dill said. 'But this is the first time I've ever backed off from a fight, and it tastes bad. Really bad.'

'I'm not a happy trooper,' Garvin Jaansma said quietly.

'Shut up,' Njangu said. 'We're hard cases, remember? Not sentimental schnooks.'

The two, dressed in combat camouflage, fully armed, stood to one side of the Camp Mahan parade ground.

At its head were three flagpoles, the center flying the Confederation flag, the other two the Cumbre ensign and the Force colors.

The officer of the guard, a ranking *dec*, and the daily guard detachment stood at the salute as a seven-man detail marched to the poles, unfastened the lines, and made ready to lower the colors. A bugler with his archaic instrument stood ready.

A shout echoed across the parade ground.

'Stop!'

A man with a blaster lurched from behind a building. He was in his forties, grizzled and hard-bitten. He was familiar to Njangu, and he puzzled, got it. The man's name was Barker, no, Barken, a long-server from somewhere out-system, who'd arrived with the Force on its deployment to Cumbre. Barken had worn stripes, had them taken away, had them given back again. He was considered a good field soldier, had won medals in the rising, had been promoted yet again, then had been reduced to the ranks for throwing a two-week drunk.

'Stop, goddammit!' He fired a round into the air, and everyone froze.

'We're not lowerin' the friggin' flag, goddammit!' He stumbled closer to the guard detail, and the *dec*'s hand slid toward his holstered pistol.

'Hold it, soldier,' he shouted back. 'Get rid of the gun, and freeze!'

'Shove that up yer ass. Sir,' Barken said, 'I've been with the Force more'n twenty years, and we've never surrendered to nobody, and we're not frigging starting now!'

'You're disobeying orders!'

'Nobody oughta be obeying those goddamned orders! What are we, winks that fold up without even one lousy frigging fight? What the hell is this? What the hell is going on!'

Another round whined overhead.

'Soldier, I gave you a lawful order,' the guard commander snapped. 'Drop that blaster!'

He unsnapped his holster flap.

'Shut yer friggin' mouth, sir!' Barken called. 'We're not taking the Hag down, not without somebody shooting me first.'

The officer had his pistol half-drawn. Someone – perhaps two someones – was going to get burnt down in the next few seconds.

'Stop!' Garvin shouted, somewhat surprised at himself. His own firearm was in his hand, and he was trotting onto the field.

Both Barken and the officer of the guard turned.

'What the hell are you doing, *Alt*?' the guard officer shouted.

Garvin paid no attention.

'You, Barken. Get rid of that stupid gun!'

Barken glowered, started to say something.

'Do what he says,' Njangu said calmly. He stood to one side of Garvin, his own pistol in hand, but held loosely, pointing down at the ground. 'You're betting into a pat hand.'

Barken's lips thinned, then he slumped and tossed the blaster away. It clattered on the tarmac.

'Thanks, *Alt* . . .' the guard officer said.

'Be quiet,' Garvin said. He wasn't sure what he was doing or why he was doing it, knowing he was breaking at least as many regulations as Barken.

'*Tweg*, bring the flags down. Bugler, we won't have any music. No triumphs, no dirges either.'

The bugler nodded shakily, tucked his instrument back under his arm. The warrant in charge of the flag detail looked perplexed. Garvin waved the pistol at him.

'Follow your orders, *Tweg*!'

The noncom obeyed, and the pulleys squeaked loudly in the silence.

'You,' Garvin said, pointing at two of the men. 'Case the Cumbre flag.'

'Yessir,' one said.

'You others,' Jaansma continued. 'Take the Confederation flag and the Force ensign. Cut them apart.'

'Sir?'

Njangu heard a sound, spun, saw one of the guards stealthily unslinging his blaster. Njangu fired, and the bolt blew a meter-wide hole in the paving behind the man. He jumped, dropped his blaster.

'Stand easy, friend,' Yoshitaro said in a mild voice. 'This is just getting interesting.'

'You heard my order. Cut the flags into little pieces,' Garvin ordered. 'Every man here is to get one.'

He spun toward the guard detail, not waiting to see that his orders were followed.

'I want every one of you to take a piece of those flags and remember what they stand for,' he ordered. 'If carrying it's too much for you, give it to a friend, someone who wants to fight. Someone who won't let anyone, not man, not Musth, take it from him without a battle.

'We lost today. But this isn't the end of the war. This is just the beginning.'

TEN

'There is a difference, young *alts*, between being a damned-fool firebrand and a warrior,' *Caud* Rao said coldly. 'Don't you realize you could have started a firestorm among the men?'

Garvin started to say something, then clamped his mouth shut. Njangu stood beside him, both in dress uniforms, both frozen statues.

'Go ahead,' Rao said. 'I meant that as a rhetorical question, but I'm curious as to your answer.'

'Yessir,' Garvin said. 'Maybe it could've. But I said this wasn't the time, the place for a fight, and I didn't think I'd be disobeyed.'

'You don't sound especially sorry for what you did,' Rao said. He tapped fingernails on his desk, glanced up at *Mil* Angara, whose face was pointedly blank.

'Very well,' he decided. 'Maybe we're going to need some firebrands, although I'm going to have a word with Hedley about the kind of officers he's created.

'Intelligence and Reconnaissance, *Alt* Jaansma, is the job description. Not Agitation and Instigation. Remember that.

'I'm going to give both of you a verbal reprimand. I could have made it a formal reprimand in your record jacket, but I won't have any trouble remembering either of you if you come up before me anytime soon.'

He didn't add that he expected the conquering Musth to vet the records, possibly looking for trouble-makers.

'Dismissed.'

Garvin snapped a salute, and he and Njangu pivoted, marched out of the CO's office. *Caud* Rao shook his head.

'There are times I wish I could be young and big-mouthed like those two.'

'No you don't, sir,' Angara said. 'It just gets you into trouble.'

'As if I'm not in it already.' Rao got up, paced to a window. 'I wonder how long the Musth will take to figure out what they want to do with us. I'm surprised, as efficiently as they came down, their war leader didn't have any contingencies for the Force.'

'Maybe,' Angara suggested, 'they expected us to con-veniently fight to the last man.'

Rao considered what he knew about the Musth, nodded slowly. 'Possibly. If you're right, that means they aren't particularly gifted at analyzing other beings.'

'We beat them once, didn't we, which might suggest something?'

'Historical precedent doesn't seem to matter much in combat.' Rao said dryly. There was a long silence.

'Grig, would you mind doing me a favor?'

'If possible, sir.'

'Could you quietly scout around for one of those pieces of our colors? I'm not at all sure we might not be called on to be like those two in the not-too-distant future, and I think I might need something to remind me how to do proper damned foolishness.'

Angara grinned tightly, reached into a breast pocket, and took out a bit of colorful cloth.

'Already taken care of, sir, by *Alt* Penwyth. One for you, and one for me.' He handed the piece to Rao, who looked at him quizzically.

'There's something pretty goddamned frightening about having an exec who knows you better'n you do yourself.'

Planetary Police announced they were 'developing several leads' to the unknown bomber, which meant they had nothing.

The bank officer looked nervously at the two officers.

'This is irregular. *Most* irregular!'

'Just about everything is, these days,' Garvin agreed. 'I assume you'll need to check this with her attorney. Here's his com number.'

'Yes . . . yes . . . that's what should be done.'

The man dithered with sensors, spoke to a secretary, was routed to a courtroom, and then waited while Gy Glenn was brought out of court.

'This had best be important,' he said. scowling as much as he could manage a scowl.

The banker explained, and now it was Glenn's turn to look astonished.

'You said the officer is there in person.'

'I am,' Jaansma said.

'Would you swivel the pickup so I can identify him,' Glenn requested. 'Thank you. That's the man. Would you step out of hearing, please?'

The banker obeyed.

'*Alt* Jaansma, you're sure that's what's best?'

'I am.'

'I assume your decision has something to do with the, shall we say, change in the current political situation?'

'Yes.'

'Would you object to my checking with Miss Mellusin, sorry, Mrs. Mellusin?'

'I wouldn't,' Garvin said. 'But I think we've got to move quickly.'

Glenn gnawed at his lower lip.

'Call that banker back over. I'll com her, but you can proceed with the transaction immediately. Our new friends from elsewhere, should they learn of this, might well object, so we'd best get the matter finished as quickly as we can.'

The banker listened, looked even more astonished, and shut down the com.

'You have proper security, I assume?'

Njangu, without speaking, lifted an arm. From outside the door, Monique Lir and half a dozen soldiers in full combat garb, doubled into the bank.

'We have three armored transports and a gunship outside,' Njangu said. 'I don't think we have to worry about being held up.'

'You appear to have this matter well thought out,' the banker said. 'In what form would you like it?'

'Five- and ten-credit coins,' Garvin said.

'Very, very irregular,' the banker said. 'But it's good that you came to the central branch. We can manage the transaction, but any other branch would have their vaults depleted.'

Neither soldier commented.

'Miss Yazeth,' the banker said. 'conduct these people to our vault. I'll give you instructions as we go.'

Half an hour later, soldiers began trundling heavy bags of coins through the bank and loading them into the waiting Griersons. The banker stood watching, the confirmation from Jasith Mellusin no comfort, for he looked like he was about to start crying seeing money he secretly thought of as his vanish into the hands of goons and thugs.

The situation.' Loy Kouro said cheerfully, 'may not be as disastrous as everyone thought.'

Jasith carefully put her fork down. They were having a late breakfast on one of the terraces of her mansion on the Heights.

'And what might *that* mean?'

'I'm starting to believe we can survive, maybe even prosper, working with these Musth. They're hardly the monsters some paint them.'

'Prosper?' Jasith said. 'Loy, they've taken us over, said anybody out after dark will be shot, anybody in groups of ten or more'll have the same thing done to them . . . I don't see how you can call that prospering.'

'Oh, that's just typical soldier talk,' Kouro said. 'Soldiers always overreact to everything. Give it a few weeks, let them see what happened to Aesc was an anomaly, they'll settle down.'

Jasith balled up her napkin, tossed it down beside her. 'What about the penalties they're planning on levying?'

'That'll just have to be the price of doing business. Look at it as just another tax. Except that it won't be levied forever.'

'Who says?'

'Why would they want to put us out of business?' Kouro asked reasonably.

'So they can own it altogether,' Jasith said. 'I don't believe you're saying this. Doesn't it bother you that anytime they want to make an announcement about anything they just waltz into *Matin*, and take it over?'

'Surely it bothers me,' Kouro said. 'But I'm enough of an adult to know you can't always kick against the pricks.'

'I wonder what your father would've done?'

'He's gone,' Kouro said, voice sharpening. 'I'm in charge now.'

'No, Loy. You're not in charge of anything,' Jasith said. 'The Musth have all the cards, and they're playing them as they want.'

'Typical miner,' Loy said. 'All you see is what's in front of you.'

'What I do see is they'll want to buy my ore, at a price they'll set, and I'll bet it isn't one that I'll laugh about.'

'As I said, some things you just have to live with.'

'So says the mighty publisher,' Jasith said. 'One who speaks for all Cumbre.'

'What the hell's the matter with you lately?' Kouro said, tone hurt. 'You're always on edge, ready to jump down my throat.'

'I merely said I thought you were talking like either a fool or what some would call a traitor,' Jasith said evenly.

Kouro was on his feet.

'So that's it!'

'What's it?'

'You and that damned soldier you were screwing before we got married . . . are you seeing him again? Playing a little hide the sausage on the side?'

'I'm not seeing Garvin,' Jasith said, coming to her feet, chair crashing back. 'I married *you*, didn't I? And you were the one who proposed, weren't you?'

'I wonder how I got tricked into that,' Kouro said. 'Maybe so you could be sleeping around with people below our class, and nobody's say anything if, oh, look, there's a child. What comes next, Jasith? You going to start bedding 'Raum, one in every orifice?'

Jasith came around the small table, slapped him. Kouro jerked back, hit her in the mouth with his fist. Jasith cried out in surprise, then stumbled and fell.

Kouro leaned over her.

'Don't you ever do that to me again! Not ever!'

He stamped from the room. A few moments later, she heard his speedster lift away from the landing deck, drive away at full power.

Jasith sat, stunned, for a time. She lifted a hand to her lips, wiped them, looked at the traces of blood on her fingers.

'No,' she said quietly. 'I won't ever do that to you again.'

'I wondered how long it'd take them to get around to us,' Garvin said. He and Njangu were 'lounging' near a seemingly unmanned gun position, in the event things escalated.

Other soldiers were close to other missile and gun stations. No one got inside the turrets or pits, remembering the antiaircraft site that'd been obliterated on that first day of the Musth occupation. Three weeks had passed since then, and the Legion had long since run out of fingernails to dine on.

Over Camp Mahan circled layers of Musth – *aksai* on high cover, a mother ship underneath it, then two *velv*, another layer of *aksai*, all escorting a single highly polished *wynt*.

'Time enough,' Njangu said. 'Now, is it gonna be catastrophe or just simple disaster?'

The *wynt* grounded, and Wlencing and his staff got out, entered Force Headquarters.

It was catastrophe, although not quite complete. Wlencing told Rao he did not propose to completely dissolve the Force. It was to be reduced to a single battalion of light infantry, two thousand men, which would serve as backup to the Planetary Police in the event of riots or emergencies. All aerial capabilities except about fifty or so Griersons for transport were to be grounded.

Headquarters would be trimmed down appropriately.

The Zhukov Gunship Battalion was to be dissolved. its ACVs scrapped. The Artillery Detachment, except for two Shrike batteries, was to be broken up. All heavy weapons were to be turned in, to eventually be scrapped.

The disarmament was to be complete in sixty days.

Rao and his staff listened to Wlencing s orders, stone-faced.

When the Musth finished, Rao asked, 'What is to be done with the excess men?'

'I thought the anssswer would be obviousss,' Wlencing said. 'Dissscharge them asss civiliansss, which they were before.'

'A good percentage of them aren't from Cumbre, and have no place to go,' Angara said.

'That isss not my conccccern,' Wlencing began, and an aide leaned close, spoke quietly.

'I have a posssssible sssolution,' he then said. 'The minesss on C-Cumbre will now be operated at full cap-accity. Thossse sssoldiersss who don't find placesss will be accepted as minersss.'

Rao considered arguing, knew it would be useless. Without reply, he rose and stalked out, his staff flanking him.

Wlencing's aide waited until the room was empty, then asked: 'Since we shamed them, will they now fight?'

'No,' Wlencing said. 'We have beaten them down too far. They might have been capable of a last stand, if we had attacked them at first. But using wisdom, we ate at them, allowed our presence to become commonplace, and now it is too late. They are truly beaten.'

'Will they obey your orders?'

'What choice do they have?'

'Well?' *Caud* Rao asked his staff. On scrambled screens were the commanders of the dispersed regiments.

'They didn't leave us any options, did they, sir,' *Mil* Ken Fong, head of Operations – III Section – said.

'No,' Rao said. 'I hoped by stalling them, pretending we were beaten, which we would've been, we could get some time to find alternatives. I was wrong.'

'What we should've flipping done,' Hedley said, 'was blow Wlencing and his staff out of the sky as they were landing. *That* would have given us some time.'

'We don't fight like bandits, like criminals,' Rao said coldly.

'Maybe we should . . .' Hedley let his voice trail off.

'So we have two choices,' Rao said. 'We fight . . . or we fold. Votes . . . although I'll make my own decision. I just want to see what you think.'

'We're still part of the Confederation,' Angara said. 'We fight.'

Rao looked at the screens, at the men and women in the command bunker. No one, not even Hedley, dissented.

'Good,' Rao said. 'We'll stall as long as we can, get the word out, then hit them hard.'

'Three officers to see you. *Cent* Hedley with *Alt* Jaansma and *Aspirant* Yoshitaro,' the Force Command *tweg* announced through the intercom.

'I should have expected them,' Rao muttered.

'Pardon, sir?'

'Nothing. Show them in.'

The three officers entered, and Hedley saluted.

'I assume this is important?' Rao asked.

'Yes, sir,' Hedley said. 'We want to offer an alternative to fighting or giving up.'

'Why didn't you mention it during the staff meeting?'

'It might not be palatable to some of the officers, sir,' Hedley said. 'It's actually these two men's ideas.'

Rao nodded to Garvin.

'It's fairly simple, sir. We surrender . . . or at least give in to their demands.'

'Let them break up the Force?' Rao said.

'Let them break up what they can,' Yoshitaro put in. 'I don't think they're fools enough to let us discharge troops into some kind of inactive reserve. But there's nothing to say those who want to couldn't join some kind of veterans' association after a few weeks.

'Sprinkle those in every city on Cumbre, and that'll give us an intel source, and reserves we can call up when we need them.'

'We?'

'Some of us go underground,' Garvin said. 'We use the dispersed locations, plus the base on Mullion Island to strike from.'

'A guerrilla war?'

'Exactly. sir,' Hedley said. 'Hit 'em high, low, and wherever they aren't strong enough. Hit them hard enough, and pretty soon they'll get tired of fighting, and start wanting to talk about some kind of truce.'

'Like the 'Raum?' Rao said distastefully.

'They came close to beating us, sir,' Yoshitaro said.

'A nasty way to fight a war,' Rao said.

None of the three answered.

Rao considered. 'Well, I don't think they'd be willing to go nuclear, not as long as they want some part of the real estate.'

'Which we can flipping give them,' Hedley said.

'After they're hammered some, and then we can come

up with some kind of truce that'll let them save face. They'll still have their victory, plus access to the mines on C-Cumbre.'

'*Aspirant*,' Rao said, 'you said "we" a bit ago. Who're your fighters?'

'Initially,' Njangu said, 'you discharge everybody in I&R who asks for one. Out of one hundred twenty-eight troops, about ninety want to keep fighting. Half a dozen wouldn't mind getting out, and we let them go. Keep the others wherever you want them.

'Plus we keep the people on Mullion like we said. That'll give us some kind of security, and we'll just have to make sure that nobody, absolutely nobody, gets tracked back to them.' Njangu's voice rang with enthusiasm.

'What about supplying those bases?' Rao asked. 'An army doesn't march on idealism.'

'I know where we can get credits and supplies, sir,' Hedley said. 'I have enough contacts with the rich to get them to kick in.'

'You assume our Rentiers are all that patriotic?'

'Of course not, sir. But it seems the late and unlamented Policy and Analysis Section of the PlanPolice kept files on almost everyone. I, ahem, seem to have found them, some months ago, which I didn't bother boring you with, since they're certainly of the seamiest.'

'Blackmail?'

'Just so, sir.' There was no smile on Hedley's face.

'That's ugly,' Rao said. 'The whole idea's ugly. Jaansma, Yoshitaro, what makes you think you could get away with having your own war, at least at first?'

'First, because we had experience with the 'Raum. No offense, and we don't mean to sound arrogant, but if the two of us had really been fighting on their side, instead of being double agents, I think we could have given *Caud*

Williams and the Force a lot rougher way to go. Also, because humans outnumber the Musth . . . that's counting civilians, too,' Njangu said confidently. 'Sooner or later the Musth'll manage to piss everyone on the planet off, and make them into fighters, or at least people who'll help us fight. That was the 'Raum strategy, and I think if they'd had support from the people, they might've gotten away with it.'

'There'll be civilian casualties,' Rao said.

Both Njangu and Garvin nodded grimly.

'Are you able to live with reprisals?'

'Sir,' Garvin said, 'I don't see any way the Musth are going to be able to maintain the present situation, whether we're fighting them or not. Sooner or later, they'll overreact, and start killing civvies anyway. When they do, every time they do, we'll have another recruit.'

'That's a price that'll we have to accept,' Njangu added. 'Otherwise, we just end up being slaves, working on their damned mines over on C-Cumbre. And I don't think the Confederation . . . or Redruth . . . is going to jump in and play Save Our Asses.'

Rao shook his head, unbelieving. 'When I was an *alt*, all I gave a damn about was my platoon, sport, and my mess bill. What's happened to the new generation?'

'We grew up different,' Njangu said. 'Maybe things were a little closer to the bone for us.'

'I would guess so,' Rao said. 'A question for you, however. You seem to be willing to accept civilian dead with equanimity. Do you think you'll feel the same way the first time you see a dead woman or child? Or see the Musth strafe a village?'

Garvin started to say something. Njangu held up his hand.

'I'll answer that. Sir, do you think that'll be anything

different than what we saw . . . what we did . . . against the 'Raum?'

Rao grimaced.

'That's in the past.' He thought for a time, then slowly began shaking his head.

'No. That's too much of a dream, and if it goes awry, this whole planet could be a shambles. Thank you, gentlemen, for trying to come up with something, but that's not the answer.

'We'll stay with the original strategy and fight them where we stand.

'That's all, gentlemen. Good luck.'

Garvin started to say something, got a hard look from Njangu, shut his mouth. Hedley saluted, and the three walked out.

In the corridor Hedley stopped, sank back against the wall.

'Shit,' he said. 'I thought for a minute we had the old man convinced.'

'So what now, sir?' Garvin asked.

'I guess we get ready to fight, try not to get killed, and hope we're able to keep the battle going after the Force gets massacred.'

ELEVEN

Caud Rao, with a skeleton staff, left Camp Mahan within the hour. He jumped from regiment to regiment, city to city, and filed regular reports back to Mil Angara. They were encoded – but the code was one that'd been broken by the Musth.

Wlencing got intercepts almost as fast as Angara's clerks were able to decode the transmissions.

All of them were much the same – Rao was successfully trying to keep the hotheads in the Force under control. Matters appeared in hand, and the Musth orders would be followed.

Some of Wlencing's warriors grumbled, wanted action, vengeance for Aesc's murder, but the Musth leader told them not to be foolish. War, fought just for its own sake, was stupidity.

If the Musth had achieved victory without casualties, this was the greatest triumph of all, and indicated clearly the human victory a generation ago was nothing but an anomaly.

If these humans were all too eager to become the puppets of the Musth, this was a clear indication of what the First Cause must have intended – for The People to utterly dominate the cosmos.

And as for revenge for Aesc . . . vengeance, he

reminded them, was a dish to be savored at length and leisure.

'Do you wish extraction?' The transmission ebbed, rose, bouncing from satellite station to station before reaching the Cumbre system, then further retransmitted by robot stations within the system.

Ab Yohns considered. Part of him wanted out. It'd been a long, long assignment, and his nerves felt sand-papered. But again, what were the chances of a Larix/Kura ship being able to enter Cumbre, pick him up, and extract successfully without being detected and destroyed by the Musth?

'Negative,' he said. 'I'll stick around, see what develops. You'll need a man on the ground.'

'We were hoping you would decide that,' his control said. 'We do need you, now more than ever before.'

'I'll expect the fee to be adjusted accordingly,' Yohns said.

'It shall be.' Without formality, the com ended.

Ben Dill strolled through the control room, set up in a hangar on Mullion Island, pausing to look at screens, control panels, sensors, cabinets. Every now and then, intent on some detail, he walked through a display terminal. Here and there the holograph was blurred, where Njangu hadn't shot pictures.

Dill was trailed by Hedley, Kang, Heiser, and Froude. Finally he stopped, stopping them all in turn.

'Interestin',' he said.

'Interesting enough for you, and some others, to start training on?'

'Hell no,' Dill said. 'Just a start.'

'We've built a simulator in another hangar,' Hedley said.

'You're expecting a lot from me, and whoever else is supposed to be a flyboy,' Dill said. 'No idea of instrument feel, what kind of readouts you get, what kind of support.

'Sorry, gents. Not nearly enough.'

'I wish,' Dr. Froude said grumpily, 'you'd at least *try* the sim. We used more than the pictures you know. We have projections of how the mother ships fly from our off-world detectors, combined with the fairly significant information you and others have provided on the *aksai,* and more data, theories really, from the stolen star charts.'

'Sounds like enough to get somebody killed.' Dill said.

'Only sim,' Heiser reminded.

Dill grunted, considered.

'What the hell. It can't hurt that much to give it a run. But I don't see what any of this is going to get us anytime soon.'

'All knowledge is power,' Froude said a bit pompously.

'And when we get our hands on one of the ships.' Ho Kang added, 'you'll be able to get it off the ground.'

'Ben doesn't feel very super these days,' Dill grumbled. 'I suppose, Ho, you'd be willing to ride the ECM seat, whichever one it might be, like in the old days? Or is it hey, Ben, whyn't you go into the deep black just for drill?'

'That's a shitty thing to say,' Ho Kang said indignantly. 'Since when have I ever not been willing to piggyback your dinosaur ass?'

'Sorry,' Ben said. 'You're right. This waiting around for the balloon to go up's gotten me a little testy. Let's see what it's like, but I can flat-ass guarantee this sim ain't gonna be enough.'

*

There were almost a hundred Zhukovs on Camp Mahan's huge parade ground, their crews at attention in front of each ACV. Their drives were humming, and their coms were on, all monitoring the 'cast from *Caud* Rao, a sentiment-dripping speech about how nobly they'd served, and how their service, their frequent sacrifice, would never be forgotten.

The Gunship Battalion's colors were cased, and the battalion was declared dissolved.

One vehicle commander and one driver doubled to each Zhukov, and, still in perfect formation, the attack ships lifted away, four aerial columns headed for the distant city of Seya, on the island of the same name.

The Zhukov crewmen and the battalion's necessary support elements were marched back to barracks, where they were immediately granted discharges, and began cycling out into the civilian sector.

It was a gut-wrenching moment, watched over by circling *aksai* and two *velv*. Wlencing was aboard one of the destroyer-like ships. He turned away from the screen with satisfaction.

'Little by little, it grows,' he said to Rahfer.

The aide's head bobbed quickly.

'It is a pity,' Rahfer said, 'there are no medals for a successful victory gained without any bloodshed, nor revenge for System-Leader Aesc's murder.'

'There will still be medals to be earned here,' Wlencing said. 'Once the humans have dissolved their fighting strength, there will be dissidents, criminals against order to handle. There will still be glory enough for everyone.'

The Zhukovs reached Seya, and were grounded in a hastily graded compound, where heavy wrecking machinery waited. Their pilots and commanders were brought back to Camp Mahan, where they joined their fellows, awaiting discharge.

The company given the task of destroying the gunships began putting out bids for various surplus items, from seats to com gear. As soon as the ships were stripped, they'd be scrapped and melted down.

Caud Rao was kept fully informed about this matter again in a code easily read by the Musth.

No Musth reported the occasional Grierson or two flying between Mahan and Seya, if they were even observed, nor were their packed crew compartments noted.

'Reporting as ordered, sir,' Njangu said. 'What's going on?'

'Tell him,' *Cent* Hedley told the com tech.

'I was monitoring the standard Force emergency freq as part of my normal watch duties,' the young man said. 'It was just 1900 hours tonight. Someone came on, a filtered voice, so I couldn't tell if it was man, woman, or synthed, asking for a response from the Force.

'Like I'm supposed to do, I responded.

'The voice said, and I'm quoting precisely, "Message for Njangu Yoshitaro. Respond on this frequency after message ends. Broadcast will be repeated nightly." It sent that twice, then shut down. I didn't have time enough to get a locator on it, don't have any idea what it could be.'

'Thanks, technician. You're dismissed,' Hedley said, waited until the man had left the office.

'You got any irons in the fire?' Hedley said. 'Running any agents that might've blown their normal contact?'

'Sir,' Njangu said honestly, 'I'm just getting ready for the shitstorm to come. I haven't and won't develop anybody until the fog lifts a bit.'

'Hmm.'

'Maybe I better be around a com sometime tomorrow night?'

'Wouldn't do any harm,' Hedley agreed.

'Message for Njangu Yoshitaro. Respond on this frequency after message ends,' the colorless voice said. 'Broadcast will be repeated nightly. Message for Njangu Yoshitaro. Respond on this frequency after message ends. Broadcast will be repeated nightly. Clear.'

Njangu touched the sensor.

'Yoshitaro here. Over.'

A whisper of static, then:

'Meeting desired. Location: fifty meters SSW from old Planning Group Headquarters ruins familiar to you. Midday. Tomorrow. No more than one escort.'

'Understood.' Njangu said. 'If I come . . . how do I recognize you?'

A noise came that might have been amusement.

'You will recognize. Clear.'

Njangu put the microphone down, looked at Hedley.

'You have any idea what's going on?'

'Nary a one,' Yoshitaro said.

'Do you know where the voice is talking about?'

'Sure. He, she, or it wants my young ass right in the middle of what's left of the Eckmuhl. the same place the 'Raum got nasty with me last time around.'

'You going to make the meet?'

'Why not? Nobody's tried to kill me in at least, oh, four days.'

'What'll you want for backup?'

'Two Griersons hanging about offshore,' Njangu said. 'Loaded for max grunt.'

'What about ground security?'

'They said one person, I'll take one person.'

'As a matter of curiosity,' Hedley said, 'who?'

'Nobody's tried to kill my fun-loving CO lately, either.'

The Eckmuhl was – had been – the 'Raum ghetto in Leggett for centuries. When their revolt moved back into the cities, after being nearly obliterated in the countryside, the Eckmuhl became the center of resistance. The planned general rising, unintentionally set off early by Yoshitaro and Jaansma, had gone awry. The Movement had been destroyed, along with most of the Eckmuhl. After the war, PlanGov had been bludgeoned into building low-cost housing for the 'Raum, which now crept over the hills north and east behind the walled enclave. Many 'Raum, particularly the younger ones, gladly fled the tenements and squalor.

But the Eckmuhl still held close to a hundred thousand people. Some lived in their undamaged if rickety apartments, some had cleared ruins and rebuilt, others lived in the wreckage itself. Life continued, vibrant, loud, vital.

Garvin Jaansma, uncomfortable in civilian clothes with body armor underneath, growled to his exec: 'In case you haven't noticed, I fit in here like a square widget. I'm neither brown, short nor do I express myself normally above 160db(A). You, on the other hand—'

'Don't be racist,' Njangu said, 'sir. Or I'll nark you off as . . . as what did they call us?'

'The Rentiers' lapdogs,' Garvin said morosely. 'Hah. We weren't that well paid. Still aren't. So who are we looking for?'

'I think I know,' Njangu said. 'And I'll even give you a clue. The person is the greatest survivor we know.'

'Impossible,' Garvin said. '*I'm* the greatest survivor I know. And I didn't send any messages for some sort of goddamned meeting in the rubble.' He wiped sweat.

'Those walls don't let any sea breeze through at all, do they?'

Njangu's eyes were darting here, there, across the square at the collapsed building. They'd found a drink cart and stayed under the shade of its umbrella, sucking down iced carbonated, limed water and waiting. Both men kept the glasses in their off hands, favored hands hovering near barely-hidden gun butts.

'It's midday and half-gone,' Garvin said. 'Shall we write off our friend?'

'Nope,' Njangu said. 'Her security's eyeballing us right now. Come on. Let's stroll over into ground zero, so they've got no chance of missing.'

Garvin set his glass on the vendor's counter, dropped a bill without looking at it, realized from the vendor's grateful babble he should've, and followed Njangu out into the blazing sun. He, too, made the waiting gunmen. There were three of them, each watching a different byway, once streets, now curling through high-piled rubble.

'I'd call this fifty meters . . . and here she comes,' Njangu said.

From a narrow alley, a woman walked unhurriedly toward them.

'I should've guessed,' Garvin said.

'You should've,' Njangu said. 'Good afternoon, Councilor Poynton.'

Jo Poynton nodded a greeting.

'Even though I owe you two my life, I'm still not sure whether I like you or not.'

Njangu shrugged.

'We don't have time to worry about the past. What's done is done.'

'You're right. I apologize,' she said.

'Forget about it,' Njangu said amiably.

'Now that the love affair has picked up with all its old ardor,' Garvin said, 'could we get out of this sun before my brain bakes, and then maybe you can tell us . . . sorry, tell Njangu . . . what you came looking for?'

'There's a café up the next street,' Poynton said. 'Some of my old . . . associates . . . own it, and can keep us . . . me, at any rate, safe.'

'We're following you,' Garvin said. 'But no more lime waters, 'kay?' He made a face. 'If I have one more, I'll wrinkle to death.'

'How about a beer?'

'Only if you aren't planning on trying to kill us,' NJangu said.

'No. I need you.'

'For what?'

'Guns. Guns to fight the Musth.'

'I didn't promise her anything, one way or another,' Njangu said, *Mil* Angara and *Cent* Hedley listening intently.

'How many fighters did she say she could muster?' Angara said, a bit incredulously.

'Somewhere between a thousand and fifteen hundred,' Garvin said.

Hedley shook his head.

'We flipping didn't do *near* good enough a job of killing 'Raum, did we? And why the hell didn't all these eager flipping young warriors join the Force like we thought they were going to?'

No one bothered to answer.

'To tell the truth,' Njangu said, 'I thought it was a pretty fine idea for some civilian Musth murderers, even if junior-class *aspirants* like me aren't supposed to do situation analysis. The thing is, I didn't know where we could come up with any spare guns, period.'

'Ignoring the fact I'm not really thrilled with the idea of arming a former enemy,' Angara said. 'What happens when they run out of Musth to kill? Are they going to want to go back to old times?'

'Who cares?' Hedley said. 'Like the old joke says, the fall's going to flipping kill us anyway.'

He scratched his chin.

'Angara, my friend, we *could* let our young friends in on a secret. Like where there are nearly two thousand spare bangsticks.'

Njangu and Garvin looked startled.

'Go ahead,' Angara said reluctantly. 'The 'Raum are who they were for in the first place. I guess the gods've got a pretty wacky sense of humor.'

'Seems toward the close of the late unpleasantness,' Hedley said, 'a flipping spaceship just happened to trundle through the Cumbrian skies, and happened to get shot down by one of our Zooks. Everybody dead in the crash, but it was easy to ID the ship and crew as coming from Larix/Kura. It appears that grand gentleman Red-flipping-ruth was trying to stir up the issue by sending guns to the goblins.

'We still don't know who his liaison with the 'Raum was, but at least we've got the guns, carefully stashed in one of our arsenals.'

'You two,' Njangu said, 'don't keep secrets half bad.'

'Of course,' Hedley said comfortably. 'That's why we outrank you. Now, the question is, do we give these perfectly functional guns to Poynton's Pistoleers?'

The three looked at Angara.

'I'm acting commander of the regiment,' he said slowly. 'But this one I think I'd better clear with *Caud* Rao. He's in Kerrier. I suspect he'll approve, on the old saw that the enemy of our enemy is our friend. So you can go ahead and prepare to get the weaponry over to the

Eckmuhl. Hedley, you'll be in charge of the whole operation.'

'I gave Poynton one of our off-channel coms,' Njangu said. 'I'll com her right now.'

'The real flipping problem,' Hedley said, 'is to make sure this little transshipment doesn't get spotted by our friends, which'd be sure to end this nonshooting situation we've lulled them into.'

'If it does, it does,' Angara said. 'I figure we've stretched their patience about as far as we can with the stalling game. The rubber band's going to go *twang* in another day or so anyway, and we're as ready as we can be.'

Caud Rao considered, gave his approval, ordered the operation to be mounted immediately.

Someone set off a bomb in a warehouse on the outskirts of Taman City, close to the Third Regiment's field headquarters, not long after full dark two nights later. The warehouse had been stuffed with waste lubricant from the Force's ACVs, waiting recycling. The bomb blew the lid off the long building, and flames roared high into the skies, attracting planetary attention.

Everyone scrambled – the holo lifters, all heavy fire vehicles. Even the Musth patrols, more from curiosity than anything else, went at full drive toward Taman City, about a thousand kilometers from Leggett.

No one saw an in-system freighter, one of the Force's unrostered acquisitions, lift from the Force's hidden base on Mullion Island, and, flying nap of the earth, soar across Dharma Island's narrow peninsula, just east-southeast of Leggett. It held low over the bay, then banked north, and came in low and fast on Chance Island, landing beyond Camp Mahan, in the maze of ammunition/weapon dumps, its loading ports yawning wide.

Two Griersons and one *aksai* flown by Ben Dill, escorted the ship. *Haut* Jon Hedley was aboard one Grierson. When the freighter landed, the escorts grounded on one of Camp Mahan's distant ranges, waiting.

A three-company-strong working party was waiting for the freighter. Cased weapons, five to a case, were hurriedly loaded aboard, and the freighter lifted off.

It stayed low, over the water, at a moderate speed, and its escorts quickly caught up with it.

The freighter lifted just high enough over the Leggett waterfront to keep from alarming anyone, then landed just inside the Eckmuhl's walls, antigrav hissing softly.

Waiting were Poynton, Garvin, Njangu, and several hundred 'Raum.

No commands were necessary. The 'Raum scurried into the ship, came out lugging cased rifles and ammo crates, disappeared into the depths of the Eckmuhl.

'They'll be broken out of the cases and out of the Eckmuhl for our other fighters before dawn,' Poynton said.

'Smooth.' Garvin admired.

'That's what worries me,' Njangu said. 'That means something's bound to go wrong on the back end.'

Poynton caught his eye, motioned him to her. Garvin saw the action, discreetly walked a few paces away, to where their Cooke waited.

'Thanks,' Poynton said. 'Although I swore I'd never say that to any soldier, even you.'

Njangu shrugged. 'Keeping things stirred up's what makes life interesting for me.' He grinned. 'Seems like you can't stay away from guns, can you?'

Poynton started to get angry, then saw the humor.

'They won't let me, it seems like.'

'Maybe you should've gone with the main chance, and enlisted like some of the others in The Movement did,' he suggested.

'I thought about it,' Poynton confessed. 'But I wasn't sure if the amnesty extended as high up as I was.'

'So you found a nice, safe hiding place . . . right in the middle of PlanGov. Subtle, very subtle, Jo.'

She smiled. 'It worked, didn't it? Nobody blew my cover.'

'True,' Njangu said. 'So what now?'

'We go to ground, and go back to what we know best,' Poynton said. 'Except we'll be sniping at Musth when the time is right for shooting.'

'They're bigger targets,' Njangu said. 'One thing. Remember what happened to Brooks?'

'He got dead,' Poynton said, voice becoming harsh.

'That wasn't what I meant,' Njangu said. 'My call is he was starting to get ideas about the future. Big ideas. I'm not sure, if you folks had won, you would have ended up with the power going where you thought it'd go.'

Poynton's lips thinned.

'And you think I could go the same way . . . even if I concede you were right about Brooks?'

'Having a thousand or so people backing whatever you say with guns can get real seductive, I've been told.'

'Don't worry,' Poynton said. 'I'm not that sort.'

'I don't think you are,' Yoshitaro said. 'But there's nothing wrong with a warning, is there?'

Poynton gave him a hard look.

'You surely know how to get back into a person's good graces, don't you?'

Njangu grinned.

'That's why you're the Councilor and I'm the guy running through the bushes. No goddamned tact at all.'

For some reason, Poynton found herself answering Yoshitaro's grin.

'Look,' he went on, 'you keep that com I gave you handy. It might be my turn to need some help next.'

'If we can, we will.'

The two looked at each other, and Njangu had a sudden desire to lean over and kiss her, and see if she wanted to remember a different night, when she'd worn a blue-velvet jumpsuit.

Perhaps he swayed a little close, perhaps she moved toward him a trifle.

But Garvin called softly.

'Let's hike! The ship's unloaded!'

They broke away, both looking a little embarrassed.

'Next time around, hey?'

Poynton nodded, and trotted after the column of 'Raum, disappearing into the ruins.

The freighter lifted off. turned, and climbed over the walls of the Eckmuhl, headed for the bay.

'Let's go,' Garvin said to his pilot as he and Njangu climbed into the Cooke. 'Hang a zig west out to sea before we cut back toward Mahan. I'd just as rather not be around that freighter. Too big an echo.'

The pilot obeyed, and the Cooke climbed above the Eckmuhl's walls. Ahead was the glistening water of the bay, and Camp Mahan's lights.

Garvin could just see the freighter, above the water as it cleared land.

'This is Toy Six,' his com said. That was Hedley. 'In the air. Climax Mass.'

Continue the mission.

Suddenly a xenon searchlight speared from the darkness, caught the freighter.

One of the coms on Garvin's Cooke scanned to the standard watch frequency:

'Unknown ship, unknown ship, this is the Planetary Police. Identify yourself at once and come to a hover, over.'

Another com came on.

'Planetary Police, this is Confederation business. Douse your light and break off, over.'

But the police, now visible in a modified Cooke, didn't give up.

'Unknown broadcaster, this is Planetary Police. We have no clearance for any operation at this time. Identify yourself at once, and obey our instructions, over.'

'This is Toy Six,' Hedley said. 'I say again, this is Confederation business, none of yours, over.'

'This is Planetary Police. Illuminate yourself or prepare to be fired on. This is your only warning.'

'Toy Baker, this is Toy Six,' Hedley's voice came on the operation's frequency. 'Take the cop out.'

'Toy Baker, roger that.'

'Oh shit,' Njangu muttered.

He saw a spit of fire from out at sea, a missile launch from the other Grierson, and the police Cooke exploded, spun down toward the water.

'This is Toy Six,' Hedley's came voice came. 'Climax Mass, over.'

Garvin clicked his mike sensor once, stomach roiling for an instant, thinking about a pair of stubborn men who'd just gotten very dead, when his driver swore, and pointed to the radar screen.

Over the tiny, spread-out flotilla was a blip, larger than anything except the freighter.

'What the hell . . . Musth, by the speed of it,' Garvin muttered. 'We're for it now.'

An instant later, the freighter blew up as three missiles from the Musth *velv* that'd appeared from nowhere, attracted by the police lights, struck home.

The com waves were a blur of surprise, shock.

'This is Toy Six, Toy Six,' Hedley's voice hammered. 'All stations, keep silence! Stand by for orders.'

But before he could give any, the action had ended.

Ben Dill, lying full length in his *aksai*, had seen the *velv* as soon as it'd fired on the freighter, fed full power into a climb, touched two controls, and missiles whispered out of his launch pods. They barely had time to arm before homing on the *velv*.

The nose of the Musth ship vanished, then its rear finning. The *velv* spun, the pilot regained control for an instant, then lost it, and dived down toward the water. There was a flash of fire, quickly extinguished.

'Son of a bitch,' Njangu said. 'That's torn it.'

TWELVE

For three days there was nothing from the Musth except an ominous silence.

Then, at dusk, they struck Camp Mahan out of the setting sun, arcing around from their base in the Highlands and coming in vertically from space, from Silitric, E-Cumbre.

Velv and mother ships held altitude, lobbing missiles down against the feeble antimissile barrage.

It was as if they'd surprised the Force garrison again, and the missile batteries were taken out within minutes.

Wlencing ordered the landing force down, and *wynt* poured out of mother-ship bays, while *aksai* flew security.

Then the real Force missile stations on Chance unmasked and opened fire. The sites that'd been suppressed had been dummies or automated. Less than half a dozen Force troops died in that first attack.

The missiles came up in swarms, overloaded the Musth ECM operators, struck home in the *wynt* formations.

For a long moment it was boiling madness in the skies. Then Wlencing and his subordinate war leaders regained control, and the invasion continued.

Wynt landed in dead ground behind Camp Mahan, or on the beaches, and Musth warriors bounded out.

The beaches and approaches to the base had been mined, and Musth screeched and died in sandy explosions.

Furies bank-launched, and the rockets harrowed the Musth ranks as Force cannon fired canister at point-blank range, shrapnel spraying the attacking aliens. The Musth were so close that Shrike operators had to send their missiles on a loop out to sea while they armed. Some were hit by Musth antimissiles, but not enough to matter.

The first wave hesitated, fell back to the shelter of their *wynt*, and Shrikes were guided in on them.

The surviving Musth commanders called for immediate support, or permission to lift off, abandon the attack.

Wlencing denied it, ordered the second wave in, preceded by an all-out aerial attack.

Aksai and *velv* strafed the island, attacking any building or possible target. Barracks, hangars, and buildings on Mahan exploded, and flames built a whirlwind into the darkening skies.

But the Force was far underground, in bunkers, gun positions, and launch stations.

More missiles came out of the smoke, and more Musth died.

The second wave came in, was riddled, and pinned down in a thin perimeter around the Force base.

Wlencing hid his rage, claws moving in and out as he paced the bridge of his command ship.

A few minutes later, his intelligence analysts reported all Confederation codes had been changed.

He needed no explanation. If the codes could be changed that rapidly, that meant the Confederation knew he'd been reading their 'secrets,' and were sophisticated enough to make sure they weren't real secrets at all, but false data they wanted him to believe.

And believe it he had, Wlencing thought in fury.

He'd thought the Confederation were passively kneeling under his whip, whereas it was obvious they were waiting for the right time to react. Perhaps they'd lost the initiative at the beginning, but now it appeared they might have been calling the shots for some time.

The first question was: How long?

Wlencing growled aloud, wanted to hurt something, anything, anyone. But he found control. A new thought came, and he almost wanted blind rage to return: What else had the Confederation managed to conceal from him?

He had no answers . . . and needed some, badly and quickly.

More than a thousand kilometers away, on Seya Island, men and women had trotted out of hasty prefabs in and around the massive junkyard the Zhukovs had been abandoned in, just as Force Headquarters reported the first incoming Musth ships. They'd been waiting for some time, after they'd been secretly shuttled back to their ACVs, with nothing to do but practice on sims and be bored.

The Zhukovs, already fueled and armed, were airborne within a dozen minutes, and, in three-ship combat elements, sped toward Chance Island.

Two hundred kilometers from Dharma Island, they climbed into the low ionosphere.

Haut Chaka, CO of Golan Flight, opened his mike and reminded his flight:

'Golan Element, we'll go straight down on 'em. Try for the mother ships, then the transports. Don't play glory girl yet, leave the *aksai* alone. Straight through, then climb, and we'll go back through 'em again.'

Other commanders gave like orders as the Zhukovs closed on Chance Island.

A fisherman, far below and out at sea who'd been staring at the turmoil above Chance Island saw, distant in the sky, gleaming in the last light of the dying sun. flashing reflections. He wondered what they were, went back to gaping at the whatever-the-billy-blue-hell was going on over at the soldiers' camp.

The Zhukovs weren't the most maneuverable combat vehicles ever built, but were among the most heavily armed.

As they dived, their gunners launched ship-killing Goddards. Most of these were taken out by Musth countermissiles, but two hit a mother ship and sent it spinning out of the fight, and four more homed on *velv*, destroying two of them.

Then the *aksai* were in the fight, slashing into the Zhukovs as the heavier craft bucked and swayed, trying to evade combat and go for the soft-skinned troop carriers.

Now it was the Force's turn to take casualties, and Zhukovs blew up, rolled, dived, smoking toward the far-below ground. But more than enough were beyond *aksai* range, covered by Force antiaircraft, and they swept over the landing grounds, missiles hissing out, 150mm autocannon thundering, chainguns chattering. *Wynt* blew up, and the third wave of attacking Musth was shattered.

The *aksai* and *velv*, on Wlencing's orders, screamed down, heedless of AA fire, intent on smashing the Zhukovs.

Then the secret ships from Mullion Island struck, everything from yachts and speedsters with improvised missile racks to close-system patrol craft to the three lovingly restored *aksai*.

The skies were swirling madness, and not even the best of the gunners in RaoForce could hold a target long enough to make a launch, nor be sure they'd be able to guide a missile in without a friendly getting in the way.

Ben Dill put two missiles into a *velv* and took his *aksai* in a tight loop, almost through the wreckage of the ship he'd brought down.

'This is Scythe Six,' he said. 'Scythe Flight, are you still with me?'

'That's affirm,' a rather breathless voice came. 'This is Three. Two's back up there going after a mother ship.'

'This is Two,' a calm voice came. 'Have a mother ship acquired, two seconds to launch, one . . . SHIT!'

The air went dead, and Dill saw a flash of red in the darkness.

'Aw, *giptel*-doots,' he swore, forgetting his mike was open, climbed toward where his flightmate had died, saw two *aksai* diving.

'Now let's see who blinks,' he mumbled, sliding to full drive. 'Come on, come on . . .

The two *aksai* banked sharply, exposing their bellies.

'*Thought* you'd back off first . . .'

Dill launched two missiles. Both homed on the rear Musth ship, and blew it in half.

He and his wingman were hard on the tail of the first Musth ship, but it was pulling away fast, in better and newer shape than the two remaining Force attack ships.

An all-ships signal blasted into Dill's speakers: 'Recall, recall, recall.' Most of the Force's ships broke contact and fled, dumping antiradar cheff and 'casting every electronic spoofery they could, for previously assigned fields, some on Mullion, others in equally secluded parts of Cumbre, some with little more than stacked fuel supplies, two or three mechanics, and an officer or noncom with a communicator. The Musth ships, shocked by the unexpected battle and the tenacity of a defeated enemy, were reluctant to track the

Force craft too closely, and so all but a handful were able to break away.

But Ben Dill was intent on his own battle, after the fleeing *aksai*.

'Oh no, oh no, I need you, I want you,' Dill growled, lifted his ship's nose, and launched three missiles, howitzer-arcing them over the fleeing Musth ship, into its projected flight pattern.

The *aksai* climbed straight into Dill's first missile, and part of its wing came off. It whipped into a spin, then lazily flip-flopped down toward the planet below.

'And aren't I Mrs. Dill's favorite son, all gifted and—'

A wandering missile that should've self-destructed but hadn't, rather tardily sensed a possibility and exploded about ten meters behind Dill's *aksai*. The ship bucked, and its drive abruptly quit.

'Oh come on,' Dill pleaded. 'I really don't want to go swimming tonight.'

The *aksai* wasn't listening. It lurched. flopped onto its back, and started down. Dill sa wed at the controls, felt nothing but mush.

'Scythe Three, Scythe Three, this is Scythe Six. I'm in a Mayday condition.'

Nothing came back at him. and he noted all the indicator lights on his com were out.

'Dunno if I'm broadcasting,' he said into the mike. 'But this is Ben Dill, punching out. Somebody be good and come get me. Out.'

He pushed a small overhead bar to one side, and the *aksai*'s canopy blew off. Wind roared into the cockpit at him, more than 180kph, pulling his cheeks back until he slammed his helmet visor shut. Dill hit the button that seared away his safety straps. Now the only thing that was holding him was the hurricane into the open pod.

His *aksai* spun on its axis once, dumping Ben Dill out

into the night sky, the dropper that'd been stuffed between his ankles behind him.

He fell about five seconds, tumbling, long enough to decide he really was going to be dead. Then the dropper cut in, and he realized he was slowing as the antigrav lowered him at walking speed toward the ground.

Dill was hanging half-in, half-out of the dropper harness, and he managed to pull the straps together, fasten them. Now the small box was above him, like an old-fashioned parachute, and he was dropping toward . . . toward what?

He looked down, saw blackness.

At a distance, there were lights. He guessed that would be Dharma Island.

That meant the blackness below was ocean.

'Crap in my hat,' he muttered. 'And I never made the swim team, either.'

Then lights came at him, blinding him, and an aircraft slashed by and Dill had a moment to see it was an *aksai*.

'I'd just as soon not be gunned down when I'm out of the fight,' he muttered, and the *aksai* banked past again and he thought, hoped, it was his wingman or maybe just a chivalrous Musth.

He held out his hands in perplexed helplessness, pointed down, made swimming motions.

The *aksai* slowed almost to its stall speed, came past again. He couldn't see inside the cockpit pod, make out the pilot.

Dill looked down again, saw greater darkness in front of him and what might have been a dim line demarking it.

Breakers? An island? If it's a mass as big as I want it to be, Mullion Island?

Who knew?

Especially about Mullion Island. Good legends – aquatic monsters, amphibious monsters, land-dwelling monsters, everything except cannibals. All that was known for sure was the area around the secret base, which, if he was triangulating himself right, would be somewhere over there. Quite a ways over there.

Then he saw a flicker of some kind of light.

The moons are obscured, so what am I staring at? A fishing boat? A village? A hopeful thought?

He found the dropper's tiny control box on the harness, pried its cover open, breaking a nail in the process, and touched sensors, steering the dropper toward the light.

The *aksai* came past again, then dived away, went back to speed, was gone.

Ben Dill saw darker blackness below, hoped he was coming in for a nice soft landing in some trees or in beach sand. The light he was steering for was not far distant, almost level with him.

Come on, be nice, be land, he thought, looked at where the horizon should be, kept his boots together, let his legs go limp, grabbed the dropper harness high, tried to remember a prayer, and struck water, salt water, his arms coming down to cover his face, and then he was underwater, roiled by the current, drowning.

THIRTEEN

'Son of a bitch,' Garvin said devoutly. 'I always thought ol' Ben was immortal.'

'So did he,' Njangu said. 'Guess you were both wrong.'

'I suppose the Musth ain't gonna stop shooting long enough to let us drink him under,' Monique Lir said.

'Not likely,' Njangu agreed. 'But when they do stop, there'll be a bunch of other crunchies with him for the wake, so we can really toast our brains.'

'What a joy and a comfort you are,' Garvin said, as an alarm on the bunker's concrete wall blared and the three ran toward their alert stations.

This time the Musth came in by sea, sending their *wynt* skidding low over the water, using Leggett City as a shield to keep Force gunners from opening up on them.

Velv and *aksai* flashed overhead, looking for targets, but found few in the smoking rubble.

'All missile stations,' *Caud* Rao ordered. 'Make your launches count. Gun stations, aim low. A splash is as good as a direct hit.'

They were. *Wynt* slammed into water bursts that flowered up, the sea as solid as concrete when a ship smashed into it. Other *wynt* pilots' nerves broke, and they climbed for a bit of altitude, exposing vulnerable undersides.

Force missile launchers popped up, launched, vanished back underground before counterstrikes could be made.

Only a scattering of *wynt* made it to the beach and disgorged their warriors, some of whom found shelter with their pinned-down brothers.

Force snipers and two-man SSW teams crawled out of spider holes and opened fire. The Musth shot back – but they were on the Force's home grounds, and generally found few targets.

Frustration begat anger begat rage, and Musth got careless – and more joined their fellows in death.

Yet another Musth attack was stopped before it had begun.

'You have our concern.' Wlencing's chief aide, Rahfer said.

Wlencing glanced from the screen he was studying to Rahfer and another aide, Daaf.

'There is a gap in the continuity without him,' he admitted. 'But Alikhan is not the first cub of mine to die in battle, and we all die in our time. It is more important that he died well, and coming from my loins, I know he did.'

Rahfer moved a paw in agreement.

'Now he is of the past, and not part of any equation,' Wlencing said. 'We should be devoting ourselves to ending this absurd situation.

'I do not believe these men can fight this handily. Certainly we saw nothing of this before, when they fought against the worms who called themselves 'Raum.'

'Perhaps that is the answer,' Daaf said. 'Perhaps they fight well with a worthier foe.'

'That is the rankest sentimentality,' Wlencing

scoffed. 'And not worth discussing. What is important is that they have caused great losses among our warriors.'

'Almost a quarter of our fighters,' agreed Rahfer.

'We could deploy nuclear devices,' Daaf suggested.

'Not to be considered,' Wlencing said scornfully. 'What are the chances of radiation striking any of the cities they fight close to? Even Leggett could be easily contaminated by winds from a strike against their base island. And I am not sure, as well entrenched as they are, such devices would have significant effect.

'Remember, we need these men for when the fighting is over, to work the mines, and other services.'

'Why don't they come out and fight, as warriors should?' Daaf grumbled. Rahfer was about to show agreement when Wlencing's ears cocked, and his eyes reddened.

'You do not serve me by serving or speaking foolishly! Why should you expect anyone to fight on your terms, under your conditions, if he is capable of doing damage in other ways?'

'Still,' Daaf said, unconvinced, 'this is not honorable.'

'I will admit to that,' Wlencing said. He looked back at the screen, showing the swirling destruction on Chance Island. Other screens showed the battles around Aire, Taman City, Kerrier. 'It is also primitive, the way groundworms fight to keep from being pulled from their burrows. It is time for a change in our strategy.

'We have two choices, I think. We can wait them out, in this battle they call, in their language, a 'sssiege,' keeping a constant pressure on them. I do not like this, because it assumes a probable continuation of the casualty rate we have been taking.

'But I have been studying some of their histories. There is another way to fight this war, and if it lacks honor, so does their fighting, as we have agreed.

'And after all, these men cannot understand real honor, can they?'

'I cannot believe this,' Jasith said.

'Darling, you're being utterly naive,' Loy said. 'They're aliens, animals. So of course that's the way they fight.'

'I'm not talking about the Musth,' Jasith snapped. 'I believe they're capable of anything, so nothing from them surprises me. What I don't believe is the way you're jumping in bed with them so happily, like you can't wait to do whatever they want next.'

'I'll tell you this again,' Kouro said. 'We don't have any choice. Our stupid soldiers are over there on their island, bottled up, so they're no good to us. What am I supposed to do? Tell the Musth to shove it? How long after I did that do you think it'd be before they shut my holo down and put all my people out of work?'

'Isn't it strange,' Jasith said, not looking at her husband. 'Rich people always seem to have the same way of talking. Something they don't like isn't bad for them, but for their employees. You'd think we got the way we are by bleeding anytime somebody said widows and orphans.'

'What do you think we're supposed to do?' Loy demanded. 'What would you do, if you were me?'

Jasith considered an answer, discarded it, found another.

'I'd let them close me down rather than give them the cameras and crews so everybody in the system is forced to look at what they're going to do next.'

Kouro shook his head.

'Your father wouldn't believe you're talking like this. He built an empire, and damned well would've died before surrendering one millimeter of it.'

'I think you can leave my father well out of this,' Jasith said. 'If he were alive, I think he'd be over there, with the quote stupid end quote soldiers. Or at any rate, trying to figure out some way to help them.'

'Well, aren't you Miss Resistance herself,' Kouro sneered. 'And what are you doing, I might ask? Besides sitting up here in your mansion wringing your hands? Perhaps you'd like to throw a benefit tea for the Force? Or maybe roll bandages, like I read they did in olden times?'

Jasith stared out the window, across the bay at the murk around Chance Island. She could see diving Musth aircraft and, every now and then, hear the dull blast of a distant explosion.

'I don't know,' she said. 'I don't know. But I'm going to do something.'

'That'll be very bright,' Kouro said. 'I can't wait to see my wife's name on the Musth Enemy List.'

'They're taking hostages,' *Mil* Rees, CO of First Regiment said grimly. The tight beam between Aire and the Force's base blurred, then refirmed. 'They took thirty in Aire, they've announced, and said there'd be others taken in other cities. I'm surprised it hasn't hit Leggett yet.'

'Have they announced any intents?' *Caud* Rao asked. Rees shook her head.

'Nothing, sir. But all the holos say there'll be a broadcast tomorrow at midday.'

Rao looked at Angara, Hedley, soliciting opinions.

'Keep the troops away from the holo sets,' Hedley said. 'Whatever it is, it won't be good.'

It wasn't.

'This is *Matin*'s Aire Bureau, broadcasting live,' the toneless, off-screen voice said. 'We are 'casting on the direct orders of the Musth.'

The screen showed a high, blank concrete wall. After a moment, there was an off-screen *thud* of a steel door slamming open. Fifteen men and women moved onscreen. They looked frightened, confused, and were staring about.

'These fifteen,' the voice continued, 'are hostages seized by the Musth, and are considered by them leaders of Cumbre.'

A mike clicked closed, and another voice, this one Musth, came on.

'Becausse of the continuing fighting, it hasss been decccided that all humansss in the sssytem onccce known asss Cumbre are to be held resssponsssive, in other wordsss, to be consssidered criminalsss.

'The fighting mussst end immediately.

'If it doesss not, all humansss held by usss will meet the end decccided by our leadersss.'

The people on-screen had a moment to show fear, and then devourer-weapons opened fire. Blood gouted, bodies contorted, and then the crawling worms began their final destruction.

The camera held steady until the last body stopped moving.

Garvin looked away from the screen, saw Njangu's face, trying hard to hold the same dispassion.

'Within a ssshort time,' the voice continued, 'if the fighting isss not ended, othersss will die, asss we promisssed. Further prisssonersss will then be taken.'

'I wonder what reaction the CO'll have to this?' Garvin said.

Before Njangu could respond, their bunker's PA set opened.

'This is *Caud* Rao. All Force personnel are advised we are launching an attack against the Musth immediately. There can be no negotiation.'

'Guess that's the answer,' Garvin said.

'Not enough of one,' Njangu said. 'I want to do something really nasty back at them.

'And a little bit more direct, maybe.'

The Legion attack came from space, from one of the manned stations on Fowey, D-Cumbre's largest moon, that the invaders had missed, since most of it was far underground, concerned with seismic development on satellites.

A research ship had its forward spaces packed with mining explosives, and a fairly simple homing device installed. The ship launched, and drove at speed 'down' toward the planet.

Its two-man crew huddled nervously over high-magnification screens as the planet grew and grew. The screens centered on the airspace above Chance Island.

'There,' the woman commander said. 'That's one of their mother ships.'

'Got it,' the man announced. 'Tracking . . . locked . . . let's get the hell out!'

The two ran for the lifecraft coupled to the nearest lock, dived into it, and shot away from the doomed research ship, clawing up for empty space.

They almost made it, but they showed up on an *aksai*'s screens. The pilot launched a spread of missiles, and the tiny ship blew up.

Two seconds later, the research ship smashed into the Musth mother ship, and, for an instant, there was a new sun in C-Cumbre's sky.

But that wasn't enough.

'One man, sorry, one Musth, leadership, right, Jon?' Njangu asked.

'So it appears,' Hedley said.

'Which would be this Wlencing?'

'Probably.'

'Here's what I want,' Njangu said, and explained. Hedley considered.

'Sure,' he said. 'That takes no signal analysis other'n a flipping abacus. But you and I&R won't be able to mount the operation.'

'Why not?' Garvin asked. 'We slither out from here and—'

'And probably get blown out of the sky before you get a klick,' Hedley responded. 'No. We do this another way.'

The Musth tried another tactic. Heavy rockets, semi-guided, not unlike the Force's Furies, but far larger, were wave-launched against Chance Island. The ground shook, shimmered as blast waves crisscrossed the ruins.

But only a handful of Force women and men died.

Underground it was dusty, dry, claustrophobic. But it was better than being on the surface.

Camp Mahan continued to hold.

'Well,' Hedley said, 'this flipping Wlencing isn't a total idiot.'

'Close, though,' Njangu said. 'Doesn't seem to worry about a general staff, or any kind of subordinating command. We act, he's the one who calls for the reaction.'

'Close enough to get killed, I hope,' Hedley said. 'We're mounting the shot in an hour. No missiles – Rao doesn't want to chance they've got spoofers. Cross your fingers.'

Njangu shook his head.

'I don't believe in luck. The other guy's the one who's usually got it.'

*

The two converted speedsters had only one weapon apiece, both huge, hastily constructed bombs. They took off from the secret airbase on Mullion Island just before dawn, made several jigs to confuse their point of origin. then flew very low, and very slowly, east-north-east across the open water toward Dharma Island, spray slashing up in their wake. They maintained electronic silence, and made visual contact with Dharma just as the sun was lightening the skies. They climbed as they came over the beach, but held bare meters above the jungle.

Ahead, the ground rose toward the great plateau of the Highlands, and mist swirled in front of them. They prayed their altimeters had height-adjusted correctly. navigated through the murk using Sat Positioning, not chancing radar, holding to less than twenty meters above the ground, just at 125kph, almost stalling speed.

Both navigators watched coordinated time ticks on the screens in front of them.

The commander finally spoke.

'Able.'

Both ships went to full secondary power, climbed sharply to two hundred meters, and turned their Target Acquisition radar on.

'Target acquired,' the first said.

'Got it, too,' came from the second.

'Beginning drop count,' the first said.

Njangu had figured if Wlencing was the Musth's single commander, it should be simple to find a single source for signals. Technicians searched, and found a blare of coms. They came from the Highlands, where the Musth had their headquarters before the war started, emanating not from the clustered buildings, but about a kilometer south and east. Wlencing, as Hedley had said, wasn't a complete fool. But he was overconfident. In spite of the Force's worries, no antihoming stations had been built.

The two speedsters smashed toward the low cluster of prefabricated buildings that was the Musth headquarters.

Both pilots dimly noted blips on their screens – belatedly, the Musth were launching.

'Beta,' the commander said, and the two ships shot up to drop altitude.

'Five seconds.'

At the count, a bulbous object fell away from the lead ship, dropped, hit the ground and bounced high into the sky.

As it did, the second ship launched its bomb, more a rectangular case than anything aerodynamic. Lifters deployed, and the weapon fell slowly toward the ground.

The first bomb hit, blew, and the shock wave rolled across the Highlands, over the base. Trees, Musth aircraft, buildings shattered in the blast.

The second case detonated about ten meters above the ground. Again, a heavy charge, but these explosives had been packed amid scrap iron, glass – anything that would make lethal shrapnel.

The charge sprayed across the swampland, a murderous scythe.

Unfortunately, the first bomb had gone off short, on the edges of the Musth base, and the second exploded exactly where it should – a few dozen meters short of the first blast.

High-ranking Musth, including three of Wlencing's aides, died, as well as a hundred of his warriors and pilots.

But Wlencing and most of his staff lived on.

Njangu's dream of a single, war-ending stroke had failed.

FOURTEEN

The exchange could hardly have been called a conversation. Even with hyperspace relay stations linking the three Musth, each signal took several hours to transmit back and forth. The three were Wlencing, Paumoto, and Keffa, Paumoto's younger firebrand of a compatriot.

'Your progress is not good,' Paumoto began.

'I am aware of that,' Wlencing said. 'I hardly need another to correct me.'

'I am not interested in correcting you,' Paumoto said. 'I merely thought, since we frequently share a commonality of interests, you might appreciate being informed of some further changes within our worlds.'

'That cursed Senza,' Keffa added, 'has been steadily pushing for a consensus calling for withdrawal, or at least an attempt to return to our further détente with Man.'

'If you had conquered Cumbre as quickly as you promised,' Paumoto added, 'he would have been digging in an abandoned burrow. But as it is . . .'

'Circumstances became different and more difficult than we had anticipated,' Wlencing said. 'Such is not uncommon in war.'

'Nor in politics,' Paumoto added. 'But changes must be allowed for, and when unexpected events happen, new strategies, tactics, must be devised.'

'Why are you so concerned about my affairs?'
Wlencing demanded.

The time delay gave Paumoto a chance to lose his
temper, recover it, and make a politic response. Such was
not the case from Keffa, whose ire could continue on for
days. He blurted, 'Because your affairs are a wedge for
Senza against both of us, and our allies.'

Paumoto's response was: 'Senza has interested himself
in Cumbre, and thereby created interest from others who
previously were unconcerned or neutral.'

Wlencing had enough sense to control his response,
and replied, in a tone that from humans might've been
plaintive:

'But why does he scurry about my trail?'

'Because,' Paumoto answered, forcing patience, 'your
manner of thinking, of behaving, is one that he and his
clan and their sympathizers have decided is wrong for the
Musth, denying our true path, our destiny.'

'What does he want? To make an alliance with Man?'

Keffa growled inarticulately.

'That is almost precisely what he does wish,' Paumoto
said. 'His projections, his analyses, incorrect, certainly,
suggest that the universe is large enough for both species,
at least for a time. We should form alliances, temporary
or for longer periods, that would be immediately beneficial to us, and need not concern ourselves with the
long-range effects.

'In the end, Senza says the Musth will prove stronger
than Man. In millennia to come, we shall conquer them,
obliterate them peacefully, merely by our presence, and
by the clear fact our destiny was predecided by our creator and they are nothing more than bumbling, lucky
genetic sports.'

'Mystical wormshit!' Wlencing said. 'Power goes to
those who seize it and remains with them as long as they

are strong enough to hold it. That is the only secret of the universe, and I cannot understand why Senza, for all his purported intelligence, cannot grasp that simple fact.'

'This is going nowhere at a rapid rate,' Paumoto said. 'I have already spent more than a full day in this transmission room, and nothing has been developed save cublike pouting.

'I shall not dictate to you, Wlencing, for you are, as you say, a powerful and admirable being, if, at the moment, you appear somewhat thick-skulled.

'Keffa and I are doing what we can to keep the situation from deteriorating, and will continue to do so. Again, this is a matter that suits us, suits our interests. If you fail, there is a great chance we ourselves shall lose a portion of the power we wield.'

'So what do you wish me to do?'

'*Win*,' Keffa said. 'Win handily, win rapidly. It does not matter what it takes. We are prepared to send selected clansmen to reinforce you, if that is needed.

'But you must emerge victorious. Otherwise, you may well have made me, and possibly Paumoto, into your enemies.'

FIFTEEN

Ben Dill hit bottom, let himself stay there for a minute as he reflexively hit the dropper quick-release tabs. *Rather not be drowned by my own rig, and it'll be a long swim back to the surface*, and he pushed up hard, swimming, and realized he was standing in thigh-deep surf.

He felt a complete fool for an instant, then a breaker knocked him spinning, and he went underwater again. Once more he picked himself up, and this time felt the straps of his dropper brush his chest. He grabbed it, not sure what he could use the damned thing for, but anything is a potential tool to a crash survivor.

He ate another wave, stumbled, but kept his feet. That gave him the direction of the shore, and he waded for it, knocked down twice before he reached the beach, gritty under his feet.

It didn't look, in the darkness, like much of a beach, no more than a few meters before the jungle rose.

He was sandy, out of breath, bruised from his pinwheeling fall, but by somebody's gods, still alive.

Forgetting himself, he yodeled in glee.

Mrs. Dill's favorite boy is still in the game!

Something roared back at him from the jungle. It sounded close, bigger than Dill, and hungry.

Dill cursed — silently — and began trying to figure what to do next.

The roaring came again, and Dill squatted, just at the waterline, and looked around. To one side, not far distant, something black rose. He made for it, found a nest of rocks, and crept into their midst, grateful for some kind of shelter.

Damned glad I didn't try to do a landing fall on top of those friggin' boulders. Now all I have to do is live until dawn.

He thought of his survival packs, took them out of his flight suit's pouches on either leg. Small pistol. Good. A very small sort of pistol when he wanted a rocket launcher for that howler in the darkness. But still good. A folding knife with several blades. Good. A flarepencil. He considered launching one, decided against it. Finally, his SatPos fumbled out. He turned it on, swore. The small panel light must have broken. Never mind. In the morning.

He remembered the light he'd seen. He scanned darkness, thought he saw a dying glimmer. He chanced going outside the rocks to find a bit of driftwood, and positioned it firmly in the sand, hopefully above the hightide line, pointing at the light. Tomorrow, that'd give him a track to follow.

Now all he had to do was wait until dawn.

He found a nice solid rock to put his back against. held the ever-more-tiny pistol in one hand, the knife in the other, and waited.

The roarer roared three times more over the hours.

Eventually, after approximately fifty-six hundred Eyears, the sky lightened and dawn came. It was gray. overcast, muggy, rain threatening.

Dill considered his surroundings. Thick jungle ahead. A narrow, curving beach of black sand stretching to either side. Behind him . . . Dill grimaced.

Long lines of breakers smashed over rocks toward him. If he'd landed in that . . .

'I am living *right*,' he said confidently. Now for a little rescue, a good meal, and some sleep before getting back to the war.

He found his Search and Rescue com, and it looked and acted no livelier than the one in his *aksai*. Dill muttered about technology, then took out his SatPos.

It, at least, was functioning. He touched the LOCATE button, and it *dit-dit-ditted* at him. Then the screen lit:

```
POSITION UNKNOWN.  RETURN TO BASE UNIT
        FOR RECALIBRATION
```

Wondering what the hell could go somewhat wrong with bubble circuitry, Dill grudgingly tucked away another bit of failed electronics with the rest of his high-technology world, in an ankle pocket where it wouldn't get in the way.

He wondered why his survival kit didn't have an old-fashioned compass, though the way his luck was going, he probably would have sat on it. But Dill decided, when he hiked home, he'd make some changes to the pack before he got shot down again.

He finally decided to go the way his stick from the night before pointed. Then the overcast lightened, and he had another option.

He stuck a twig in the sand, noted the dim shadow it cast, then checked his watch finger for the time. Before the clouds obscured the sun again, he hastily scribed an old-fashioned analog clock in the sand, with fourteen hours, a bit more than half a day on D-Cumbre.

He positioned the current hour at the twig, numbered around as evenly as he could. Between fourteen and that hour was, roughly, south.

Which was approximately the direction his stick of the night before pointed, which meant Dharma Island was over there somewhere to the east-southeast, across the heaving sea, gray as the sky. Just a hair westerly of south would be the direction of the secret base, deep in the jungle. So all he had to do was hike south until some convenient god told him where to cut inland to find the base.

That was for later, he thought. He found dry rations in the survival pack, which needed only fresh water for them to be edible. Unfortunately, he didn't see any fresh water.

Let's go look for that light first, although with the way things are going, it'll be some scrap metal reflecting something or other I didn't notice.

The dropper's pack was seven-eighths charged. Not knowing what he'd do with not quite enough antigrav to lift him, but just ease him down slowly, but also not wanting to discard anything possibly useful, just as he'd been taught, he slung the pack over one shoulder and started up the beach.

He followed the beach through two small bays, and was beginning to think he was chasing after some sort of illusion when he saw the *aksai*.

It was the one he'd downed in the dogfight – missing half a wing, some of its tail section, weapons pods, and the canopy of the pilot's pod gone. Dill was hoping the pilot had successfully ejected when he saw something . . . someone . . . dangling out of the cockpit, still held in by shoulder straps, its head about half a meter above the incoming tide.

Ben Dill, in spite of having killed his share and some, never had much interest in collecting scalps, ears, pictures, or any other trophy connected with corpses, thinking such association could be contagious. He was about to hurry on when the body moved.

Still worse, something else moved just beyond the breaker line, something dark and tentacled that wasn't an illusory rock.

Shit, shinola, and little green apples, he thought, dumped his dropper, and waded out toward the *aksai*. The tentacled one, still not showing anything except black ropes Dill knew would be slimy and strong, edged closer.

There was matted dark fluid on the Musth's fur that he guessed was their equivalent of blood. A wave came up, splashed the pilot's face clean, and Dill recognized him, as the Musth opened his eyes.

It was Alikhan, Wlencing's cub.

Alikhan saw the pistol, dwarfed in Dill's paw.

'Good,' he said. 'To go now is better than to wait to die.'

'Shaddup,' Dill said, sticking the gun in a pocket of his flight suit, taking out the folding survival knife, and spring-opening a saw blade. 'Don't worry about me, but about Ol' Ropy out there.'

He looked for the harness quick-release, saw it had been bunged up in the impact, and started cutting at the harness.

'Is anything broken?'

'Not that I am aware of,' Alikhan said. 'But I have been dangling here for some time, and am numb, so don't know if, in fact—'

The last strap broke, and Alikhan dropped onto Dill's chest, and both of them fell into waist-deep water. Spluttering, Dill surfaced, just in time to feel a tentacle, as slimy as he'd expected, tentatively stroke him.

Remembering a childhood cellar full of slimy things that bit, Dill's mind yammered, while his hand clawed the minuscule pistol out of his flight suit. He pointed back over his shoulder, pulled the trigger, and a surprisingly loud blast came. The tentacle whipped away, and Dill, through salt-water-filled eyes, saw something big and black submerging as it swam away.

Then he was on his feet, muscling Alikhan up.

The Musth was hissing in amusement.

'Very goddamned funny,' Dill said. 'It wasn't you Slitherpuss was trying to add to his larder.'

'I was merely pleased by seeing two such great pilot-heroes as ourselves stymied by something simply animalistic.'

'On an animal's turf,' Dill said, 'always bet on the animal. Now, you got anything in this busted-up ship that could keep either of us, preferably me, alive until we reach civilization?'

'A few things,' Alikhan said, paw moving smoothly toward a pack clipped to the remains of his seat. Dill had the pistol aimed.

'Uh-uh,' he said 'Keep your hands away from that.'

Alikhan obeyed, and Dill grabbed the pack.

'Anything else? Just point, and Daddy will get.'

'Nothing. I did not assume I was going to lose the engagement,' Alikhan said.

' 'Kay,' Dill said. 'Now let's get our asses on dry land and we can debate what happens next.'

He waved the pistol, and Alikhan waded ahead of him to the beach. Dill, keeping one eye on the Musth, opened the pack and found one of the small ultra-acid pistols, and three wasp-grenades.

'No food, just weapons, huh?'

'What did your supporters pack for you?'

'One gun, a knife, a day or so's worth of dry rations and a bunch of beep-boops that didn't work, plus other junk,' Dill said.

'I suppose they think after a day a good pilot lives on the purest oxygen and courage?'

'Knock off the humor for a minute,' Dill said. 'We've got a pecking order to establish.'

'I do not understand, not having a beak?'

'I mean, who's in charge.'

'You have the gun, do you not?' Alikhan asked.

'Yeh,' Dill said. 'But sooner or later I've got to get some sleep, and I'd just as soon not have you jump me the minute I nod off.

'So let's start at the beginning: I'm the ranking badass, right?'

'I assume you mean that since you were lucky enough to shoot me down, you make the rules.'

'Lucky my left testicle,' Dill said. 'You flew right into my missile, so I guess that makes me the winner.'

'This time,' Alikhan said. 'But there will always be another.'

'That's what we're discussing,' Dill said. 'Do you Musth recognize parole? That's when you give your word, your promise, not to either try to bash my head in or escape until I release you from that promise.'

'That is an amusing concept,' Alikhan said. 'Why would you not promise an enemy anything he wants?'

His back fur ruffled a bit.

'I can finish the thought,' Dill said. 'Until you get a chance to drygulch him from the rear.'

Alikhan inclined his head. 'You understand well. Musth are not in the habit of taking prisoners. However, there are exceptions. For instance, you did me a service by not permitting that unseen beast to pull my head off, or do whatever disgusting thing he had in mind. We Musth recognize a debt such as that.

'So if you wish to have that debt repaid by me giving this parole, then I shall. And I shall honor that promise.'

'We've got ourselves a start,' Dill said. 'Now. Who's gonna come looking for you? An *aksai* . . . I don't know if it was the last one we've got flying or one of yours . . . did a flyby on me last night, while I was hanging in the dropper. Suppose it was yours?'

'It probably was not,' Alikhan said thoughtfully. 'You killed Yalf, which means the pilot coming past you would have been Tvem. He is constantly talking about wanting to destroy all humans, so I assume he would've killed you as you hung there.'

'You're not thinking he had a bit of mercy for a helpless being?'

Alikhan moved his paws from side to side, discarding the improbable concept. 'Perhaps he was out of ammunition.'

'Let's say that was the case. And let's say this Tvem knew you weren't killed. Will your people send out a search party?'

'I would not think so,' Alikhan said, 'unless they saw me land safely. We Musth, especially one who is Wlencing's cub, are meant to die nobly when we die, but we certainly *must* be dead, not fallen into the enemy's hands. Already four of my den brothers and sisters have gone on,' he said, and Dill thought he could detect a bit of mournfulness in the Musth's voice.

'So Daddy won't come looking,' mused Dill. 'So suppose that was Jacqueline flying that heap. She sees I'm alive, and goes back to the Force, and they start looking for me.

'Only problem is, they'll come looking from . . . from somewhere you don't need to know about, and will have to wait until you folks aren't hanging about. Which could be today, tomorrow, or next week.

'Which means neither one of us have got our nursies screaming around the bushes looking for us wandering babes. So we might as well take a hike, God helping those who help themselves and so forth.'

'We might as well.' Alikhan agreed. 'Which way?'

Dill pointed.

'We follow this beach long enough, and we'll be able to see Dharma Island, over . . . there. Then either we get help from my friends, or else we build a raft and put to sea.'

'You actually think we can survive this experience?' Alikhan said. 'That we shall not leave our bones bleaching on this forgotten strand?'

'Who taught you Basic?' Dill demanded. 'Edgar Allan Poe? Of course I don't. Hup-ho. Let's hike.'

The beach, unfortunately, didn't continue forever, and was interrupted by streams, mudflats, and headlands twice. Each time the two had to cut into the jungle until they could pass over or through the obstacle. Intermittent rain made the going more difficult.

When they made it back to the ocean, the first order was to sluice off the mud and insects.

'You know,' Dill observed as he waded out of the surf, 'next time around, I think I'll arrange to have a tail, even a stubby one like yours. Makes life easier when you've got to toddle through the tules.'

'You have that option?' Alikhan managed. 'Why hasn't your race arranged for that before?'

'I was making a joke,' Dill said. 'Not a very good one, but the best I can manage under the circumstances.'

'I admit,' Alikhan said, 'I am not that pleased with the course of events.'

'Shows what happens when you go and start a war,' Ben suggested. 'No guts, no glory, like they used to say.'

Alikhan looked at him for a moment, then got up.

'Let us go on.'

At some time around midday, they found a spring, and

mixed up two of Dill's rations. One was labeled BEEF WITH JUICES, the other GIPTEL AND BEANS.

'You're the enemy,' Dill said, 'so you get the beans.'

Dill opened his pouch, let water trickle in, then resealed the pouch and hit the heat tab at the base. The pouch got hot, and steam came out.

Alikhan awkwardly did the same.

'We eat with our fingers?'

'Should be a spoon on the side. Pull it away.'

'Ah. Clever.'

They chewed in silence.

'Since you are eating along with me,' Alikhan said, 'I assume you aren't attempting to poison me with this.'

'The theory is,' Ben suggested, 'these rations make you so damned mean you can survive anything.'

'An excellent theory. I think I am now ready to walk on water across to safety, or perhaps sprout wings.'

'Those *gip* 'n' unmentionables aren't *that* bad.'

'Yes they are.'

Dill pushed a vine aside, looked for a nongloppy foothold, stepped forward, hastily changed his point of aim as a creature about the size of his head that looked like an earth frog that'd had something large land on it hissed.

Dill went one way, the creature went another.

Then it roared at him – the same roar that had sent him cowering for the rocks the night before.

'I'll be dipped,' he said. 'Little guys sure make a lot of noise.'

Alikhan, who had leapt back in alarm, unbristled his fur.

'Perhaps it is now time to discuss returning my gun.'

'I'm still pondering how much I believe your parole,' Dill said. 'I'll report back to you on that one.'

*

A river curled into the ocean, dotted with deep pools. A crag rose next to it, with a shelf that hung out far enough to give shelter against the rain, which had become a steady downpour.

Dill dragged fallen branches into a pile, then found a decaying stump. He kicked it open, scooped dry sawdust into his hands, put that next to his firewood. With his pistol set at low power, he sizzled the sawdust into life then patiently fed branches, smaller, then larger, into the blaze.

Alikhan huddled on a log, watching.

'I am impressed,' he said. 'None of my training gave me this.'

'Your training evidently didn't figure you'd ever lose,' Dill said. 'We're more realistic.'

'I'm not sure that a little practice in losing might not be good,' Alikhan said. 'When I studied under Senza of the *Polperros*, he and his cadre were forever going on about how the Musth were hurting themselves by failing to gain from the past, particularly the past's defeats.

'My father thought that was nonsense, and antidestiny. We Musth should only concern ourselves with the future, and with victories.'

'The problem with rhetoric, either way,' Dill said, 'is that it don't put beans in the belly.'

'I suppose we are going to have another of your dried feasts again, which is slightly better than nothing,' Alikhan said. 'Although I despise always being in your debt.'

'Don't worry about it,' Dill said. 'I'm real comfortable with folks owing me. But I'd rather save the rats for an emergency. C'mon.'

'And I was just beginning to become dry,' Alikhan said, but followed the hulking man back toward the river.

'This is fishing lesson number one,' Ben said.

'I know how to fish,' Alikhan said. 'Shall I cut poles, or do we make nets from clothing threads?'

'I said fish, not play about,' Dill said. 'First, we need to know whether any body of water got fish. Ah-ho. I see something moving. Hopefully it's not something that's interested in eating Ben Dill or his buddy.

'Now, we need a nice pool. Not a deep one, because you being the pupil, me being the master, you're going wading.'

They went a dozen meters upstream.

'This one looks about right, especially 'cause there's some narrows here. I take my little gill net from the pack, string it across here, so there's no escapees. But that's incidental. Watch and listen closely, class, and feel free to ask questions, because this is the hard part.'

Dill took one of Alikhan's wasp-grenades from his pocket.

'Pity this isn't a blast-grenade or a hunk of Telex. According to what we learned about your weaponry, you thumb this little doodad here, which gives you a count of, oh, six or seven before it goes whammy and weasels eat your flesh.'

'Be careful,' Alikhan said. 'If the insects do not find a ready target, and you're too close, you can be stung to death by them.'

'They'll be too busy drowning,' Dill said. 'Now, I pre-pare for the cast, keeping excellent posture and stance, thumb the fiendish thingy, and delicately place the fly directly upon the swirling water where we last saw our magnificent prey.'

The grenade went into the pool and half a dozen seconds later there was a muffled blast and a small white column of water frothed. Seconds later, fish floated to the surface.

'And now we harvest. Get your furry butt in the pool. Toss all of them onto the bank, and you'll see a lot more, stunned, down on the bottom. They'll recover, so don't fart around grabbing them.'

Some minutes later, they had an impressive pile of fish.

'Next we gut them and throw the guts back into the river. Notice, we're not taking the finny ones back to the camp to clean, because Lord alone knows who haunts this wilderness, and we don't need to be setting out bait.'

'This is an incredible number of fish,' Alikhan said. 'I do not know if even I can eat half.'

'We would have a choice here,' Dill said. 'If we knew we were going to be out here in the bush for very long, we should lay over a day and smoke 'em in the fire. Or, if we had more of your little bangies, we could be wasteful and just move on, fishing as we go.

'I dunno which'd be the best idea. I've got some hooks and line in my gear, so maybe we should just honk up what we can tonight, and keep moving.'

In the early afternoon of the next day, they heard a high whine, craned upward, and saw, shooting in and out of the clouds, a Confederation-design speedster.

'Hot damn,' Dill exulted. 'Here comes rescue, if I do things right.'

He fumbled through his pack, found a mirror with a hole in its center.

'I just sorta peek through here, flash back and forth, hoping that bastard up there dreamin' among the clouds happens to look down and YOWP he did!'

The aircraft banked into a dive, and Dill began jumping up and down, waving.

'I am not pleased,' Alikhan said.

'Better my people than getting et by whatever's in this jungle,' Dill said.

'Possibly.'

Dill went back into the survival pack, found the flare pencil, cocked and fired it. The flare shot up for three meters, hit a tree branch and spun, sizzling red, on the sand, then was smokily extinguished by a wave.

'Goddammit,' Dill swore.

But the speedster kept on coming.

'Come on, baby, come on, baby, come . . . aw, goddammit, you blind friggin' bat!'

The speedster climbed and leisurely disappeared into the clouds.

'Maybe he's going up for altitude to call in help,' Dill said.

The Musth looked at him.

'You aliens aren't supposed to be able to look askance, whatever that means,' Dill complained.

They waited another handful of minutes, but the aircraft never reappeared.

For two days more they moved south along the ocean's edge. They saw no more aircraft in the skies, saw no boats on the water. For two days they lived off the fish they'd caught, then used the fishing gear to catch other, larger fish from the ocean.

'Enough,' Alikhan announced at the end of the third day. 'If I eat one more of these swimmers, I'm going to sprout fins.'

'I've about had enough,' Ben agreed. 'So let's try something different.'

They used line from his survival kit to make small nooses, which they hung from a longish pole. Then they went back into the jungle, found a tree that animal noises were coming from, and planted the pole against it.

'Animals are like people, and lazy, taking the easy way, which generally gets you killed,' Dill explained. 'We just built whatever furry sorts lurk around here a runway getting in and out of their homes in this-yere tree. They go up or down the pole, stick their silly fool heads in the nooses, and it's Jack Ketch time, followed by Dill's Special Stew.'

That night they ate the last of the fish, and at dawn eagerly went into the jungle to see how they had done.

Their pole-snare had done well – four of the five nooses they'd left held the heads of small mammalian-looking animals. Unfortunately, there was nothing but the heads, still dripping a bit of gore.

'This they didn't tell me about in Basic Survival.'

'Annoying,' Alikhan agreed. 'But worse is wondering just how big the creature that ate the heads off is? I have no particular desire to have *my* carapace munched upon.'

'Would you care to retire to our camp, my friend,' Ben said, 'and see if we can't find some nice morsels of fish in yonder ocean?'

'Certainly,' Alikhan agreed. 'But first it might be practical if we consider relocating our camp a distance or two?'

'An excellent plan. The ambience around these parts ain't what I thought it was gonna be.'

A day and a half later, they came on a village. Or, the remains of one.

It'd been thoroughly razed. From the air, Dill estimated. There'd been a couple of dozen fishermen, their wives and families when the aircraft showed up. The remains of their boats were still beached nearby.

Alikhan looked at the ruins, at Dill's face, and somehow reasoned enough about human psychology to say nothing and go to the edge of the village.

Ben wandered through the ruins, numbly counting the blackened twists that'd been people. He finally came back to himself, realizing there was nothing at all he could do about it, and not having the stomach to sift through the ashes for anything they might be able to use, he went to where Alikhan waited.

'My people did this.' It was not a question.

Dill nodded.

'These people were not fighters?'

'Not likely.'

'Then this is not honorable.'

Dill had enough decency to reply: 'War ain't honorable.'

Alikhan held out his paws, signifying rejection of the comfort.

'Why do you think it was done?'

'I couldn't answer that,' Dill said. 'Maybe things have gotten nastier than they were before. Maybe your father's decided nits grow up to be lice.'

'What does that mean?'

'Never mind.'

They went on in silence.

Just at dusk, Dill saw a *giptel*, a scaled Cumbre native kept by villagers for its tender white meat, drinking at a stream. Perhaps it had been one of the villages' meat animals. In any event, it showed little fear of Dill as he crept up on it with a heavy rock.

He gutted the animal, built a fire, then a spit from thick green branches, and roasted the animal, basting it with fruit from nearby bushes he recognized from stores, using broad leaves for plates.

They ate, still not saying anything beyond the necessary.

After Alikhan buried the leaves and bones of the *giptel*,

they sat, staring at the dying fire as darkness grew around them.

'If it is permitted,' Alikhan said, 'I would like to talk about what we saw today.'

'Maybe you better not. I've got a short temper.'

'I think I must take that chance,' the Musth said. 'I believe I mentioned I studied with a Musth named Senza. He is leader of a clan called the *Polperros*, whose call is to be Reckoners.

'Those are the ones who decide whether an enterprise is worth doing, and whether it is permissible as part of our destiny, and finally whether it is allowable within our codes.'

'Lawyers,' Dill asked.

'When my tutor was giving me instruction in Basic, he said that would be a correct analogy.

'I told you that Senza spoke about the necessity to learn from our defeats, such as the one we suffered when we fought against the Confederation, in my father's father's time.

'He taught that this was not merely rooting about in the shame of the past, but giving us lessons, guidance for the future. He frequently wondered if our willingness to do instant battle, which gave us dominion over the other beasts when we were evolving, might not be a hindrance, or even a fatal flaw now that we are civilized.

'Although what we saw today was certainly not an example of civilization.'

Dill nodded, forcing away his smoldering anger.

'My father, of course, believed that Senza and those who thought like him were betrayers of our race. When he discovered I had been interested in Senza's teachings. he required me to leave the course of studies and the planet I was living on to find some other pursuit.

'I knew he would want me to be a warrior, and indeed

I have always loved flying. So I thought I would please him. It is not easy having a parent who is a war leader,' Alikhan said. 'What of your parentage?'

'Not much to tell,' Dill said. 'My mother was a rancher, someone who raised meat animals on a pioneer world. My father was a musician, who charmed her right out of her socks, and I was the product. When I was three or four, he left her. Damned if I know where he went. Never felt much like looking.

'I didn't know much, growing up, except that I sure as hell didn't want to be a rancher. You never stopped working, and you could never go anywhere for longer'n a day. The animals were always needing feed, water, dragging out of a ditch, whatever. But there didn't seem to be much of an alternative.

'When I was fifteen or so, my mother was out with a lifter, chasing some beasts toward a stock pen. I guess she wasn't watching the ground around her, because she went in hard against a pinnace, got thrown out, and the xebecs stampeded over her body.

'I put the place up for auction. and some bastard thought he was taking advantage of me, offering fifteen points on the credit. I was just damned glad to get out.

'Made my way to the planet's main port, tried to figure out what to do next, walked past a recruiting post, and, like they say, the rest is all ro-mance and ratshit.'

Dill shrugged. 'So really I don't know nothing about no fathers, one way or t'other.'

'Pardon,' Alikhan said. 'I still have trouble with many words in Basic, but I think I understand well what you said. My apologies. There are always worse situations than the one you're in.

'But let me return to the point I was trying to make, and please realize I am thinking as I speak, trying to cut through the thicket of what I was told to believe was right by my father and my clan members.

'I do not like what I've seen since I've been in this system. I do not like it at all. I see no reason why we Musth should want more of Cumbre than what we already have. I see this war, this fighting, as nothing more than what cubs do, when they first realize their claws are growing, except there are bodies instead of little pride cuts. I just wish there was something I could do about it.'

'You could always change sides,' Dill said.

'And fly against my own people? Kill for you humans?'

'Sorry,' Dill said. 'I was being a shithead. That was a crappy thing to say.'

'It shall be as if you never spoke,' Alikhan said. 'But there should be *something* that could be done.'

'If you happen to figure it out,' Dill said, 'be sure and let me know.'

A storm slammed in the next day, the trees of the jungle whipping and tearing, spindrift obscuring water from air, the world gray, wind whipping the sand against their faces so they sheltered under a tree they thought might stand against the winds, and talked, or tried to talk above the booming of the nearby waves.

They reached no conclusions save neither of them much gave a damn about killing, that they would have been happy playing combat games without missiles, without rockets.

But war seemed the nature of the universe.

'At least so long,' Alikhan said, 'as the old ones begin the wars they don't have to fight in.'

'Maybe,' Ben Dill said, chewing on a bit of jungle fruit, 'we should recruit soldiers oldest first.'

Alikhan made sounds of amusement, then held his paws out in negation.

'No. Somehow, even if we could do that, the old ones would find a way for the fighting to be done at home, and they would sit in front-line meat-parlors with their friends, talking about how terrible war is back at home.'

'How long,' Alikhan said, 'will it be before we reach a place such as you have been so mysterious about, where we can attempt to reach civilization? I find these jungles wearisome, and I am tired of being hungry all the time.'

'Don't worry,' Dill said. 'Only five more miles, Ranger.'

Alikhan wondered what the word 'Ranger' meant, what a 'mile' was, and why Dill exploded in laughter, though he maybe understood when, at the end of the long day's walk, they were still on that interminable beach surrounded by water and wilderness, and Dill had used the ancient lie favored by march leaders four more times, laughing uncontrollably each time.

A long finger of rock stuck out into the ocean, and they surveyed it dourly.

'Looks like we go back into the bush and try to get around it,' Dill said.

'Is that the best way?' Alikhan asked. 'It appears to me the formation goes on and on toward the interior.'

'So it does. But I don't exactly like the look of those waves bustin' over the point. You got any other options?'

'Perhaps we could work ourselves out onto the rock, using that formation there. Then scramble to the top, and then find some way down on the other side.'

Dill sighed.

'As good as anything else. Let's go. We've got nothing to lose but our fingernails . . . and your claws.'

He slung the dropper harness on, turned it to full power, walked over to the rocks, found a foothold, a fingerjam, started up. Alikhan was behind him. They scrabbled up the formation, finding the going not that bad – the rock was old, cracked, and there were cracks for foot- and handholds.

The Musth was a lot better at climbing than Ben Dill.

'This is too much like I&R training,' Dill managed. 'I'm a rocket jock, not a crunchie. And how in hell am I supposed to get over this . . . hang on . . . I wish to hell we had a rope . . .'

He stretched far out for a dubious handhold, just about the time the dropper's charge ran out. Dill screeched once, overbalanced, and dropped ten meters into an ocean pool created by a tiny jetty. Dill surfaced, floundering, splashing.

'I am coming,' Alikhan said, and made his way down toward the water's edge, where waves slapped against the rocks.

'I'd . . . appreciate it . . .' Dill managed, splashed his way to the jetty, clung to it. 'Safe now. God *damn*, but I wish I'd learned to swim better.'

Alikhan was not far above him, on a level rock.

'Here,' he said, extending far. Dill reached for his arm and his foot slipped, and he belly flopped, went under for an instant, then surfaced, his arm flailing.

'I have you,' Alikhan said, and did, pulling.

Then there was something else in the pool, something hissing like waves as they slide back from a beach, something that was gray, beaked, with a single vertically slit eye. Dill scrabbled with one hand for his flight-suit pocket and pistol, Alikhan pulled, and the beast, whatever it was, had a clawed mantislike arm on his leg.

'Put your head down!' Alikhan snarled, and Dill obeyed reflexively, face underwater.

There was a sharp thud behind him. and Dill felt an instant's hard pressure on his eardrums, eyes, nose, body, anus. Then there was nothing, the claws were gone, and Alikhan was pulling him hard.

'Come! I do not know if I killed it!'

Gasping for air, the two dragged each other back up the finger, climbing frantically, not sure what holds they were using, then were on top of the finger, looking back at that pool as something thrashed it white, terrible tearing arms, beak, ruptured eye appearing for a moment and then gone.

'Jesus Schmidlap with a foreskin,' Dill managed. 'What the goddamned hells was *that*?'

' I do not know,' Alikhan said. 'Our briefing manuals said there were unknown beings in the sea, in the jungle, and we were to be cautious.'

Dill was eyeing Alikhan very skeptically.

'Better question. What did you kill it – or anyway give it a rough way to go, since it's still thrashing around – with?'

'There were actually *three* wasp-grenades in my *aksai*,' Alikhan said. 'You did not notice one.'

'So you could've waited until I fell asleep anytime, killed me, and kept on going?'

'I could have,' Alikhan said. 'But I had given my honor.'

'Son of a bitch,' Dill said, sticking out his huge arm.

'What am I supposed to do with that?'

'You didn't study enough local customs. Take its end and shake it up and down.'

'Like this?'

'Like that. And here's your goddamned pistol back.'

Late that day, they heard machine noises and scanned the skies.

'No,' Alikhan said. 'On the water. Look.'

'A boat,' Dill said.'

'Perhaps you might try your mirror once again,' Alikhan suggested.

This time, it worked. The fishing boat altered course and headed toward them, drifting to a halt when it was about twenty meters offshore.

A public address system clicked on.

'I see you two. You look like you're pretty beat up. Who's in charge?'

'I am,' Dill shouted. 'And yeh, we need rescuing. We're both pilots. Crashed a few days ago.'

'You mind if I blow the shit out of that furball? I had some friends downcoast at Bocage Bay.'

Dill saw a woman come out of the cabin, brace herself on a bridge railing with a rifle.

'No!' he shouted. 'He's one of us! We're both with the Force, over at Camp Mahan, Chance Island.'

The woman kept staring through her sights, then went back into the cabin, back to the PA set.

'You better not be lying, friend. Or under some kind of alien drug spell.'

'I'm not. Look. I've got the gun! He's perfectly safe.'

'Awright. I see. Can you swim?'

'He can. I'm not so good at it.'

'I'm as far inshore as I can get,' the woman said. 'You better be able to get out to me.'

'We'll try.'

Dill dived in, and Alikhan swam easily after him. Ben saw a man come out of the boat's cabin, go to the railing, and hold out a gaff.

'Take hold of this,' he ordered, and Dill managed to grab it, and pull himself over the rail.

Alikhan was at the railing, claws pulling himself up, and Dill saw the woman's teeth grit, and the rifle come up again.

Somehow Ben had the gaff from the crewman, and flailed upward. The gaff caught the rifle barrel, knocked it up as the gun went off. Then Dill had his tiny pistol out, leveled on the boat's captain.

'I'm sorry, lady,' he said as Alikhan pulled himself aboard. 'But revenge isn't on the ticket these days.

'Thanks for the rescue, anyway.'

SIXTEEN

Wlencing ordered yet another assault on Camp Mahan, but this time something a bit more subtle than the previous frontal attacks.

Mahan was sledgehammered by the rocket artillery and the aerial-strike units, but no ground troops were initially committed.

He held back a flight of *aksai*, and three *velv*. These were flown by his best pilots and gunners. and he had to force back a pang for his lost cub, who should have been among them. They had very specific orders to refrain from firing until they had a definite target.

Mahan's underground firing positions were hazed with dust, the air almost as gray as the faces of the men and women manning the missile and gun sites, the walls, the ground itself shuddering.

Wlencing next sent in a flight of *wynt*. But this was a feint – the ships held no warriors, just gunners and pilots. They came in straight and level, and the missile sites popped up to launch.

The *wynt* dived away, only losing three ships, regrouped over the bay, and attacked again.

Once more the launchers rose, and this was exactly what Wlencing wanted. The *aksai* and *velv* had not made counterstrikes as before, but concentrated on precise targeting of the human sites.

Now the *aksai* and *velv* fired instantly, as the launchers came up. Three were hit while still extruded, and the fireballs racked the underground tunnels.

Wlencing ordered the rocket artillery on Dharma Island to shift targets and put their entire fire in and around those three blown-open sites.

The *velv*, and other attack ships, strafed the area, and two other missile sites were destroyed. Wlencing committed his entire strike reserves to the attack, and by early afternoon had fire superiority over the Force.

Then he ordered the *wynt* in, to land troops. This time, in spite of the infantrymen and -women fighting from their spider holes, the Musth gained and held an inland strong point on Mahan Island.

Wlencing sent more *wynt* in, both reinforcing the recent landing and expanding the fingerhold the Musth had already gained on the beachhead.

By nightfall, a tenth of the island was in Musth hands, and the Force was powerless to stop other Musth combat elements from landing downisland, where the ranges and outbuildings had been.

The issue was no longer in doubt.

'You're aware of what happened?' *Caud* Rao asked.

'Yessir,' Garvin answered. He and Njangu kept from looking at each other – their CO looked twenty, maybe thirty years older than he had when the siege began. *Mil* Angara, *Haut* Hedley and *Alt* Erik Penwyth didn't look much better.

'I'll keep this brief,' Rao said. 'It'll be a matter of a few days, perhaps less, before the Musth take the island.'

Garvin had to blink hard, fighting for control, refusing to let his exhausted emotions take over.

'Yessir.'

'You remember, some time ago, when you two suggested we should immediately institute guerrilla tactics, rather than fighting a more conventional war, as we have.' Rao rubbed his hand over tired eyes. 'Perhaps you were right.'

Neither Garvin nor Njangu said anything.

'Let me ask an impossible question,' Rao went on. 'Is it too late to do that now?'

Garvin looked at Njangu.

'Damned hard, sir,' Yoshitaro admitted. 'We're down to ninety-three fighting men in I&R. I don't know how many other women, men, would volunteer now to go with us. The troops are pretty worn-down. The war we'd be talking about fighting is pretty goddamned nasty, sir. And I don't think the Musth will be taking prisoners.

'How many effectives are there here on the island, if I can ask?'

'About twenty-two hundred,' Angara said. 'That's as of today's morning report.'

'The biggest question I'd have,' Garvin said, 'is how to get as many volunteers as we can off the island. We'd try to get them across into Leggett, then hide out there.'

'I've got a plan for that one,' Hedley said. 'I think it might even work.'

' 'Kay, sir,' Njangu said. 'What about the other regiments?'

'They're pretty well decimated,' Rao said.

'But at least they're on land,' Garvin said.

'If you want to play the cards our way, sir,' Njangu went on, 'you'd better give orders for them to break into small fighting elements and exfiltrate if they can.

'Get beyond the Musth lines, and go to ground anywhere they can. If any of them know safe villages, go there. Go to friends, relatives, whatever. Take any weapons they can, particularly pistols, grenades, and so forth. Have them convert as many blasters to carbine configuration as they've got kits for. If they think they can get away with heavier stuff, give them our blessings. Tell them they're probably safer in the cities, but if they've got relatives, contacts in the country, go to them.

'We'll call them when the time is right.'

'How'll you do that?'

Garvin looked at his partner. They hadn't discussed that idea.

'We've talked about that, sir,' Njangu said. 'Tell them to keep monitoring *Matin – Loy* Kouro's holos.'

'You've got a way of subverting him, or some of his people?' Hedley asked, incredulously.

'Sir, we'd rather not say anything right now,' Garvin managed, trying to keep from laughing at his friend's brazen lie. 'When the time is right, we'll tell you how to do it.'

Hedley hesitated, then nodded. 'But I want to see just how before you put anything into flipping motion.'

Rao actually let a moment of hope show on his face.

'If we break up the regiments,' he said, 'that'll cause a little chaos, make them pay a little less attention to Camp Mahan, which'll give us a few extra hours or even days.

'All right. Here's the chain of command: *Mil* Angara takes over the Force. Mullion Island will be Force head-quarters for as long as you can keep it a secret. Hedley, remain in charge of II Section, but I want you to be a bit more of a free agent than before. Oh, by the way, you're now a *mil*, effective immediately.

'Both of you are given complete freedom of action. You are to carry the war to the enemy as long as you can, as best you can. If you decide there's come a time to surrender . . . that'll be your decision. Erik, you're

now under Angara. Please serve him as well as you did
me.'

'But what about you, sir?' Erik asked.

'I'll remain in command of Camp Mahan.'

'But—'

'Those are my orders, gentlemen. Carry them out.'

Angara, Hedley, and Penwyth came to stiff attention.

'Just a moment, sir.' It was Njangu, denying the knee-
deep emotion of the moment.

'Yes.' Rao's voice was brusque

'Do we still have com with the other regiments?
Secure com?'

'Of course. I'll be addressing them before we begin our
final action.'

'Request permission to make a broadcast. I hope
within the hour.'

'You have it,' Rao said irritatedly. 'Is there anything
else?'

No one said anything.

'Dismissed,' Rao said. 'Make your preparations at
once, and notify me when you're ready.

'And the gods help us all.'

' 'Kay, sir,' Garvin said to Hedley, outside Rao's office.
'What's your addition to the scheme?'

Hedley told him.

'Putting all the yolks in one egg, isn't it?'

'We have a slight shortage of flipping ships at the
moment,' Hedley said, 'in case you haven't noticed.'

'Strong point,' Njangu said, bracing against a wall as
a salvo of rockets crashed in above them.

Hedley turned to Angara. 'Opinion, sir?'

'I admire people who can keep coming up with straws
to grasp at,' Angara said. He looked back at Rao's office
door. 'I think the old man's run out of them.'

Neither Garvin nor Njangu replied.

'What's going to happen is gonna happen,' Angara said. 'So let's get the shit flowing downhill.'

Static crackled, then Jo Poynton's voice came clearly:

'Go ahead.'

Njangu continued explaining.

'So I'll record what you want, blurt-cast to you. and you'll bounce it out to the other cities?'

'Sure,' Njangu said. 'That way, if the Musth have tracking stations, they won't be able to pick you up, wherever the hell you are.'

Silence for a moment, then a low chuckle.

'I'll bet you never thought you'd be asking me for this.'

'To be real honest,' Njangu said, 'you're right.'

'Why not?' Poynton said.

'Why not indeed?'

'I'll be ready in five, no ten minutes,' Poynton said. 'I'll com you back.'

'Standing by.'

'One other thing. Try to stay alive. We might have something to discuss about the old days.'

'I've got every intention of doing just that,' Njangu said. 'Clear.'

'That's a lot of money. Sir,' Baku al Sharif said.

' 'Tis, 'tisn't it,' Garvin agreed. 'Use it well.'

'Sir . . . what's to keep me from, say, taking off with all this,' al Sharif asked. 'Not that I would, mind you. But I was just curious.'

'Nothing at all,' Garvin said. 'Except your basic honesty, hatred for the Musth, the fact that you're a good soldier who wants to continue the war, and to live a clean and moral life.'

'Plus,' First *Tweg* Monique Lir grated, 'if you touch one lousy goddamned credit for anything except keeping your decayed ass alive and continuing the war any way you can, I'll hunt you down, tear your guts out through your asshole, and watch while you parboil 'em for my supper.'

'Right, First *Tweg*. Understood, First *Tweg*. I was just curious.'

'Next man,' Garvin said, hiding a grin, and the next I&R soldier in line stepped up to the table, and eyed the pile of credits that had been Jasith Mellusin's with some awe.

'All stations,' the tech said, *en clair*. 'Stand by to record and rebroadcast to all serving soldiers who're members of the 'Raum, *Caud* Rao's orders.'

He looked at Njangu, who nodded. The tech touched sensor.

A woman's voice, calm, assured, came from the speakers:

'This is Jo Poynton. I am a 'Raum. Recently I was one of the Planetary Government's Councilors. I left the Council and went underground, because I foresaw that Council would become no more than an echo, a puppet of the Musth.

'So it has become.

'Before I was part of PlanGov, I was in The Movement, a member of the Planning Group, working with first Comstock Brien, then Jord'n Brooks. We fought for a cause we believed in . . . and we lost.

'Perhaps we changed Cumbre enough so our Task wasn't a complete failure. Perhaps not.

'But now we face a greater foe, one who cares little whether we're 'Raum or Rentier. Under the bootheels of the Musth, all humanity is threatened. What the future might bring, under their rule, slavery or worse, is unknown.

'So I call upon you, my fellow 'Raum, to rise against them. Not in foolish mobs or frontal action, but the same way we fought . . . and almost won . . . against the Rentiers and the Confederation soldiers.

'Now they are our allies, and I call you, in the name of past and future generations of 'Raum and other Cumbrians, to fight back, fight secretly and by stealth, until we gain in strength, in power.

'Find your old comrades, your old officers, and again form the secret army. If you cannot fight, then help those who can with credits, shelter, even food. Seek out Confederation soldiers, shelter them, and if you know more than them about being a warrior in the shadows, teach them well.

'This day is dark, and it may grow darker.

'But if we stand together, if we fight together, there may be light.

'For Cumbre! Cumbre and Freedom!'

'Where did *that* come from?' Loy Kouro demanded.

'From Camp Mahari, we think. It was on one of the Force's standard frequencies,' Vollmer said. 'How do you want *Matin* to play it?'

'What in the holy name of nothing do you mean?'

'I mean,' his editor, Ted Vollmer, said patiently, 'do we play it big, do we rebroadcast it, or . . .?'

'You're mad,' Kouro said. 'If we rebroadcast it on our channels, the Musth would seal our doors shut, maybe with us on the inside.'

'Three other holos so far have retransmitted it,' his editor said.

'Obviously they don't have a goon's worth of sense,' Kouro said. 'How could anyone listen to that drivel, let alone believe it? Talk like that does nothing good, nothing at all, but stir the wrong people up to do the wrong things!'

'I assume, then, you want a nice editorial condemning such foolishness?'

'Yes! No, wait! We shouldn't dignify this rubbish by giving it notice. We'll have no reaction whatsoever.'

'You're sure, sir?'

'Of course I'm sure! Damn, but I wish you people would learn to think for yourselves!'

'Yes, sir. Thank you, sir.'

That night, the Musth hit Third Regiment, based outside Taman City, hard, in a night attack without preparatory artillery or airstrikes. They broke through the perimeter, and Wlencing fed in fighting elements to sweep wide.

Before dawn, the last signals, plaintively asking for help from anyone, anywhere, knowing there was nothing to send, had stopped.

Caud Rao made his last com in code to all Force stations. It was very short:

'Force men, women. You've been given my final orders by your commanders.

'Obey them as best, and as long as you can. Fight on, fight as soldiers in a new campaign, but fight with the honor you've always held close. If you are forced to give in, hold your heads high.

'You may have lost, but the battle will continue

'The Force dies.

'It does not surrender.'

'We have a reported broadcast,' Wlencing's chief aide Rahfer said, 'origin Camp Mahan, in code, picture scrambled. It was preceded by a very long 'cast, also coded. Both of these were in variants of the humans' new code, which we have not yet broken.

'That was a very short time ago. Since then, all human units we monitor have maintained com silence.'

'I will assume,' Wlencing said, 'the message was not one of mourning for the broken unit. We'll maintain full alert, but take no action until we determine just what they are up to.'

But nothing happened, or rather appeared to happen for a while, and the night grew deeper.

Earlier that day, one of the two transports Hedley had 'acquired' for his navy lifted away from Mullion Island. Escorted by the remaining *aksai* and one Zhukov, it flew nap-of-the-jungle east, away from Camp Mahan, then turned north in a convenient canyon that led south to the sea. It flew equally low over water, slowly, since it was a balky pig to pilot, until it was west-southwest of the mouth of Dharma Island's great bay. Then it lowered into the ocean, submerging completely. Spacecraft, even though they're not generally considered in that category, can make perfectly acceptable submarines, even if they generally have the floatation-at-rest capability of earth sharks and their heat signature is fairly marked.

The freighter moved steadily and slowly into the bay. following the dredged ship channel.

About five kilometers from Camp Mahan, it bottomed and lay doggo, waiting for the signal.

The three surviving regiments obeyed Rao's orders from their bases outside Leggett, Aire, and Kerrier. A company-sized probe was made against the encircling Musth positions, not necessarily at the weakest points. The Musth, as was their common strategy, withdrew slightly, regrouped, and prepared for a smashing counterattack. As they did, the remaining Force ground-mounted rocketry and artillery opened fire.

It appeared major attacks were being mounted. Wlencing ordered his commanders to reinforce the attacked positions and drive the humans back.

The Musth obeyed, just as the regiments made their second attacks. These were at the best points for exfiltration.

First and Fourth Regiments broke through handily, Second was about half an hour behind. The companies at point swung left, right, holding open the gap in the lines.

Force women and men, taking only what they could carry and reluctantly abandoning all wounded not capable of travel, leaving medics to take care of them, moved through these gaps in small elements, generally no more than squad size.

First Regiment, proud of always being a little better than the others, managed to take some small lifters and Cookes loaded with Fury launchers and missiles.

Wlencing listened to the confused yammerings from his commanders, realized, to considerable astonishment, what was going on, and ordered the gaps closed at all costs. The Force must not be allowed to escape to fight on.

The three battles across Cumbre were total savagery fought in darkness momentarily illuminated with flaring lasers, flares exploding and then dying out, men and Musth screaming, dying, fighting with grenades, blasters, claws, and clubs.

Then the Force aircraft swarmed again, rising from their hidden fields to slash into the Musth ships darting over the battlefields in confusion, unable to find clear targets.

Again, Wlencing threw his reserves in.

This would be, must be, the final battle.

One or two Musth observation craft saw the freighter surface off Camp Mahan, but their reports were blanked by a blast of static on all known Musth frequencies. One *aksai* tried to come in for an attack, and one of three lurking Zhukovs blew it out of the air.

The freighter hurtled across the shallowing water, over the first Musth landing position. Behind it were Griersons, guns yammering, missiles firing until the racks emptied.

The freighter slammed down in the rubble of the parade field, skidding sideways, almost rolling. Its ports opened, and Force troops swarmed out of their bunkers and weapons positions and ran toward the ship. None came unburdened – some carried a couple of SSWs, others missiles, still others helped the walking wounded and sick hobble aboard.

A Musth warrior saw opportunity, fired a missile, and it struck the freighter near the stern. Crewmen smothered the flames, and no vital control systems were struck. He tried a second launch, and a 35mm burst from a Zhukov obliterated him.

'Go, let's go, let's go,' Angara chanted, standing near one of the gangways, and men and women doubled up them, not quite in panic, but not quite in calm order. Other Force officers were at other locks, positions, cramming the troops aboard.

Then there was no one on the ground, and Angara shouted to button up and lift off.

The freighter pilot and crew obeyed, and the hulk came off the ground, yawing, then drove hard across the bay, lifting over the peninsula, then down again, vanishing into the darkness of Mullion Island.

There was no one left at Camp Leggett.

No one except *Caud* Prakash Rao, seventy-eight volunteers, and the desperately wounded who had been unable to travel.

They grimly waited for the Musth.

'This is impossible,' Wlencing said, eyes scarlet in fury. 'You cannot win a battle by losing it! What are these beings thinking! This is not the way to fight a war!

'Where are they going?'

'We don't know,' Rahfer said. 'None of them seems to have a definite destination. They're moving in small groups, most of them into the cities their positions were close to.

'We're trying to land troops, but none of our warriors are familiar with the ground. Even with night-vision the situation is confusing. When we do trap a group of them, sometimes they surrender, sometimes they fight to the end, more often they stop our warriors long enough to make good their escape.'

'What about their aircraft?'

'We are still tracking where they disappeared to,' Rahfer said. 'They're thoroughly dispersed, but we're finding small landing areas here and there, and attacking them.'

'This is like trying to pick up mercury in your paws,' Wlencing said. 'We cannot allow this opportunity to slip from us.'

'Sir,' Daaf said, 'calm yourself. Consider — what damage can be done by these stragglers, these fragments? Wars cannot be fought by one or two warriors.'

'No,' Wlencing said. 'But Musth can be killed in that way, just as those worm-'Raum killed the Force warriors before you came to us, and make a rule of law very difficult. Now, be silent, and do not further parade your uneducation.'

*

At first light, the Musth on Dharma Island moved against the shatter of Camp Mahan. They moved confidently, sure there'd be no more than a handful of humans in the ruins to winkle out.

Their formations closed up as they reached the parade field. Fire from a dozen hidden positions exploded toward them.

They dived for shelter, fought back. But the Force soldiers had rolled to other positions, fired again

The Musth commanders called for air, and *aksai* rolled in to the attack. A *velv* targeted the biggest pile of rubble, once the main headquarters, and made a straight-in attack, missiles about to launch.

Striker Barken, who'd held a guard formation at gunpoint, slid from cover, pushing a crude Fury mount in front of him. He touched a delayed firing switch, rolled back. The Fury hummed to life, beeped as it acquired the *velv*, and shot toward the Musth warship.

It hit dead on, just below the main canopy, and exploded, wiping out the crew inside. The *velv* went out of control, spinning end for end, then smashing down into the middle of the Musth before it blew up.

In the confusion, Force gunners and snipers took advantage, and killed warriors where they could.

The Musth fell back, regrouped, came on.

They closed with the ruins, and again the fighting was hand-to-hand, and the Force soldiers slowly were forced back, meter by bloody meter, back into their tunnels.

The Musth went after them.

Suddenly, fifteen men and women, *Caud* Rao at their head, broke from a hidden bunker and charged into the main tunnel, shooting as they went.

Most of the Musth went down in the first volley, but the trapped warriors fought back tenaciously.

A wasp-grenade bounced near Rao, and he tried to

duck as the device exploded, and horror-insects tore his skull apart.

The fighting raged on, but slowly the shots, explosions, came less and less often.

Then there was silence.

A Musth officer staggered out of a tunnel, ten Musth, all wounded, behind him. He'd gone in with fifty.

He looked around, dazed.

A dozen meters away was the Force's flagpole, its flag, a lance with shock waves exploding from the tip, hanging defiantly, the slight offshore wind moving it gently.

'Cut that down,' he ordered.

Four of his warriors stumbled to obey.

A grenade came from nowhere, exploding in midair and sending the Musth howling to the ground. As Barken appeared from a crevice in the ruins, the officer whirled, lifted his weapon, but was too late as Barken shot him down.

A moment later, two other Musth blasted Barken as he swung his weapon toward them.

The six surviving aliens stared up at the flag, then turned away numbly, faltering back from the nightmare toward their positions.

'The Force dies . . . it does not surrender . . .'

SEVENTEEN

After the cataclysm, Cumbre lay quiet. Relatively so, at any rate.

No one knew what would come next.

The Musth ships continued swooping around the empty battlefields, chasing the remnants of the Force, and they even chanced sending heavily armed patrols into the cities. Sullen humans stared, and the Musth nervously kept their weapons ready.

Occasionally one of the Force stragglers would be discovered, and either shot down or taken prisoner.

A dozen times larger groups of soldiery were found, attacked by the Musth. About half the time they drove the aliens off before they vanished into the jungles.

There were many, many soldiers who'd escaped the tooth-combs of the aliens, but no one knew how many, who or where they were, or their plans.

Leggett civilians nervously looked at the still-smoldering rack of Camp Mahan, while other Cumbrians considered the ruins of battle in their own area. No one with a child, lover, parent, friend in the Force knew whether to mourn or keep worrying – there were no casualty lists available for the last week of the battle.

Sometimes there was sudden joy when a surreptitious

midnight tap on a door became the prodigal one, who was feasted and then hidden.

Some had guns to hide, or a friend, others had nothing but shuddering memories and an unwillingness to follow Rao's final orders.

So far, the Cumbrians had no quislings to worry about, who'd reveal the hidden warriors in their midst.

So far.

'Now that you're victorious,' Loy Kouro probed. 'what exactly are your plans for Cumbre?'

Kouro, elegant in evening dress, was one of two dozen or so Rentiers who'd responded to the Musth 'request' for their company at a 'Feasting to Celebrate the Coming of Peace.'

The gathering was in the penthouse dining room of the Bank of Cumbre, a sixty-story spire overlooking Leggett.

Wlencing, wearing harness made from the fur of some black-and-white-striped animal, with only a holstered pistol and grenade box, took a moment to respond:

'The firssst order,' he said, 'will be to ssstabilize thisss human sssociety.'

'Of course,' Kouro said. 'Without that, we might as well still be at war. I just hope that stability will come easily.'

'Now that isss a matter for you humansss to determine, isss it not?' Rahfer said, hissing in mild amusement.

'Well, I suppose so,' Kouro said. 'Are there any specific plans you'd like to tell me about?'

'We ssshall allow the moment to dictate exactly what ssshall be done,' Wlencing said. 'The firssst priority will be to bring the minesss on what you named Ccc-Cumbre. which will now be known asss Mabasssi, jussst asss thisss world will be Whar, back to their full work-ability.'

'Of course.'

'We ssshall be hiring workersss here on Whar, and . . . other sssources of labor will be found.'

'Such as?'

Wlencing gave Kouro a look, didn't answer.

'Of courssse, we ssshall devote every effort to hunting down thessse banditsss who were onccce sssoldiersss, to prevent the upsssetsss they will bring to you humansss.

'We ssshall continue what we termed our counccilss-shipsss, but the buildingsss will be enlarged. Other Musssth will be arriving from our home worldsss to gar-rissson, or rather, to ssstaff them.

'We ssshall need buildersss to work on thessse enlarge-mentsss. And there ssshall be new conssstruction around our bassse in the Highlandsss, on Sssilitric, and on Mabasssi, to replacce the headquartersss dessstroyed by the 'Raum. We ssshall compensssate thossse workersss, of courssse.

'Asss time fulfillsss, we ssshall probably inssstitute other waysss that will improve order, sssuch as central identity cardsss. We are consssidering hiring cccertain of your humansss to asssisssst usss, probably giving each of them an area, a block, to be resssponsible for, ssso no diss-sidency can develop.'

'Are you willing to be quoted on that?'

'Of courssse,' Wlencing hissed exasperatedly. 'I sssaid it, did I not? I would not have sssaid it if it were not the truth.'

'I'm sorry,' Kouro said. 'That's merely a formality meaning is it all right if I mention what you told me in a story.'

'It isss all right.' Wlencing's head snaked back, forth. 'I do not sssee your mate. Where isss ssshe?'

'She, well, was feeling very sick, and sends her apology.'

'There were many of thossse,' Rahfer said. 'We have noted their namesss, and will remember them.'

Kouro smiled nervously

'Thank you for your time. I'm sure you'll be pleased with the way we'll continue to cover the, umm, change of government.'

'I'm *sssure* we will,' Wlencing said. 'I foresssee making no changesss in the manner of the human propaganda machine, at leassst for the presssent.'

On Mullion Island, the Force began regrouping, sending out cautious probes looking for stragglers.

Awards were made and wounds were licked. And there were promotions:

Grig Angara, as per the sealed orders given him by Rao, took command of the Force and was promoted *Caud*;

Jon Hedley became both his executive officer and remained head of II Section:

And; among others, Garvin Jaansma was made *cent*, Njangu Yoshitaro promoted *alt* and Erik Penwyth made *cent*.

The new fad in Leggett, which quickly spread to the other cities on Cumbre, was postering. Any child's computer could produce a three-dee, high-color item, and run off a few dozen. The real game was to post them close to where the Musth would see them, but not close enough to get caught.

The only problem was, no one spoke Musth, so the posters were all in Prime. But then, a sufficient number of Musth officers could read the human tongue, and the creators put some thought into their message:

MUSTH
YOUR CUBS GO INTO HEAT
WITH EACH OTHER
AS YOU DID BEFORE
WITH YOUR DEN-MATES

Others made equally defamatory (if sometimes wildly
inaccurate) claims about Musth biology and habits. But
many had the desired effect: The Musth were sufficiently
sensitive about their passions if left uncontrolled during
the period of heat to explode in rage when they saw such
a poster.

At first, they were just torn down. But that didn't
stop anything. The Musth, thinking a building's occu-
pants should be able to control what was pasted on its
walls, started arresting anyone found inside a building so
decorated.

The already-full prisons got more crowded.

The poster makers grew more clever, and the posters
appeared on the rear of Musth aircraft, their 'consulates,'
and even, once or twice, hung on the harness of the last
Musth in a patrol.

A strange aircraft was picked up by the radar watch at
the Mullion Island base less than two weeks after the fall
of Camp Mahan. The aircraft grounded about a kilometer
beyond the base before it could be IDed.

I&R, still rebuilding itself from volunteers, went out
as the reaction force.

They found a shabby agricultural lifter, anodized a
dozen colors and held together with good intentions, in
a clearing, with no one around it.

Lir put the patrol on line at the edge of the clearing,
motioned the point woman to her.

'You, me, we'll have a look.'

The point woman, after adjusting a sudden blockage in her throat approximately the size of a battleship, nodded, readied her blaster.

Lir slid out into the clearing, waited for movement, for fire. Nothing came. She crept forward, followed by the point woman. The patrol's weapons were ready.

She made about five meters, when the shout came:

'Lir! First *Tweg* Lir!'

The voice was human, and somewhat familiar.

She went, very fast, to the lifter, used it for cover.

'Yeh,' she shouted back.

'It's me. Ben Dill.'

'You're dead.'

'The hell!'

' 'Kay. You're not dead,' Lir called. 'One man . . . you . . . out. Slow and unarmed.'

Ben stepped into the clearing, very slowly, hands half-raised. He wore the ragged remains of his flight suit cut down into shorts and held up by a length of rope, home-made sandals and a billowing, multicolored top that might have been a fat woman's skirt twenty years or so earlier.

Lir got up, weapon not pointed much of anywhere in particular.

' 'Kay,' she said. 'What the hell are you doing?'

'Trying to come home,' Dill said. 'I got shot down a month or so ago—'

'I know,' Lir said. 'I was waiting to go to your wake.'

'It'll have to be postponed,' Dill said. 'Got ashore. walked up the coast, got picked up by some fisher-woman, and she took me to her village. I managed to put this piece of shit back into running order, then flew on upcoast until I saw one of our ships haulin' for home.

'I took a heading, and followed it for a while, then sat down, and waited for another boat to fly past, followed it another way. Couldn't keep up — that frigging lifter's got no hum to its bones and no goddamned radio, either, so I couldn't screech for help.

'Your security blows *giptels*. When I got where I remembered a couple of hills, I did a popup so you people'd get me on screen, but not long enough for some beaver to pull a launch. Then I put it down and waited for company.'

'Can I kiss you?'

Lir managed a quick grin.

'Officers don't fraternize.'

'Then you kiss me. I made it. Oh yeah. There's one other thing. I got a friend.'

'Have him come out.'

'Do me a favor. Put the blaster on safe and point it somewheres away, 'kay?' Dill said.

Monique did as requested.

'Alikhan. Come out. Slowly.'

Monique's finger was on the safety as the Musth came into the open. He, like Ben, held his arms spread wide, visibly empty. She tensed, then relaxed.

'Son of a bitch,' Lir swore. 'You got a prisoner.'

'Uh . . . it's . . . he's . . . a little bit more than that.'

Both Alikhan, Dill, and their junk heap were swept with every known pickup before it was agreed they weren't bugged and probably hadn't been followed. Still, the base remained at full alert.

The two pilots were taken to Angara and Hedley, and Dill explained what had happened.

'You speak Basic perfectly, Alikhan,' Hedley mused. 'Convenient.'

'You think me to be a double agent.' It was not a question.

'That should be a possibility,' Hedley said.

'Don't you think, sir,' Dill said, 'it's a little preposterous for the commander of the Musth to put his own kid out there? And doesn't that mean I'd have to be a part of the plot, helping him get shot down?'

'You're right,' Hedley admitted. 'My brain's fogging.'

'Let me try to understand,' Angara said. 'You want this war to be ended.'

'Correct.'

'Why?'

'It is not showing honor to any of us.'

'None of your brothers seem to feel that way,' Angara said. 'They seem to think what's happened is some kind of fulfillment of destiny.'

'I suppose some do,' Alikhan said. 'Why should they not? Have they ever been offered an alternative, another perspective? I am a rare exception, having chosen, for a time, to study the ways of the Reckoners, of Senza. But most of us accept the beliefs we are given by our elders. Almost all in this system come from warrior clans, so we think only like fighters.'

'Would you be willing to help change their minds,' Hedley asked. 'Maybe by doing propaganda coms?'

'I do not think that would be effective,' Alikhan said. 'Other than possibly causing my father to die of shame. I would not know what to say, in any event.'

'If you won't do propaganda,' Angara said, 'of course you wouldn't be willing to fight on our side.'

'Or, for instance, guide a group of our warriors to a target within a compound of yours,' Hedley added.

'No to both ideas,' Alikhan said.

'He's a warrior, sir, not a friggin' turncoat,' Dill growled.

Angara gave him a look, was about to say something, decided not to.

'Very well,' the *caud* said. 'I do not have any idea on

how you could be of use, at least not without conditioning, and I surely don't have any idea of how to condit a
Musth, even if I thought it was ethical.'

Hedley looked at Alikhan consideringly, as if he
might be willing to try programming an alien, but
didn't say anything.

'Would you ... will you ... attempt to escape?'
Angara asked.

'Not until Ben Dill releases me from the parole I
gave.'

'Very well,' Angara said. We'll treat you as an honored
guest, although there will be restrictions. *Alt* Dill, I'm
going to put you in charge of Alikhan. Stay with him.
Some of our people are a little trigger-happy these days.

'I'm sorry I can't put you back in a ship, Ben,' he finished. 'But this is more important, I think.'

Dill came to attention, saluted, and the two pilots
went out. Angara shook his head.

'This goddamned war gets screwier every minute.
We've got a pacifist monster. the only goddamned one
who's ever been taken prisoner, and no goddamned idea
on how to use him.'

'Welcome to the asylum, sir.' Hedley said.

The Highlands around the Musth base was a swarm of
human-operated construction equipment. The marshland was being leveled and filled. and landing pads built
at regular intervals.

Wlencing watched with some satisfaction. Daaf stood
beside him.

'Are you certain we shall get the aircraft replacements
to fill these slots?' he asked. Not to mention their pilots?'

'Of course.' Wlencing said. 'Why would our fellows
not respond, not want to be involved in this great adven-
ture?'

Daaf thought of the over sixty percent casualties the Musth had endured, but decided not to argue with his war leader. Besides, any objections he had would be wrong – he knew himself to be uneducated.

Jasith Mellusin stared, shocked, at the screen. On it was Hon Felps, the executive in charge of mining personnel.

'They can't do that, can they?'

'If the Musth subscribed to any sort of warfare rules such as humans try to adhere to, which they evidently don't,' Felps said tightly, 'our lawyers say they'd be in violation. You can't make a prisoner of war work for you. But the Musth haven't signed any of our treaties and, technically, no state of war exists between the Confederation and the Musth.'

'So I'm supposed to stand there and let them use the Force prisoners as . . . I guess you'd call them slave labor?'

'The Musth are willing to pay small wages,' Felps said. 'Plus they'll absorb all living expenses once they're on C-Cumbre. Sorry, I find it very hard to think of it as Mabasi.'

'Don't bother,' Jasith said. 'It's still C-Cumbre to anyone I take seriously. I guess, then, there's not much we can do about it.'

She looked to either side, although there was no one in her mansion's office. 'Would you do me a large favor and see if any of the prisoners is named Jaansma? Garvin Jaansma?'

'Yes, ma'am.'

'That's a personal request,' she said. 'and I want you to handle it yourself, and mention it to no one.'

'Certainly, Jasith.' The executive reached for the cutoff sensor, stopped himself. 'Oh yes. One other thing, which I forgot. This order from the Musth has me somewhat upset.'

'As if you're the only one.'

'The Musth also advised me we can expect them to provide other workers. Human workers. I asked from where, and they said they saw no purpose in criminals sitting in prisons if they could be doing something useful.'

Jasith Mellusin blinked at Felps.

'Crooks, too?'

'So it appears.'

'And, again, there's nothing we can do to stop it.'

'Not if we wish to retain even partial control of Mellusin Mining.'

'Very well,' Jasith said and, without saying good-bye, cut the connection.

She got up, paced to the window, looked out at the bay, at the ruins. She considered swearing, realized that wouldn't do any good. She went back to the com, started to call Loy, caught herself.

'And what would that get me?' she said aloud, knowing the most likely answer.

She thought about crying, but wouldn't allow herself to, got up once again, and walked out of the office. She stopped at the black-framed portrait of her father, stared at it.

'What the hell would you do if you were me?'

No answer came from there, either.

That night, a Musth patrol challenged a young boy, twelve, putting up a poster. Instead of surrendering, he ran. Two Musth opened fire. The boy's legs were nearly severed by the blasts. The Musth debated what they should do.

The boy bled to death before they decided to notify a human hospital.

*

'There is an unanswered question here,' Wlencing said in a half growl as his *wynt* orbited over the crowded streets of Leggett. 'How did all these learn of that cub's death so quickly? Do we not control all the holos?'

'We do, sir.' Rahfer said.

'And you reported all other cities report equal numbers of fools mewling about that young criminal?'

'That is what I've been told.'

'How did they learn about it so fast?'

'I don't know.'

There was a simple answer – during the Rebellion both 'Raum and their opponents had learned not to trust holos, and Cumbre had developed a very efficient, very rapid, if frequently inaccurate, jungle telegraph. Someone heard something, called five or more numbers, reported. Each of them called five or so coms, and so on. For better or worse, every city, village, hamlet, fishing boat, or hunter was plugged in to a systemwide rumor mill.

The parents of the boy had been original builders of that telegraph and, as always, the death of one person, one real person, meant more than the most horrifying numbers of anonymous casualties.

Wlencing stared down once more.

'What response should we make?' Rahfer asked.

'None,' Wlencing said. 'They'll get tired of shouting at closed doors and aircraft in a few hours and things will return to normal.'

But they didn't.

There were five Musth, keeping to the center of the street as they'd been taught, patrolling the area around the main landing field in Launceston.

They wore night snoopers and looked about constantly. They had heat sensors on their belts and were fully alert.

Neither snoopers nor sensors read through a stone wall, where ten men, nine of them 'Raum, the other a schoolteacher's son, crouched. One 'Raum held a mirror on a stick just beyond the wall.

He saw the flicker of the oncoming patrol, sharply tapped his fellow. The taps went down the line, and each man counted to ten to give the Musth time to get closer. Then they jumped to their feet and ran into the open. Each carried one of the simple projectile weapons provided by Redruth of Larix/Kura and given out by Gavin

The startled Musth were less than four meters away.

There were no commands given—each man picked a target and fired until his weapon was empty.

One Musth managed to get a shot off, and burned a 'Raum on his side before he convulsed and died with the others.

The wounded 'Raum crouched in silent agony while the others hastily stripped the Musth harnesses of weaponry.

Another 'Raum knelt beside him.

'Can you run?'

'Of course. It just hurts.'

'Then come. They'll be looking for their fellows soon.'

The wounded 'Raum got up and, with the others, disappeared into darkness.

Other Musth were attacked, but none as successfully as in Launceston.

Wlencing ordered more hostages taken the next day. The media, particularly *Matin*, were ordered to play the taking big.

'I'm looking for one flipping volunteer,' *Mil* Hedley said.

Cent Erik Penwyth looked about the tent, saw no one but the two of them.

'I s'pose I'm the candidate?'

'You s'pose right.'

'I'm not much on volunteering,' Erik said. 'The hours're shoddy, and sometimes the work conditions're pretty hazardous.'

'These hours are excellent, the pay is whatever you can make it . . . and I've no flipping idea what the hazard level is. Pretty low I'd guess at first.'

'What would you be interested in me doing?'

'Going back home.'

'Beg pardon?'

'The Force needs an agent with the Rentiers. We want you to slither back into your family and do the dissolute young man role, through with his frightening fling with the Force, ready to return to serious decadence with no flipping interest in Musth or Man. As you're lounging, we want you to get a feel as to the Rentiers. Who's playing the Musth game, who's taking them seriously, who can we get to play on our side. The usual flipping subversion on any victims you deem worthy.'

'Mmmh.' Penwyth considered. 'I don't think I've made too many rabid patriotic speeches, and Buddha knows my fellows are too dumb to wonder where I've been and if I'm for real, so nobody'd be ready to nark me out. Certainly the family's no bother. Advantages, one supposes, of being an only child.

'And I *am* getting tired of having one uniform and a change. It'd be nice to have a proper wardrobe again.

'But I think not.'

'Why flipping not?' Hedley said.

Penwyth took a deep breath.

'Because I'd feel like I was running out on the others. Goin' back to champagne and all that, while you're sweatin' over here. No, the more I think 'bout it, the less I like it.'

' 'Kay,' Hedley said. 'We'll try another approach. I'm detaching you to independent service, where I flipping want to put you.'

'Guess, when you put it like that, I haven't much choice. What support will I get?'

'We'll insert you in the next day or so back on the outskirts of Leggett. We'll give you a standard transceiver, which you're to keep well away from you, and check every two or three days for messages. Also you'll have a coder and compressor, which you'd be advised to keep closer at hand.

'Your reports'll be coded and blurted back to us. Mostly we'll want to use you as an eye, no more. Until the flipping situation gets worse – worse for the Musth, anyway – I can't see bringing you into the open. We'll keep a channel open and try to extract you if you step in it.

'Any questions?'

Penwyth considered.

'S'pose not. I guess it will be interestin' to have a bath oftener than when it rains, now won't it?'

'It's occurred to me,' Njangu said evenly, switching off the com's newscast, 'that there's a rising going on and we seem to be getting left out, and that ain't the way it's supposed to work, us being the moral arbiters and that sort of shit for this here system.

'I think I want to go play.'

'How?' Garvin asked.

'We tried for that frigging Wlencing once,' Njangu said. 'I think it's time we try again.'

'What makes you think this time'll be any luckier than the last?'

'Because I'm going to take this team in myself,' Njangu said. 'We'll give it a shot without all the supertech, and see how he likes playing with the big boys.'

'As your commanding ossifer,' Garvin said, 'I give my permission. I assume you're going to clear things with Jon and Angara.'

'But of course, my leader.'

'Which means you'll leave me here in the goddamned jungle with nothing to do but play with my pahdoodle,' Garvin said.

'Oh, I'll bet, given my inspiring example, you'll manage to come up with something obnoxious.'

Four days later, two women and two men showed up at the Seya labor exchange. They considered various possibilities offered, decided against the mines on Silitric, opted for common labor jobs on the Highlands of Dharma Island, building the new Musth base.

They didn't seem much interested in the employment terms or the hours, shouldered their oddly heavy packs, and boarded the cargo lifter that took them across a quarter of the world, onto the mist-covered heights.

Some of their fellows had never seen a Musth except on the holos, and reacted with fear or anger when their employers materialized on the landing field. But the four didn't seem bothered.

The workers were told off in teams by human overseers, assigned to rather shoddy barracks, given a list of rules and regulations, told their shift would start at dawn the next day and that work hours were thirteen on, thirteen off, and the extra hour was for transport to and from the work site.

The four never showed up for their first day on the job. But no one noticed – there'd been a fire that night in the personnel office, and that day was spent chaotically trying to sort out who was supposed to work

where, and how much seniority and credits they were
owed.

The four – Njangu Yoshitaro, Monique Lir, *Finf* Val
Heckmyer, and Darod Montagna – had slid out of the
camp through the rather casual security into the marsh-
lands after they set the incendiary in the personnel office,
and gone to ground.

They found a burrow against a hill, crawled inside
with weapons ready, and found it opened into a
respectable room, almost big enough to stand in. They
speculated glumly about what sort of creature on this
still-unexplored world made the cave, and hoped it had
moved on to better locations or at any rate was noncar-
nivorous.

Nothing disturbed their sleep, and the next morning
they moved closer to the workings and began observing,
looking for their target.

They muttered at the almost-constant fog, but it
made their task easier. Very seldom did the Musth sweep
with light-enhancing devices, and they never seemed to
use heat sensors in their complacency in this distant
place.

They built several hides around the base, and moved
from one to another, in pairs, both awake during the day,
alternating watches at night.

Regularly, *aksai*, *wynt*, *velv* swooped overhead, landed
at the ever-growing field. The only troops they saw were
perimeter-checking aerial patrols and ground crews
inside, not interested in anything beyond their tasks.

After five days, they reconvened at the burrow and
allowed themselves the luxury of using heat tabs on their
rations.

'I don't have much of anything,' Njangu said. 'The
Musth keep way too far inside their perimeter. Way too
far for me to be able to hit them. I know we got outside

of the perimeter without problems, but trying to get back in and get closer might be a bitch. Besides, I didn't see anybody who looked like he had any rank, let alone Wlencing.'

'Same here,' Montagna said. 'As the team sniper, I was hoping maybe we could get a longarm dropped in or maybe use a scoped SSW, but that goddam' fog doesn't help that.'

'Same thing with a missile,' Heckmyer said. 'Assuming we could get a supply drop, who'd lug the bastard around?'

'Not to mention who'd want to fire it off and hope to haul ass before counterfire leveled his ears a couple of meters or so?' Lir finished.

'I hate like hell to just quit,' Njangu said. 'We could chance having an explosive drop, work our way inside their guard, and blow up a bunch of shit, like aircraft. and take any shots we could on the way out.'

'Is that the best use?' Lir asked. 'This is sort of a one-time operation, isn't it, boss? I'd hate to set off a bunch of bangs, then figure out next week or next month that we could've done something serious while we were here. Already we've learned a KT and a half about the way these Musth operate up here. Pretty sloppy, as far as I can see. I guess they figure out here in the tules they don't have to worry about goblins like us. I'd sure like to come back with a better idea and a bigger bang.'

'The same thoughts occurred to me,' Njangu said.

'So we just abort?' Montagna said 'I'm just a newbie, and you guys have all the experience, but that idea really blows stobor.'

'You're telling me?' Njangu said. 'Not to mention Garvin'll be all over us. He's probably out there having all kinds of fun and getting medals.'

'There's always another party,' Heckmyer said.

'Yeh,' Yoshitaro said. 'And that makes me feel a *lot* better. 'Kay. I'll signal for extraction.'

Two Musth were savaged in an alley, and Wlencing declared a dawn-to-dusk curfew, no exceptions. Anyone seen outside their quarters would be shot.

Garvin wasn't able to harass Njangu at all. He hadn't been able to come up with any scheme that wasn't either pointless or suicidal.

I&R troops stayed out of the way while their officers and first *tweg* alternately sulked and tried to come up with something interesting.

The window washer had never been a soldier, nor had he served with the 'Raum or been a policeman. He was a quiet, sober, solitary man, whose main pleasure was shooting very small, very fast. very old-fashioned projectiles at very long ranges into very small targets.

He had no opinion about the Musth one way or another, until the children in the neighborhood had decided it would be fun to throw a few rocks at the next Musth patrol.

They did, and the Musth opened fire. Two little boys were seriously wounded, one girl killed.

The window washer became interested in the Musth, and studied them as he worked his solitary job in Leggett's main business district.

No one paid the slightest attention to the man who showed up with his battered lifter, attached lines to a building, then used them as guides to spider up and down in his bosun's chair. equipped with two modified droppers.

He made an interesting discovery:

Musth officials seemed to appear at the PlanGov

buildings on the first day of each week, no doubt to give the latest chapter of the law to their Council puppets.

He took three weeks to verify that was indeed a nice precise, dangerous schedule, decided he knew enough.

The next time Wlencing's *wynt* landed near the still-unfinished PlanGov buildings, no one noticed the little man ten stories up, about five hundred meters away. If they had, they might've found it odd that his chair wasn't at a window, but at a blank stone wall, where no one could notice the little man open up his tool kit, take out two wrapped tubelike objects, and put them together. A third object, a rather large optic sight, went atop the two pieces, and the device set on a bipod. Even then, the object looked so little like a contemporary blaster or laser many wouldn't have found cause for alarm.

He lay full length on his chair, moving slowly to avoid swaying, positioned himself comfortably, and eased a single round into the chamber of his weapon.

He swept the sight across the square, across the *wynt*, across three human policemen, found a knot of Musth.

The man inhaled, breathed out, held his breath, and pressed the trigger.

Without waiting to see the results of his shot, he unhurriedly broke his weapon down and moved his chair around the side of the building, then lowered it to the ground. Ten minutes later, his lifter was headed back toward his modest home. He never mentioned what he'd done, returned to his normal work the next day, and no one ever talked about the outrage to him.

The square outside PlanGov was a scream of rushing cops and Musth.

Wlencing sat on his tail next to the sprawled body of his aide, Rahfer. The Musth had a small entry hole in one side of his head, and most of his skull was missing on the other.

Daaf stood next to him.

'That shot was intended for you.'

'Perhaps,' Wlencing said. 'Perhaps not. Perhaps the worms merely wanted to kill any Musth.'

'This was not a brave action.'

Wlencing looked at him, then said:

'So it is appropriate that my response will not be, either.'

Again, the holos were commandeered, and again frightened men and women were murdered by firing squads.

The Musth announced more hostages would be taken, and the same response made to any other crime against them.

'I think,' Garvin said, we should think about doing something criminal.'

'Time and past,' Njangu agreed. 'Have you finally got a plan?'

'Yeh. Let's go see the old man.'

EIGHTEEN

Langnes 65443/Reckoning

Senza stared at the multicolored figures. data, hanging in midair over his workplace. He swept a hand, studied their replacements. scanned another set of data.

'*This*,' he demanded of his assistant. Kenryo, 'is the reality of what that rock-brain Paumoto and his crew are calling a triumph?'

'Yes,' his assistant said in a neutral voice.

'He's either a jelly-thinker, or he plans to keep this information secret. Monstrous, truly monstrous! Aesc killed, somewhere over half of his warriors casualties, more than that in equipment loss.

'Keffa we know to be a fool. He can't count his paws and get the same figure twice running. But Paumoto! He's not that stupid!

'Is he?'

The assistant, one of Senza's own cubs, made no reply.

'Did you run a projection of how many Common years it would take, given these losses, before the Cumbre system becomes profitable?'

'Yes.'

'And?'

'Somewhere between eight-eights and twice that,

depending on whether they merely seize the minerals or whether they're attempting to keep Cumbre a stable, producing system.'

'Someone is mad.' Senza proclaimed. Or else . . . or else this is a trap, intended to get me to move rashly, and then the real data will be presented, or some better interpretation we have all missed.'

'None of us have seen any alternatives.'

'As I said, something we have all missed.' Senza moved his paws in bewilderment.

'I wish . . . I want . . . to do something. To use this as a lever against Paumoto, quiet him, and hopefully trample that imbecile Keffa before he tries to have me slain.

'But this is too absurd, too unbelievable. I need something better.

'Something,' Senza said again. 'But I know not what.'

NINETEEN

D-Cumbre

'You know,' Ben Dill said to Alikhan. 'I feel like one of those old-timey generals, whose R&D people came to him with a new kind of spear or something, and he sat there stewing, staring, not knowing how to use it, and the war got worse and worse for him, and then some frigging barbarian snuck into the back of his tent and whomped him upside the head with a rock and the war was lost.'

He tossed a pebble out the tent flap at an inoffensive Mullion Island lizard, and growled.

'That was quite a speech,' Alikhan said. 'Am I making a jump in logic to assume you're thinking of me as this new kind of spear?'

'Not even a little bit,' Dill said. 'You say you want to help end this goddamned war, but we can't do this, can't do that, can't do the other thing.'

'Don't become angry,' Alikhan said. 'If you were in my position, what would you do?'

'Dunno,' Dill grunted. 'Go find a bar and try to get in a fight. Relieve some of the stress.'

'I don't think that's practical,' Alikhan said. 'First, I do not touch alcohol, which would make it boring for me;

second, if we brought along some of my decayed meat, your fellows would find that somewhat disgusting: third, I am not enamoured of the idea of bruising my paws in a melee; and last, if we *were* in a place where alcohol was served, wouldn't someone grab for a weapon when he saw a Musth, listening to no explanations?'

'That does not sound like an attractive evening to me.'

'Plus,' Dill grunted, 'I don't see any goddamned drinkin' dives on this goddamned island.'

'I'm sorry I don't seem to have any ideas about my possible deployment,' Alikhan said. 'Why don't you consult some experts?'

'Such as?'

'I'm sure there must be someone who knows something about the Musth here. Isn't it well-known that any army can always produce an expert on any subject?'

'I have some pleasure in having sight of you,' Danfin Froude said in Musth.

Alikhan waved a paw in negation.

'And I greet you,' he said in the same language, then switched to Basic. 'But perhaps we could communicate more readily in your tongue.'

'Is my accent *that* terrible?'

Alikhan, politely, chose not to answer him.

'Your friend here thought I could maybe be of service,' the mathematician said, 'and he's spent some time with me, trying to remember your conversations as precisely as he could.

'Something he said did give me a bit of an idea. You once told *Alt* Dill that your fellow warriors weren't given the opportunity to think otherwise about what they're doing than what war leaders like your father told them.'

'This is true,' Alikhan said. 'It is taken for granted that we learn to reason for ourselves in the den, with teaching from others and from our parents. Once we leave, become adults, once we take on service with another Musth, it is assumed we have chosen correctly after considerable thought, and henceforth should serve with absolute dedication.

'Such is the way of honor.'

After a moment of consideration, Alikhan added, and Ben wondered if there was a bit of melancholy in his sibilant voice, 'Maybe that is why we keep betraying each other, rather than really working together. It's very hard for any of us to say we made a mistake, that we should do something different.'

'It's easier,' Ben asked, 'just to shoot someone in the back?'

'Does it not save explanations?'

'You obviously don't have the same kind of court system we do,' Dill said.

'If you two trucks would shut the hell up,' Froude snapped, 'I think my idea can be made to work. Alikhan. You know that a voice can be filtered so no one can identify it?'

'Certainly. We make great use of such devices in our ruling bodies.'

'Do you think, if you had the opportunity to sit down with another warrior you could maybe make him come over to our side, or at any rate start questioning his orders?'

'No.' Alikhan said. 'Only a great talker, one like Senza, who I studied with, might be able to do that. And there would have to be the seed of a doubt planted beforehand.'

'Seed of a doubt, eh?' Froude mused. 'Ben, why don't you hunt up some nice decayed *giptel* for Alikhan. and some sort of firewater for me, then make yourself gone. Alikhan and I have some free-associating to do.

The merchants' associations in Leggett, Aire, Launceston,

and Seya were surprised — business wasn't *quite* as awful
as they'd anticipated under the Musth, even though most
people didn't have many credits, and those who did were
reluctant to spend them until the situation clarified
itself. But at least no companies had been seized out-
right, at least not yet.

Profits were down as anticipated, but there were many
new businesses opening. All were small many seemed a
bit improbable, but all were adequately funded, their
owners paying for everything in hard currency.

It was also interesting that the profile of these new
businessmen was pretty much the same — young to early
middle-aged, mostly single men and women who kept to
themselves. Sometimes their store shelves seemed not as
fully stocked as they could be, but what of that?
Cumbrian manufacturing hadn't even begun to rebuild
after the 'Raum uprising.

These shop owners joined their local merchants associations, minded their own business, and led quiet lives.

A few merchants theorized that these new retailers
were ex-service, and were impressed that the Force had
evidently made them put some of their pay away, for
times like these.

It was also interesting that these store owners all
seemed interested in electronics, and all put in rather
expensive com gear.

One of the most popular new businesses was the
Hammer And Thud Blowout Boys, a fourteen-piece
band that began playing in Leggett to great acclaim,
then asked for permission from the Musth to tour the
cities of D-Cumbre. Musth security searched their gear
and possessions thoroughly, found nothing, and
approved. It would be good for human morale to be
entertained even though this seemingly arbitrary
arrangement of noise did little for the aliens.

The H&T Boys – actually as many young women as men – had quite an entourage on the road, friends, equipment handlers, and so forth as they zigged across the planet, evidently willing to play any venue that wanted them.

The band leader, a jovial beanstalk of a man named Hedley, was unusual in that he played none of the main instruments, but only banged a tambourine and sang in the chorus.

The party began a little nervously, and it was noticeable that some of the invited Rentiers didn't materialize, especially those who'd been willing to remain on the Musth Council.

It was thrown by the enormously rich Rentier, Bampur, somewhat vaguely in honor of Erik Penwyth's successful return from the dead, 'or wherever he's been hiding himself,' following a banquet by Erik's parents.

Penwyth seemed little changed by his time in the military, still drawlingly casual, handsome in a rather dissipated way, and taking little if anything seriously.

No one noticed that he drank a great deal less than he had before, and smilingly refused any drugs offered. He drifted here, there, perhaps a bit quieter, more interested in listening than he'd been before, dancing with anyone who asked.

Redheaded Karo Lonrod guided him onto the floor, pressed close.

'I assume,' she said breathily, 'you have incredible tales of heroism to whisper in my pink shell-like ear.'

'Nary a bit,' Penwyth said. 'I was sent to some stupid radar station on one of the out-islands, saw nothing, heard nothing, made my way home when I thought the shooting was over.'

She pulled back, looked at him skeptically.

'I thought you volunteered for something dashing . . . what did they call it, R&I or something?'

'Briefly,' Penwyth admitted. 'But they were too terribly heroic for my tastes. Man can get killed, y'know.'

'No, I don't know,' Lonrod said. 'But something I do know, is you and I never went home together.'

' 'Sat so?'

'It is. Are you interested in changing that?'

'Why certainly,' Penwyth said. 'A man should never refuse an invitation like that, not and remain a gentleman. Or woman, either.'

She giggled, was about to whisper something, when Jasith Mellusin touched his shoulder.

'I believe it's my turn with the wandering lad?'

'We were just getting into an interesting discussion.' Lonrod said, but moved out of Erik's embrace. 'Can I consider that a promise?'

'You certainly may,' Erik said. 'We'll discuss the details in a bit.'

Jasith moved into his arms, and they danced away.

'I assume Karo was interested in mattress games,' Jasith said. 'She told me she wanted to see what you'd learned in the army.'

'I'm afeared she'll be disappointed,' Erik said. 'Nothing but saluting everything that moved, and painting everything else white.'

'Right,' Jasith said, disbelievingly. 'I remember you from before I got married, before . . .'

She broke off, and her smile vanished.

'And where's your husband tonight,' Erik asked, changing the subject.

'Not here, of course. His lords and furry masters might get angry if he had any association with a soldier.'

'That's Loy,' Erik said. 'Always very careful.'

They danced silently for a while.

'Do you know what happened to Garvin?' Jasith asked.

'I've heard some stories,' he said. 'I'm fairly sure he's alive, if I don't know where he is.'

'I asked around,' Jasith said, 'and found out a whole lot of soldiers haven't come home yet.'

'Jasith,' Erik said, 'I understand it got very nasty with the Musth. Hell, there are men and women from the Force who're still missing after that disaster with the 'Raum.'

'I know that,' Jasith said. 'But why have so many of the officers not shown up?'

'I think because they were trained to lead from the front, and that's generally a fairly good way to get killed.'

'Maybe. Or maybe not.'

'Maybe, or maybe not,' Erik agreed. 'This band's quite good, isn't it?'

'Erik Penwyth, I think you're fencing with me.'

'Not a chance,' he said. 'Didn't bring any fence posts, for beginners.'

'You know, I'm not a complete bubblebrain,' Jasith said 'I think we can assume *some* of Daddy's genes got through.'

'Now don't go getting serious on me,' Penwyth said. 'I've come back with a firm plan to devote myself to nothing but carryin' on relentlessly from now on.'

'No doubt,' Jasith said. 'But if you happen to run across Garvin in your travels, tell him to call this number,' and she gave him a slip of paper. 'I'm the only one who'll answer it, I keep the com with me, there's no recorder, and nobody knows about the number. Especially not my husband.'

Penwyth waggled his eyebrows. 'Now, that sounds most full of intrigue.'

Jasith looked at him.

'That word's got a whole bunch of meanings.'

'It does,' Penwyth said blandly. 'Now, doesn't it.'

Ab Yohns had chanced two trips into Leggett since the fall of Camp Mahan. He made small purchases, visited coffee bars, saloons, and restaurants, listening to people talk. He noticed the wave of new, small businesses, and their owners, tried to chat with them, but found the women and men rather close-mouthed.

Interesting, he thought, considering whether he ought to involve himself in what was developing, decided not. There would be little profit in it, and he knew well the first to resist generally get killed being noble.

Besides, his main client was still Protector Redruth.

He did admire the subtlety of whoever was running Confederation Intelligence, or at least this scheme – he doubted if the Musth were familiar enough with humans to watch businesses as closely as they should.

But sooner or later he knew their puppets would get curious.

Wlencing hid a distasteful reaction, turned away from the four vee formations of recruits to Daaf. He spoke in a low tone:

'Am I showing signs of incorrect emotion, or are these warriors less than those who have joined us before?'

'Referring to their records, which I did during the insystem flight, no, you are not. Few of these have been properly trained, either by their dens or by the masters they chose to follow. Almost none of them have any fighting experience, beyond acting as guards for their first masters.

'Also, there was something I found more worrisome, if I may speak freely?'

'Go ahead,' Wlencing said. 'It will do these good to wait in the rain at the pleasure of a leader.'

'Few of them come from a respected clan, and the half dozen who do are not impressive. I took the moment to speak to them, ask them about their masters, and they said their clans did not wish them to engage with you.'

'What clans were these?'

Daaf consulted a handheld panel, named them.

'Two I know not,' Wlencing said angrily, 'but three of those are clans that supported our claims to this system when we first met.'

Wlencing thought back to the meeting on 4Planet, in the building called Gathering. It was two system-years gone, no longer, yet seemed even more distant, buried in the bloodshed and fighting that had gone on since. He thought for an instant of his dead cub Alikhan, shut off that area of thought.

'I await your words,' Daaf said

'Never mind,' Wlencing growled. 'Those three clans who were on our side now are not. That is enough for you to know. Did you ask what their clanmasters or their aides said?'

'I did. Very carefully,' Daaf said. 'With each one away from the hearing of the other. They said, and I am choosing my words with exactitude, that their clanmasters were increasingly convinced there was no glory, no honor, no gain to be reached by serving this far from the Musth worlds.'

'Senza's poison,' Wlencing hissed. 'We should have found a way to deal with him before . . . never mind. You did not hear what I just spoke.

'What of the new equipment that arrived with these recruits?'

'That, at least, is first-rate.'

'Good. How many of this intake have experience as pilots?'

'No more than forty, and those are barely qualified.'

'That will be the first order. Turn them over to the training masters, with orders to find any that might be capable of flying our attack ships.

'The others . . . all the others . . . are to become warriors, no matter what they thought they would be serving as. We have enough meat cutters, clerks, already.

'When you have given the orders, I want you to communications. I need to have speech with Senza and Keffa as soon as possible.'

The com shuddered against Jasith's side.

She stood, and the analyst looked down the long table. startled at the interruption. The half dozen other board members in the meeting were just as surprised.

'Pardon me,' she said, trying to sound apologetic. 'But there is a com I must make that I forgot about. Please forgive me for my rudeness.'

Without waiting, she hurried to the door behind her, past her two waiting bodyguards, into the corridor as the com fluttered again.

She pulled it from her pocket, keyed it on.

'Jasith Mellusin.'

'Garvin Jaansma.'

'You re alive!'

'I'm alive.' She could find no emotion in his voice.

'I want to see you.'

There was a silence.

'I can't. I've got . . . business I'm involved with.'

'I think maybe your business is mine. And I'm not thinking of, of anything else.'

Again a pause.

' 'Kay.'

'What about—'

Garvin interrupted her.

'No names. What about . . . where I saw you last.

Tomorrow night. When you were about to go to dinner with him. The same time. Go for a walk on the pier.'

'There? But that'll be dangerous. It's close to close to them.'

'Don't worry about it.'

The connection went dead.

Jasith stared at the com for a time, then pocketed it, returned to her meeting.

TWENTY

Langnes 889234/Tenacity

'You are overly worried,' Keffa said, a bit of a purr in his voice. 'Those who vacillate, those who have fallen away from commitment to your cause, are unworthy, both for their race and to share in any benefits from this undertaking.'

He waited while the transmission bounced around the galaxy, had enough time to watch two more bouts in his private arena and the start of a third before the reply came from the system once known as Cumbre, now Redon.

'I think I am still correct in my concern,' Wlencing said. 'Remember I am here on the fringes of nowhere, and by the time an action occurs where you are, and its effects reverberate to me, much time has passed.

'So this is why I want something to be done now. One thing that would aid immeasurably is if there is some way to silence Senza. I would also be grateful for any help you or your clan might be able to make, particularly in the way of warriors, good trained warriors, or equipment.

'I attempted to contact Paumoto, but was told that he was not available. I would appreciate it if you would convey my respects, and also my needs, to him.'

Again, the long wait.

'You may be assured you have my every sinew to assist you,' Keffa said. 'Even though I must say I am somewhat taken aback at the reports of the cost of this subjugation, in warriors, equipment, money.

'Still, it is important to we Musth that we are victorious, and I shall personally make it my business.

'Remember, War Leader Wlencing, you are not alone.'

Keffa nodded to an assistant. and the connection was broken. He tried to return to watching the bout, but other matters kept intruding.

So Wlencing was not able to contact Paumoto. Keffa wondered – he had communication with the clan leader within the past three days, and Paumoto had said nothing about traveling. Was Paumoto avoiding the war leader?

As for silencing Senza . . . that had been tried by many, and, Keffa thought, it would be as impossible to cut off radiation from an exploding sun. He wished he knew of an assassin more competent than the two he'd tried previously.

Was Paumoto beginning to reconsider his commitment?

Keffa thought not. He *certainly* would have contacted Keffa if he thought a change in strategy was worth considering.

Would he not?

Perhaps a visit to this strange system that had belonged to Man might be in order, might suggest a better way of dealing with the matter, might even provide a clue to Paumoto's behavior.

TWENTY-ONE

D-Cumbre

Jon Hedley finished reading the translation, lowered it. 'Seems pretty flipping strong,' he said. 'But there's a couple words I don't understand. *Lert*, for instance.'

'I do not think there is an equivalent,' Alikhan said.

'There doesn't seem to be,' Danfin Froude said. 'Sort of a combination between pride, defiance, an assemblage of what they consider military virtues. Try warrior-thinking. Something you can teach others or, if you're a mystic, inherit as part of a racial thing.'

' 'Kay,' Hedley said. 'What about *krang*?'

'Laws, but more than laws,' Alikhan said. 'Customs are part of it.'

'Code would maybe come close,' Froude added. 'Or so Alikhan tells me.'

'*Brahda*?'

'Fate, career.'

'Another question,' Hedley said. 'You didn't make any call for anyone to join us. Why not?'

'Would you respond to a call for desertion from your enemy, especially if he was an alien?' Froude asked.

' 'Course not.'

'Well then.'

' 'Kay,' Hedley said. 'And I like the way you have of disseminating it. I'll make a few mods, to make sure we suddenly don't get a homing missile up our flipping heinies before we go off-air, clear it with the old man.

'But I'm pretty sure we have a go on this one.'

'I won't bullshit you,' Njangu said, his voice echoing across the square. The village of Issus was filled with fishermen from Dharma and a dozen nearby islands. The square was guarded by I&R gunmen, and Shrike and Shadow portable launchers were set up on the village outskirts waiting for a Musth aircraft to show.

'We're going to fight back, and we're going to need you. We'll need you for courier boats, to smuggle various things. I don't think we'll have to train you for that. We'll need you to move troops back and forth between one place and another, maybe, as things progress, we might want you as gunboats.'

'What's in it for us?' a boat driver asked.

'Damned little,' Njangu said. 'Seeing Cumbre out from under the Musth, if you give a stobor's nostril about that. Getting your boat sunk and maybe you dead if you screw up or get unlucky.

'The infinite gratitude of the government if we win.'

There was laughter, boos. Njangu grinned, and there was more laughter.

'You see? I said I wasn't gonna try to run anything up your butts you weren't expecting.'

'The Musth sure like fish,' another fisherman called. 'Good market there.'

'They sure do,' Njangu said amiably, relaxing against a porch railing. This wasn't much different than hustling his clique back when he was a gangster into doing something he wanted and they weren't sure about.

'They like 'em so much they'll probably want you to

go back to their worlds and teach 'em how to shoot a net.'

Some laughter, but there were wry mutterings.

'Or teach 'em how to use someone for bait, eh Njangu?' a woman called.

That got laughter — most of them had heard about Yoshitaro being used in exactly that capacity when he came home with Ton Milot, a long time ago, when he was a trainee, and almost becoming dinner for a voracious *barraco*.

Now you know why I'm fighting,' Njangu said. 'I don't want to go back to being bait. Especially for some aliens. But what about you? You think you'll do just fine, hanging about, throwing your nets, and the Musth'll live and let live?'

'Never known a government to do that for fishermen,' someone called. 'Why should we expect a buncha furry aliens to do different?'

'*I* wouldn't, if I were you. But I'm not. My personal call is they're going to get more and more demanding. harder and harder to deal with. And I know it's easier to get rid of a hard-ass master **before** he gets all his hooks seated in you.

'The Musth still have got their thumbs up, wandering around on their elbows. But they aren't dumb. Little by little, day by day, they'll get more secure, know us better, and we'll be farther and farther up that creek.

'Think about it. If you want to join us, there'll be people around. If we need you for a specific job, we'll call you. There won't be any problem from us if you say no.

'But don't go and sing to the Musth about us, about what I said, about what you maybe'll see your friends and neighbors doing.' Njangu's voice changed, became soft, dangerous.

'If you do that, you and I'll have a chat. And I don't think you want that to happen.'

He slid off the porch, slung his blaster. Someone in the crowd — he thought it was either Ton Milot, who he'd brought along for exactly that service, or Alei his brother — cheered, and there were some other cheers. Not everyone, but some. Most of the crowd was silent, thinking about what Yoshitaro had said. about what they'd seen already of the Musth, about what the future might bring.

His *tweg*, Stef Bassas. came up.

'Are we pulling out tonight, sir?'

Njangu glanced at the lowering sun.

'Negative. I'd just as soon not chance the rust bucket in the air when it's getting dark. Too big a goddamned signature, and I don't like meeting *aksai* in the dark. Or anywhere else, come to think.'

The team's Grierson was under cam nets about half a kilometer outside Issus. This was the fourth speech Njangu had given that day in as many villages, and he was tired. He'd deliberately chosen Issus as the last stop because he felt it was as much of a home, besides the Force, as he had on Cumbre.

'We'll set up camp outside the village,' he decided.

'I'll have the men detailed off, sir. And I'll have rations distributed from the Grierson. Maybe we'll be able to get some fruit from the people to supplement them,' Bassas said.

' 'Lo, Njanju,' a shy voice came.

Njangu turned, saw Deira. She'd lost a bit of weight since he'd last seen her, but was still voluptuous. She wore, like a lot of the fishing women. a comfortable wrap that, Njangu knew, comfortably unwrapped. He felt a stirring somewhere south of his weapons harness

'Are you staying the night?'

'Uh, yeh.'

Deira smiled.

'With me?'

'Umm,' Njangu said cleverly, looked at Bassas, who was considering the ground.

First your men, then yourself, he remembered the adage.

'The village will be feeding your men if you do,' Deira said. 'We don't have many feasts these days. and we'd surely like to have one in your honor.'

Njangu noticed Ton and Alei to one side, with an impressively bearded man who had to be the clout in Issus, looking approving.

Bassas smiled at the idea of a night without issue rations.

'We thank you,' Njangu said. 'But we cannot drink. If the Musth show up, we have to be able to do more'n throw rocks at them.'

'I've already told everyone that,' Ton said. 'They'll go along with the water-and-juice ritual, even though they don't like it.'

Njangu looked at the sky, looked at Deira, thought about duty, thought about Deira, thought, *Screw duty.*

'We'll do it.'

'Good,' Ton said. 'Some of our boys were admiring your girls.'

'And don't forget about us women,' Deira said. 'It'll be nice, uh, talking to somebody who doesn't have fish breath.'

'Thanks a lot,' Ton said.

'You be quiet,' Deira said. 'You're married.'

'I know that,' Ton said indignantly.

'Lupul told me to make sure you wouldn't forget.' Deira came up, took Njangu's arm.

'You, I have a special dish cooking. Just you, me, and Babeu,' she said in a low voice. 'That's her, there. We're good friends, and I told her *all* about you, about us. If you like her, it'll be like it was before, hmm?' Deira indicated a slender blond-haired woman about Deira's age. 'I had a lot of fun then, more than the last time you were here. You think you won't get bored?'

'I'm not worried about that,' Njangu said. 'I'm worried about getting any sleep.'

'Don't worry,' Deira said. 'You won't get any.'

'Oh Abu running zigzags in the desert,' Njangu murmured.

'Come on.' Deira urged. 'The fish won't be ready for an hour. And we don't want to waste any time, do we?'

Njangu moaned.

Tomorrow he had another four speeches scheduled, these in mountain villages, recruiting aircraft watchers.

The team landed quietly about half a kilometer from the transmission relay station. The four technicians. helped by their gun guards, turned the antigrav pallet's power on, and muscled it out of the Grierson's rear hatch and up the mountainside toward the low buildings just over the crest. Alikhan and Froude, even though their work was finished, insisted on seeing the mission through. Froude had been given a blaster, and someone started to tell him how to use it. Froude got indignant. He might be a civilian, but that didn't mean he knew *nothing*.

Ben Dill, following orders and accompanying Alikhan everywhere, had flown the Grierson in, and now was quietly bemoaning his fate at being once again a crunchie as he took point and led the team upward.

They saw no one as they approached the site. Two techs, specialists in security devices, examined the fencing.

'Nothing, sir,' they reported to Froude, not knowing what rank he held, but assuming anyone who could dress as shabbily as he did, and in civilian clothes to boot, certainly outranked them. 'Just some buzzers and the fence is electrified to keep critters off. It's clear now, and we've cut the lock off.'

They muscled the bulky transmitter through the gate, waited while the techs opened the control-room door brought it inside.

'Just like I thought, sir,' another tech reported. 'Pretty standard, no security devices I can see on the operating net. We'll need fifteen, no ten minutes to wrap this up.'

Well within the time frame the retransmission point's power was shunted through the transmitter, and it was powered up.

The transmitter was tuned to the Musth's main watch frequency, and was using the station's power to blast its message across the planet and into space.

It was not coincidence that the station was one of *Matin*'s.

'Anytime, sir.'

'Start it up,' Froude said, and the recording hissed on, beaming into a hundred or more disbelieving Musth coms, from ships to stationary units.

The team left the station, trotting down the path to the Grierson and lifting away from the site before anyone could respond.

The production qualities of the recording were somewhat lacking, no more than a carefully filtered voice, speaking Musth in a gentle tone:

'Remember when you were a cub, how you fought, played, looked up at the stars, saw them gleaming promise?

'You fought hard in your den, showed you were the strongest, the best, the most lert. You held your own and more in the warrens, then went out, into the world.

'You became a warrior, knew the ways, the sacred krang.

You fought your brothers on the training grounds, proving your-self again. Or perhaps you listened to the blood singing within, and came to Redon without your claws blooded.

'*You were proud, brave, with all your* lert, *all your honor.*

'*But what has happened since then?*

'*You have seen your brothers die, killed from behind or from a burrow. You fought back.*

'*Against what?*

'*Cubs? Females? Nothing?*

'*Is this honor?*

'*Has your* lert *grown?*

'*Many, too many, of your fellows are gone, with only the death ceremony for remembrance. Some lie rotting on a jungle path, others' bones are turned, swept by the tides, others . . . others are simply vanished, with no one to know their deaths.*

'*Will their dens remember them? Will their clans? Will cubs thrill to their honor?*

'*What about you?*

'*Will cubs pray to inherit your* lert?

'*Or will you be like so many, many others, die here on this forgotten end path, this green nightmare of a planet?*

'*Dead*

'*Forgotten.*

'*Without honor.*

'*Or is it time to leave, to return to worlds that are as they should be, to find proper brahda for yourself, for others, for your clan?*

'*You can make your own decision about that.*

'*You are a warrior. You know how to think.*

'*Don't you?*'

A continuous low growl came from Wlencing as he lis-tened to the recording twice through.

'I am assuming that transmission source had been taken over by these worms.'

'It must have been,' Daaf said. 'I cannot picture this Kouro person being that far removed from reality to allow it.'

'No, he is not,' Wlencing said. 'I assume you sent a team out to secure the location, and make full analysis.'

Daaf hesitated.

'You did not?'

'No,' Daaf said. 'An *aksai* flight commander located the source of the transmission, and he and the other craft destroyed it.'

Wlencing's growl grew larger.

'I want his guts . . . no. I cannot punish bravery. But make sure he does not enter my sight for a time, until my anger is gone. Also, deal with this Kouro. He may not have anything to do with this filth, but it is still his fault. Punish him in some appropriate way. Take some of his credits. I would think that would hurt him more than anything physical.'

'It will be done.'

Wlencing touched a sensor, listened to the 'cast again. What did the bandits hope to accomplish? There was no call to change sides or mutiny. Just that bleak promise of eventual death and nothingness.

It would not be good for warrior spirit to listen to it. Wlencing was about to order that anyone caught listening to this would be punished, caught himself. That was stupid, and would do nothing more than make it a forbidden, and therefore attractive thing.

He listened again.

The language was perfect. No human could have made the recording. Certainly whoever created it understood Musth thinking But no human could understand Musth honor. But no Musth would work with worms. And there were no reports of a prisoner having been taken . . .

Who, then, was responsible?

Jasith walked back and forth on the finger dock outside
the Shelburne. She kept looking at her watch finger.
Garvin, if he was going to show up, was half an hour late.

A brisk wind that tasted of ash from Camp Mahan was
coming off the bay, so in spite of the sun there was
nobody on the docks except a fisherman sitting with his
back to a bollard, using a glue gun to repair a net; and a
small dark 'Raum boy, scrubbing lazily at the gangway
leading down to the docks.

She didn't see the bulge of a pistol hidden in the dock
boy's shorts, who was actually about fourteen, and had
been a courier for the 'Raum during the rising; or the
gleam of the blaster hidden under the fisherman's nets.

She started to get angry, remembered that whatever
Garvin was doing, it was probably something that could
get him killed. And things didn't always happen the way
they should in that business, she had learned from the
'Rising. She decided to give it another half hour.

A sleek water runabout, all gleaming wood and
chrome, which looked like it was two or three centuries
old, cut sleekly in from the bay, leaving a great rooster
tail as it drove toward shore.

Jasith thought the boat was about to ram the dock
when the whine of its engine died, and the boat's course
straightened. Water churned at its stern as the engine
reversed, and the runabout drifted to a stop exactly next
to the dock.

Garvin Jaansma, immaculate in white shorts, shirt,
and a cream-colored sweater, jumped out of the boat's
cockpit and deftly moored it to a piling.

Jasith's eyes were wide.

'My-oh-muffins,' she managed. 'Where did you get
that boat . . . and that outfit?'

'Some of your fellow Rentiers donated them for the afternoon,' he said. 'Rather dapper, aren't I?'

'You are. Where did you learn to handle a boat like that?'

'Didn't I ever tell you about the time I ran a water show for my circus?'

Jasith looked at him closely, couldn't tell if he was lying or not.

Garvin looked at an old-fashioned wristwatch.

'It's a bit late for lunch,' he said, behaving as if he were Erik Penwyth's unknown brother, 'but perhaps a glass of wine or some tea would go well. Care to?'

He extended an elbow. Jasith took it.

'What happens if we run into some Musth? They come here sometimes,' she asked.

'That'd be unfortunate,' Garvin said. 'For the Musth.'

He didn't explain that the runabout was loaded with close to a ton of Blok explosives, and he had the detonator in his pocket; nor that the fisherman and dockboy were only two of the platoon of gunmen in and around the Shelburne.

Jasith studied Garvin. He'd changed since she'd last seen him. His face was harder, his eyes seemed to look a little beyond or through what he was seeing, and were never still. He was leaner, and moved more quickly, as if anything his foot touched might explode.

'I didn't know if you were going to go inside the hotel when you showed up,' she said. 'But I had two of my security men check two tables in the restaurant, and make sure they didn't have any listening devices.'

Garvin half grinned. That was the reason he was a little late – his own men had seen the security team at work, and had snatched them as they left the hotel, found out who they were, and then made sure *they* hadn't planted any bugs.

'And you don't have to worry about my husband showing up and asking embarrassing questions.'

'I know,' Garvin said. 'He'll be busy with War Leader Wlencing the rest of the day.'

'You didn't have anything to do with that, did you? I mean, picking a *Matin* tower to do that from?'

'Honestly, I didn't.' Honestly, Garvin hadn't, but he thought Hedley's idea a capital one.

'I wish you had,' Jasith said. 'I thought it was funnier than all hell.'

Garvin grinned, a real grin, and the two laughed. It was a nice sound, he thought, remembering when it'd come at better times.

Jasith's laugh stopped suddenly.

'Loy and I . . . aren't getting along that well these days.' Without realizing it, she touched her face, where Kouro had struck her. 'Next time, if there's a next time of one kind or another, *do* have something to do with it.'

The maître d' escorted them to a table near a window, and didn't show by the slightest lifting of an eyebrow that he knew the man with Jasith Mellusin most certainly wasn't her husband. The Shelburne wasn't the best hotel and restaurant on D-Cumbre because the staff gossiped.

Jasith ordered the same white cordial she had the last time; Garvin asked for an herbal tea.

'Are you living the clean-cut life now?' Jasith asked.

'I'm working,' Garvin said.

'Which, of course, means I should get to the point of why I wanted to talk to you,' Jasith said. 'Did you manage to get away with the money I arranged?'

'We did,' Garvin said. 'And thanks. It's being put to very good use right now.'

'Don't tell me how.'

'I hadn't planned to.'

She reached in her belt pouch, took out a small, blue-plastic chip, gave it to him.

'Mellusin Mining is very, very big. Not as big as it was before everybody started shooting, but still big.'

'I'd kind of understood that already,' Garvin said. 'Seemed fairly obvious to me.'

'One thing my father had, which he never told me about, was a handful of people who'd do just about anything for him. Hon Felps, he was Daddy's first assistant, had to tell me about them.'

'A lot of very rich types seem to need their own private muscle,' Garvin said. 'You're not shocking me.'

'I've still got the people. Maybe, the way things are going with the Musth, I'll need them, sooner or later. But that's not why I brought them up.

'Look at the chip.'

Garvin did.

'Looks like an old-fashioned hotel key fob,' he said. 'With a number on it.'

'The number's the thing. GT973. Remember that.'

' 'Kay.'

'Every one of my key executives has been told if anybody contacts him and uses that number, give him or her anything they want,' Jasith said. 'I mean anything.'

'That'd sure make embezzlement an interesting proposition.'

'I guess it did a couple of times, Hon said. Or maybe some other ways some people wanted to take advantage. He said it didn't happen more than twice, and I didn't ask him for the details.'

Now it was Garvin's turn to consider Jasith. She, too, seemed to have grown up, her expression older than it should be at twenty. There were little wrinkles at the corner of her mouth. Garvin wished he could make them into smile lines, ignored the romantic thought.

'You've got the number,' Jasith said. 'If you need it for anything . . . go ahead and do it. Just tell me if you need me to cover what happened.'

'Thanks,' Garvin said, and the key disappeared as their drinks came.

'What about money?' she asked. 'Do you need more?'

'I don't think so.'

'Again, ask if you do.'

'Again, thanks.' Garvin wondered if he should say anything, wondered why he shouldn't. 'You've changed some.'

'*Things* seem to have changed, haven't they?'

'Yeh,' Garvin said, sipping tea. 'They surely have. Something else that just came to me. Sometimes we run a little short of transport. Mellusin Mining has a lot of spaceships, transporters.'

'Just ask.' Jasith put her drink down, leaned across the table to him, said, fiercely, 'Garvin, it's going to get worse, a lot worse, before things get better, isn't it?'

'Yeh.'

'What about the Confederation? Are they ever going to show up?'

'Damned if I know,' Garvin said. 'I wouldn't expect them, or anybody else in high-anodized armor anytime soon.'

'What about Redruth?'

'I don't think he'd want to tangle with the whole Musth empire, or even the chunk we've got hanging around here, so don't worry about him for a while. I'd guess he assumes there's a gabillion of them in-system, although I wish to hell I knew why they *haven't* swarmed all over us,' Garvin said. 'I know we would, if we'd grabbed a system from the Musth that had things we wanted.

'I guess we all screw up, thinking that just because

somebody's weird-looking, way down deep they think the same, or sort of the same as we do.'

Jasith managed a smile.

'That's the advantage of being a woman. We know better. We learned the hard way.'

Garvin laughed.

'Anything else?' he asked.

Jasith looked around.

'I really wish we weren't here,' she said.

'Where would you like to be?'

Again, a smile came.

'I remember a lim, floating around Camp Mahan. Or a flower bed at my house.'

Garvin, when he'd arranged the meet, had one of his men rent a room upstairs for emergency purposes. The balcony fronted on a roof ideal for a sudden exit, and the room could have been . . . could be . . . used for other purposes. He almost said something, stopped himself.

'That'd be nice,' he said gently. 'I'd like that a lot, too.'

He took money from his pocket, put it on the table.

'Maybe . . . another time.'

He bent over, chastely kissed her lips, hurried out.

Jasith lifted her drink, then didn't want it. She stood, watching Garvin move quickly down the dock into the runabout, bring the lines inboard as the engine throbbed into life. Foam frothed at the stern, and the boat moved away from the dock, then, at full power, sped off, lifting to the step.

She watched until it disappeared to the east, along the coast, into the haze. Jasith realized the haze was her making, found a handkerchief in her purse, dabbed at her face, checked her makeup, then left the room.

A waiter checking table settings and a maid folding napkins at a table near the exit waited until she was gone. The maid took a tiny com from her pocket, keyed it.

'Both clear,' she said. 'No tail, no probs, no action. Team withdrawing.'

'Interestin',' Njangu said. 'So we've got Mellusin Mining in our pockets. All we have to do now is figure out what we can use 'em for.'

He eyed his friend skeptically.

'You done good, little brown brother. I'd make lewd suppositions about how you did it if I hadn't read the cover team's report.' He caught Garvin's expression.

'Something delicate there. Sorry. Forget I spoke.'

'Didn't mean to be touchy,' Garvin said. 'I'm just not sure what happened . . . what didn't happen . . . meant.'

'Like I said,' Njangu said. 'Forget about it. You want to clear your head even more, I've got a nice, nasty little bit of nastiness about to ripen. Nothing but in, bang, bang, bang, and we go home.

'This clever operation emanates from careful study of my stumbling around a few weeks or so ago trying to pot ol' Wlencing that didn't play out like it should've. But I always knew something good'd come out of that.'

'You mean Lir figured something out?'

'Sharrop,' Njangu said. 'If you want to come, you're a straphanger, and I'm in charge. Better . . . big strong lad like yourself can be commo, and lug the set.'

'I'm your boy. Gimme ten to put a harness together.'

Actually, the idea really was Njangu's. A husband-and-wife team, going to work for the Musth at the Highlands base took some uninflated metalloid-coated balloons with them, together with a can of gas. They had an elaborate story all ready, involving a birthday and absent friends, and were somewhat disappointed when their gear was barely glanced at, and the balloons ignored. They also had, hidden in the handle of a suitcase, a tiny transceiver, set on a single frequency.

Njangu's team, inserted about two hours' hike from the base by Grierson, consisted of half a dozen gun guards from I&R, together with ten men and women from an infantry company's combat support platoon. Each carried a light mortar and an apron pack of rounds.

They reached the cave Njangu had found on his previous trip, holed up. At dusk the next day, they ate and washed from a nearby pool.

Njangu checked the wind direction. As always at that hour, it was blowing from the southwest, at about four knots. Perfect. And, as always, the fog hung close about them. He had trouble seeing ten meters in any direction.

The team moved by compass to the location Njangu had picked, just behind a low hillock. Two hundred meters on the other side of the rise the base perimeter began, with its guards and alarms.

The mortars were carefully positioned by SatPos. sandbagged, their aiming stakes set. They would fire on predetermined azimuths and ranges.

Three rounds per tube were fused, the correct increments set, and the guns were ready.

Garvin touched a sensor on his transmitter, and the transceiver inside the camp beeped once. The woman holding it glanced around the barracks again to make sure everyone except her partner was sleeping. twisted the handle, and waited until a responding beep came. Then the pair filled the balloons, opened their barracks window, and freed them.

Sixteen silvery blobs floated away, across the base toward the runways . . .

Njangu waited ten minutes, then tapped two I&R

women. They doubled across to the mortar teams, clicked fingers, came back.

Ten gunners held rounds over the tubes, pulled safety pins, and dropped the rounds. Nearly simultaneously. the guns CHUNG*ed*, and small bombs lofted into the Musth base. Another volley, and a third.

The first alarm was shrilling as the team broke their tubes down, shouldered them, and trotted away, keeping the hillock between them and the Musth base.

Njangu, on point, touched sensors as they retreated, and tiny lights they'd clipped to bushes along the path lit for a few seconds, then burned out, leaving nothing but a trace of ash to mark their presence, fireflies guiding the attackers back toward their aircraft.

Meanwhile, mortar rounds slammed in across the base, and the Musth went to full alert. A rocket battery managed to get a location on the mortar launches and ripple-fired a return volley, then corrected and sent hell flaming around where the mortars had been.

Aksai, wynt, velv all followed alert plans and their pilots and scurrying ground teams got drives started, and the ships lifted, getting away from danger.

Lifting blind, on instruments, the ships moved smoothly along the short approach lanes to takeoff points, readied for lift.

Then more alarms went off – unknown aircraft had somehow penetrated outer security, obviously acquiring targets as they flew slowly toward the runways. Evidently no one had those balloons on visual as they drifted toward the runways, or couldn't get through on the jammed coms, so their radar images worked exactly as hoped for.

It still might not have been catastrophe if there hadn't been some luck in the game. Too many of the ships were flown by half-trained, inexperienced pilots. Alarms, danger, yammering on the coms, and it took no more than half a dozen fliers to panic and decide to break up, to blazes with clearance, and go for open sky where they could see, not have to rely on these still-unfamiliar instruments.

An *aksai* smashed into a *velv*, and the destroyer exploded. More pilots broke, and there were other collisions. Traffic control, the formation commanders were screaming, trying to bring order, making things worse, and other ships smashed together, lost orientation, and ground-looped or just flew into the ground, or into buildings, and the runways were flaming confusion.

The Force team was halfway across the water to Mullion Island before the lead Grierson's electronics specialist reported any Musth on her radar, and by that time the attack ships were safely under Zhukov cover.

And then they disappeared.

The Musth base was a disaster of fire and death, and it was two days before normal air traffic resumed.

The real casualties weren't the dead or burnt pilots or ground personnel, nor the ruined hangars and buildings. but the morale and confidence of the Musth who heard about the debacle.

Another propaganda broadcast was prepared, and a team went out. But the Musth weren't imbeciles – the relay station they tried to take over, not one of Loy Kouro's, had been boobytrapped. Three members of the technical team were killed, two badly injured, the survivors barely extracted before the Musth reaction force arrived.

'We went to the well once too often, my friend,' Froude said.

'There must be something more effective,' Alikhan said. 'Something more conclusive we can arrive at.'

'Dig out the rotten meat,' Froude said. 'And this time,

let's get Ann Heiser in with us. Maybe another scientist can thicken the stew.'

The shaped charge of Telex was hastily plastered to the heavy gates of the main Cumbre prison in Leggett, and the two sweating, scared 'Raum darted along the wall to safety. One triggered an alarm, and sirens screeched inside the prison, but it was too late.

The charge blew one gate off its hinges, ripped the other half-away.

A rocket team slid out of the office building across from the gates, crouched, aimed, and sent first one missile, then a second, through the gateway to explode against the inner gates.

One of the gun turrets above it swung around, but two SSW teams took it under fire. Rounds smashed, then blew in, the supposedly bulletproof glass, and the human guards inside died. There'd been some discussion about the impact of killing these guards, which ended with a cynical 'Raum saying that no one cared about prison guards, not even their brothers.

Another rocket crashed through the gateway, and the inner gates were open.

The rocket team ducked out of the way, and the assault force, seventy-five experienced 'Raum, attacked. Jo Poynton was at the head of the force until someone tripped her, holding her down while guns chattered and the leading 'Raum were cut down.

Another rocket went through the gap, blew up in the main compound, killed the guards who'd gotten a tripod-mounted blaster into action, then the attackers were inside the prison.

Poynton, cursing the man who'd saved her life, ran through the smoking ruin, found three survivors of her special group. She unclipped a small demo pack from her harness, and the three hosed rounds at the administration building, cut their fire on her signal. Poynton zigged forward, tossed the demo pack, flattened as the charge blew the building's door off. She rolled a grenade through the smoke and sent a burst after it.

There were screams. then someone shouted. 'no more, no more. We surrender.'

Poynton and her three were inside, and at the cell controls. They were very familiar – one of the guards had decided to change sides two weeks earlier, and Poynton had been practicing on cardboard cutouts.

Automatic voice commands crackled as prisoners milled around their cells, listening to the gunfire and blasts.

'All prisoners, all modules, stand back from your cell doors . . . cell doors coming open . . .'

Then a real voice, a woman's voice came:

'The gates are down! Anyone who wants to be free, run for it now. Move!'

Most prisoners obeyed, but a few, sure it was some kind of trick by the prison guards to kill them, stayed in their cells.

Prisoners, political, criminal, swarmed into the streets of Leggett.

Some were political hostages. The 'Raum had guides waiting, tried to identify the political prisoners, hurried them to safety. But they missed all too many, who scattered in panic through the streets of Leggett. Some found safe hiding places, others were picked up by police and Musth patrols.

A handful, sadly, stayed where they were, and, within the day, were shot down as part of the Musth reprisals.

'Little by little,' Poynton told her subordinates. 'We're grinding them down, slow but sure.'

*

Ted Vollmer morosely chewed on an antacid, thought about quitting, remembered his mortgage and the new Musth policy of sending the unemployed to the mines. and tried to hide a glower at Loy Kouro.

'Yes,' Kouro went on, 'a major policy review's in order I do believe. We're allowing these renegades. these bandits, to control our holo, dictate what the main features are going to be.'

'You mean, we don't want to run real news.' Vollmer didn't make it a question.

'I wouldn't put it quite like that,' Kouro said. 'But I think we'll have to reevaluate the emphasis on certain items. For instance, major accomplishments by our Musth allies could be featured more prominently, and this continuing violence downplayed a little, perhaps during the second take after the commercial messages, in a section we'll call "Police Matters," perhaps.

'I think—'

What Kouro thought was a mystery as the elevator doors crashed open, and five men, hooded, wearing black, with blasters ready, leapt out.

The men, or women, Vollmer corrected himself, were screaming at the top of their lungs to 'Freeze! Move and die! Stand where you are!'

Vollmer, after that, never wondered why witnesses to an armed robbery so frequently disagreed, as everything got blurry and frightening.

Loy Kouro shouted, 'Who are you! What are you doing in my holo!'

He yanked out a small pistol that Vollmer never knew he carried, and two of the men swung blasters toward him, aimed.

Ted Vollmer then did something he cursed himself forever after for, and knocked Loy Kouro headfirst into a filing cabinet, the gun flying away, Kouro lying motionless.

Amazingly, neither of the two gunmen shot Vollmer, and he swore one of them laughed

'Stay frozen,' one of them said, his voice calm

Three of the black-clad gunmen hurried through the newsroom, toward the broadcast studio.

The elevator door closed, and a moment or maybe an hour passed, then it came open, disgorging more armed men.

They, too, ran toward the studio.

Kouro moaned. Vollmer saw that the two guards left in the newsroom weren't exactly watching him, and carefully kicked his boss in the head, almost as hard as he could. Kouro slumped back into unconsciousness, and Vollmer felt the happy glow of a task well-done.

Inside the studio, Garvin Jaansma held the three 'casters at gunpoint. Monique Lir held a gun on a technician, handed her a cylinder.

'This goes out. Now.'

The technician's head bobbed up and down, and she shoved the disk into a slot.

'You're on.'

The holo sets around the room blurred. then cleared.

On-screen was a Musth, then he vanished, and the green/white/brown colors of the Cumbrian flag appeared. the planetary anthem swelling over it. The music faded, and a confident voice spoke:

'This is the voice of Free Cumbre speaking. We have taken over *Matin* for this broadcast.

'Men, women of Cumbre. You now live under the iron bootheel of the Musth. But nothing is forever. Some of us, many of us, are fighting back.

'We fight the best we can. Some of us know how to build and plant bombs against the hated foe. Some have guns and aren't afraid to use them.

'Others are forced to work in their factories, and know

that a bolt torqued just a little too much ... or too little ... will ruin that part, without anyone ever suspecting. A bit of dirt on a bubble can make a great machine self-destruct.

'Still others oversee shipments to the Musth or merely work on a loading dock. A change on the bill of lading, one misstroke of a key, and the supplies will go somewhere else, anywhere else, to be lost at a forgotten waystation.

'Brave boys and girls put up posters, telling us what the news really is, now that the holos are controlled by the aliens. Their teachers aren't afraid to tell the truth, not the pap the Musth insist on.

'Some of us can't do anything, we think. But there is much you can do. Don't speak to the Musth unless forced. If you see something that appears none of your business, don't report it. Don't gossip to anyone.

'If you have a block captain, do all you can to make his task as difficult as possible.

'If you are a block captain, remember what we said at the beginning of this 'cast. Nothing lasts forever. Sooner or later, the Musth will be driven away.

'Then there will a reckoning for those who groveled to the invaders, who informed against their own.

'For those of you who've fallen under the spell of the aliens, it's not too late to change, to refuse to cooperate further.

'The war goes on.

'It shall never end, until the Cumbre system is free and the last Musth driven off.

'Free Cumbre! Free once, Free again!'

By the time the 'cast ended, most of the raiders had vanished, leaving only one in the newsroom, one supervising the cast. Those two — Monique Lir and Garvin Jaansma — not willing to chance the elevators, darted up the steps to the roof, where a civilian speedster waited.

They piled in, and the speedster dived down at full speed, leveling below office buildings, and vanished into the night over the bay.

Loy Kouro was treated for concussion, and spent the next week recuperating at his mansion. Unfortunately, his wife was too busy with problems on C-Cumbre to spend as much time with him as she wished.

'Perhaps,' Daaf ventured, 'our policies aren't as clearly thought out as they should be. They seem to be having little effect in calming the populace.'

Wlencing's fur ruffled, and he glared at his aide through reddened eyes.

'Our policy, *my* policy, has been carefully made up. I see no reason at all to change to something ill defined, something that will appear as if we're making cowardly concessions to these worms.

We must continue the course, and intensify the severity of our response!'

'I think,' Alikhan said, sounding, for the first time like the rest of his race, 'we have a possssible anssswer.'

'To what?' *Mil* Hedley asked, widening the pickup. Danfin Froude was slumped back in his chair, an overturned glass beside him. Ben Dill was on the floor, snoring loudly. Only Ann Heiser appeared sober.

'We think,' she said, voice very precise, then marred by a massive hiccup, 'we might have figured out a way to end this goddamned war.'

TWENTY-TWO

'How drunk were they when they came up with *this* one?' Njangu asked.

'Very,' Hedley said. 'Stinko, to be exact.'

'And the old man bought the idea?' Garvin asked.

'As a forlorn hope,' Hedley said. 'In every sense of the word.'

'Um,' Njangu said. 'Why are we gonna try stealing this particular mother ship?'

'According to Alikhan, it's a semiobsolete model, which is why it's mostly parked where it is on C-Cumbre. No more'n a standby watch aboard.'

'But it's fueled, ready to roll?'

'Alikhan says it was carried on the boards as on standby. But probably without charts, rations, or anything not needed for in-system deployment.'

'So we lug human rats, water—'

'No water,' Hedley said. 'That's on board as part of the coolant system. The Musth ships recycle.'

'Humans can drink Musth pee?'

'Evidently.'

'All right,' Garvin said. 'So we've got our fat little paws on this ship – then we've got to figure out what troopies to use on the op. Then what?'

'Then we use the star charts we've already got to go visiting.'

'Who?' Njangu asked.

'There's a Musth clan leader named Senza. He's the main one preaching pacifism, Alikhan says. Or, at any rate, not wanting to fight humans this flipping century. Alikhan studied . . . I guess we'd call it philosophy . . . under this guy.

'Seems the Musth aren't exactly the most cohesive folks around. Only a handful of their clan leaders backed the late Asser.'

'So we go chitchat with Senza,' Njangu said. 'What does that give us?'

'Alikhan says with hard evidence of what a disaster this whole flipping mess has turned into, Senza will use his clout – I guess these Reckoners are what pass for Musth diplomats – to call off Wlencing.'

'What does the fact Alikhan is Wlencing's kid do to things?'

'I guess it improves Alikhan's credibility. Anyway, Senza's been in a pissing match with the Musth warhawks for years, always looking for a chance to pull their chains. Alikhan thinks he can give Senza that chance, which should make the Musth declare a cease-fire, and then we can force some sort of talks,' Hedley said.

'I guess the Musth must have got the fear of the gods put in them the last time they went roundy-roundy with the Confederation,' Garvin said.

'Or else Alikhan fancies himself as having a tongue of the purest iridium,' Njangu said. 'Has anybody considered what we do if our road maps don't happen to go to this Senza's house? I mean, we're all blessed with the luck of heroes and such—'

'Already thought of,' Hedley interrupted. 'We'll use

the charts we have to make a planetfall somewhere and Alikhan looks for the local map store.'

Njangu gave Hedley a somewhat incredulous stare. 'Just that simple, eh? 'Kay. Let's go back to something that's in our arena. I assume you assume I&R'll be your raiders?'

'You assume right.'

'And after we grab the ship, we trundle off with Alikhan, becoming his bodyguards and the guys who bring the pilot coffee?'

'Right. We'll have Ben Dill and anybody else who's got anything resembling starship experience along. About fifteen more.'

'Not enough,' Garvin said flatly.

'I'm trying to keep my effectives as high as possible,' Hedley complained. 'We'll still have a war to fight while you clowns are out playing Space Rangers Against the Flipping Galaxy.'

'Nemmine about that, Garvin,' Njangu said. 'I know where we can score more shooters – and they're already in place,' Njangu said. 'What I don't particularly like is this elaborate scheme you've got for the insertion. Puttputt freighter. The last *aksai* with phony signals . . . uhuh. Too easy to get dead.'

'You know a better way?' Hedley asked.

'Remembering who else is on C-Cumbre, I do. And my cute, lovable colleague here with the forty-centimeter tongue is the key.'

'Now wait a minute,' Garvin protested.

'Go take a shower and tuck a flower behind your ear . . . *sir*,' Njangu said. 'Froggie's gone a-courting doo-dah, doo-dah.'

'This is exciting,' Karo Lonrod told Erik Penwyth as he neatly grounded his speedster at the steps to Jasith Mellusin's mansion. 'I've never been a blind before.'

'And you make a gorgeous one, too,' Erik said.

'Or else,' Lonrod said, 'I could think there's something else between Garvin and Jasith?'

'Like?'

'Like something to do with the war . . . which also might explain why you're so mysterioso about your comings and goings, and why my father wrote you a really big check last week that he wouldn't explain.'

'The war's over,' Penwyth said

'I'm a good little bimbo, so I know that. Which is why I'm excited about being a blind, since that's the other option.'

Sometimes I wonder,' Erik began, gratefully broke off as Jasith and her husband came out the door. Jasith kissed Loy briefly. hurried to the speedster. Erik rolled down his window.

'Sorry you can't come with us, old boy,' he called. 'The new gallery's s'posed to be enormously educating.'

Kouro forced a smile, went back inside as Jasith squeezed into the backseat.

'Let's lift! I swear, he gets to be more of a fussbudget old coot every day.'

'Documentsss,' the first Musth demanded, as the second stepped back, blaster ready.

Njangu, moving very slowly, held out a plas card with his left hand.

'Documentsss,' the Musth repeated more loudly, probably the only Basic he knew.

A thin tube in Njangu's right hand thudded once, and the Musth gargled blood. Njangu spun the empty single shot weapon into the second Musth's face, swept-kicked his blaster away as it went off, crouched, and leapt up. head slamming into the Musth's face. The alien squealed, slashed reflexively with a claw, catching Njangu's upper arm.

Yoshitaro spun to the side, smashed two strikes into the alien's side, turned again as the Musth flailed at him. He blocked the Musth's claw, was inside his guard, lunge-struck into the being's throat, felt something crunch. The Musth staggered, fell, lay motionless.

'Very good,' Jo Poynton said, coming out of nowhere. 'You moved before we could shoot.'

'Thanks anyway for the backup,' Njangu said, examining the slashes and the slowly spreading darkness that was blood on his jacket.

'I think I'm gonna have to set up a forgery section.' he said. 'I could have guessed he wasn't going to take my officers' mess card. C'mon, Poynton. Get me to a bandage and a beer before more fuzzies materialize.'

It still felt odd to be drinking and socializing in the early afternoon, but Cumbrian society had learned the Musth dusk-to-dawn curfew was meant for everyone, even Rentiers.

Penwyth, Lonrod, and Jasith appeared at the gallery, were joined by the owner and, after Jasith bought two assemblages from the exhibit, he took the three into a back room with the artist. Both, ex-members of the Force, would swear the trio had been with them until whenever.

Waiting was Garvin Jaansma.

'We'll be back in two hours,' he said.

'Why not three,' Penwyth suggested.

Garvin puzzled, then shrugged. 'Three, then.'

He led Jasith out a side door.

'Wonder why Erik wanted me to be gone longer?'

'I thought you were a better spy than that,' Jasith said. 'What do you think Karo thinks we're doing?'

'Oh.'

'A good adultery takes a while,' Jasith said. 'Or so they tell me,' she added primly.

Garvin, making sure there wasn't a tail, took Jasith a few blocks away into the middle of the prewar rich shopping district, into an expensive furniture store's back room. He locked the door into the showroom, barred the freight door into the alley.

Jasith watched, leaning back on a gold-lace-embroidered, wildly overstuffed couch

'And what is it I can do for you?' she said.

'I need one of your ships to deliver some of my men to C-Cumbre.'

'You have it.'

Garvin was a bit surprised at her immediate agreement.

'Also, one of your lims.'

Jasith nodded.

This time, since she might end up implicated, he explained what he needed the lifter for.

'I can do better then that,' Jasith said. 'I'll set up a meeting with the Musth, and that should guarantee we can get into their base.'

Garvin noticed the 'we.'

'But what happens to you when the shooting starts?' he asked.

'That'll be no problem,' Jasith said airily. 'You can tie me up . . . I'll say I was kidnapped. Don't worry about me. The owner of Mellusin Mining still has a little bit of respect with them.'

Garvin was skeptical, but said nothing.

'Is that all you need?'

'Yeh,' Garvin said. 'No, goddammit! I want to kiss you.'

'Well, thank a goddess,' Jasith murmured. 'I was starting to wonder if it'd been shot off.

'Now, slowly. We've got over two hours, and I want something to remember.'

'What about afterward?' Poynton asked.

'Your people disperse back to the mines and look innocent, along with my troops,' Njangu said.

'The wounded?'

'Walking, or any that you can carry out on stretchers — the Force'll supply a med team at the mines for them. The others . . . they'll have to be left to the Musth. Just like any of our troops in the same boat. We can give out lethal-pills, if you want.'

Poynton eyed Yoshitaro. 'We taught you well how to fight this kind of war, didn't we?'

'I learned from you,' Njangu admitted. 'But I got basic nastiness back on an armpit called Waughtal's World.'

'What about me? I get stuck on C-Cumbre?'

'Not a chance. You're needed here. We'll spirit you back after the smoke settles, probably on one of Mellusin's ships, when my team comes back.

'That's if you want,' Njangu said. 'Personally, I've got a helluva better use for you. Go out with our Musth friend. You're still a member of PlanGov, still on the *real* Council. If there is any hope to Alikhan's plan, you'll be there, able to speak for the humans in the Cumbre system.'

Poynton looked at him wryly. 'Aren't you a little young to be playing interstellar diplomat?'

'Politics hates a vacuum, I read somewhere. Why not seize the moment? Better than waiting for the Rentiers to get off their asses. And what's this "young" shit, anyway? You aren't more'n couple of years older than me.'

Poynton laughed. 'I forgot you're somebody who calls a spade a frigging shovel.'

She was about to go on when a 'Raum slid into the room and, without apology, whispered urgently to Poynton.

Njangu finished his beer, considered the room he was in. It was about ten meters underground, reached by a narrow passage down through rubble. It was long, fairly low-ceilinged, with carefully fitted stone walls, ceiling, floor. Other rooms opened off it. There were bedrooms, a kitchen, a 'fresher, workrooms. Poynton told him it had been one of the Planning Group's hides, and the bombing of the building above only made it more hidden.

It was immaculate, and a whispering air conditioner kept the hide fresh-smelling, comfortable. Some might have found it claustrophobic, but Njangu Yoshitaro, a creature of alleys, shadows, and the night, was very much at ease.

The 'Raum finished, hurried out.

'The Musth,' Poynton said, 'have deployed into the Eckmuhl in strength, looking for the murderer who killed their soldiers. So I wouldn't think you'll be wanting to leave for a while.'

'I guess not,' Njangu agreed.

'We'll get you out of the Eckmuhl after dark. There's dozens of passageways, old sewer lines, abandoned power ways.'

'So all we have to do is figure out a way to pass the time 'til nighttime?'

'Do you have any ideas?' Poynton asked.

Njangu remembered her body's smoothness. 'I could think of a couple.'

'So could I,' Poynton said. 'After all, you did save my life. Sort of.'

'That's a crappy reason,' Njangu complained.

'Then . . . how about just I remember you as feeling good when you were inside me?'

Njangu realized his lips were quite dry.

'That'll manage just fine.'

Three ore transports, the normal safety-conscious formation, guarded by a pair of overhead *aksai*, lowered toward the Musth-guarded dock area on D-Cumbre. Each ship carried the orange-outlined-in-black logo of Mellusin Mining.

Musth guards had already checked the warehouses for contraband. But the check was fairly perfunctory – who in a proper state of sanity would want to go to the dry, hot, dusty waste of C-Cumbre/Mabasi? The stevedores were robots, and the loading went smoothly, except for the problem around the lead ship, which was carrying both Mellusin Mining's owner and a long, highly polished lim, also in Mellusin's colors.

If anyone wondered why Jasith needed this monstrous lim, considering she was traveling with only one bodyguard, they didn't say anything. Jasith was in a temper, raving loudly at the human stevedores moving the lim into a cargo hold, swearing that if there was a ding, one damned ding, she'd make sure none of them dot-and-carried on this planet again. There were mutters about frigging Rentiers, but quiet ones – Jasith had more than enough influence to unemploy the lot of them.

The Musth guards thought this was quite a show, far more interesting than their regular duties, and gathered around watching.

As a result, no one saw nearly one hundred men and women, heavily laden, stream into the middle ship, hidden from overhead observation by convenient rain shields.

Loaded, the small crews of the transports began the normal ship/traffic control chatter, and lifted for space.

Out-atmosphere, the guardian *aksai* were replaced by

a single *velv* and, on secondary drive, set an economical orbit toward C-Cumbre.

The command group assembled in the flight leader's owner's quarters. Garvin Jaansma considered them. Jon Hedley had assumed he'd be in command, but Angara refused to release him, pointing out everything was in Alikhan's hands, rather paws, and all that would be needed in charge was a good headbanger.

He'd endorsed Njangu's idea of taking Jo Poynton to add legitimacy. Besides Alikhan, Ben Dill, Poynton, and the two I&R commanders. Ann Heiser, Ho Kang, and Danfin Froude were in the cabin.

'There's nothing to do,' Garvin announced, 'until we hit C-Cumbre. The troops in the other ship have been told they'll have no duties for the four ship-days in space but to make sure their weaponry's clean, and they're rested.

'I suggest we do the same. There'll be enough to worry about after we land.'

Good advice – but not followed by either Garvin or Njangu, in spite of Jasith's and Jo's presence.

Nor did Alikhan relax. He kept going over and over what he should, might say to Senza with Dill and the two scientists until Dill threatened to throttle him if he heard either the words 'Senza' or 'peace' again.

They closed on C-Cumbre, and *aksai* closed to meet them, escorted them to their landing places in the vast Mellusin Mining yards.

'So they want us t' fight their wars, do they?'

There was a rumble of anger from the women and men in the rocky chamber, a kilometer underground. The miners were filthy, exhausted, an hour before shift's end. Many carried hand tools, and all had breathing masks around their suit necks.

'Who's they?' Poynton shot back. 'I guess I'm they because I'm with them.'

'Wouldn't be the first to sell out yer sisters for the Rentiers' credits,' a heavy woman sneered.

Poynton held the woman's eyes until they dropped.

'Just so,' she said coldly. 'Taking the Musth money, I am. Maybe they'll buy me an estate somewhere for selling you out.'

There were a few humorless laughs.

'Say we do what you want?' another miner said. 'You haven't given us much in th' way of details.'

'And I'm not going to,' Poynton said. 'All you need to know is you'll get a chance to kill some Musth, maybe get killed yourselves. All of you were out during the rising – you know why things are kept secret.'

'And if whatever we're going to do works?'

'Maybe we'll get a chance to end this crap. Bring things back to normal.'

'I wonder,' a bearded miner said softly, 'what th' hell normal is. Sure wasn't any with the Rentiers, and then bein' underground, then the rising. I thought maybe things were gettin' to the point of not bein' too bad when the goddamn Musth showed up and we was back in th' crapper.'

There was silence in the cavern.

'Aw hell, Poynton,' the man said. 'I'm in. The *soh* always told m' dad I was born to be shot.'

He stepped forward, then another man, then the stocky woman, and Poynton knew she had them.

'So that's our baby,' Garvin said, peering through the dirty side port of the survey ship as it slowly flew along the Musth base's perimeter.

'Does look a bit abandoned,' Njangu said hopefully.

'It just better not be *too* forlorn,' Garvin said. 'Like the drive's shut down.'

'Don't worry, boss,' Njangu said. 'It'll prob'ly turn out that Alikhan's never flown anything actually like this barge, and we'll be screwed before we start.'

'That's the I&R tradition,' Garvin said. 'Utter cheeriness.'

'Here's the cheap lie, Jasith,' Garvin said. 'You schedule a one-on-one conference with the Musth muckety in charge of mining—'

'Pilfern,' Jasith said. They were in her suite at Mellusin Mining's Planetary Headquarters.

'Pilfern. Make it as late as you can. You'll stop by this ship to check something—'

'I'll be checking how soon that ruptured hold will take to be repaired so we can load ingots at the refinery.'

'Good. To your dismay, you found the ship had been seized by bandits, who took your lim and tied you up and left you in a shed.'

'Who took my lim and me as a hostage, and ordered us to do whatever they wanted. That will make it more authentic. Tie me up before you take off.'

'Goddammit, Jasith, you don't know what you're getting into!'

'Maybe not. But it's past time for a Mellusin to get into *something*! That's the way it's going to be, Garvin!'

Garvin realized the subject had been suddenly closed.

'All right,' he said. 'I'm too tired to argue.'

'Does that mean you're too tired to mess around a little?'

Garvin glanced at his watch finger.

' 'Kay. Fifteen minutes for messing around, then I brief the assault team.'

'How'd I ever get lucky enough to end up with the last of the romantics?'

There were seven in the first strike team – Garvin, Ben Dill, Monique Lir, Ho Kang, Darod, Montagna, and Alikhan. The Musth refused to carry a weapon.

'But what if somebody starts shooting at you?' Dill asked.

'If he hits me, our enterprise was not meant to be,' Alikhan said equably.

Dill snarled wordlessly, and added a second pistol to his combat harness.

Jasith sent word – the meet was set, just before third-meal.

As the sun settled, her lim landed beside the ore transport. Jasith at the controls. She explained to Njangu that she didn't want her driver endangered.

Njangu winced – another bit of irregular behavior the Musth might uncover. But he said nothing.

As soon as Jasith had notified Garvin, lighters began trickling in from the mines. Each carried a handful of hard-faced men and women who were issued black coveralls, weapons, their faces blackened, and given brief orders – 'When you off-load around a Musth ship, kill anything that looks like a Musth. Listen to anybody in uniform or any of your people wearing a white arm-band.

'When the ship takes off, or when ordered, retreat back to this ore transport.'

Poynton had named certain of the miners to leadership slots, and they got the armbands.

There were about two hundred raiders, 'Raum and Force, in the ore transport's hold.

Garvin wished he had some kind of speech, finally managed, ' 'Kay. It's time to go help some Musth die for their empire,' trotted down the ramp, and climbed into the crowded lim.

The canopy slid closed, and, without orders, Running Bear lifted.

Then things started to go wrong.

The lim came across the Musth perimeter fast, broadcasting the recognition signals given Jasith. Each of the AA batteries it overflew responded automatically to the signals. A simple device in the lim bounced these acknowledgments back to the ore transport. On the flight deck of the transport, these were triangulated by Dr. Heiser. Another signal, and the transport took off after the lim.

Musth headquarters sent an *aksai* to escort the lim. mostly as a courtesy to a high-ranking human. They did not bother to notify Running Bear, pilot of the lim.

Running Bear banked the lim away from its Musth-assigned course as planned, went to full power, and flew toward the targeted Musth field.

Ahead, the mother ship's nose was outlined in fire by the rapidly setting sun.

The off-course lim was challenged once, twice, made reply.

'Two kilometers,' Running Bear reported. 'On final.'

He brought the lim in fast, flared it, and slammed the antigrav on at the last minute. The lim bounced once, was down, and the canopy flew open.

The mother ship was about fifty meters away, two guards in front of its lock. They gaped, then one lifted his weapon. Alikhan shouted for him to surrender, but the blaster was aimed. Ben Dill dropped him, and the other Musth ducked behind barrels. Garvin lofted a grenade after him, and there was an explosion and a dying scream.

Alikhan stopped, paws moving in confusion.

'Move,' Dill shouted, and the Musth went up the ramp through the open airlock, the rest of the first attack team behind him.

Overhead, the Musth pilot, barely out of training, dropped down to take a closer look.

Running Bear heard the whistle, saw the oncoming *aksai*, grabbed Jasith, threw her over his shoulder, and ran across the flat tarmac toward the barrels. The *aksai* pilot decided something was wrong and climbed, arming his weapons systems, then dived and launched two missiles.

One went wide, the other blew the lim into fragments.

Jasith sobbed, close to the evil-smelling tarmac as the blast rang around her. She lifted her face, realized she was lying in a pool of Musth blood, and not two meters away was the shattered body of the guard.

The *aksai* pilot low-flew the field, saw no movement, snarled across the perimeter. Only one AA site fired and the missile was late, never acquiring its target.

Then the transport was down, locks sliding open, and raiders streaming out.

The *aksai* skidded through a turn, came back low.

Striker Mar Henschley swung her Shrike launcher, centered the *aksai* in her sights, and touched the trigger. She was the first to launch, and her missile blew the fighting craft in half. Another missile fired by another gunner flew through the cloud of expanding gas, decided there was nothing solid enough to be worth exploding for, and flew on until it self-detonated.

Henschley yelped in sheer glee, then reloaded.

On board the ship, the strike team moved steadily upward. They found half a dozen Musth, about the size of the maintenance crew Alikhan had thought to be aboard, and called for their surrender. Only one was armed, and Garvin shot him. The others charged gun muzzles, trying to close. They died either bravely or stupidly, depending on perspective.

Occasionally the team heard dim explosions from the outside, wondered about the fighting. Then they were on the bridge. The watch officer was down before he could draw his blaster, and the ship was theirs.

Alikhan walked forward, toward the controls, the scuffing of his pads loud in the silence.

'Well?' Dill asked.

'I can fly this,' Alikhan said firmly.

Half a dozen *aksai*, more *wynt*, were wrecked around the field, their green pilots no match for the Force's missile-men.

They gave welcome cover to the raiders as Musth warriors debarked from other *wynt* and attacked.

A canny *velv* captain flew a roundabout course, popped up, and acquired a target and launched, just as a Shrike blast tumbled his locators and sent him spinning into a hillside.

His missile, at full speed, crashed into the drive area of the transport, and it blew up spectacularly, the fiery ball illuminating the near-night sky.

Almost twenty-five raiders and the transport's crew were killed in the blast, and the Musth mother ship rocked.

Wlencing, on D-Cumbre/Whar saw the blast on one of the field's many remotes, and knew what the worms were intending.

'No, you hatchling sports, they're after our ship! Kill the ship!' he roared into a closed com, then swore again, wondering why he seemed to be the only one who could figure out the human strategies.

Garvin stared out of a port at the boiling chaos around the ship.

'How long 'til you can lift?'

'Five of your minutes,' Alikhan said calmly. 'I have it now on antigravity.'

Garvin reached a decision.

'Dill! Get everyone aboard. I mean everyone! We'll have to take 'em with us.'

The big man ran for the airlock.

Njangu spat blood from the explosion, got up, hearing Dill's shouts:

'The ship! Into the ship!'

He staggered, realized what was going on, echoed Dill's commands, and the shouts were picked up by others.

'Raum and soldiers went for the mother ship, some in calm retreat, others in blind panic.

He saw an incoming *aksai*, saw a Shrike gunner standing calmly in the open.

The *aksai* and Mar Henschley fired at the same time, and both vanished in the double blast.

Njangu wondered who the unknown hero was, went back to pushing the last few raiders aboard. One of them was Running Bear, carrying a semiconscious woman in civilian clothes, her face hidden by dark Musth blood. Njangu realized who she must be.

'How is—'

'Just shocky, sir.' Running Bear went on into the ship.

Njangu realized he and Lir were the only two left not aboard, and the ramp was humming, moving.

'Goddammit, Top, quit playing last standing hero!'

Lir gave him a single-fingered salute, sent half a drum stammering through a wave of Musth.

Njangu gave up, jumped through the lock, Lir just behind him as the hatch slid shut.

The mother ship came off the ground. teetered, and climbed.

A flight of *aksai* banked after it as the ship sped upward.

One launched, missed, then the mother ship was out of range.

Seconds later, it was on the fringes of C-Cumbre's atmosphere, and recklessly vanished into stardrive.

Wlencing looked again and again at the images from the remotes, saw the lim approach, land near the mother ship and beings leap out.

He no longer bothered to bring up a close-up of the renegade Musth.

Very well. The cub was a traitor. He knew why, who had poisoned him, where he was going, even his intention.

Wlencing got up, turned to Daaf. The aide flinched away from Wlencing's terrible gaze.

'I want immediate contact with Keffa.'

TWENTY-THREE

Langnes 77837?/World unknown

The world was thrice-ringed, one red, one brown, one green, or so the mother ship screens showed.

Alikhan hissed a response into the mike that hung, unsupported, in front of him. His three screens flashed data, then blanked, in keeping with the Musth practice of not worrying a pilot until something started going wrong.

A voice came back to him and a staccato conversation began.

A large screen appeared, and the other three obligingly moved aside for it. The screen showed clouds, then went infrared, and there were landmasses below.

Alikhan spoke without turning his head, as his fingers brushed sensors on the panel in front of him, and the humans felt the drive hum change, deepen. 'You may speak if you wish,' he said. 'We have been cleared to land.'

Garvin, Njangu, and the two scientists watched silently from a corner of the control room, and Ben Dill sat in a control chair behind and to one side of Alikhan, his fingers echoing, tentatively, Alikhan's movements, without ever touching the panel in front of him.

'This is gonna work?' Njangu asked suspiciously.

You're just gonna ground, stroll out, buy the right chart, and off we go again?'

'Why not?' Alikhan said. 'We have done nothing to cause alarm, and the ship's trading account is very plus.'

You Musth don't have to worry about customs, health quarantine, security clearance?' Ann Heiser asked.

'Why? My clan's business is its own, until we show some intent to harm those who own this system.'

Garvin and Njangu exchanged looks. 'Oh to be a pirate in these sunny climes.' Garvin chanted.

'First let's make sure, bucko,' Njangu said, 'the Musth have goodies worth pirating.'

The screen went back to normal vision. Alikhan found a sensor, and the view came in to about five hundred meters above the ground, swept across veldt, small wooded copses, ponds, and the occasional small settlement.

'Now this,' Alikhan said, 'is what a proper world looks like, not all those revolting greens you prefer.'

'We never invited you in the first place,' Dill said.

'True,' Alikhan said. 'Now, silence. Even though I am without question the finest pilot the cosmos has seen I still lack sufficient experience with this wallower. And be grateful for slaved emergency power controls that override my momentary lapses.'

On-screen, a scatter of buildings appeared that grew into a small, high-towered city. Alikhan brought the mother ship vertical, and another screen opened, showing a wide landing field studded with other starships and support buildings. Alikhan brought the antigrav up, reduced the secondary drive, and backed down. About 150 meters above the field, he cut the secondary drive, and grounded without ajar.

'Was that not smooth?'

'For a beginner,' Dill said.

'Now, I shall attend to business,' Alikhan said. 'You might not want to admit any curious visitors.'

Off D-Cumbre and in N-space, Alikhan had taken the first two jumps on the star chart he'd chosen from Njangu's thievery.

The Force medics were occupied with the wounded, and Garvin, Njangu, their noncoms, Poynton, and her appointed leaders were busy sorting out I&R's seventy survivors and the slightly more than a hundred 'Raum, and exploring the ship for compartments to house them.

There was no need to discuss options – the raiders would have to stay with the ship, their fate linked to Alikhan's success.

Alikhan, Dill, Ho, and the scientists sorted through the mother ship's charts and discovered, unsurprisingly, there wasn't one for Senza's homeworld, known as 'Reckoning,' aboard.

'So we use this chart to make the first planetfall. It's a system well within our area of influence, and then we get the chart we need.'

Dill had goggled. 'No overconfidence *here*.'

Half a dozen times, casualties died, and were buried in space. Alikhan was surprised, wondering why they simply weren't recycled into the ship.

He was similarly perplexed by Garvin's refusal to allow the dead Musth to be recycled.

They, too, were treated as the human dead, and, even though Garvin wasn't sure they, or anyone else, had a soul, he whispered the unfortunately all-too-familiar words of the Confederation's burial ceremony as the lock cycled.

*

The first pleasure for the miners and the insufficiently clean soldiers, was bath after bath after bath. The Musth 'freshers were entire rooms, with rain-shower ceilings that could be set from mist to typhoon. The water's taste, as human wastes were cycled into the system, tasted less coppery as time passed.

Less enjoyable were the Musth toilets, being mere holes in the deck. Garvin was muttering about these jakes, and Poynton said, smugly, 'See the advantage of growing up poor, without any luxuries like being able to sit down? Or a tail?'

Njangu added, 'Easy for me to live with, too, *sir*, not having grown up with a silver crapper in my . . . never mind the rest.'

Also unsatisfactory were the stored Musth rations. Alikhan said the Musth fed their crews well, so the meals were highly seasoned and properly aged.

'Like a friggin' rotten corpse,' one striker said after disobeying orders and unsealing a pack, then promptly going into projectile vomiting mode.

Dr. Froude calculated that, given the rations the Force had carried aboard, they could survive for a while. 'Maybe three weeks, maybe a little more. Then we turn to cannibalism.' He seemed rather ghoulishly interested in that eventuality.

But a solution was found – Alikhan spent some time in the ship's larder, found something acceptable for human palates. It was nourishing in a bulky sort of way, nearly tasteless, with the texture of pablum when mixed with water.

They supplanted the human rations. Lir, having taken a course in nutrition once, thought there'd be enough necessary trace elements in their own packs to keep everyone alive, not enough of the Musth trace chemicals in the musth rats to kill anyone that quickly.

Alikhan told Dill these were the rations for the punishment details, deliberately intended to provide no more than nourishment. Dill didn't share the information with anyone except Garvin and Njangu.

Fortunately the ship had an efficient autopilot, so, except when it came out of hyperspace and its navigational computer needed a little fine-tuning, the bridge could be left with only a single watch officer.

Dill and Alikhan corralled the surviving Shrike gunners, plus volunteers, and started learning how to use the mother ship's missile array.

Twice, in normal space, they chanced launching – the medium-range bombardment weapons, the close-range antiship missiles like Shrikes, and the long-range heavy missiles that could be programmed to have nearly the evasive ability of an *aksai*.

Musth gunners wore helmets, as did human missilemen, to give a rocket-eye perspective, but used eye motion for guidance instead of the human joysticks. That, plus the fact that Musth helmets weren't configured for human skulls, didn't help human accuracy.

Every time a missile exploded, lighting up emptiness, Njangu moaned about another deathblow to his promising career in interstellar piracy.

Garvin was starting to think he was serious.

One nice thing about the Musth ship was the number of viewscreens. Human ships generally had screens only in control rooms, with a scattering in other compartments, generally showing either nothing or the stomach-wrenching color swirl of N-space 'reality.'

Musth screens, and there were many in nearly every compartment and corridor, translated the pickup into rapidly changing pictures of the normal space around them.

Many humans found this fascinating, and sat, tourist-
ing the stars, for hours.

Others did not – 'Raum who'd made only a few trips
back and forth to C-Cumbre, even a handful of
Forcemen. Combining claustrophobia and agoraphobia,
they crept whimpering into screenless compartments and
huddled.

'I'd knock 'em out,' the medic Jil Mahim said, 'but we
don't have the drugs to spare. All we can do is hope they
don't go completely mad before we get onplanet somewhere.'

Even though the men and women had been told off to
specific compartments, some found lovers, and places to
be alone with each other; some Force people, some
'Raum, some intermixed

First *Tweg* Lir wanted to bring that to an end, but
Garvin nixed the idea, so long as nobody was screwing
inside the chain of command

Not only was Lir's notion senseless petty tyranny, but
he, Jasith, Njangu, and Jo were among the compart-
ment-creepers.

Garvin and Jasith stared at a screen, looking at the
Musth ships on the airfield, star, in-system and onplanet
and at the sweeping plains of this unknown world.

'Wouldn't it be nice,' Jasith sighed, 'if we were visiting here on . . . on some kind of vacation, maybe?'

Or on any purpose other than war, Garvin thought.

About two E-hours after they'd landed, a lifter
grounded beside the mother ship.

Alikhan got out, carrying a parcel, and the lifter took
off.

Ben Dill met him at the lock.

'Just that simple?'
'But what else should it have been?'

After the strange ship had taken off, a Musth clearance clerk ran the ship's numbers through a registry.

His head darted, and he hissed in surprise as he read the on-screen scroll.

TWENTY-FOUR

N-Space

It was ship-night, and there were only a few awake on the mother ship.

Two were Alikhan and Ben Dill. Dill was determined to 'qualify' as pilot, and be the first human to have a Musth starship in his logbook. Alikhan was obliging and, as he taught, became more skilled himself.

Besides, there wasn't much else to pass the time. The few books that had been brought on board were religious in nature, and both beings had decided what they believed or didn't believe in years earlier.

The ship broke out of N-space, and the two checked the computer for the next jump.

'Five more jumps, and—'

Quite suddenly, there was another starship in the utter emptiness.

Alikhan's paw flashed to a sensor, and N-space swirled, as Dill saw a flash from the other huge ship.

'What . . . who was that?'

'It looked like a clanmaster's ship,' Alikhan replied. 'Who it is, where it came from, I know nothing.'

'It sure wasn't our friend. Sucker went and launched at us!'

Alikhan slapped sensors, and the mother ship went back to normal space, then jumped again.

Numbers,' he growled. 'Give me human random numbers!'

'Three . . . one . . .. EVERYBODY UP, battle stations, and the sleeping Forcemen on the bridge came awake, and the com man, the 'talker,' readied his infantry back-pack set, '. . . one . . .. eleven . . .'

Dill realized Alikhan wanted human values to key his jump times to, hopefully foxing the pursuer.

On the eleven count their huge enemy came into the same space, fired again as the mother ship vanished.

'Gunners to stations,' Alikhan managed. 'Have them try to destroy that other ship.'

'One more time: Who the hell is it?'

'Colors are gray . . . red . . . you have no word for the third,' and a missile exploded close enough to blank a screen for a moment. Another missile went off, and Dill felt shock roll through the ship.

'We're hit,' he announced unnecessarily, and Garvin and Njangu were on the bridge.

'We've got a big fat enemy all over our asses,' Dill announced. 'Looks like—'

Description wasn't necessary as the ship reappeared. Alikhan hissed, ears cocking, and again they were in hyperspace.

'Ben, take the controls and count again.'

' 'Kay,' Dill said. 'Three . . . four . . . nine . . . sixteen, son of a bitch, can't give 'em that much time, that one almost got us . . . Garvin, you might want to get every-body saddled up for debarkation . . . four . . .

'Missile stations manned,' the talker reported tone-lessly.

Alikhan was at a secondary board for an instant, con-sulting records. 'Gray, red, *plat* . . . not good. That is

Keffa's clan. One of Paumoto and my father's fiercest allies.'

'So how in blazes did he find us?'

Lir was on the bridge. 'Boss, that rocket that hit us appears to have done some damage. We've got compartments all through the ship self-sealing. So far, nobody's gotten trapped, but . . .'

Garvin gnawed a lip.

'Ben,' he said, 'leave us out in normal space long enough for somebody to get a clean shot. Talker, all stations, anybody near a missile launcher, tell 'em to shoot anytime they want to at that big bustard.'

'I think,' Alikhan said. 'I should be looking for an emergency landing place.'

'A short jump first,' Garvin ordered. 'Now a long one.' Dill obeyed.

'Bring us out . . . Gunners, SHOOT!'

Missiles spat from the mother ship.

'JUMP!'

'The fiche shows a haven,' Alikhan said. 'Three more jumps.'

Their pursuer emerged, fired as the mother ship jumped, and hit again. The ship lurched, and the com crackled.

'Boss,' the talker reported. 'Irthing reports one of the compartments that was hit . . . we lost some people in there.'

Garvin grimaced, said nothing, and the ship jumped again. Once more he ordered the missile crews to fire as Keffa's ship emerged, saw two flashes as they jumped back into N-space.

'I would imagine,' Alikhan said, 'that someone back on Silitric recognized me, notified my father, and he would probably be able to theorize where I might be going. He would notify his allies, probably have a bulletin sent out to all ports of some sort of disaster, and our stop for a chart didn't go as well as I thought.'

'Old news,' Njangu said impatiently. 'Alikhan, can you com Senza, tell him where this landing place is, ask him for help?'

'I can send a message, we will not have time to know if it was picked up, let alone receive a reply,' Alikhan said. 'Ben, when we break out this time, we should be close to the world we want. Take us closer. Be bold in your navigation. I shall ready that message.'

He swept off the bridge.

'Here we are, here we go again.' and Dill hit the sensors.

When the mother ship emerged again, it was in the middle of an E-type system. A light green world hung not far distant.

Keffa's huge ship popped into being, took a hit, and went back into hyperspace.

'Now, young Musth, I'll show you a trick I'll bet you don't know,' Dill muttered, fingers tapping sensors.

'Now, we're either going to be a part of that there planet, or . . .'

He hit a sensor and the mother ship jumped in, out of N-space. His stomach lurched.

'Brilliant, Ben, if I do say so myself,' Dill said. 'That big chubby planet is now between us and that ugly shit. Repress nausea and admire me.

'Now I guess we put it on the ground and take things from there.'

'We have a hit in the stardrive section, serious, and another in the main fire control,' the officer told Keffa.

'What of the traitor's ship?'

'He became lucky, was able to interpose the planet

between us and him. We suspect, since he has also taken damage, he will land.'

'What about that world?'

'Normal to the nth place, but thus far uncolonized.'

'Go after him,' Keffa ordered. 'Destroy his ship before he can land. If he already has . . .' Keffa paused, wishing he had taken a full complement of warriors aboard.

'. . . we shall land as well, and destroy this cub, and all his fellows while repairs on our ship are made.'

The mother ship was shouting madness as laden men and women scurried away from it.

Alikhan had brought the ship in on its side near a large lake, with vertical buttes around it. Woods dotted the rolling hillside before the mountains.

'Away from the ship . . . come on, let's move . . . get your asses into line and let's get moving . . . that shithead'll be along shortly and we want to be invisible . . . come on, ladies, hustle your butts,' noncoms and officers raved.

Columns were formed, and started away, as fast as possible, into the hilly ground.

'You notice,' Alikhan puffed as he passed Ben Dill who was carrying one end of a stretcher and a tubed Shrike on his back, 'what a perfect world I found.'

'And I'll be the first to move that it be named after you. I just hope you got your goddamned message away and momma comes quick and kisses bruises.'

An E-hour away from the ship, the sky boomed and shook, and Keffa's ship crashed overhead.

Garvin ordered the raiders to take cover and, while they obeyed, trotted up a promontory and lay flat. He could just see their ship about four kilometers distant.

Keffa's ship hurtled back into view, dived at it. Garvin ducked, expecting nuclear fire, but the ground rumbled with blasts of conventional explosion.

'The bastard wants to crucify us personally,' he snarled.

He chanced looking up as the command ship came in for a vertical landing about a kilometer beyond the flaming ruins of the mother ship.

Monique Lir sprawled beside him, scanned the command ship with a small pair of binoculars.

'I think,' she said, 'we have the sons of bitches right where we want them.'

There was a tight, pleased smile on her face.

TWENTY-FIVE

D-Cumbre

'Your mate'sss behavior isss intolerable.' Wlencing said. 'What sssort of sssspecies are you, when one of the high-essst in your sssociety losssesss all control and becomesss a bandit?'

Loy Kouro squirmed, not wanting to offer his belief that Jasith was nothing more than a typical woman, besotted with a damned soldier.

'I can't explain,' he said. 'She's been behaving strangely lately. I think she is having problems with her mind.'

'I am not unfamiliar with madnessss,' Wlencing said, not allowing himself thoughts of Alikhan. 'But it doesss not matter, for ssshe will be desssstroyed when Keffa find-sss the ssstolen ssship.'

Kouro started, fought for control.

' Good,' Wlencing said. 'You took that like a warrior. Now, who will become in charge of her interessstsss, particularly the minesss?'

'Why . . . I suppose I shall,' Kouro said, brightening noticeably.

'And ssshould anything happen to you?'

'Like Jasith, I have no immediate family.'

Wlencing considered him for a time

'Then it ssshould be bessst for the two enterprisssesss you have inherited for there to be peaccce between our ssspecies, would it not?'

'Of course!'

'You are advisssed, then, to do all possssible to keep order, for I am placccing you on our lissst of potential hossstagesss.'

Kouro held back fear and anger, wanting to snarl that it'd be really goddamned convenient for them to shoot him, as they had so many others, and end up with all that he had, but he kept silent.

Finally, he said, sullenly, 'I think the record will show that I have gone out of my way to help you and your people, War Leader.'

'Then now we are asssssured you will do even more,' Wlencing said.

If Kouro had known more about the Musth, he would have realized that the following hiss from the back of Wlencing's throat indicated amusement.

'Erik,' Tregony, a very rich Rentier sputtered, 'I never thought you were capable of this.'

'I'm *sure* I don't understand,' Penwyth drawled.

'Bringing these terrible, terrible holos to me . . . trying to blackmail me.'

'Now, Mister Tregony,' Erik said, 'that's a terrible thing to accuse someone of who grew up with your sons. I ran across these holos, which I'm sure are fakes, and went to a bit of trouble and expense to acquire what I b'lieve are the only copies. And I give them to you now as a present. Where's the blackmail in that?'

Tregony scowled. 'But if I chose to reimburse you that wouldn't go amiss.'

'If you wish.'

'How much?'

Penwyth named a figure, and Tregony goggled.

Gods, man. Do you think I'm Croesus?'

'That figure is exactly twenty-five percent of the annual bonus Tregony Holdings gave you this year, no more.'

'How'd you learn that?'

Penwyth smiled, didn't answer.

'I'll issue a draft,' the older man growled.

To Bearer, please, which'll not be me. Also, if you'll be a gem and notify your banker that the sum should be available in smallish bills?'

Tregony nodded jerkily.

'One other thing. Some friends of mine might want to use your island for a retreat for a time. They're a bit irregular in their ways, and might arrive without announcement and there might be more'n two or three of them. So if you'd notify your staff not to be s'prised at anything out of the ordinary . . .'

'How many of your dissolute friends will we have to put up with?'

'Five, six, or two hundred.'

Tregony jerked. 'This *isn't* blackmail, is it?'

'I *said* that at the beginning.' Penwyth smiled.

Angara blanked the screen. 'I see what you mean about time's goddamned wing-ed chariot, Jon. We're losing men almost as fast as we would if we were in full combat.'

'Not so much time as this flipping jungle, sir. The men don't have a truly stable base – even the people here on Mullion Island are always looking over their shoulders, waiting for a flipping Musth to come out of nowhere.

'Jungle rot, accidents, shitty food, no passes . . . this nibbling gets to people.'

'Them and us,' Angara added. 'And using that island Penwyth hustled up for a day or two of relaxation isn't enough.'

Hedley sighed.

'I wish, sometimes, I was religious, like when I was a sprat, and could believe in flipping miracles.'

'Like our pet Musth being able to pull off his trick.

'I say again about flipping miracles. Hell, I'm even hoping Redruth shows up and stirs things up a bit, on the dumb-ass theory that new trouble can be better'n the old stuff.'

Angara got up from his field desk, went to his cot in a corner of the bunker, and opened a footlocker. He took out a bottle, gave it to Hedley.

'Here. You're on a one-day pass. Don't share it with anybody of our sex, and no more than two of another. The hangover'll give you something else to snivel about.'

'Thanks, sir. With my flipping luck, I'll just have gotten buzzy when the bastards throw an attack.'

The Musth weren't much more cheerful. There was peace, but warriors kept dying. In the cities, the aliens were always watched, always followed by packs of grim-faced children – the Musth hadn't figured a way to reopen schools that didn't violate their 'no crowds' policy.

After curfew the streets were empty, but a patrol could expect the flat smash of a single blaster bolt from nowhere, then feet scurrying into silence, while a warrior writhed in agony.

They were watched even more closely than they knew. An aircraft would be spotted by someone, and its flight path passed on to one of the 'merchants,' and its passage tracked across D-Cumbre as closely as if a thousand radar were following it. If opportunity came, a Shrike might soar out of nowhere.

The Eckmuhl, and the centers of other cities, were no-go zones, unless the Musth went in company-sized formations, with tactical air support. Even then, they'd be sniped at, and take a casualty or two.

Only the main islands were firmly held by the aliens.

But little by little, the Musth were winning. Some humans fell sick, a few were captured or killed. But most of the steady drain was a man or woman giving up, slipping away and vanishing into the civilian sea. No one blamed them much, no one sought these deserters — there's not much tougher than fighting a guerrilla war with no forseeable end.

But the Force fought on.

Wlencing's screens gave no more cheerful a set of figures than Angara's. It wasn't the continual casualties so much as other hard figures.

Cumbre cost more, vastly more, to occupy than it gave back in profits to the clans exploiting the system. Only a trickle of ships took back minerals, luxury goods to the Musth worlds.

The clanmasters who'd backed Asser and Wlencing would not continue the course into bankruptcy.

Something must be done. Wlencing wished he had a clue as to what.

The block warden was quite proud of himself. He'd spotted the ambush team, two men, two women, waiting below his building for the security patrol, and notified the Musth on the special com he'd been given.

The team was efficiently counterambushed by three dozen Musth warriors. Probably the assassins wouldn't have tried to surrender, but the Musth didn't give them the chance, blasting the four until their bodies were unrecognizable lumps of flesh.

The warden was rewarded with credits, and begged the aliens not to praise him publicly.

They agreed, but two nights later, just after midnight, the warden's apartment was fire-bombed. He, his wife, their four children, and his wife's mother died in the flames.

His successor was a great deal less ambitious and more nearsighted.

The ten-man human patrol was trapped against cliffs in the piedmont near the Highlands. Unable to break contact, they fought back.

Wlencing ordered his attack ships in. The crags were rocketed, bombed. But when the ringing explosions died away, and the dust settled, a defiant blaster would open fire from rocky concealment.

Wlencing sent in warriors on the ground. Three days later, the last of the ten were killed. The Musth lost four *wynt*, an *aksai* and forty-three warriors.

Both sides considered the engagement a defeat.

There was an explosion in one of Mellusin Mining's deep shafts on C-Cumbre, of unknown but almost certainly natural causes.

The surface had contact with the survivors down the mine, trapped in one of the stopes two kilometers underground, water rising from lower levels.

The frantic rescue teams, realizing they couldn't open a rescue shaft in time, called on the government for help.

'Who are these miners?' Wlencing asked Daaf.

'Mostly 'Raum. A scattering of military prisoners and some criminals.'

Wlencing thought for only a moment. 'The request is denied. The present emergency forbids the expense.'

Daaf chanced it: 'War Leader, is that an honorable response?'

Wlencing hissed rage, reflexively moved his claws in, out.

'Do not ever use insolence like that again, or I shall have you returned to your clan!'

Daaf stared at Wlencing for a moment, then left the compartment without an answer.

Wlencing stared out at Silitric's desolation, watched a storm building against the mountains, wondered what his response might have been a system-year ago.

But that was then. Wlencing had never left a task unfinished, and this one would be no exception. There were too many Musth lives spent here, from Aesc to the lowest engine wiper, just to give up.

As a cub, he'd wondered if the human-Musth war might not have ended in victory for the Musth if only his race had kept fighting, pushed harder.

Now, on Cumbre, he would not let himself think about becoming a shirker like they had been.

The slow drowning of almost a hundred miners sent a shock wave across the Cumbre system. Rumor spreaders and Force merchants spread the word for a general strike.

Wlencing heard of it, forbade it on the pain of reprisals.

But on the set day, only a handful of businesses opened. Wlencing sent troops into the streets to force merchants to open their shops, but there were almost no customers.

Worse, few of his human administrators, clerks, janitors, translators showed up for work.

Wlencing raged, ordered all of them discharged, and his underlings obeyed.

The strike ended, but the Musth stayed frozen without

the human grease for their alien wheels. A few Musth appealed the ruling, but Wlencing announced firmly that once he had issued a dictat, it could not be rescinded.

Very quietly, the more capable Musth leaders rehired sometimes under false names, most of their old staff, and life returned, mostly, to as before.

'It doesn't look like there's any surprises here,' Angara said.

'I haven't found any,' Hedley said.

Angara reran the computer speculation, then got up and paced the underground command center on Mullion Island. 'Damn,' he said irrelevantly, 'but it's stuffy down here. I'd make a shitty 'Raum.'

Hedley was still staring at the screen.

'We need to do something big, for our own sakes if nobody else's,' Angara said.

Hedley nodded. 'The plan's approved. Let's move the day after tomorrow.'

Hedley's agents had noticed a swarm of ships around the Highland base. Other agents found out these were the first of the freshly trained fliers, newly assigned to the fighting zone.

Remembering a ghastly moment in Man's history. Hedley named the plan Operation Nits.

Just after dawn, as the Musth pilots were assembling. preparing for the day's assignments, a wave of Zhukovs, armed yachts, and the Force's sole remaining *aksai* attacked the Highland.

They hit the field hard, rocketing anything they saw, strafing AA positions, aircraft still on the ground, any-thing moving. One pass, then another, and they fled, back toward their hideouts.

But there were human casualties, ships shot down crashed, or just crippled. One led to total disaster.

Jacqueline Boursier, high overhead in her *aksai* cursed as she saw a yacht, trailing smoke, limp over Mullion Island's narrow beach, a *wynt* and two *aksai* harrying it.

'Come on, you shitheel, bail out, goddammit, don't let 'em follow you home!'

But the yacht's pilot wasn't listening, and pancaked his ship down in the middle of the secret base's landing field, skating out of control, ripping away camou nets over bunkers, tents, gun emplacements, and revealing the long-held secret.

Boursier swept down, fired, knocked out the *wynt* and with a second launch, blowing an *aksai* out of the air. But that was her last missile, and she watched the last Musth ship disappear back toward Dharma Island.

Three days later, the Musth attacked Mullion Island in full force – it'd taken that long for Wlencing to move troops from Silitric, and ready his formations for battle.

They found no one – the Force had dispersed two days earlier.

But they left machine shops, aircraft under repair, supply dumps and armories.

The Force had lost its headquarters, its only effective base.

TWENTY-SIX

Unknown System/Unknown World

'Poor bastards,' Monique Lir said, watching the two columns of Musth warriors trudge toward them from Keffa's ship. 'They outnumber us what, two to one?'

'At least,' Njangu said. 'Duck your heady-bone. Here comes their air.'

Two aircraft soared out of a lock about halfway up the ship's hill. They were small flits that could carry no more than four warriors.

'Guess they went and forgot their *aksai*,' Monique said. 'Shall I have a team Shrike 'em, boss?'

'What's the chance of their pooh-bah, this Keffa, being on one of them?'

'Eh,' Lir guessed, waggling her fingers, 'six to five, either way.'

'Then we'll let 'em stumble on in ignorance for a while. 'Sides, Garvin gets the next moment of glory. But let's slide out of the line of fire, on the off chance those lifters have got heat detectors and somebody who knows how to use them.'

The two trotted down the rise, to the clump of trees, strange bleached-green growths more like fungi than real woods.

About twenty-five 'Raum and a scattering of I&R soldiers waited. Njangu noted Jasith, looking lost and a little scared, Poynton talking to her in low, soothing tones. He also noted that Jasith was firmly clutching a small pistol, a hideout gun one of the 'Raum had given her.

At least she wasn't being a rich idiot and vaporing around.

On the reverse slope, the enemy marched closer. A dozen men and women came up from hiding, spattered bursts across the right column, ducked away.

Garvin and another ten came from a nest of low boulders that didn't look like they could hide anything, fired in turn while the first set fled up the hillside in the cover of a ravine and over the hill to safety.

The Musth were firing back, but there wasn't anything to shoot at.

One of the flits swooped low, hovered.

Finf Heckmyer put half a belt through an SSW, and the lifter shuddered, slid sideways, and, trailing smoke, limped back to the command ship.

Garvin, just at the top of the hill, nodded in satisfaction. ' 'At's right, boys. Learn how it works the hard way.'

The humans moved in twenty-man groups, keeping in touch by com, occasionally joining up for attacks against the Musth, but moving, always moving.

The weather was mild, with no more than occasional sheeting rain.

'Something's real wrong here,' a troopie observed. 'Nobody ever goes sojering in good weather. Where's the ice? Where's the snow? Where's the frigging typhoons?'

A column of warriors patrolled carefully through a long patch of trees. A blast tore the middle of the column apart, and warriors savagely opened up, spraying everything and nothing.

Finally realizing no return fire was coming, they sheepishly stopped shooting, and aid-givers and officers ran toward the wounded

Then the second booby trap went off, less than five meters from the first, decimating the command group and medics.

Ten 'Raum stood, pumped five rounds each into the swarm, ran. One wasn't quick enough and was shot down.

The Musth *were* learning. An I&R team stalked a fifty-warrior sweep, and was skillfully led into an ambush, with no human survivors.

Garvin, after surveying the body-laden field, ordered his subordinates to sermonize on what happens when you let yourself think your enemy's stupider than you.

None of the human groups spent more than a few hours in one place, one eye on the sky, the other on a possible ambush site. They endlessly circled Keffa's ship, closing for a fast attack on the warriors tracking them, then vanishing into the wilds.

Little by little, the soldiers were memorizing their fighting ground.

But so were the Musth.

Keffa felt utter frustration. He had a ship that could nearly blow a planet out of its orbit, but he didn't have sensors delicate enough to detect one sniper hiding on the hillside.

He could remain airborne, but how could he hunt his prey?

He refused to consider admitting withdrawal, returning with a larger, more suitable force.

A Musth never retreated, after all.

*

'Try this,' Alikhan suggested.

Dill looked skeptically at the bit of orange growth. but put it in his mouth, chewed tentatively.

'Sort of like, oh, a real dead potato,' he said. 'But it's staying down.' He wrote a description in a notebook

'Now this.'

'This' was quite appealing – green with white striations. Dill chewed twice, then his eyes bulged and he stumbled to the nearest bush and vomited. He rinsed his mouth from his canteen, came back.

'This one's next,' Alikhan said mercilessly.

'Gimme a minute.'

He drank more water, felt his nausea subside.

'Thus far,' Alikhan said, 'we have seven plants we both can eat, four neither of us can stomach, and eleven you can't tolerate.'

'What fun I'm having in the name of science,' Dill said.

'Well, since we are not infantrymen, we must serve in some way.'

'And what good little crunchies we be. But nobody's ever gonna give anybody a medal for puking above and beyond the call of duty.'

Dill scratched his burgeoning beard, which he thought made him look distinguished, but most others thought looked like a wire brush that had lost an engagement with a wildcat.

'So,' he said, 'you being a canny analyst, how's all this nonsense gonna play out?'

'Either Keffa will call for reinforcements and destroy us; Keffa will give up and abandon us; Senza will have gotten my message, and decided it's in his interest to help us; or we shall destroy Keffa. In descending order of probability.

'I can live with those odds.'

'Yet another, more likely than the others, is that Keffa will destroy us without assistance.'

'Wonderful. The dice are loaded, as usual. The best option is being marooned. *Best?* What did I just say? I wish I could claim bein' stuporous.' Dill changed the subject. 'I wonder why we haven't seen any critters bigger than my head yet? Especially ones that'll fit on a grill over a nice fire.'

'Perhaps there are none. I am not an ecologist.'

'I surely miss a steak that isn't prefabbed and dehydrated,' Dill mourned.

That night, a sentry saw movement, woke his sleeping team up. He pulled a grenade, and something twice the size of a Musth, with, as the sentry said, 'more legs than God,' made a purring sort of noise, then leapt away.

'Perhaps,' Alikhan suggested, 'someone else is as interested in steak as you, without worrying about the niceties such as a fire.'

'Shaddup,' Ben Dill said.

Thirty raiders were surprised, pincered between two columns. They shot their way out, but still lost ten.

'I'm sorry, Garvin,' Jasith apologized. 'I just haven't felt like it.'

'Who has? Terror doesn't make me real lustful, either.'

'Do you think we'll make it?'

Garvin hesitated, then said, 'Of course.'

'You're kind of a crappy liar.'

'I guess it's the military life. I *used* to be a great shill.'

Jasith looked across the pond their element was camped by, at the vegetation outlined by the setting sun.

'I don't think I could ever get used to a world where the colors aren't what they're supposed to be.'

'Sure you could,' Garvin said. 'After a couple three you figure out nobody knows what supposed to be really is.'

Silence for a time, then Jasith said, 'I wonder what Loy's doing now?'

Hopefully, Garvin thought, *being hung by his nonexistent balls by the Musth for associating with a known bandit, but more likely making sure Mellusin Mining is now part of his holdings.* But he said nothing.

'I get horny when I'm scared,' Njangu breathed into Poynton's ear. They were curled together some meters from the rest of their group.

'Again? No wonder you were a criminal.'

For some reason he couldn't figure out, Njangu hadn't been bothered telling Jo Poynton about his normally hidden past as a junior thug on Waughtal's Planet, nor even about his abused childhood. Perhaps it was because of Jo's honesty about her own less-than-stellar past.

'Of course again,' he purred.

Two scouts were following a Musth column when a missile came in from nowhere and killed them in mid-transmission. A reaction team found the site, quickly reported, then ran fifty meters and went to cover, as Dr. Froude had asked them to. Another rocket exploded where they'd been.

'I've been expecting this,' Froude told Garvin. 'We've been too fast, too loose on the com, and they've finally been able to track our signals.

'We'll have to change policy, and go to limited casts. changing frequencies regularly. Also, move after transmitting if you want to live. If that doesn't work, we'll have to start using messengers. Or perhaps semaphore flags.'

The noose was tightening.

'What're we like, Monique?'

'Food enough for, oh, thirty days, more if we can really cut the rats with local edibles. About two units maybe a little more, per man.'

A unit of fire was a soldier's basic ammunition need for one battle – 150 rounds for a basic blaster. 500 for a Squad Support Weapon, two Shrikes per team, and so forth.

'Not good,' Garvin glummed.

'Not good at all,' Lir agreed.

The Musth had, the two scientists figured, a total of five flits on board their ship. Careful observation by a Shrike team produced an interesting fact – when the flits were taking off and landing in the hangar lock, the team's antiradar detectors went dead. The ship was shutting down its sensors when they landed or launched aircraft. Evidently the Musth didn't have much faith in their ship's friend-or-foe recognition abilities.

The Shrike team crept to within range and waited until nightfall. The flits buzzed around the command ship, and the hangar dock slid open.

The team fired, and the Shrike slammed into the lock, exploded.

The blast rocked the great ship, and smoke boiled out. Then, nothing more. The waiting flits were boarded through a secondary lock, and this time the Musth's tracking radar stayed up.

Sometime during the night, repair crews put a big, ugly patch over the blackened hole in the skin, and the fight went on.

*

A day later, with no warning, the command ship launched a dozen long-range missiles in all directions. They exploded against trees, boulders, empty ground.

None of the teams watching the ship was hit.

'System failure? Panic? They thought they saw something? I don't have the froggiest,' Froude said.

'Insufficient data to theorize,' Heiser said, sounding a bit more professional.

Contamination from the hyperdrive missiles pocked the land around the ship, and Garvin wondered if Keffa was intending to create a radioactive moat.

Two days later, the ship lifted and awkwardly grounded three kilometers away, and warriors began looking for the humans again.

The incident remained a puzzle.

Heiser and Froude disappeared for a day, came back with one of the ship-observation teams.

'Did you two ever hear of military discipline?' Garvin snarled. 'Or that we might worry?'

'We went out,' Heiser explained, 'without clearing it with you because we knew you wouldn't approve.'

'Don't punish the troops,' Froude added. 'We said we were under orders, highly classified and such.'

'Not that I think you'll be that angry,' Heiser said. 'I think we've got a way to get rid of this Musth.

'The only drawback is it'll probably irretrievably strand us here on this planet.'

'We were rather hoping we could find a way to seize the ship for our own purposes,' Froude said. 'But, unfortunately . . .'

Garvin and Njangu were wondering why the scientists seem to have all the good ideas, then both turned white when Froude explained how they'd done their 'research.'

'Nobody's that loony,' Njangu said in wonderment.

'I guess they are.'

'Now,' Njangu said, 'all we need is a dozen or so other loons to try it out.'

'A dozen,' Garvin said grimly, 'and I&R's two best climbers.'

'Me and Lir.'

Garvin nodded.

'And this one isn't likely to be one of those laugh ho-ho in the face of danger vacations.'

'You'd rather hang around here,' Njangu said, 'getting whittled and eating trees while we're waiting for Keffa's backup goons to materialize?'

Froude and Heiser's investigation *had* been thorough. They had kept with the observation team for a couple of days, and noted that the Musth, like most soldiers, were unfortunate creatures of habit.

At dawn and dusk, the traditional times of attack, warriors took fighting positions outside the ship in hasty trenches, no more than knee-high packed dirt parapets, that snaked, like molehills, around the command ship. Then roll was taken and tasks assigned.

After the dawn assembly, the warriors moved off on their missions. At dusk, they filed back into the ship. A few minutes later, noodlights came on, and the observers' telltales showed infrared, radar and amplified light swept the area until near dawn

But not, evidently, around the ship's base – some sort of creature evidently hid near one of the fins during the dusk assembly, then, once the Musth had vanished, streaked for the nearby woods. It didn't make it, caught by the searchlights, and then a missile was wasted blowing whatever it was into oblivion.

'I'd imagine a ship built for onplanet warfare wouldn't

have such a dismaying gap in its defenses,' Froude theorized. 'Which shows again you should always use the proper tool for a task. This deep-space elephant is a risk to its crew.'

Njangu considered who was really at risk from the ship, but said nothing.

After Froude and Heiser had developed their theory, the next night, as the warriors were pulling back for the night, the two scientists crawled from their cover up the entrenchments, until they were only a few meters from one of the bullet-tipped fins, and considered matters as the searchlights began sweeping the perimeter.

Since the command ship wasn't intended to be an inatmosphere speedster and, in any event, had more than enough power, the ship only looked aerodynamic from a distance.

Up close, the ship's skin was an eczema of radiation plating, radar and other flat arrays, and here and there extruded other sensors.

The pair, survey complete, waiting until the lights went out at false dawn, then scuttled back the way they'd come. With the observers, they headed for the RP with Garvin's command group.

'Will it work?' Jasith asked Running Bear as they watched the attack team disappear into the woods.

'Maybe.'

'And if it doesn't?'

Running Bear shrugged.

'Do you think Alikhan's friend is going to show up?'

Running Bear kept from snapping, 'How in hell should I know?' Instead:

'Old AmerInd fable,' he said. 'Going all the way back.

'A long long time ago, there were things called flims.

They were like entertainment holos today, but not even three-dee.

'Anyway, my people used to watch them, and their favorites were called 'Natives and Cowmen.'

'The cowmen sometimes were soldiers, sometimes just people. But they were always trying to steal my people's — we were the natives — land. And all of these flims ended the same way — the cowmen would finally be trapped somewhere and about to face justice, my people were about to triumph, and there'd be bugle music, and the leader of my people would look around, and coming over the hill, always, always, always would be more goddamned cowmen.

'I could never understand why my people would have wanted to watch something like that.'

'I don't get it,' Jasith said. 'Oh. Yes I do. Boy, you're sure a morale booster.'

'Us sour-mushes wouldn't want you to get too cheerful,' Garvin said, having come up unnoticed.

'I swear, I'll never understand soldiers,' Jasith said.

'Welcome to the crowd. You might want to pack — we're getting ready to go after Njangu.'

There were twelve of them slinking toward the ship, following the zigs of the Musth parapets.

All except Lir and Yoshitaro carried heavy packs, holding fused demolition chargers, and other gear. None of them looked at the knot of Musth waiting to enter their ship and safety, superstitiously afraid of alerting the aliens.

The lock slide closed behind the aliens, and the soldiers double-timed, bear-walking on hands and feet, to directly under the huge ship's drive tubes. Njangu looked up at the grid above them.

If I was a Space Ranger Against the Galaxy, we could crawl up those tubes and find a nice human-size hole to hunker

*through and shoot up them baddies. I'll just be happy if the bas-
tard doesn't go and take off on us.*

The climb promised to be interesting, since nobody
had planned for any mountaineering, any more than
they'd planned on being aboard the mother ship in the
first place, and all the exotic gear was somewhere back on
D-Cumbre

Njangu and Monique had made climbing harnesses
the rope every I&R soldier carried as part of his basic
load, found pebbles for chocks, and would climb in
double-stockinged feet. Most of the soldiers carried cara-
biners for nonclimbing purposes, so that was one thing
they didn't have to improvise, as well as ropes of various
sizes for climbing, slings, and so forth. They also didn't
worry about pitons they didn't have – Njangu thought
it'd be fairly impossible to nail their way up through a
starship's hull.

They roped up, five meters separating them. Njangu
reached up, found a hand-jam, pulled himself up, had a
toehold, was moving, slowly at first, then faster as his
body remembered training, hours of practice, even some
time wasted in recreational climbing with various I&R
crazies.

They crept slowly up the starship, finding, now and
again, antennae or nameless protrusions to tie off on, and
belay the other.

They changed lead twice. Njangu knew Monique to
be the stronger climber, but she evidently preferred to be
second on the rope.

Once he slipped, slid three meters before braking
himself.

He didn't look down, not wanting to see how far away
splat was, nor Lir to notice how scared he was, kept
climbing. His shoulder muscles tore, his feet were raw,
his fingers were disjointed.

He pushed a pebble into a notch between shielding plates, tied a sling with a carabiner into it, clipped his climbing rope on, and motioned Monique past him, climbed after her, painfully, monotonously.

His head bumped Lir's foot, and he thought she was having problems, then realized they'd reached their goal, that hangar lock the Shrikes had blown open, hastily patched almost three hundred meters above the ground

He saw Lir grin in the darkness. She crabbed sideways and found a jagged lip she could actually stand on. Njangu clambered up beside her.

The two-centimeter lip was big enough to throw a parade on. Better, there were two stud mounts a meter above them. One gave them a secure anchor for their rope. Lir dug into Njangu's pack, took out a fat coil of very thin rope, rated for hundred-kilo strength. She uncoiled it, let it fall to the ground.

There were pulls, then two strong tugs, and they reeled the line in, had a crude double pulley carved from a hardwood tree.

The pulley was securely tied to the second stud mount, and the cord went back to the ground.

Then it was endless hauling, as demo charges were tied on, reeled up, and positioned across the patch.

Njangu had hauled up a hundred, a thousand, ten million charges when he realized they'd brought up all twenty.

He bleared at the horizon, hoped it wasn't starting to lighten.

It was time to go.

They rappelled back down the ship, using the slings they'd left in place. Monique almost got inverted, kicked hard at the hull, and recovered, hoping thuds didn't transmit.

Then they were on the ground.

Njangu wanted to collapse for a week, realized he could make out people's faces, and signaled. They crept back out as they'd come, then, when the lock slid open, before the first Musth came out, ran for cover.

'Your honors, I believe,' Njangu said, handing the det box to Garvin. The command element had been nervously waiting atop a hill some distance from the ship.

'Give it to the good doctor,' Garvin said. 'This was his discovery.'

Froude took the detonator, then peered at the distant ship. There were Musth in formation in front of it, and it was almost full daylight

He licked his lips, shook his head. 'No. I, uh—'

Garvin took the detonator back

'Don't worry about it,' he said. 'Your decency is something I wish I still had.

'First *Tweg*, since you did most of the work.'

'What 'bout me?' Njangu said, as Monique took the box, slid the safety over, pressed hard on the sensor.

Keffa had decided to take the morning formation himself, and was pacing down the ramp considering his warriors, wondering why he hadn't been able to wipe these wormlets out, wondering when his ordered support would arrive, when one of his officers stopped, pointed up.

His thoughts broken, Keffa irritatedly looked up, saw a snarl of small objects somehow fixed to his ship, wondered what they could be.

There was a sparkle of light, Garvin thought from the sun for an instant, then the blast mushroomed.

Fire erupted from the lock, then a jet of flame, quickly subsiding. Smoke poured out and rumbling began, grew.

Garvin and Lir swore they saw the skin rip right around the ship, red glaring fire showing. The rip widened in less than a second, and the upper third of the ship blew apart. The ground reeled, and shock waves rolled across the sky.

The humans were up, running, falling, staggering drunkenly as blast after blast deafened them, and streamers of colors they couldn't imagine arched high through the sky.

Alikhan stared into nothingness. The raiders had assembled, fleeing from the Armageddon they'd set off.

'Come on,' Dill said. 'Keffa would have done the same – or worse, slowly – to you.'

Alikhan didn't respond.

Dill left him alone, staring back the way they'd come. as the explosions continued.

It was three days before they couldn't hear the sound of Keffa's ship dying.

Garvin sent two volunteers back to observe the ship, with a radiation meter. The device buzzed warning more than a kilometer from the ruins, and the scouts returned.

Whether any of the Musth who'd been outside the ship survived, no one ever knew.

Five days after the scouts returned, another Musth ship entered atmosphere. It overflew the wreckage of Keffa's ship, then the burnt-out mother ship the humans were now using as a base.

Alikhan peered up at it, using one tube of Lir's binocs as a telescope.

'Well?'

'More goddamned cowmen,' Running Bear muttered.

'Blue, with a yellow stripe,' Alikhan said. 'That is the emblem of Senza and his Reckoners.'

Some anonymous striker in the rear ranks spoke for them all:

'What took him so frigging long?'

TWENTY-SEVEN

D-Cumbre

Wlencing held his blinding rage tightly to him as his flit landed.

Senza was taking his full revenge, landing at the human port at Leggett rather than Silitric or the Highlands, humiliating Wlencing and his soldiers in front of the worms.

His transmission had come as a surprise – Wlencing had not had the time to reestablish the outer-world stations, and had been very precise:

> Recent developments within our worlds suggest you might wish to confer with me on the strategic direction now considered optimal for the system known as Cumbre. It might be wise to also take minimal action against the humans until our new course becomes clear.

Wlencing read through the diplomatic vagueness like a laser.

Keffa had failed and Alikhan had succeeded.

Senza had won, evidently destroying Wlencing's and

Asser's fragile coalition, and assembling enough clan-masters to force Wlencing to do . . . to do what?

The very least would be a return to the old order. Wlencing knew, if the humans were restored to authority, he and his fellows would be driven out of the system.

Probably they would allow Senza and his mewlings access to Cumbre's riches.

Not that it mattered. Cumbre was an impossible dream, best abandoned.

Wlencing wanted to take revenge, to kill Senza when he came before him, but knew he'd never get the chance.

He hoped his cub would not witness his father's humiliation but knew he would.

At least, he thought wryly, *Alikhan probably has my determination, even in a cause as foolish as the one he chose.*

The cub must die for his betrayal . . . but that too was foolish thinking.

He would never see Alikhan again. He should, must, be thought of as dying when his *aksai* was shot down into the sea so long ago.

The future was all that mattered: rebuilding his clan, having more cubs when mating season came, attempting to reestablish his relationship with Paumoto, finding a new direction.

Wlencing got out of the lifter, flanked by Daaf, other aides, and stalked toward Senza's ship.

He saw the small crowd of humans nearby, was surprised the wormlings weren't shouting scorn, but just staring, cold-faced.

Intent on his thoughts, he barely noticed the old man, once a fierce 'Raum rebel, step out of the crowd and, almost casually, lob, underhand, a small ball.

'You can always take one with you . . .'

The grenade went off, blew Wlencing almost in half, killed two aides.

Daaf, desperately wounded, managed to claw out his *devourer-weapon*, and shoot down the old 'Raum.

The landing field was hushed for a moment, except for the dull hum from Senza's ship.

But only for a moment.

TWENTY-EIGHT

It was a soft, tropical night. Garvin Jaansma, in dress summer whites, wearing the tabs of a *Mil*, leaned against a deck railing of the Shelburne Hotel, sipping a tall chill drink.

Njangu Yoshitaro, nursing a beer beside him, wore the same uniform, with the tabs of a *cent*.

Caud Angara had promoted Garvin and had made him head of II Section.

Njangu, for what Angara called 'theft above and beyond the call of sanity,' got bumped two grades and given I&R Company.

'You see,' Garvin whispered during the long ceremony when the Force licked its wounds with panoply, promotions, and medals, 'how virtue triumphs? I expect you to be properly respectful of my increasingly greater rank.'

'Don't hold your breath on that one,' Njangu answered. 'I'm quite happy letting you have the light-of-lime, whatever that is, and also be the conspicuous target.'

Now, inside the Shelburne was soft music, enticing smells, and easy laughter.

The two were waiting for their dinner companions making sure they stayed a drink up on them.

'So what's your guess on what Senza's going to do?' Njangu asked.

'No guess,' Garvin said. 'He gave the old man the hot skinny a couple of hours ago. With Wlencing dead, no face-saving talks are necessary. The old crew of Musth will get shipped back to their clans in whatever they call disgrace.

'We'll be doing business with Senza. Somebody, most likely Mellusin Mining, will front for him, so there won't be Musth traipsing around Leggett, at least for a while.'

'That'll still piss some folks off.'

'Tough. Who else are we going to trade with? The Confederation still ain't come riding to the rescue lately.'

'Strong point,' Njangu said. 'It grates, but I guess that's best. Just like there probably won't be much of a war-crimes trial for collaborators.'

Garvin's lips tightened. 'That's what Jon said. Maybe they'll lynch a few block wardens, a few other blatant assholes, but not much more. I surely doubt if any Rentiers will be for the high jump.'

'Which leads me,' Njangu said, 'to be delicately nosy about, ahem, *your* circumstances?'

'Loy Kouro's going to stay in jail as long as I can keep coming up with phony charges. Maybe three more weeks. I'm trying to bribe some jailbird to put a length of sharpened bedspring between his third and fourth ribs, so far without success. Jasith's filing a divorce petition tomorrow.'

'Which means what for the two of you?'

Garvin was silent for a while.

'I guess . . . it means what it means. I don't know.'

He saw dark bulks down by the water, recognized Alikhan, Ben Dill, two other Musth.

'I wonder what will happen to him?'

'Ben said,' Njangu answered, 'Alikhan won't stay with

his father's clan. I guess there might be some ugly whispers about him setting Wlencing up for what happened, and nobody loves a patricide. Ben told me he'll either become a Reckoner or else join the Force.'

Garvin looked astonished.

'Huh?'

'First, there'll be some Musth who haven't gotten tired of war. Second,' Njangu said, 'Hedley told me there's always people who want to join the side that beat 'em up. Not my style, but what the hell?'

Garvin recovered.

'Sure. Why not? We always need pilots, warriors. Maybe that's what those other two furries are talking to Ben about.'

'Especially since we are going to be buying modified *aksai*, probably some *velv*, and sure as hell, since we're a little short of navy, some mother ships from the Musth,' Njangu said.

'Well, kiss my moneymaking ass,' Garvin said. 'Wheels within wheels.'

'Always.'

Njangu finished his beer, set the glass on the railing.

'PlanGov goes back to the way we had it set up,' he said. 'And we start rebuilding, rearming in a big fat blur. You know what comes next.'

'Yeh,' Garvin grunted. '*Protector* Redruth. It might be nice, if he's out of the way, to see about fun things like what's going on with the Confederation, hell, if there even still *is* a Confederation.'

Two women came through double doors onto the deck, saw the soldiers, started over.

'It will be interesting to see,' Njangu said, 'if *we* can start a war for a change, or if we've got to wait until somebody knocks our dickstrings loose.'

Jasith Mellusin wore a froth of green lace, ending at

mid-thigh, with a nearly transparent purple torso stocking under it. Jo Poynton wore a more sober pantsuit in black that clung to her body, left her arms bare, was slit on either leg.

The two men made appropriate compliments.

'Come on,' Garvin said, taking Jasith's arm, 'just once, let's pretend we are civilized humans, instead of underpaid murderers.'

The four went into the Shelburne, out of the night, and the bright lights, music, and laughter swallowed them.

APPENDIX

The Cumbre system has a medium main sequence sun, about 1.5 million kilometers in diameter.

There are thirteen planets in the system, named, rather unimaginatively, after the alphabet. A- and B-Cumbre are too close to the sun to be habitable, with limited atmospheres, and have only solar and astronomical observation stations.

Mineral-rich C-Cumbre is the reason for both Man and Musth colonizing the system. Its riches include manganese, tungsten, vanadium, niobium, titanium, godarium, natural gamma iron, and some precious metals.

Mines, worked by both races, stud the arid landscape. It's uncomfortable for both races, more for the Musth than Man. It has a single moon, Balar.

E-Cumbre is chill, just habitable for Man, comfortable for Musth, who know it as Silitric, and consider it the center of the system.

F-, H-and I-Cumbre are ice giants.

G-Cumbre a half-destroyed world from an out-of-system asteroid, and moonlets litter its orbit.

J- and K-Cumbre are small planetoids, and have small observation stations.

L- and M-Cumbre are little larger than J- and K-, and

are almost certainly trapped asteroids, with extremely irregular orbits.

D-Cumbre is – mostly – Man's world. It has three small moons: Fowey, Bodwin, and Kailas. Only the largest and nearest, Fowey, affects D-Cumbre's tides.

D-Cumbre is about thirteen thousand kilometers in diameter at the equator, and its axial tilt is fourteen degrees. producing a more even climate than Earth's. Unlike on Earth, there are no continental masses, but many, many islands, mostly in the temperate and tropical belt, although two significant landmasses are at the poles. Some of the islands are large and of volcanic origin. Their peaks have been worn into plateaus with an entirely different climate than the lowlands – still wet, but chill and mist-hung, with the vegetation fernlike, from tiny to enormous. The Musth make their headquarters on the largest of these, the Highlands on Dharma Island.

Man settled at sea level, mostly in the tropics, with his capital, Leggett on the northwestern portion of Dharma and three smaller islets. There are two dozen smaller cities. some not more than villages, on other islands in the temperate or tropical zones.

The climate is balmy, and there are few weather hazards, although open seas away from the island masses produce enormous globe-circling waves, and the stormy season can be uncomfortable.

The environment must be considered benign, although there are still-unclassified predators in the jungles and several species of fish, from large sea serpents to marine carnivores to coelenterates, that must be considered hazardous to life.

Chris Bunch is the author of the Sten Series, the Dragonmaster Series, the Seer King Series and many other acclaimed SF and fantasy novels. A notable journalist and bestselling writer for many years, he died in 2005.

Find out more about Chris Bunch and other Orbit authors by registering for the free monthly newsletter at www.orbitbooks.net

STORMFORCE

The Last Legion: Book Three

Chris Bunch

There's more to war than combat training . . .

On the outer fringes of civilization, a lone military force struggles to keep the peace in a volatile star system. With no incoming communications from the Confederation Empire as guidance, only the Legion can stop a grasping tyrant from expanding his territories.

The dual system of Larix and Kura is controlled by dictator and self-styled Protector Alena Redruth, and he now has his eye on the Cumbre system. His spies monitor the Legion's activities, but information can flow both ways. Legion Intelligence Officer Njangu Yoshitaro will pose as Redruth's agent and infiltrate the upper echelons of the dual system's government. It is a corrupt hierarchy comprised of petty autocrats vying for control. Njangu can use these shifting loyalties to his advantage — unless the dictator discovers his identity first.

HOMEFALL

The Last Legion: Book Four

Chris Bunch

A search for truth, and a race against time . . .

The Last Legion has questions that need to be answered. And one question has now become a priority. Why has there been no word from the Confederation – the Legion's own government and the power behind a thousand star systems?

Against all odds, the Last Legion managed to reclaim the volatile Cumbre star system. Isolated at the edge of the galactic empire and outnumbered, it was a hard-fought war. And it was won without any help from the human Confederation government. The Confederation remained ominously silent throughout. Now, to answer these questions, the Legion must travel across galaxies to gather information. But can they keep their mission a secret from enemy forces – and will they have time to discover the truth?